THE MURDER OF A MAN
NOBODY WOULD WANT TO KILL

SUNSPANGLED

A DI JIMMY MOLASH INVESTIGATION

LUKE GLADSTONE

The Book Guild Ltd

First published in Great Britain in 2022 by
The Book Guild Ltd
Unit E2 Airfield Business Park,
Harrison Road, Market Harborough,
Leicestershire. LE16 7UL
Tel: 0116 2792299
www.bookguild.co.uk
Email: info@bookguild.co.uk
Twitter: @bookguild

Typeset in 11pt Minion Pro

Printed and bound in Great Britain by 4edge Limited

ISBN 978 1915352 408

British Library Cataloguing in Publication Data.
A catalogue record for this book is available from the British Library.

For Emily and Katie
Who make my life sunspangled

With thanks to (retired) Detective Inspector Chris Dovey for
all his patience explaining police procedure

1

The young man walking up the stairs with a song on his lips and a song in his heart was being murdered. He did not know it.

There are around seven hundred recorded murders in Britain each year. A sizeable majority of the adult victims live in some degree of fear of being killed. They may be involved in street gangs where fatal stabbings are common. They may have been regularly abused by their partner, suffering a catalogue of injuries before the lethal blow is struck. Even where a murder is committed on the spur of the moment, such as an argument between strangers leading to a fatal assault, the victim will usually sense danger.

Occasionally someone is murdered in the pure bliss of ignorance. As the young man opened the door to the sole bedroom on the top floor of the house, he was blissful. He sensed the joy of the final few weeks of term to come. Exams were over, they'd gone smoothly and there were merely a few introductory lectures to attend, which were setting the groundwork for their final year at university.

There had been a party atmosphere in the Union Bar that evening, with a much higher proportion of the student population out to play. It was a sign of the days to come and he relished the prospect. A life of almost infinite opportunities lay in front of him, but he thought of this only subconsciously. Live in the moment. There were years and decades to decide which of those opportunities to grab.

He emptied his pockets and took off his clothes, throwing them casually onto a chair, and connected his phone to a charger. Had there been anyone there to see it, which there was not, they would have observed a tanned, athletic and powerful body walking naked across the room to the bed. The body of a sportsman in the early part of his prime blessed with good looks and topped with a mop of blond hair.

The day had been warm but still with the freshness of the start of summer. The temperature in the bedroom was pleasant and the window remained shut and fastened. He got into bed, relishing the prospect of every remaining day in June, all of which he would be spending at Middleham University.

He had been blessed not just with looks and intellect, but also with compassion. During his A-level years he had used his free periods to set up and run a voluntary group, which cared for elderly residents in his hometown. At university he had regularly helped man the call line for students with mental health issues, having spent much of the Easter holidays in his first year undergoing training.

Very few of his friends knew about this. Naturally a man who kept his cards close to his chest, he couldn't abide the pious platitudes and self-satisfaction of some of his peers. When the reciprocal adulation began he would flash his bright smile and fade into the background.

The last person anyone would want to kill?

In the few days since exams had finished he'd begun to get an instinct that all was far from well with one of his fellow students. His voluntary work had made him develop a natural intuition for spotting when people had serious problems. He was increasingly worried about something he couldn't quite define in his mind.

Normally, when he got into bed he would read for a while or lay on his back with his hands behind his head, thinking about the events of the evening. That night he was trying to think about some of his fellow students whom he'd spent the evening with and of plans for the next day. He couldn't concentrate and that instinct kept bubbling back up to the surface of his mind. He knew help was needed but he hadn't yet evaluated the problem.

Weariness gradually came over him and he decided to tackle the issue in the morning. He yawned and a mischievous thought darted across his mind, which he decided would create a perfect opportunity for good-natured banter at the expense of one of his housemates.

Drowsy now, he turned onto his side and, with a smile on his face, his eyes closed for the last time.

Our lungs contain lots of small, elastic air sacs, which are called alveoli. Each time we breathe, the alveoli absorb oxygen and release carbon dioxide. This exchange of gases is fundamental to our bodies functioning. The oxygen-rich blood flows to the heart and is pumped round the body, fuelling our organs.

What the young man, who had just gone to bed for the last time, had ingested that evening changed the way his lungs worked. The alveoli were irritated and slowly began to fill with fluid rather than air. This caused less oxygen to be absorbed into the bloodstream and so in turn led to his organs not receiving the fuel they required.

Gradually his breathing became shallower as his heart pumped more slowly. His vital organs were ceasing to function. The pressure on what the previous morning had been a perfectly functioning heart became too great and it stopped. Mark Gower was dead.

*

*M*ark Gower's killer lay exultant in bed, brain racing like a Formula One car being pushed to the peak of performance and eyes like dinner plates in the darkness. It felt as if life had been leading to these moments, knowing that this might be the precise second when Mark's life would end – a time not to be wasted by sleeping.

Guiding a pathetic weakling along the tracks they would probably have trod anyway was one thing. Destroying a man like Mark would be quite another. The euphoria was intoxicating in a way that made alcohol or MDMA seem like a child's sweets.

It was tempting to get up, to run, to make the noise that this gladiatorial achievement so merited. There would be no suspicion so how could you act suspiciously?

Too fey to be able to rationalise caution, there was somewhere in the subconscious, a reserve, a self-preservation trigger. No matter, lying in bed with a million thoughts a second rocketing around your brain was exhilarating.

Anticipation lapped the mouth like the first taste of a gourmet meal. In the morning Mark's death would surely be confirmed – that knowledge, that certainty might lead to a yet higher plateau of ecstasy.

Thoughts swirled for what seemed like hours around a mind suddenly fixated with destruction. Eventually the adrenalin burned out and dreams ensued.

A Roman Emperor stood majestically, deciding which Christians should be thrown to the lions.

2

On the morning of Wednesday 12 June 2019, Sam Taylor had known that the chances of anything approaching a lie-in were non-existent, so he had allowed himself to half wake up as soon as Chloe Hartwell got out of bed. He opened the slits of his eyes just a little and watched her walking naked around his bedroom. By any standards she looked amazing and he decided once again that it was absolutely worth it.

Chloe had started keeping a few things in Sam's room as the majority of the nights they spent together were at his rather than her house. The clothes she kept in his wardrobe represented a wide range on the spectrum of sartorial elegance. The previous week they had attended one of the array of summer balls the university held each year. Done up to the nines, as Sam put it to himself, she had been *the* head-turner of the night, in a classically elegant way. He had loved every minute of it.

Today was near the other end of that spectrum. They were going to London to join a protest march and Chloe was dressing herself in what Sam privately described as her grunge mode, despite the grunge scene having died out before either of them was born.

Chloe had put on a 'Trump Hands Off Our NHS' T-shirt and was climbing into a pair of jeans, which consisted almost as much of patches and rips as denim. Both were about two sizes too big for her and did a good job of hiding her figure. She put her hair up into what could best be described as a mess and applied some vaguely gothic-looking dark lipstick.

Sam's characteristic shrewd stare was on this occasion more libidinous than appraising. Chloe was well used to being ogled, but she was also getting used to Sam's manner of staring piercingly at others, often during conversations, as he assessed what they were thinking.

When she turned to see Sam's eyes on her, the hint of a self-satisfied smile on his lips, her smile was internal. Given that most of Chloe's hair was tied up, the flick of a few beguiling strands that landed over her forehead and eyes was more subtle than usual. The slight pursing and then opening of her lips that had sent shivers down so many spines was not.

"Time to get up, handsome. We're going in a few minutes. I want to be there early for the coach. You could go and see where Owen is, we're not waiting for him." Chloe's voice was liquid and alluring whilst simultaneously, as usual, leaving him in no doubt about the priorities of the day. Sam inhaled deeply and the spell was broken, temporarily at least.

He got up, sprayed on some deodorant and then dressed quickly in an old T-shirt and faded jeans. This ensured he would not be smartly enough dressed to be out of place but still distinct from the look Chloe and her mates would be flaunting in London. Sam was indeed handsome. He was tall and powerfully but not heavily built. Had it not been for a short, straight nose there would have been more than a touch of the eagle about the first impression Sam Taylor made. Without needing to be combed his sleek black hair fell naturally into perfect place and in less than a minute he was ready.

He went downstairs and, given that it was not the sort of

house where the ceremony of knocking on bedroom doors was observed, opened Owen Lloyd's bedroom door.

Owen was already dressed and ready, looking at his phone, checking various social media feeds regarding the day's protest. Owen Lloyd had nothing of the eagle about him, resembling more a little owl as he stared at his phone through prescription glasses perched halfway down his short beak of a nose. His five housemates ranged from decent to very good-looking, and all played sports. Owen Lloyd was neither sporty nor had he any pretensions to good looks, being short, pot-bellied and possessing a mop of unruly mousy brown curls that he had never sought to tame.

Coming from a traditional, middle-class family, who dressed conservatively and voted Tory, the concept of student protests became a new avenue for Owen to explore when Sam had started dating Chloe Hartwell. Chloe had been on every protest march organised at the university and attendance had become compulsory for Sam. Chloe had entreated his housemates to participate, but only Owen had been lured.

Sam Taylor yawned and said, "I'd better know what we are protesting about today, mate, don't want to be baffed when Chloe is talking to me about it."

"I've just been reading up, it is the underfunding of social care. Theresa May's manifesto in 2017 was to get the people to pay for it directly rather than via government funding. That was before she had to backtrack on the 'dementia tax'. Now she's going, whoever takes over will have to grasp this nettle," Owen replied.

"Right, thanks, mate. More importantly, who is providing the beer for the coach trip?"

"You keen to get back on it?" Owen said with a smile. "I fancy a quiet, gentle drink through the day myself. We'll take an Augustinian approach – Lord makes us abstinent but not yet."

Owen's smile broadened. "Don't worry. I checked with

MacInnes and he is sorting it so it'll be something decent, not that bloody home-brew cider we had last time. I think we're getting dropped off in Bloomsbury again and marching down to Trafalgar Square. Once we are there the different groups will be planning future protests and Chloe will be busy. We ought to be able to get at least a couple in at that pub down on Villiers Street by Charing Cross."

For the previous minute or so they'd heard Chloe calling from somewhere near the front door. Now she shouted that she was leaving, whether they were ready or not. "Once more unto the breach…" said Owen with a smile.

Owen and Sam left their house to travel to London and register their brimming disgust at the government's refusal to spend enough money to deal with the social care needs that were due to mushroom over the next couple of decades.

The three students walked along Newton Street towards the campus in unusual silence, and with each step nearer the university all three were increasingly crowded in by their own desires.

For each, the kaleidoscope of those desires in their own mind had been shaken a different way and formed a distinct pattern. For one of them, as that pattern settled, the face of Mark Gower dominated it.

3

The chivvying of Sam Taylor and Owen Lloyd by Chloe Hartwell had reached almost hectoring tones by the time it woke Danny Wilson. Then the front door slammed.

Danny woke feeling slightly jaded but given how accustomed they were to large quantities of alcohol, this didn't qualify as a hangover. He reasoned that a couple of pints of water and a cup of coffee would have him firing on all cylinders again.

He got up, stretched and walked downstairs in his boxer shorts to the kitchen. At six foot five inches Danny was the tallest of the residents at 12 Newton Street and was built like a bear. Not a grizzly bear but a giant panda bringing an affectionate smile to the faces of people when they saw him. There seemed a frankness about him that would entice you to trust to a bear hug.

He put the kettle on and downed a couple of pints of water, exhaling strongly as a result of the second pint. He had filled the pint glass a third time for more leisurely consumption when Ryan Sandling walked in, already dressed.

Ryan was a shade under six feet tall and of unremarkable medium build. His clothes were smart but functional, worn with reserve rather than as an expression of personality. He was quite good-looking with regular chiselled features but his most remarkable attribute was his eyes. They were deep, chilly pools of unusually dark blue, seemingly guileless yet uncommunicative, his expression betraying neither kindness nor cruelty.

"Morning, mate," Danny said. "Coffee? Tea?"

"Have the anarchists gone to change the world?" Ryan responded. Smiles ghosted both their faces. The subject of protesting being a regular topic of debate in the house since Sam had started seeing Chloe Hartwell early in the previous term.

"Coffee after last night, thanks," said Ryan. "Large and black."

"Anyone else up and around who wants one?" asked Danny.

"Doubt it," Ryan replied, showing no inclination to go and ask. "Do you reckon Jack and that Annette are upstairs picking out wedding patterns?"

Danny guffawed, a joyous laugh from deep inside his being. The household was famous throughout the university for laughing, both for frequency and volume. Danny's belly laugh was indicative of his natural inclination to find enjoyment in everyday life. "That lad is smashing it," he said, pouring the coffee.

Ryan smiled and replied, "Can you imagine what he'll drag in next?" Sipping coffee, Ryan continued, "I'm going to go up to the campus and get next year's textbooks. You coming?"

"Christ, you're keen," said Danny. "What's the hurry? We've got weeks yet."

"Nothing really," said Ryan, shrugging, "It's just that the end of term is going to be one long party based on last year, so I'm keen to get all the boring admin done now so it doesn't reduce valuable drinking time."

"Sure, why not, mate. I'll chuck some clothes on and we'll wander up. If I have a look round what's available today, Mark and I can probably get it done quickly when the final list of third-year texts comes out," Danny said, pausing and then adding, "I'll shower later before we go out to the bar."

Ryan smiled. "Yeah, that's a good plan, I'll do the same."

A few minutes later they were on the way to the campus. Ryan Sandling, walking unnaturally quickly, was trying to keep his mind in step with his breathing. *The tasks ahead*, he told himself, *you must focus on the tasks ahead.* He reminded himself how straightforward they should be.

Danny Wilson was forcing the pace. His body, totally relaxed when he had left the house, was feeling tenser with every step. He had done it again and whilst the previous time all had worked out well, there was no guarantee it would this time. This time he was determined that fear wouldn't make him look guilty.

4

Jack Freeman lay in bed, immune to the hubbub of noise in the house. The first time the front door had slammed he had woken briefly and immediately gone back to sleep. About fifteen minutes later it had slammed again and he had opened his eyes for a few seconds. Remembering that he had no introductory lectures that day relating to his final year's courses he closed them again and slept.

It was sometime later that he really woke up. In no hurry, he lay back and thought of the unique events of the previous evening.

A fortuitous meeting really; he'd no idea she had just done her finals. For some reason he had assumed that she was a fresher. It had been as extraordinary as he had hoped and he wondered whether she had been a virgin, an unempathetic smile playing on his lips.

He tried to remember as much as he could. Eventually he had exhausted his memory banks and got up. The room smelt of sweaty bodies more than sex. Jack opened a window and then swaggered naked across the landing to the bathroom. He turned on the shower and as he waited for the hot water he gave a shiver that had nothing to do with the air temperature. He suddenly felt a need to cleanse himself and having got into the shower he vigorously lathered his body with an excess of shower gel.

A few minutes later he re-entered his bedroom and dressed immaculately in a fashionable T-shirt and tailored shorts. Just over medium height, Jack was lean but strong, his body toned at the gym. When his enchanting smile greeted you, his moss-green eyes were always alert, constantly soaking up his surroundings in the manner of a trained watcher.

As he was alone, his face remained serious and he spent several minutes examining his short, immaculately trimmed beard in the full-length mirror on the inside door of the wardrobe. His hair, light brown with a hint of red, fell naturally into a luxuriant quiff, needing little attention. Satisfied with what the mirror showed him, he went downstairs.

Twelve Newton Street was not one of those student houses with a culture of low-cost culinary creativity. Breakfast was usually limited to toast. Butter was generally available and on a good day either Marmite or jam. The haute cuisine could be washed down with tea, coffee or water.

Someone had obviously been shopping recently as butter, Marmite, jam, milk and sugar were all available. He opted for toast with just a scrape of butter and a sugarless cup of tea. The house was quiet. He knew that Sam, Chloe and Owen were due to go to London, but where were the others? He picked up his wallet and keys and left by the front door.

He returned about fifteen minutes later and put the kettle on again. He poked his head round Owen's bedroom door just in case. The room was empty. He walked up the first flight of stairs and looked in all of Sam, Ryan and Danny's rooms, which were also empty.

He climbed up the second flight of stairs, opened Mark's door and life duly changed forever.

Jack Freeman stared at Mark Gower's inert form in the bed in the attic of 12 Newton Street. Mark lay on his side, facing Jack as he stood on the threshold of the room. The duvet was wrapped around Mark from the midriff downwards and his body looked rigid.

Studying chemistry, Jack was the only scientist living at 12 Newton Street. Instantly he knew what he was looking at. The horror of an actual corpse froze him to the spot. He was shivering more vigorously now.

He hyperventilated, unable to drag his eyes away from the body. The only thought his brain could process was that this was what a dead body actually looked like.

He walked towards the bed, the few steps seeming to take an eternity, his limbs feeling as if they were those of a puppet on strings being manipulated by a clumsy child. He reached the bed and put his hand on Mark's face, which was cold.

Jack shied away from the bedside. He stared transfixed at the contents of the bed. At what had been a fellow human, someone who breathed, laughed and joked. Someone who had breathed, laughed and joked with him, Jack Freeman, for nearly two years and was now just a heap of flesh and bones, ready to rot.

His brain was scrambled by what he'd seen and couldn't process obvious simple tasks he'd always taken for granted. Was it wise to call the police or should he get as far away from the house as feasible?

Sometime later he walked stiffly downstairs, picked up his mobile and called 999.

5

Major crime investigations are analogous to using a map to go on a journey. If you go in the wrong direction at, or near, the start of the journey the consequences can be much more severe in terms of the time required getting back on track.

For example, if you go the wrong way at the end of a journey to a friend's house by arriving at the street they live in and turning the wrong way down it, it takes very little time to correct the mistake. By contrast, if you go in the wrong direction along the motorway near your house early in your journey, much more time is lost correcting the error.

In the case of a major crime investigation this is compounded because evidence is not there permanently, as roads are. Mistakes at the start of an investigation can lead to evidence never being gathered and the crime remaining unsolved. This is known within the police as the 'golden hour' principle. It was Martin Huttley who took Jack Freeman's 999 call and he didn't make any mistakes.

The natural shock of finding a dead body or seriously injured person means that hysterical 999 callers are common. Whilst Jack was in shock and felt he was struggling to articulate himself, Huttley's long experience meant that he had little trouble with the conversation.

Jack explained that he had gone to Mark's room and found him apparently dead in his bed, his cheek cold to the touch. Huttley asked whether he had touched the body other than briefly on the cheek. When Jack replied that he had not, he was firmly told not to do so.

Huttley asked when Mark had last been seen and Jack explained that he had not seen him since Mark went to bed the previous night between what he guessed was midnight and one o'clock. As far as he was aware nobody else had either. As far as he was aware Mark did not have any physical or mental health issues.

Having established that Freeman was alone in the house, calling from his bedroom, Huttley told him to remain there. He took the address and told Jack that a police officer and a pair of paramedics would be sent and he was to let nobody else into the house. If his housemates returned they were to either join him in his bedroom or go to their own. On no account were he or they to go into Mark's room. He should not use his phone and in particular he was requested not to call or message anybody or go onto social media.

Huttley knew that the killer calls in a disproportionately high percentage of murders. Often this is for pragmatic reasons. It provides justification for being at the crime scene and potentially for DNA being found on the victim or elsewhere at the scene. Sometimes it is the killer's ego wanting to make themselves centre-stage or an attempt to divert suspicion by appearing helpful. Huttley therefore added a note that Jack Freeman had seemed in shock but had not behaved suspiciously.

Newton Street was near the centre of Middleham. The police

station was less than a mile away, whereas the hospital was built on the outskirts. Police Constable Adam Coleman arrived before the paramedics.

Huttley had briefed Coleman that it was an unexplained death of a young student who had apparently died in his sleep. There was no reported evidence of how he had died. Given that Mark Gower apparently had no health issues the death was unexplained.

Coleman arrived at 12 Newton Street and rather than ringing the doorbell, which might potentially have relevant DNA on it, he knocked on the door. He heard the sound of someone running downstairs and the door flew open. Jack Freeman stood in the doorway wild-eyed. Coleman was in fact only four years Freeman's elder, but after six years as a policeman he had plenty of experience of crime scenes. He politely took control of the situation.

"Jack Freeman?" he began, and upon getting a nod continued, "Police Constable Coleman. Please could you show me where Mark Gower is?"

Jack rediscovered the power of speech and said hoarsely, "In the attic. His room is the only one on the top floor."

Coleman walked past him and said, "Please could you follow me, Sir? Touch as little as you can and stay behind me." The pair walked briskly up the two flights of stairs and found Mark Gower's bedroom door wide open. Coleman instructed Jack to wait on the landing and entered the bedroom. Ideally Coleman would not touch the body at all, but it was important to confirm whether Jack's impression that Gower was dead was correct. If it were not, maximising the chances of recovery would become the overwhelming priority.

Mark's arms were both exposed above the duvet and Coleman felt for a pulse. There was none and the wrist was cold. Sensing that Jack was waiting for confirmation he said, "I am afraid you were correct, Mr Freeman, he is dead." He turned round quickly and looked keenly at Jack. What he saw was horror, but nothing that obviously implied guilt.

Coleman had been involved in a murder inquiry once before but had never been first on the scene. His senses went on to full alert and he looked round the room. The window was shut and fastened. Even if it had been opened, it would have taken a professional burglar to get in or out by it without a ladder. There was a sheer drop outside with no conveniently available downpipe.

Coleman sniffed. There was no sign of drugs or tobacco in the air, nor was there any perfume implying Mark had had a companion in his bed the previous night. The odour was of stale alcohol. "Had Mark been drinking last night?" enquired Coleman.

Jack had got a better hold of himself now, the initial shock passing. He replied in a more even tone, "Yes, we all had. We spent the evening in the Union Bar and had the usual drink when we got home as well." At this point there was another knock on the front door. Coleman sent Jack down to answer it but only to allow paramedics or housemates in. It was the former.

To Middleham police officers, Millie Dean and Mike Luff were a well-known double act as local paramedics and Luff greeted Coleman in a friendly manner as the duo reached the attic, asking, "What have we got?" Coleman replied that it looked as if the occupant of the room had died in the night. The paramedics took one look at Gower's body, felt for any sign of life and, seeing there was no call for their skills, confirmed the fact of death and prepared to leave. The fewer people at the scene for as short a time as possible, the lower the chances of contamination of evidence.

Coleman said tentatively, "His lips and fingernails look a bit blue. That's cyanosis, right? Could he have taken cyanide?"

"Good spot. Lots of drugs cause cyanosis, though. He looks a bit peaceful to have taken cyanide to me, but the pathologist will tell you more. He doesn't look a candidate for having had an ongoing heart condition that might have caused cyanosis naturally," Dean responded. Coleman nodded and took out his phone as the paramedics made to depart. He sealed Gower's bedroom with tape and called the Criminal Investigation Department.

Unexplained deaths have to be attended by an officer of at least sergeant rank and ideally by one of inspector rank. There is therefore usually a 'Duty DI' on call. In this case it was Detective Inspector Alan Clinton. He listened to Coleman's report and said he would be at Newton Street in a few minutes.

Standing next to Coleman in the hall by the front door as it closed following the departure of the paramedics, Jack walked into the kitchen and turned the taps on in the sink and squirted washing-up liquid into the bowl.

Whilst some of the crockery was chipped, reflecting the state of the house more generally, Coleman noticed that the kitchen, like the other rooms he'd been in, was relatively clean. The linoleum in the kitchen was hardly shining as it did at his mother's house, but these clearly weren't the archetypal students who within a few months turned their accommodation into a hovel.

Coleman suddenly remembered Jack's mention of 'the usual drink' and asked about it. Jack explained, saying, "It is a house rule when we've been out drinking at the Union Bar or a pub. Last night we'd been in the Union Bar and got back here about half eleven, maybe quarter to twelve. When we get home we always all have one nightcap in the lounge. Everyone has the same drink, which is chosen by a different one of us in rotation. It is usually a shot and mixer combination but sometimes it's something more exotic."

"What was it last night?" asked Coleman.

Jack had been explaining in something of a daze. Coleman sensed he had explained the house nightcap rule plenty of times before and was virtually reciting from memory. Faced with a specific question about the previous night Jack had to think long and hard. Eventually he seemed able to focus his mind. "Gin and tonic. It was Mark's choice and we had gin and tonic."

Coleman walked over to the sink and turned off the taps. "Don't wash anything up or touch any of the bottles, glasses, etc. It's just in case there is any evidence on them." Jack blinked at Coleman, still not absorbing facts efficiently.

Coleman carried on regardless. The more information he could obtain the better and whilst there was no reason at this stage to believe Jack was responsible for Mark's death, if he was, this was the time he was most likely to give himself away. "Did you have just the one nightcap?" asked Coleman.

Jack was back on automatic pilot now. "Yes, that's the rule. It's a pint, though. Then we typically go to bed. If anyone wants to carry on drinking they usually congregate in a bedroom. I don't think anyone did last night, though. We all went to bed after the house nightcap."

Coleman looked in the lounge. There were various glasses scattered about the room. "Did Mark mix the drinks in here?" he asked.

"No, the house nightcap is always mixed in the kitchen. The person mixing it tests it, you know, to make sure it is not too weak, and then brings them in on a tray. Mark did that last night."

Coleman switched his attention back to the kitchen. There were a whole host of bottles on the work surface, amongst which there were some containing gin and others tonic. More glasses, mugs and plates that may have been this morning's breakfast or yesterday's dinner were also lying around. A number of plates and mugs had been washed up and were on the drainer, but no pint glasses were amongst them.

Coleman sealed off both the kitchen and the lounge. He asked whether Jack had already washed up any of the glasses from the nightcap and, getting a negative answer, was about to ask whether he knew if anyone else had when there was another rap on the front door.

Detective Inspector Clinton introduced himself, Detective Sergeant Cheryl King and Crime Scene Investigator ('CSI') Keith Bourne to Jack. All were wearing the standard scene suit, facemask, overshoes and protective gloves. Given the simplicity of the potential crime scene a single CSI was allocated rather than a team under a crime scene manager. The initial role of the CSI is to control everyone at the crime scene so as to maximise the harvest of evidence. The Duty DI is in overall charge and they work together and then advise the investigating team on examination strategies and priorities when the latter arrive.

Clinton asked Jack if he would mind going to his room whilst they began their investigation, adding that they or their colleagues would want to speak to him in due course.

When the four police officers were alone in the hall Coleman went through the facts he had to date. He emphasised the apparent cyanosis and the fact he had sealed off the lounge and kitchen. If the victim had consumed some sort of drug it could have been at the Union Bar or in his room but equally it could have been in the nightcap.

Clinton nodded approvingly and instructed Coleman to man the front door to ensure nobody got in and contaminated the evidence. Clinton explained he would shortly be asking Jack Freeman for the mobile numbers of Mark's housemates so Coleman could contact them and request that they come home immediately and, like Jack, remain incommunicado in their rooms.

Clinton, King and Bourne then went up to Mark Gower's room. Without touching the corpse more than necessary they looked, under Bourne's instructions, for anything that might imply an assault, whether physical or via, for example, an injection. They did not turn the body over to make a thorough check as that could have released bodily fluids and contaminated the evidence. That would be for the forensic pathologist in due course. They found nothing.

Bourne examined the room for any sign of forced entry or disturbance. There was none. There was no suicide note. After a brief discussion with Bourne, Clinton took Mark Gower's mobile phone, which was connected to a charger and resting on his bedside table.

Touching the iPhone as little as possible, even with gloves, Clinton discovered that Mark didn't password-protect his phone and that his social media was open to viewing. Clinton checked text, voicemail, WhatsApp, email, Instagram, Snapchat, Twitter and Facebook. There was no sign of a cry for help, let alone an online suicide note. On the contrary, Mark Gower appeared to have been an unusually positive and happy young man. Once the forensic team had finished with Mark Gower's phone they could take a proper look.

Clinton thought for a moment and then asked King, "Anything more we can do here, Cheryl, before we call it in?"

King stood up from where she had been checking drawers to see if any suicide note was laying hidden. "No," she replied. "I'm pretty much done. Let's leave it to Keith and whoever ends up investigating this." King looked around the bedroom, her professional antennae twitching. *There's something really wrong here*, she told herself. *Happy, healthy-looking young men just don't die like this.*

6

Detective Inspector James Molash sat with his feet on his desk and stretched, stifling a yawn. Thirty-one, he still possessed the suppleness of youth and so slouched with his posterior halfway from the back of the chair. Had there been a physiotherapist present they might have given a lengthy lecture on the likely consequences in middle age, but that would have invoked a serious bout of yawning.

An inch or so over six foot tall, broad-shouldered, with a naturally high muscle mass and very low body fat, physical issues hadn't yet intruded on Molash's life.

His current problem was boredom. An unusual outbreak of lawfulness had left him with little option but to catch up on the seemingly endless amount of paperwork that modern policing seemed to involve.

Brilliant when presented with a complex puzzle, ferociously hard-working when faced with a mass of routine detection – the internal paperwork contained in endless strategic initiatives and information collations flummoxed him. His powers of concentration deserted him, even when he tried to bring them to bear.

It wasn't even that he had the old-fashioned copper's disdain for administration. During an investigation his usual principle of delegating as much discretion as he could to junior officers didn't extend to HOLMES, the Home Office Large Major Enquiry System. Molash insisted all relevant information was input onto HOLMES rather than being left in paper form.

He had seen plenty of cases fall apart in court or torn apart by the Crown Prosecution Service due to poor recording of information. When a new, junior officer joined the team he would tell them to investigate with their nose but record all information as the court needs to see it. Apart from the humiliation of a clearly guilty offender walking free as a result of a lack of attention to clerical detail, careers were made or broken on such points.

Molash had been promoted to the rank of inspector before his thirtieth birthday. He had been told in no uncertain terms that this marked him down as a high-flyer and that it was the mixture of investigative flair and attention to administrative detail during an inquiry that had gained him that early elevation.

He had also been told that if he were going to continue his climb through the ranks then he would need to start forming relationships throughout the broader police service. Molash had no intention of undertaking that sort of networking and suspected that he hadn't disguised the fact particularly well. Jimmy Molash loved being a senior member of a team investigating serious crimes. In June 2019 he was the Deputy Senior Investigating Officer ('DSIO') in a squad based at Middleham Police Station.

As Molash surveyed what he considered the organised chaos of his desk, he reflected, by no means for the first time, that internal politics and endless paperwork were for people like—

His internal phone rang. It was the high priest of police politics and fashionable initiatives, Molash's boss and the Senior

Investigating Officer ('SIO') of the team, Chief Inspector Edward Eliot.

"Morning, Jimmy, could I have a word when you have a moment, please?" Eliot's none too dulcet tones came through the earpiece. Molash surmised from the peevish note in Eliot's voice that it was something completely trivial. Still, he reasoned, it would break up the monotony of the paperwork and he said he would come straightaway to his superior's office.

Eliot's office was ultra-modern, fitting for a man for whom every new theory was embraced as potential alchemy for criminal investigation. He sat in an executive chair behind a light pine desk, the combination the last word in ergonomic design.

The desk was neatly ordered, in stark contrast to Molash's. A small number of files were neatly piled and both laptops and tablets were open. Molash wondered, once again, why so many different screens were necessary. It was as if Eliot had seen a film about city traders and fancied himself as master of a very different universe.

A fleeting image of Richard Osman on the television quiz show *Pointless*, with his never-used computer, swept through Molash's mind. The irony of thinking about a man with nominally pointless but actually relevant information to impart caused a brief smile to pass his lips.

The clock in Eliot's office had just ticked round to midday as Molash entered and he bade his superior officer a cheery, "Good afternoon, Sir." Eliot looked up and frowned. He continually reminded his subordinates to 'call me Ted'. This was the result of a course Eliot had been sent on to improve his dealings with junior ranks. It had been a bewildering experience with two days of discussion about camaraderie and team building.

A man with few interests outside his job and even fewer friends, Eliot had felt horribly out of his depth as he floundered in every role-play designed to help Chief Inspectors understand the motivations of a team of junior officers.

Like a drowning man unable to swim to the life raft of understanding his fellow humans, he clung to whatever jetsam had been cast into the water by his peers who possessed the skill of empathising. The result was predictably inept. Lacking the interpersonal skills to create genuine warmth, Eliot had sought refuge in the suggestion that the calculated use of informality could work well, even in a hierarchical organisation like the police force.

He returned with a mantra that he would be a pioneer in bringing the police force into the modern age by disposing with the use of 'Sir' or 'Boss' or 'Guv', endlessly reminding his team to 'call me Ted'. Perhaps inevitably this led to a game played throughout the station called 'Call me...', which did nothing for Eliot's respect from or credibility with the junior ranks.

"Sit down, Jimmy," Eliot said, his voice nearing squeaking pitch. Eliot topped Molash by a good inch and, mid-forties, retained a thick thatch of light brown hair, which was invariably beautifully combed. Whilst not as powerfully built as Molash, Eliot was by no means puny. When agitation caused his voice to rise towards the level where squeaking took over, it sounded ridiculous coming from a big man.

Molash knew the danger signs and tried to pour oil on troubled waters. "Thanks, Ted," he said, sitting upright, by his own standards almost to attention. "What's the latest on the crime figures?"

This was akin to asking someone from the temperance society what the latest was on alcoholism in the area. Eliot had spent a good proportion of the previous few years engaged in his pet project of how to cut data more efficiently to make the crime figures clearer, so as to enable action to be taken (by others) to improve them.

Buoyed by some encouraging remarks from a deputy chief constable he had never met regarding his initial thoughts, Eliot had proceeded to make a pest of himself. Ignoring the fact that much of the value a non-expert individual brings to a task is typically their early thoughts and impressions, Eliot had chosen to dig deeper and think further. With every quarterly round of crime figures there would follow an Eliot analysis using new data-cutting techniques. Given that he always titled the email 'New and innovative ways to evaluate the crime figures' all the senior officers who received it simply deleted it unread.

Inviting a monologue on Eliot's pet subject was usually a long odds-on shot to replace the troubled waters, which might otherwise mount to a torrent, with the comforting babbling of a stream.

There is no such thing as a racing certainty, though, and instead Eliot took a deep breath. "We can discuss the crime figures in due course," he said, still trying to get his voice under control. "I'm still waiting for your contribution, by the way. Given you were on the Faulkner case I cut you some slack with the previous quarter's data but there are no excuses at the moment. By the end of the week, please."

"In the meantime, I wanted to know your thoughts on this." Eliot's voice reached a crescendo, with the final word of the sentence sounding as if it had been spat out by an angry grass snake.

Eliot passed Molash a piece of paper, which was headed:

Team Building at the Middleham Nick as a Result of Senior Officers Attending Team-Building Courses

Below which was printed:

Team-building Ideas flowed down like waters and righteousness like an everlasting stream.
And feedback, ever more feedback, was sought.
And so the Constables went unto the Sergeants and said, "It is a crock of shit and it stinketh."

And the Sergeants went unto the Inspectors and said, "It is a container of excrement, and it is very strong such that none may abide by it."

And the Inspectors went unto the SIO and said, "It is a vessel of fertiliser, and none may abide its strength."

And the SIO thought deeply and went unto the Deputy Chief Constables and the Assistant Chief Constables and said, "These team-building initiatives will actively promote the growth and morale of the police, with powerful effects."

And so the Ideas became Policy.

And darkness fell on Middleham Nick.

Ordinarily Molash would have smiled, but a sixth sense told him that Eliot was really incensed, so he sought the refuge of playing innocent. "Where did this come from, Ted?" he asked.

Eliot's voice went up an octave again. "I'm reliably informed it's been doing the rounds for the last week. Are you telling me you haven't seen it? It's apparently been on notice boards, in the canteen, you name it. This morning I found it amongst my copy of the national crime figures."

Molash opted for literalism. "I hadn't read it, Ted." A statement that was literally true since he'd only needed to see the first few lines to get the gist when he'd seen it the previous week.

Eliot's phone rang. He looked at it in an irritated fashion and ignored it, continuing, "I specifically tasked you with ensuring that there were no inappropriate attempts at humour on email or WhatsApp groups in my team," Eliot said in something close to a shout. "And we now get this, part of which seems to be directed at ridiculing me."

Molash saw an exit route and chose his words carefully. "Ted, look, this is as old as the hills. It's called 'How Shit Happens' and has been round every big organisation in the country. It points out that it's incredibly hard to get feedback through a hierarchical system – we're no different."

Eliot hesitated and Molash pressed home his advantage. "Google it, Ted." He continued using Eliot's forename at every opportunity, like a politician trying to sound sincere and empathetic when facing questioning from a member of the public.

Eliot had already reached for a tablet. His eyes were glued to the screen and he flicked through a few (similar) search results, which appeared to mollify him a little.

"Thanks, Jimmy. All right, so this isn't original—" he began.

Molash was keen to seize the initiative and interrupted. "When I was a teenager my old man showed me a version that had once done the rounds at his father's office. It's old hat."

"Well," said Eliot, hesitating, "I suppose this was only a shortened version of what normally does the rounds according to the Google search. Perhaps that indicates we're not perceived to have too much of a problem with reporting feedback compared to other organisations."

Molash blinked. The usual version of 'How Shit Happens' has seven stages of Chinese whispers, each changing the message with some degree of subtlety. Eliot was once again demonstrating his gift for hitting the nail squarely on the thumb. The additional point being made by the anonymous member of Eliot's team was to highlight the gulf between the feedback the SIO received and that which he fed to the powers that be.

Molash realised he'd hesitated too long and the silence had fed Eliot's paranoia. The anger was back. "Right, Jimmy, I want the perpetrator found and made an example of." Molash, who had a shrewd idea of where the guilt lay, was frantically thinking of how to play the situation tactically, when there was a knock on the door.

Lucinda Carew, a young and attractive detective constable, recently recruited from the uniformed ranks by Eliot, put her head round the door. "Sorry to disturb you, Sir," she said with a flash of a smile that would have lit up a much less drab room than Eliot's office.

Eliot became avuncular and beamed back. "That's all right, Lucinda, come in. Jimmy and I were having a discussion about team bonding. What can I do for you?"

Clinton had called Mark Gower's death in as suspicious and therefore to be handed over to the relevant SIO. He found that Eliot was the SIO on duty. Eliot wasn't picking up his phone, but Clinton knew where Eliot was based. He called and got through to Carew, who told him that Eliot was in his office and she would ask him to call Clinton back immediately.

"The Duty DI, Inspector Clinton, has called in a suspicious death in Newton Street, Sir."

Molash was on his feet in an instant, buoyed on several levels. "I'll get Woody, whilst Lucinda fills you in Sir," he said, out of the door before Eliot could utter another word.

Whilst Eliot sat behind his desk smiling benignly at Linda Carew and prattling on, the first sniff of the hunt filled Molash's nostrils as he roamed the corridors of Middleham Police Station.

7

At any given time there are around thirty-five to forty forensic pathologists (historically referred to as 'home office pathologists') in the country. They provide a twenty-four-seven service to the police and coroners. Given the relatively small number of deaths that require a pathologist, SIOs tend to deal with the same one or two pathologists that look after that geographical area.

In this case Eliot spoke to Dr Grace Patel and once the formalities were completed, she agreed to meet Eliot and his team at 12 Newton Street. She asked Eliot whether he wanted an expert toxicologist at the scene. Eliot suggested that Dr Patel attended alone initially and they would review the need for a toxicologist once the initial examination had been made.

Whilst Eliot was liaising with Dr Patel, Molash found Woodcock, who had heard that Molash had been summoned to the SIO's office. Woodcock asked chirpily, "Hello, Guv, how is Ted this fine afternoon?"

Molash replied drily, "Luckily for you he's been distracted

from the detective work of hunting through this department for second-rate comedians, as we've got a body to go and see."

One of the myths concerning murder investigations is that the SIO spends their time out and about, gathering evidence, interviewing those connected with the crime and so on. This makes for good television crime drama but in reality the SIO spends the vast majority of their time in the incident room. More junior members of the team largely do the information-gathering.

One of the main exceptions is that the SIO always attends the initial crime scene, usually with a couple of members of their team. Eliot's policy was that he, Molash and Detective Sergeant Woodcock attended the initial crime scene.

Eliot, Molash and Woodcock put on the same scene of crime suits that Clinton, King and Bourne had worn and set out for 12 Newton Street, Eliot briefing Molash and Woodcock on the way. He concluded by saying that Dr Grace Patel was the pathologist assigned to the case.

"Excellent news, we've got Dr Patel, rather than Dr Goodworth," opined Woodcock with a twinkle in his eye. Goodworth was efficient, but dry and uncommunicative, only answering direct questions, and he rarely offered any helpful suggestions. Patel by contrast, had a razor-sharp manner and the verbal jousts between her and Molash were legendary.

Woodcock could never work out whether they were flirting, genuinely antagonistic or simply enjoying the verbal cut and thrust. His theory was the last named one, partly on the basis of the stark contrast in the manner in which Dr Patel dealt with Eliot, which was very formal. Woodcock suspected that this was nothing to do with rank. Patel seemed to regard Eliot as a bureaucrat without the intellectual ability to make a meaningful contribution to the solution of murder cases.

The fact that Eliot delegated attendance at post-mortems to Molash (there were rumours Eliot had once vomited during one) probably didn't improve Dr Patel's opinion of him either. By contrast, Molash's track record of solving major crimes seemed to make Patel enjoy catching him out. Whatever the answer to the question, the Molash/Patel dialogue qualified as entertainment in Woodcock's book, when compared to the humdrum legwork that comprised the bulk of a typical investigation.

Molash looked across at Woodcock, thinking that his trusted sergeant was likely to be in enough trouble as it was for pushing his sense of humour too far.

8

"What are our initial theories then, lads?" said Eliot as they surveyed the front of 12 Newton Street. This was all part of Eliot's desire for informality and encouraging subordinate officers to offer opinions. It had the fringe benefit of covering up the fact that he was usually slower than Molash to assess a situation.

Molash decided that on this occasion it was better for him, rather than Woodcock, to take the initiative. "We'll see what Dr Patel says shortly but it seems likely there was no physical assault on the victim. If ingesting some sort of drug caused the cyanosis, rather than it occurring naturally, then either he took it himself or someone poisoned him. Either way, the three obvious times for him to have ingested it were at the Union Bar, whilst having the nightcap in the lounge or in his room when everybody went to bed.

"We'll need to put together an evidential timeline. Given that they were drinking quite heavily, many drugs would have caused a pretty obvious change in alertness, which suggests it is less likely to have been ingested early in the evening. We'll question his housemates on how Mark was behaving.

"It's possible someone could have got into the house after everyone went to bed, and gone upstairs and given him an overdose. Once Dr Patel has done an initial examination, we'll look at CCTV and what sort of house-to-house is appropriate."

Neither of Molash's colleagues had anything to add to that initial plan and they were preparing to seek entry to 12 Newton Street when a young man, very tall and heavily built, came running up the street. Danny Wilson looked in good condition and was barely out of breath when he asked, "Are you here about Mark? Is it true that he's dead?" Even when faced with the potential death of a housemate, Wilson's friendly manner was still in evidence.

"Do you live here, Sir?" Eliot enquired, and on obtaining an introduction he asked Danny to follow them into the house.

"Anyone unauthorised trying to gain entry, Constable?" Molash asked Coleman, who replied in the negative.

Clinton had heard the door open and had come downstairs. He exchanged a brief greeting with Eliot and suggested Danny go to his room, with the same no-contact drill he had issued to Jack Freeman. Eliot then went through his understanding of the information so far in painstaking detail with Clinton.

Since calling Eliot, Clinton had asked Jack Freeman who else lived at 12 Newton Street and, on obtaining a list, had got Coleman to call them all and tell them that there was a police request to return to the house straightaway. If they demanded an explanation Coleman was to tell them that Mark had died and on no account were they to communicate that fact.

Clinton had asked Jack whether any girlfriends had stayed the previous night and Chloe Hartwell's name had been added to the list of those requested to come to 12 Newton Street. It seemed that a girl called Annette had also stayed the night, but it wasn't known where she lived or what her mobile number was.

35

Clinton was summing up that nothing they or Keith Bourne had discovered so far gave any suggestion of suicide, when the door opened again and Dr Patel walked in clad in the same outfit as the police officers. "Good afternoon, Chief Inspector," she said formally to Eliot, then added, "Good afternoon, team," looking at Molash, eyes twinkling. "Where is he?"

It was Clinton who answered, "Top floor, it's the only room up there. He's lying in the bed." Dr Patel nodded and made her way up the stairs.

"Anything more you need from us, Sir?" Clinton asked Eliot.

Eliot shook his head. "Thanks, Inspector," he said. "Can you attend the 8am briefing tomorrow, please? I'd like you to hear everything we've got at that stage to see if it triggers anything from what you have seen. Given we're so close to the station, the incident room will be there."

Clinton acquiesced and, looking at Molash, added, "We'll get everything onto HOLMES this afternoon." Molash gave a nod of thanks as King emerged from the shadows and the pair left.

Before Eliot, Molash and Woodcock walked up the two flights of stairs to Mark Gower's bedroom, they opened the doors to the downstairs rooms and gave swift, appraising glances around them.

It was Molash who took the longest, walking round both the kitchen and the lounge. They bore the hallmark of a typical, thriving house. Not that messy considering six male university students were living together. Not run-down but not luxurious.

When they reached Mark Gower's bedroom on the top floor Dr Patel was taking a swab from Mark Gower's mouth. Eliot was always at his most jovial when faced with a dead body, even one as peaceful as Mark Gower's. "Any surprises for us, Doc?" he asked.

Dr Patel straightened up and gave Eliot a look that intimated that she had no idea what he might have been expecting, making that an impossible question to answer. "There are no signs of any sort of physical assault nor any injection marks, new or old. I've taken a sample from his nose, but there's no evidence he was in the habit of snorting anything like cocaine. I've taken a hair sample which should confirm the position.

"There is cyanosis which suggests that death may have been caused by lack of oxygen in his system. I'll be able to tell you more after the post-mortem, but from the look of him, he was in good condition. Not just fit," she said with a look in the direction of the policemen as she pointed to Mark Gower's muscled torso, "but with the natural health of youth that young men have at that age which only lasts a few years," she added pointedly. "I'd be surprised if I find that he had any serious ongoing health issues when I open him up."

"Keith tells me that there is no sign of a suicide note and that the evidence of the victim's phone suggests he was a happy, well-adjusted young man with no reason to take his own life."

"There is therefore nothing at this stage to point strongly towards suicide, murder, natural causes or an accidental drug overdose. Post-mortem at noon tomorrow if that suits you all?" Patel concluded, emphasising the final word.

Anxious to ask a question rather than answer one, Eliot replied, "If it was some sort of drug that killed him, it was probably taken either in the Union Bar during the evening, around midnight here when the residents apparently had a nightcap or in his room. Is there anything from the time of death to give a pointer?"

Patel shook her head. "Not at this stage, though later rather than earlier would make more sense. If he's taken a fatal dose there aren't many drugs where he would be fine for several hours and then die in his sleep. Keith tells me the glasses and bottles that were used for the nightcap haven't been touched so they'll be bagged for forensics."

Woodcock asked, "If something was slipped into a drink, there might be traces on the person who had done that?"

Dr Patel looked as if she was about to make a barbed remark but remembered Eliot was there and so instead said, "Good question, Sergeant. A search of the house for anything that looks like a receptacle for any form of drug or poison would be a good idea. It's possible clothes would have been contaminated too so the clothes they wore yesterday should be tested. If we find any drugs in the post-mortem, that is."

"On that subject," Eliot asked, "what priority can we have for the forensics?"

"Very little until the post-mortem, Chief Inspector," Patel replied. "If we find something that suggests this young man was poisoned then we can get it towards the top of the pile."

With a final sad glance at the corpse, Dr Patel rose and gathered her belongings. As she prepared to leave the room she stopped by Molash who was, characteristically, leaning against the wall by the door.

Whilst he'd been listening, Molash had been assessing Mark Gower's room and how it fitted into the bigger picture at 12 Newton Street. His initial impression was that the evidence which Clinton had related from Gower's phone, that Mark was an unusually cheerful individual, was likely to prove right.

Yet this was a house into which Molash thought evil had come. It hadn't inveigled its way into the walls as dry rot does, but evil had been here, poisoning the heart of someone – before they had poisoned the young man whose shell remained recumbent on the bed.

Someone who didn't know Molash as well as Patel did might have mistaken his slouching for inattention. Patel knew it indicated that Molash's mind was likely to be in top gear and she said quietly but pointedly, "You'd better gather your wits, Jimmy, I reckon you're going to need them on this one."

9

Molash asked Coleman whether he'd been able to contact the other three students living at 12 Newton Street, Ryan Sandling, Owen Lloyd and Sam Taylor. Coleman replied that he'd spoken to Sam and that Sam and Owen were catching the first train back from London. He wasn't sure what the position with Chloe Hartwell was as Sam had said he would speak to her. He'd called Ryan a couple of times, but his phone was off. He'd left a message.

Eliot, Molash and Woodcock went to look at the kitchen and lounge. Woodcock looked round and sniffed, saying, "I'd expected it to be a complete mess, six twenty-year-old lads living together. It's been bashed about a bit but it's not too bad."

"Coleman has done a good job protecting the evidence here," said Molash. "If there has been foul play and Gower's nightcap was poisoned then that could be crucial."

"If that happened why didn't the killer wash up? They've presumably had plenty of chance?" asked Eliot.

"That's definitely on the list of questions that need answering," said Molash. "It may be that they thought it wouldn't matter. There was always going to be a post-mortem. It might be that by establishing the poison was in the nightcap that it pointed more to suicide as Mark made the drinks." He turned away with a dissatisfied look and added, "If he was poisoned at all."

Eliot tended to get twitchy when away from the station for any length of time and his two colleagues sensed he wanted to agree the next steps and leave. He started running through the typical golden hour(s) checks.

"What level of house-to-house do we think is worth doing at the moment, Jimmy? This is your turf." Molash reflected, not for the first time, that the entire town appeared to be his, rather than Eliot's, turf.

House-to-house enquiries are often a crucial part of a murder investigation where there is no obvious suspect who was close to the victim. One of the most high-profile murder cases this century was the abduction and killing of thirteen-year-old Millie Dowler in 2002. Her killer, Levi Bellfield, lived right by the point of her abduction. When during the house-to-house enquiries there was no response from Bellfield's home the police didn't try to contact him again. Bellfield killed at least two more people and committed multiple other serious crimes before being imprisoned. He was convicted of Millie Dowler's murder when in prison in 2011. A well-organised house-to-house enquiry operation might have stopped Bellfield offending again.

Molash replied thoughtfully, "If Gower was murdered then it looks likely he was poisoned either at the Union Bar or in 12 Newton Street. House-to-house is likely to be of limited value."

Woodcock said, "Half the people living in Newton Street must be students. The house backs onto Stuart Street which is similar. We can ask the university for a list of addresses of students and visit as many of those as we can that were in close vicinity. As soon as the news has been broken to his parents we can start the house-to-house."

Molash nodded and added, "It might prove a waste of resource, but let's do it. We'll reassess in the morning once we've got some decent preliminary information on Gower. In the meantime we could do with some CCTV on the house, especially of the front door last night and ideally of these students walking back from the Union Bar. We'll go outside and have a look in a minute."

Eliot nodded and Molash continued, "Woody is going to stay here and do a preliminary interview with the students as they get back. We should find out what happened at the Union Bar last night. Let's identify the manager and speak to him first. Also we should speak to one of the lecturers who knew Gower well. The other issue is getting the social media checks started, including getting all their phones to digital forensics."

Woodcock chipped in, "Knowing Keith he'll be doing it anyway, but I asked him to look for any receptacle that might have had drugs in it. If Gower used it to commit suicide then it may well still be in the house, likewise if someone poisoned him here."

Eliot thought for a few moments and nodded. "Sounds good. Are we all agreed that there is no obvious wider threat to the public? We have no reason to suppose that there is a maniac on the loose poisoning random members of the public?" As SIO this should have been Eliot's decision to make, but he wanted Molash to agree and so phrased it as a consultation.

Molash sighed inwardly but said evenly, "Agreed, but we'll discuss it at the initial briefing in the morning," to which Eliot replied, "Good. I'll see you both back at the station."

After Eliot had left, Molash and Woodcock conducted a preliminary walk around of the area surrounding 12 Newton Street. Newton Street backed onto another set of similar houses in Stuart Street with only a brief alleyway between them. Neither had gardens, which when combined with the large number of bedrooms made them ideal for student lodgings.

The rear door of 12 Newton Street was locked and bolted, and it took Woodcock three attempts to open it, his hands getting grimy in the process. The windows to the alleyway were too small for anyone except perhaps a child to get through. The possibility of an assailant entering 12 Newton Street the previous night from the rear of the building was quickly ruled out.

By contrast, if the front door had not been locked, anyone could have walked into 12 Newton Street. There were also two big windows on each of the ground and first floors plus a slightly smaller one in the attic, all of which were big enough for an adult to enter by, albeit a ladder would have been needed to reach all but the two on the ground floor.

On the other side of Newton Street, a couple of doors down from being opposite number 12, was an old-fashioned, family-owned hardware store. The store had two CCTV cameras, one of which was pointing in the direction of 12 Newton Street. Molash called into the station and was put through to the newly set-up incident room. He arranged for one of the team to visit the hardware store straightaway to maximise the chances of obtaining CCTV footage from the previous night before it was recorded over.

"OK, Woody," Molash said, "you go back into the house and start the preliminary interviews. I'm going to the incident room to ensure all the initial lines of enquiry are up and running. I'll see you back there."

10

Eliot's lack of interpersonal skills meant that it was invariably Molash who was the senior officer that went to see the victim's family. However, given that it was nearly a two-hour drive to Mark Gower's parents' house, Molash wouldn't be the first officer to visit them. Before departing for 12 Newton Street, Eliot had spoken to Constables Sally Fordham and Alexander Sayer, who would be the Family Liaison Officers ('FLOs') with the Gower family.

Eliot briefed them on the facts as known to that point, and they set off for the Gowers' family home immediately. Shortly before they arrived they would call the incident room to check for any updates. With the crime scene indoors and Mark's housemates instructed not to use personal devices to communicate with anyone, there was little risk of Mr and Mrs Gower hearing of their son's death before Fordham and Sayer arrived.

In this instance Mr and Mrs Gower would have no idea what was coming. It was a completely different scenario from, for example, where a person goes missing and relatives fear the worst when the police arrive.

Fordham rang the bell at the spacious-looking semi-detached house where the Gower family lived. The front garden wasn't large but well kept, and several rose bushes were in full bloom. A car was parked in the drive and they were in luck: both Mark's parents were at home.

Bob Gower opened the door and before he could say anything Fordham began briskly, producing her warrant card, "Good afternoon, Mr Gower, Detective Constable Fordham, this is Detective Constable Sayer. Would it be possible to have a word with you and your wife, please, Sir?"

Bob Gower was taken aback but was a calm and intelligent man in his late forties with plenty of worldly experience and he invited them in. He led the way to a large open-plan living space where he had clearly been working. An Apple Mac computer screen, wireless keyboard and mouse were on the kitchen table next to a pile of A4 paper. It looked as if Gower was annotating a draft report. Mrs Gower was carrying a washing basket in the direction of the utility room.

Bob Gower told his wife Lydia, who looked a few years younger than him, the police officers' names and explained that they wanted to talk to them both. Mrs Gower put down the washing basket and offered tea and coffee.

Fordham didn't want to delay telling them their son had died, and kettles aren't the ideal contraptions to be handling when told your only child is dead, so she politely declined, adding, "Perhaps you could both sit down, this will take a little while."

In their last seconds of normality the thoughts of Bob and Lydia Gower were similar to those of the average law-abiding citizen when the police unexpectedly turn up at their house and ask to talk to them.

Bob wondered whether he'd failed to pay a bill such as his

road tax, despite knowing full well that he was up to date with all such invoices. Lydia, who had a penchant for speed, wondered whether there had been a complaint about her driving.

They sat next to each other, with nothing more than the natural apprehension most people would feel. Lydia smiled. "How can we help you, Constable Fordham?"

When breaking the news of the death of a loved one, police officers use clear, unequivocal language. The use of softer terms such as 'passed away' can confuse the issue. FLOs talk compassionately but directly, and Fordham said, "I'm very sorry to be bringing bad news to you. This morning your son Mark was found dead in his bed at 12 Newton Street, Middleham."

Lydia Gower let out a sound halfway between a low scream and an exclamation of 'My God' and instinctively clutched at her husband's arm. Bob Gower stared, uncomprehending, at Fordham.

Neither could articulate any response, so Fordham continued, "Mark looks to have died peacefully and apparently alone in his room. He'd been drinking in the Union Bar that evening. He was cheerful and went to bed in good spirits according to his friends. I'm afraid there will have to be a post-mortem, but it doesn't look at this stage as if Mark was the subject of any sort of physical assault."

"But how could he have died then?" asked Lydia in a shout, her voice out of control. "He hardly had a day's illness in his life. He didn't use…" Her voice trailed off.

Fordham moved in swiftly. "We'll obviously get a definitive answer from the post-mortem, but from an initial examination I can confirm that there was no evidence of recreational drug use past or present." She paused to evaluate whether either of Mark's parents wanted to comment on that, and when they didn't, continued, "It is possible that Mark's death was due to natural causes."

Rapport can sometimes be built through the bereaved family

members feeling that FLOs are listening to, and ideally agreeing with, what they are saying, especially when they are defending the honour of the family member who has died.

Fordham therefore quickly added, "However, as Mrs Gower pointed out, Mark was in excellent health so that doesn't seem likely. Equally Mark was as cheerful and positive as usual yesterday so there's equally little reason to believe he took his own life. At the moment we are keeping an open mind, which means we have to treat the death as suspicious."

Bob Gower was as still as a statue on a plinth, his brain as cold and unmoving as frozen stone. Suddenly the tears came for Lydia and they surged from her as she started to shake. This woke her husband from his reverie and he threw his arms round her and held her, rocking gently to and fro.

Fordham and Sayer had seen it many times. Their instinct was that the Gowers would recover quicker than most – but it was the shock, the terrible, unparalleled shock.

Fordham waited until the Gowers looked back up at her and then explained that Sayer and herself were family liaison officers and the police's point of contact for the Gowers. As such they would be visiting the Gowers regularly to update them. They would be available at any time to take the Gowers' call should Mark's parents wish to discuss anything or remember any useful facts.

Fordham added that one of the senior investigating officers, a Detective Inspector Molash, had asked if he could visit them later in the day to ask them some questions. There is a natural human preference for dealing with the boss, which is magnified significantly during a police investigation into the death of a family member, and the Gowers accepted, subconscious gratitude behind their numb nods of the head.

There was a short silence whilst Fordham gave the Gowers the chance to digest what she'd told them. Suddenly Lydia asked, barely piercing the deathly hush, "Can we see Mark?"

It was one of the most common questions or Fordham and Sayer might not have heard well enough to understand. Fordham nodded her head gently and said, her voice a touch quieter, "Yes. We will need someone to formally identify the body after the post-mortem tomorrow. Perhaps I could arrange for you to come to Middleham on Friday?"

Lydia thanked her in a whisper and Fordham continued, "We'll also help arrange for the return of Mark's body after the post-mortem. I am afraid that we can't ask you to the house Mark was living in at 12 Newton Street at the moment as it's still a potential crime scene, but of course we will look after Mark's things and get them back to you as soon as we can.

"I'm sorry we don't have anything more to tell you, but Constable Sayer and myself will be providing regular updates. Is there anything you'd like to ask at this stage?"

That particular elephant, of course, filled the entire room. What both the Gowers wanted to scream was, "Why? Why Mark, who had everything to live for? Why are we the ones to suffer this?" Bob took Lydia's hand and shook his head on behalf of both of them.

Sayer had spotted the kettle in the kitchen and, having quietly refilled it and flicked the switch, gently suggested a cup of tea. Lydia raised her head from where she had burrowed into Bob's shoulder and neck and nodded, immediately changing her mind.

"I'd like some coffee, please. Bob, we should have some coffee," she added. Bob Gower, gradually regaining the power of speech, agreed and thanked Sayer.

A few minutes later four coffee cups were nearing empty and Fordham and Sayer had gained the impression that they were a devoted couple. Whatever challenges they may find that Mark Gower had faced in his short life, a dysfunctional family upbringing didn't look like being one of them. The request to see Mark's room had met with no resistance and Bob had roused himself and shown them upstairs.

Mark's room was relatively tidy but unremarkable. Even though he'd celebrated his twentieth birthday only a few months before, it was emphatically the room of a twenty-something rather than a teenager. There were no posters of footballers or musicians. The small desk was almost empty except for a portable television that faced the bed. The room contained a myriad of different sports kit. Rugby was the most common but by no means a dominant theme, and a hockey stick, squash racket and set of golf clubs were all in a corner with various sets of sports clothing.

A good part of the room was taken up with bookshelves. Mark was clearly a prolific reader on a wide range of subjects, but there was nothing suggestive. Books relating to the law degree he was studying for formed only a very small section of his library. There was a half-empty litre bottle of Sainsbury's own-brand vodka and a shot glass on a space on a bookshelf between a copy of *A Room with a View* and the rugby star Billy Vunipola's autobiography *Wrecking Ball*.

Sayer went over and inspected the vodka. Bob Gower moved uneasily in the doorway and said, "He always enjoyed a drink. Was that what killed him?" There was a hint of guilt, as if Bob Gower had encouraged his son about the social benefits that could be associated with alcohol and was now wondering whether his drinking had got out of hand.

Sayer shook his head. "I don't think so, Mr Gower. Mark had been drinking at the Union Bar as Constable Fordham mentioned but nothing out of the ordinary. We won't know for sure until the post-mortem."

A few minutes later they were back downstairs drinking more coffee and building the early strands of a relationship with the Gowers. The conversation was largely a repetition of what had gone before. When people have had an unexpected and serious shock, they often struggle to absorb and memorise what they're being told. Fordham and Sayer reckoned the Gowers were doing a better job than most.

They finished their coffees, reiterated that the Gowers could call either of them at any time and that Inspector Molash would be visiting later, and prepared to leave.

Having been shocked into silence for much of the FLOs' visit, after he'd opened the front door and caught up with the reality that Fordham and Sayer were leaving, Bob Gower burst out, "You think someone deliberately killed Mark, don't you?" After a brief silence, during which Fordham and Sayer quickly scrutinised him, he added, more quietly but forcefully, "Don't you?"

Both FLOs had plenty of experience of breaking the bad news of the death of unlikeable offspring to equally unlikeable parents. Both had warmed to the Gowers and Fordham paid him the compliment of honesty, giving a sad smile and saying, "We don't know yet, Mr Gower, but yes, that's our starting assumption."

Before she could continue, Bob Gower's incredulity exploded like a volcano erupting for the first time without warning from seismologists. "But that just can't be true. Who on this earth would want to kill Mark? He didn't make enemies; he made friends. He was kind, he was funny. I know I'm his dad but he wasn't just a good lad; he was a fantastic human being – everyone said so. Teachers, sports coaches, other parents, even. A car crash or other accident, God knows that would be hard enough. But wanting to snuff out the life of someone who had so much to give and wanted to give it. That's evil, that's…"

His voice trailed off and Fordham and Sayer gave him a moment to compose himself before the latter responded, "You're right, Mr Gower. It seems incredible. Perhaps we'll find another explanation. We're only at the very start of the investigation. Inspector Molash may be able to tell you more later today."

Gower's voice had deserted him again, but he nodded in understanding and the FLOs left. Once they were back on the motorway, they called Molash's mobile and briefed him. Molash listened to Fordham's account, thanked them and asked them to attend the 8am briefing the following day.

11

At 12 Newton Street Woodcock began the business of talking to Mark's housemates. Given that he had found the body, Woodcock spoke first to Jack Freeman.

Despite the events of the day Jack's hair remained immaculate and his beard didn't have a hair out of place. Jack was in no way dishevelled. He looked ready to go out on a date.

He had what Woodcock's mother called 'cheeky-boy charm'. Woodcock's initial impression was favourable but also that Jack was nervous about something. He was open-minded about whether it had anything to do with Mark Gower's death.

Jack explained haltingly that he was studying chemistry and had just finished his part-one exams. Woodcock began by covering ground he already knew fairly well, the events of that day. This seemed to have the effect of relaxing Jack and his answers became increasingly fluent.

However, Jack's manner changed noticeably when the subject turned to the previous evening. He rushed his replies, seemingly trying to get to the end of his answers as quickly as possible. Woodcock wasn't concerned about the lack of factual detail; there were (at least) the rest of Jack's housemates from whom to obtain an accurate picture of the previous evening.

Woodcock's priority was to discover what was making Jack so edgy. The nervousness hadn't been consistent, which would have been indicative of someone who was naturally uneasy or who had reacted more severely than is typical to finding a friend dead. It seemed connected with discussing the events of the previous night. It might be concern about giving himself away if he had killed Mark, but equally it might be something else.

Jack had explained that the six of them had left for the Union Bar shortly after six o'clock. They'd sat on the table they often occupied in the centre of the main bar area and drank and talked for the next five hours or so.

Woodcock asked, "Other than going to the bar or the toilet, did the six of you leave the table much?"

Woodcock fancied that a hint of concern came into Jack's eyes. He replied, "Not much, hardly at all in the first half of the evening. A few people came over to talk to us but nothing out of the ordinary." He paused and ran his tongue over his lips. Woodcock sensed that by remaining silent he would more effectively force Jack to talk about whatever was concerning him.

"Mark, Ryan and I left the others to talk to Zara Allen, Maddy Church and Hannah Lewis for a while. That would have been about an hour from the end of the evening."

Woodcock replied, "You three went over to talk to them? They didn't come over to your table?"

Jack hesitated. "Yes, well, we knew them and I saw them having a drink together and suggested we went over to say hello."

He paused and Woodcock said, "It was your suggestion to leave your table and go and see these girls?" He wouldn't have been pressing the point but for Jack's obvious unease.

Jack nodded and seemed reluctant to say more, and

51

Woodcock was forced to continue. "Tell me about the time you spent with these three girls?"

"There's nothing to tell. They are girls we know and we chatted to them. It was all friendly, there was no hassle."

"So the girls were all on good terms with Mark then?" asked Woodcock.

It was palpably obvious that Jack had been thinking about his interaction with the girls, not Mark's, but after a pause he agreed with Woodcock's assertion. Woodcock continued, "What happened next?"

There was a long pause. Having left it too long not to be obvious that he was tense, Jack said, "I left because I saw a girl I knew." A few seconds later he added, "A girl I liked." Woodcock nodded but remained silent. After another pause Jack said, "She was dancing and I motioned to her offering her a drink. I owed her a drink and she nodded, so I went to the bar."

Again there was a silence. Woodcock figured Jack Freeman had had several hours to get his story straight and that he was making a mess of it. Jack took a deep breath and continued, "We sat chatting over the drink, just the two of us, and then I invited her back here and she said she wanted to."

It was an odd choice of words to end the sentence, implying some sort of justification of Jack's proposition. Woodcock asked, "So who went back to 12 Newton Street when the bar shut?"

"All six of us, Annette, who came back with me, and Chloe, who is Sam's girlfriend."

"Can you give me the girls' surnames and mobile numbers, please?"

Jack looked more nervous than ever. "I've got Chloe Hartwell's number in my phone. You said you wanted to take our phones so you can contact her from this," he said, offering over his phone. Woodcock took out a forensic bag and let Jack drop his phone into it.

"Is Annette's number in your phone too?" he asked.

"Er, well, no. I'd never asked her for her mobile number. I hadn't wanted to seem too…" Jack tailed off, realising he was caught between a rock and a hard place.

"That's alright, Sir," said Woodcock calmly. "We can trace her easily enough if she's a student here. What's her surname?" Jack licked his lips again. Woodcock looked faintly amused. "Do I take it you don't know the young lady's surname, Sir?"

Jack Freeman was literally wriggling as he sat on his bed. "She was doing history of art. She'd just done her finals. I was more interested in that than her surname."

"She stayed the night?"

"Yes, well, part of it. She was gone when I woke up this morning."

Woodcock wondered why Jack Freeman was so apprehensive about the one-night stand he'd just had. It was hardly unusual in student life. If Jack had guilty knowledge he might be trying to conceal it behind faked nervousness.

Woodcock decided to test the water by changing the subject. "What can you tell me about your housemates, Mr Freeman? Did everyone get on here?"

Jack was like an eager spaniel, keen to help and seemingly delighted to not be talking about Annette. "We're mates, we have been virtually since day one. They're a great set of boys. We work hard and play hard. It's our time to have fun, right? We go out on the beers a fair bit and there's never any trouble between us."

Woodcock thought this all sounded too good to be true. "Never any trouble? Usually when a bunch of young lads go out drinking there tends to be the odd argument, even amongst friends."

"I never had an argument with Mark in the two years we've been here, Sergeant. He isn't the rowing type. He is, was, very laid-back."

"So you've never seen Mark arguing with anyone?"

Jack thought for a moment. "Not really. He had a few words

with Ryan last week. We were in a pub and we'd all had a few. It didn't come to anything. Ryan had been getting a bit above himself, I think, ordering people around. Mark put him back in his box. It was nothing."

"Which pub?" asked Woodcock.

"I'm not sure. We were on a pint-a-pub all-dayer to celebrate the end of the exams, so it wasn't as if we were in one pub. It might have been The Swan in the High Street, I think. Look, Sergeant, Ryan wasn't gassed about where we were drinking, that was it. It didn't matter. None of us would want to hurt Mark, or each other for that matter."

"Tell me about the nightcap."

Jack recited what he'd told Coleman. He explained that he went to the toilet whilst Mark was making the drinks. He'd seen Sam go into the kitchen as he was heading for the toilet, but Sam had been back in the lounge by the time Jack returned. He himself hadn't gone into the kitchen. He'd wanted to get back to Annette in the lounge, as she was a bit shy.

He hadn't wanted to leave her, but he'd needed a pee for a while. He hadn't noticed what the others were doing whilst they drank the nightcap in the lounge because he was talking to Annette. The two of them hadn't left the sofa until after Mark finished his drink. The nightcap rule was that once the person who had chosen the nightcap finished, everyone else had to as well.

Woodcock had one final question. "Did Mark's behaviour change at all during the evening, in particular towards the end of it? If he'd consumed some sort of drug then he would probably be less alert as a result of the mixture of it and alcohol, so it would be different from the natural effect a few pints of beer has."

Jack considered this for a while. "No, I don't think so, but then as I said I wasn't really paying much attention to Mark from the time I met up with Annette. Owen, Ryan and Danny were chatting to him as we had the nightcap, I think. They will probably be more helpful."

Woodcock thought he'd heard enough. There was an element of Jack protesting too much with the 'I only had eyes for Annette' routine, but Woodcock figured there was a grain of truth in it. They'd probably get more from the girl. Jack's mind had seemingly been solely focused on getting her into bed. He explained to Jack that they would be asked to come in to the police station and make a statement over the next few days. In the meantime, he asked Jack for the clothes he'd worn the previous night and bagged them.

Jack Freeman stared at Woodcock's retreating figure as the policeman left the bedroom. Jack wondered whether Woodcock had comprehended what he had been doing the previous night.

12

Woodcock's conversation with Danny Wilson was more straightforward. Danny was saddened and nonplussed by Mark's death but was calm and answered questions readily. He explained that Mark and he were both studying law so he knew Mark from work as well as play, as he put it.

He had nothing bad to say about Mark. He told Woodcock that Mark was nailed on for a first and that he himself was optimistic of a strong two-one. There was no hint of envy in his tone and Woodcock warmed to him. He asked Danny to tell him about his movements that day and received a simple, clear account.

"I was planning on having a lazy day. The forecast is good for the next few days, it's due to be hot at the weekend and I just wanted to relax. The exams were full-on and we'd had a few big nights since we finished last week. Ryan was up with the lark for once, though, and had a good idea about going up to the campus to start getting the textbooks for next year. If you get in fairly quickly you can get them cheap second-hand from those who have just done their finals.

"Ryan is doing economics, which is at the far side of the campus, so we parted by the law faculty which is at this end. I suggested he give me a buzz when he was done and we'd wander back together. He'd forgotten to charge his phone, though, and it was dead. He said he'd pop his head in the law library on the way back to see if I was there but if not he'd see me at home.

"Anyway, there was a notice board by Old Man Bates' room with a list of books and other stuff we need for next year. Outside there was a trestle table and a few of the third-years were manning it, selling second-hand books. There were stacks there and so it didn't look as if we needed to make an instant decision. I noted a few prices and went to the bookshop to compare the prices with those for new books. I had chatted to some mates and was making some notes to discuss with Mark when PC Coleman called and told me."

"Why didn't you wake Mark up and suggest he went with you and Ryan?" asked Woodcock.

Danny shrugged. "It's a boring job so there was no point both of us doing it. I wasn't going myself but when Ryan suggested it I thought it was a good idea. I thought if I had a list of new and second-hand prices, it would save Mark a job. We could discuss which, if any, were worth buying new and go up and sort it out later in the week."

Woodcock smiled briefly. He got the impression that Danny Wilson would always be the type to help others out. It was probably a natural instinct, one that Danny did without thinking about. Woodcock was touching six foot in his socks, but Danny towered over him as they both stood talking in Danny's bedroom. Whilst Danny's freckled face wasn't handsome, it was attractive, a good part of the attraction laying in his naturally helpful, friendly manner.

"What can you tell me about last night?" Woodcock asked.

"We went to the Union Bar not long after it opened. Maybe half-six. It was busy for a Tuesday but lots more people are out once the exams finish. We were there early so got a good table and we drank and talked. It was just a normal night out."

"How was Mark?"

"In top form. He's typically the life and soul of the party but he was particularly so last night." He stopped and looked shrewdly at Woodcock. "If you're thinking he might have killed himself, forget it. He was the most positive person I have ever met. This is either an accident or..." He petered out, not wanting to articulate the possibility that someone would want to kill his friend.

"It may be an accident, of course. Are you aware of anyone with a motive to kill Mark?"

Danny looked about to laugh and then realised the seriousness of the situation just in time. "No way. Everyone liked Mark, we all get on well here. We're just a bunch of lads studying and enjoying ourselves. Nobody could want to kill any of us."

Woodcock switched tack. "Were you with Mark all of last evening?"

"Pretty much. I went to the bar and to have a piss from time to time, but otherwise yes. We were on a table in the middle of the bar and people came to chat to us, but nobody actually sat down at our table until Chloe, that's Sam's girlfriend, near the end of the evening. Mark got up once or twice and stood talking by our table to a couple of lads, from the rugby club, I think, but that was it." He stopped suddenly. "Actually, that's not right. Mark did get up late on and went to talk to those tennis girls.

"I don't know them. One of them is called Hannah, I think, and Mark thought she was quite fit. Jack and Ryan went with him, but Mark and Ryan were back after about ten minutes."

Woodcock told him that Jack had given him the names of the three girls. He asked Danny for his account of what happened then.

"We all left. Chloe was staying with Sam, they've gone on a protest march in London today. So has Owen. We all walked

58

back chatting as normal. The only difference was Jack was a little bit behind us, with the girl he'd hooked up with. Annette, I think her name was."

Woodcock asked, "Did Mark, or any of you, consume anything on the way home? Do you carry hipflasks, for example?"

"No, we never use hipflasks. We came straight home and the next thing we had was the nightcap. I think Mark was on his own in the kitchen, but I'm not sure – he certainly brought the tray in on his own. I was chatting to Mark, Owen and Ryan whilst we drank it. To be honest I was keeping half an eye on the sofa too – it was amusing seeing how Jack was getting on. Ryan was laying bets."

"What was the big deal about Jack and Annette?" Woodcock asked.

Danny grinned ruefully. "Well, you'll see when you meet her, Sergeant. She was a bit shy and, well, not the normal type of girl that spends a night here. Knowing Jack, he just wanted the challenge of seeing if he could get her into bed."

"If someone had put something into Mark's nightcap, would you have seen?"

Danny looked as if he was about to tell Woodcock that none of them would do such a thing but thought better of it. "Maybe. The general house rule is that if you're not drinking your drink you put it down. So our glasses would have been left on the table behind us most of the time. It's possible someone could have put something into Mark's glass. Into mine too, for that matter.

"I remember Ryan saying that Jack was breaking that rule. He was holding his glass and once he clinked glasses with that Annette. Owen was saying Jack should get a penalty drink for that rule breach and we agreed we'd sort something for him for what's now tonight.

"I think Mark still had half his left when he suddenly decided to neck it. The rule is that when the person who mixed the nightcap finishes, so does everyone else. We finished the nightcap and went to bed. We left Jack and Annette downstairs on the sofa. Jack's room is next to mine and I heard them coming up a bit later, but I sleep soundly and didn't hear anything else."

"You were with Mark whilst the nightcap was drunk. Was there any change in his manner to suggest he'd consumed some sort of drug and it was starting to have an impact on him?"

Danny's response was prompt. "Not that I noticed. We were all half-cut but Mark was his normal self. He certainly wasn't looking spaced out."

Woodcock thanked Danny and explained about wanting to take his phone and previous day's clothes. Danny nodded in understanding and handed over his without protest and agreed to come to the station to make a statement when requested over the next couple of days.

As he was handing over his phone, he said, "Under the Police and Criminal Evidence Act technically we don't have to give you our phones unless we are under arrest?" Woodcock confirmed that this was the case and explained that the police were requesting voluntary assistance and thanked Danny for his co-operation. Danny smiled and said that at least he'd got one question in his recent law degree exams correct.

13

When Molash arrived at Middleham Police Station the process of setting up what in official police parlance is the major incident room (generally referred to as simply the 'incident room') was in full swing. Eliot was bustling about talking to members of the team, handing out roles.

Even though it was possible an explanation that didn't involve criminal behaviour would explain Mark Gower's death, Molash had the scent of the chase in his nostrils. An instinct told him that someone had deliberately killed Gower and that it would be far from straightforward to work out who or why.

Molash shook himself out of his reverie. He was in danger of believing something for the most common reason any of us believe anything. The reason that makes us believe that the football team we support will win the league this year, despite all the obvious evidence to the contrary. Or leads us to trust someone who we strongly suspect is being unfaithful to us. He had been bored and so was desperate for a proper investigation to get his teeth into? Was he believing it was murder because he wanted to?

He closed his eyes and thought for a moment. Was he making something out of nothing here? The more he thought about it the more he was confident that he wasn't. It looked pretty clear that Gower wasn't the suicidal type. Molash doubted he was anything other than an occasional recreational drug user, if at all. Not a candidate to overdose but then again you never could tell... They'd check with his GP but he looked the picture of health. Murder for reasons unknown looked the most likely by a process of elimination.

Perhaps Gower had had a weak heart and hadn't wanted to tell his friends. Perhaps his joie de vivre was born out of the knowledge that he had to cram as much enjoyment in whilst he could. Molash thought this unlikely, but it needed checking out. He walked over to a desk where Detective Constable Yasmin Shah was setting up.

She was labelling files when Molash arrived and explained why he wanted an immediate check on the victim's GP. Shah nodded and said, "I'll start with his GP at home. If he had any serious health conditions, he'll probably have registered with a surgery here too, or via the university. I'll cover that too." Molash thanked her and went to view the erection of a huge clearboard.

Eliot's love of new technological ideas always ensured that his incident room had all the latest gizmos. In the view of Molash and almost all of the rest of the team most of them were of negligible value, but Molash did like the state-of-the-art, giant perspex writing board that Eliot had invested in. It was portable and could be divided into different sections or used as a whole.

Eliot always seemed to be impressed by lots of different-coloured arrows pointing in different directions, illustrating different lines of enquiry. It looked as if his team knew what they were doing. By contrast, Molash saw the true power of it. He liked visual aids and would stand and look at it, seeing how all the elements of the enquiry interlinked. The break in more than one case had come when he suddenly realised the missing link in the chain of evidence whilst standing staring at the clearboard.

Having ensured the clearboard was where he wanted it, Molash went and spoke to veteran Detective Constable Roy Clark. After more than thirty years with the police Clark had foregone the opportunity to retire because he enjoyed the job and took the view that someone with all his experience shouldn't be pensioning themselves off in their mid-fifties.

Clark had a reputation for getting on with pretty much anybody and greeted Molash in friendly fashion. "Afternoon, Guv, any particular pointers from the crime scene you want me to keep an eye out for?"

Molash in his turn liked Clark's simple efficiency and replied cheerfully, "It's an interesting one, Roy. I've got a gut feeling that it might take an odd turn, so keep your eye out for anything out of the ordinary. It's possible he was poisoned.

"Woody is bringing in the phones of those living at 12 Newton Street, assuming none of them object, plus the clothes they wore last night. A couple of girls stayed the night too, so we'll look at getting theirs as well. Keith has bagged the victim's phone, iPad, etc. Let's get everything to digital forensics quickly and see if there are any clues on social media, etc. If the digital forensics boys can get that done tomorrow then we'll use the return of phones to lubricate the process of getting them all in for interviews on Friday."

Having satisfied himself that the initial lines of enquiry were being pursued efficiently, to maximise the golden hour(s) harvest of evidence, Molash left the incident room.

Climbing into his car, he began the drive to Mark Gower's family home, determined to find out what Mark was really like.

14

It was half past two by the time Ryan Sandling arrived back at Newton Street. He seemed bemused to find PC Coleman on the door and, having identified himself to Coleman, gobsmacked to find out why. Opening the door, Coleman called out to Woodcock, who'd been wondering where Ryan was.

Woodcock asked Ryan which was his bedroom and asked if he could talk to him in it. Ryan Sandling had the air of someone who thought it might turn out to be a spoof with Mark jumping out of a cupboard at any moment.

Woodcock wondered whether this was all an act and decided to take on a more formal tone. "I appreciate this must have been a big shock, Mr Sandling. Do you feel up to answering some questions?" Ryan looked at him as if to imply that was a stupid question and said that of course he was.

Woodcock began by asking for Ryan's movements that day. Ryan's story was the same as Danny's and he'd carried on to the economics building. A similar sale of second-hand books for prospective final-year students was occurring as it was for the law students. He'd spent the morning looking for bargains and brandished the contents of the rucksack he'd been carrying as evidence. He'd also bought the recently published fifth edition of Romer's *Advanced Macroeconomics* new from the bookshop.

"I was hoping to get everything in one go, but there were a couple of books that I couldn't find second-hand and I didn't want to buy them new. I kept looking but eventually I gave up and it was lunchtime so I thought Danny would be long gone and he was. I couldn't call him as my phone was dead and I was hungry. We hadn't had any breakfast and I was a bit jaded after last night so I stopped and had lunch in the Wetherspoons in town. Had a couple of pints to take the edge off. Then I came home."

"When did your phone run out of battery?" Woodcock asked.

"During the night. I'd forgotten to charge it when we got back last night and only realised when I checked it when we got to the law faculty."

"What can you tell me about last night?"

"What do you want to know? It was just a normal night at the bar. We drank and talked. Nobody had a row with Mark if that's what you are insinuating. He was his usual buoyant self. No depression that half the world seems to have these days. We're not the types."

Woodcock felt slightly irked by the arrogant dismissal of mental health issues and Ryan's apparent lack of awareness of the fact that they can afflict anyone. He put it down to the ignorance of youth, but he looked at Ryan with interest. There was something very self-contained about him. Woodcock framed his next question slightly differently in consequence.

"If anyone had put something in Mark's drink towards the end of the evening at the Union Bar or back here when you had the nightcap, do you think you're the sort of person who would have noticed?"

Ryan shrugged his shoulders. "Maybe. If you were getting someone a drink at the Union Bar I guess you could slip some Rohypnol into their drink on the way back without anyone seeing. It'd have been trickier with us last night, though, as the six of us were in a round and we all drink the same lager at the Union Bar. You couldn't know who would take which pint when you put the tray down on the table. Anyway, I didn't see anyone put anything in Mark's drink, or anyone else's, for that matter."

Woodcock asked about the three girls from the tennis club, but Ryan Sandling became uncommunicative. Jack had seen them entering the bar. They didn't come in often. The two of them and Mark had gone over and chatted with them for a few minutes, but the girls had drunk their drinks and gone.

Ryan's memory appeared hazier about the end of the evening. Woodcock asked him about the nightcap.

"Mark made the nightcap in the kitchen and brought it in on a tray as usual. Gin and tonic. I think he was on his own in the kitchen making them, though I couldn't swear to it. I didn't go into the kitchen."

"If anything was slipped into Mark's glass could it have been done in the lounge?" Woodcock asked.

"It's possible, I suppose," said Ryan slowly. "There were eight of us in there though. You'd think someone would see. I didn't. I was keeping an eye on Jack and the girl he'd brought home, though. We were having a bet on whether he'd manage to get her pants off. She looked like she might be a virgin so it wasn't the certainty it usually was where Jack was concerned."

"Who were you betting with?"

"All of us were discussing it. Except for Sam. He was marooned on the sofa getting a pep talk from Chloe about today's protest march. We weren't actually betting money, you understand. It was just banter, us discussing the likelihood of her falling for Jack's charms."

"How did the nightcap end?"

Ryan thought for a moment. "The rule is that when the mixer, in this case Mark, finishes, everyone else finishes. Mark suddenly produced an empty glass and we all followed his excellent example. We then went to bed."

"Did all of you go to bed then?"

Ryan considered again. "I did, I was ready for it. Mark certainly did as I followed him upstairs. I think the others did too."

"Did you notice any change in Mark's behaviour towards the end of the evening beyond the normal impact of a few pints?"

Ryan's eyes narrowed. "You mean as if he'd taken something that might have caused him to overdose? No, I didn't notice any difference. I wasn't at my sharpest at that stage, though."

Woodcock sensed Ryan had a bit of an ego and so asked an extra question. "Have you any idea how Mark died?"

Ryan suddenly became sombre. "No. I can't quite believe it. He always came across as the personification of the healthy, sporty student. Maybe he took something when he got up to his room and overdosed."

It sounded a bit thin, but then as yet there was no explanation that was any more convincing. Woodcock requested Ryan's clothes from the previous night and his phone. Ryan handed his phone over with a wry remark that it hadn't been much use all day anyway and dug out the relevant clothes.

As Woodcock left the room Ryan Sandling stood deep in thought. *What*, he mused, *are the police making of such an extraordinary situation?*

15

The Union Bar at the university opened at six o'clock and Detective Constable Yasmin Shah had spoken to the manager, Les Christie, and arranged for a brief interview at half past five, whilst the bar team were setting up.

The Union Bar was a large concourse with laminate flooring and sturdy-looking but inexpensive furniture. Whilst no connoisseur of drinking establishments, Shah looked around her thinking that it had all the atmosphere of an aircraft hangar. She mused that perhaps when it was full of young students it would be different.

Les Christie was of medium height with the classic hard beer belly of a man who had spent decades managing bars. He also had the natural friendliness of a good publican and greeted Shah warmly. With Shah not being an attractive woman, her face badly pock-marked from severe teenage acne, Christie's manner remained merely friendly. She declined his offer of a drink and he guided her to a corner table and pre-empted her.

"I was very sorry to hear about Mark Gower. He and his

mates were regulars in here and a good bunch. How can I help you?"

Shah was a very methodical police officer. She wasn't given to flashes of brilliant inspiration but rarely made mistakes. One of her talents was an ability to get witnesses talking comfortably and to ask the right mixture of open and closed questions to maximise the amount of information gathered.

She began by asking an open question. "Thanks, Mr Christie, we really appreciate your help. I think we're going to need it too. At this early stage there seems no reasonable explanation for how Mark Gower died, so we're in the dark. Could you begin by telling us a bit about Mark, and his friends, from what you'd seen over the last couple of years in here?"

Les Christie's life in bars had caused him to be as well used to talking as he was listening and he spoke fluently. "The six of them were always together. They probably came in about three nights a week and usually fairly soon after we opened. They knew how to enjoy themselves, Mark especially. It was good, honest fun, though, never vindictive. They enjoyed a drink, several pints on a typical evening. Sometimes a few shots mixed in, especially at the end of the evening. A bit of a throwback to the days when students came in every night and drank properly," he concluded wistfully.

Shah smiled encouragingly and Christie continued, "There just isn't the culture nowadays. I don't think it's all down to drugs either. There were plenty of drugs around back in the day too, but lots of students came out drinking in the evening as a matter of course. When I started there was a bar in each of the five halls of residence. They've all gone – this is the only watering hole in the whole university and half the time it's like a mausoleum.

"Tuition fees have been a big part of it as well. Students are scared about how much debt they are saddling themselves with and so are less profligate. I think there's a lot of health-conscious youngsters these days too. I don't see it myself. If your number's

69

up, your number's up. You might as well enjoy yourself and have a few beers whilst you're here."

Belatedly conscious that Shah might object to alcohol on religious grounds, Christie switched tack. "Anyway, the point is that those lads are a good bunch. There was rarely any trouble even though they drank plenty. They were always playing games, singing, anything to have a good time. They were popular too as most of the students who came in regularly thought they were good fun. If there was something happening in here they'd be at the centre of it."

Shah decided it was time to be more specific. "So Mark was pretty popular amongst the student community? Anyone not like him?"

Christie nodded. "Yes, certainly amongst the students that came in here. I imagine that the po-faced types who never come out and socialise might have been less keen. Mark and his mates were loud and enjoyed being the centre of attention, so some might have thought they were too big for their boots, I suppose."

"Nobody specific then?"

"Not that I'd seen. I can barely remember Mark having an argument with anyone, other than maybe someone who was slow getting their round in! Certainly I can't recall any arguments he had recently. When they were freshers last year there were a few third-years who thought they had a bit too much to say initially. That didn't last long – the gang of them soon proved they could back the talk up, drinking and having a good time. Mark didn't have enemies here as I far as I could see. In old-fashioned language he was too cheerful to get into rows with people."

Shah decided to switch approach and opened out the discussion again. "What can you tell me about the five lads he lived with?"

Christie shrugged. "They were all pretty similar socially, which is probably why they get on well. Sam Taylor is the other ringleader. He's a public-school type, but without attitude. To be fair you wouldn't last long with that lot if you had a false sense of superiority. He's a good-looking lad and the girls used to flock round him and Mark a bit, but he's got a steady girlfriend now. Girl called Chloe Hartwell – proper eye-candy, she is."

"Did Sam and Chloe getting together cause a change in the dynamics of the group?"

"Not much. Sam was still out with the rest of them virtually every time they came in. He wasn't the type to bin his mates off to spend the evenings with a girlfriend. What did change was that the Mark/Sam double act wasn't there in terms of attracting the girls. Sam sometimes looked at pains to make it clear he wasn't available. He didn't see himself acting as Mark's wingman."

Shah asked cautiously, trying to avoid a leading question, "Did Mark and Chloe get on?" She needn't have bothered with the caution as Christie sailed on.

"Yes, all right. Chloe fancies herself, admittedly with good reason. She's choosy who she talks to, though. She was quite friendly with Mark and also Danny Wilson but a bit cool with the others." Christie thought for a moment about how to describe Danny Wilson. "Danny is one of the good guys. Never has a bad word to say about anyone. If there is any tension amongst those boys, or with any other students, Danny was always the peacemaker. It helps he's a big lad, but he's a gentle giant really. I've never seen him start a fight but he's finished one or two and I reckon a few of the hotheads have taken a look at him and calmed down rapidly."

"Who do you have in mind, Mr Christie?" asked Shah.

"Don't get me wrong, Constable. It was never any more than beer-fuelled bravado. There are a few who come in and fancy themselves as bigger, smarter or funnier than those boys. Occasionally some of them would go looking for a row with Mark and his mates, but it was the sort of young lads stuff that meant nothing in the morning. Like I said, Mark had no enemies as far as I can see."

Shah nodded and Christie carried on, "The others aren't so easy to evaluate. I like Ryan Sandling. He always chats to you at the bar. He's cheeky, though, always trying to jump the queue or get me to serve him when I'm not behind the bar. Owen Lloyd looks a bit out of place when you first meet them but he's a bright lad once you get behind the slightly pompous exterior. He'd got a good head for alcohol on him for a little feller, unlike Ryan. I've seen him pouring part of his pint away surreptitiously more than once."

Christie paused again, cleansing his mind of sin. "Jack Freeman is good company, but these days he'd be called a bit of a letch. He's always chatting women up, anything will do. Recently I've seen Jack, Mark and Ryan as a trio with the girls more. That might be partly as a result of Sam tying up with Chloe, but something doesn't ring true about it." He frowned, thinking hard. "There's something I can't put my finger on, but it's almost as if Jack is trying to get into the girls' knickers, but the others were almost keeping an eye on him."

Shah considered for a minute. "Had Jack Freeman been in any trouble then for his behaviour with women?"

Christie shook his head emphatically, seemingly regretting his remarks. "Absolutely not, Constable. There have been no complaints as far as I'm aware and I usually would be. A few years ago he'd have been described as a healthy young man. Things have changed and I'm not knocking that. I'm just trying to paint a picture to help you."

Whilst she privately thought that the tone Christie set in the bar had probably slowed the pace at which such things had changed, Shah smiled at him in a friendly manner. "Absolutely, Mr Christie. I'm taking what you are telling me in exactly the spirit you're sharing your thoughts with me. They're confidential too. It's been very useful so far. Could you tell me about last night now, please?"

Satisfied that they were on the same page and he wasn't about to be beaten metaphorically about the head with what he still referred to as 'women's lib', Christie continued enthusiastically, "Those boys got here about half-six. They sat on that big table in the middle of the bar until chucking-out time. We're licensed until later, but on ordinary nights last orders is ten to eleven. In theory drinking up is by twenty past but given the licence we're not strict on it. It was probably just gone half past when we shut. Mark and the boys were amongst the last to leave."

He paused and Shah wondered if he was considering the merits of opening up to a police officer. In her most persuasive tone she said, "Thanks. This may be really important, Mr Christie. Can you tell us anything that was slightly unusual about last night? Anything, no matter how small, might be crucial in finding out what happened to Mark." Shah wondered if she'd overdone it, but she had judged her man perfectly.

Christie nodded soberly. "I know what you mean. I can't imagine anyone wanting to kill Mark, much less could I imagine him killing himself. I never saw him stoned, much less on the Class A stuff. I just can't get my head around the fact that he's dead." Shah gave a slight nod and remained quiet, encouraging him to continue.

"It was a busy night. The students are just finishing their exams, most finished last week. There's usually a mood of celebration at this time of year. The stress of exams is over and so there's less likely to be any conflicts. I was in here circulating all last night and there wasn't a hint of trouble.

"I probably saw less of their table than usual as there were so many people in, I was keeping an eye on the whole place." Christie paused and squinted, trying to recall any small detail. "Rich Waters, who is the rugby club captain, was chatting to Mark for a while fairly early on. Chloe Hartwell came in a bit before ten, but she didn't sit with them much. I saw Mark get up with Ryan and Jack and talk to some of the tennis club girls a bit after that. Then I saw Jack with a girl I don't see much in here,

I'm not sure of her name. She didn't look much, but it was late on, and any port in a storm, I guess."

Shah asked for the names of the tennis club girls and Christie provided them. Shah played her last card. "If anything untoward happened it was most likely to have been right at the end of the evening." She paused again and waited.

Christie thought long and hard. "I was in the main bar area from about eleven. Mark and Ryan were back at their table by then. There was almost certainly no sort of altercation during that period or I would have seen it."

"What about someone slipping something into Mark's drink? Would you have seen that?"

Christie considered. "Possibly. The drinks were on the table and it would have been a hell of a risk to try and poison his glass. I saw Jack Freeman bring a tray of drinks over just before we stopped serving. I don't think Mark went anywhere after that until they all left."

Just for completeness she said, "It's a daft question but I assume all the glasses from last night have been washed up?" Christie confirmed that they had, possibly several times, and Shah knew there was no point in trying to trace the glasses Mark had drunk out of at the Union Bar the previous evening.

They couldn't rule out someone tampering with Mark's drink in the Union Bar, but it didn't seem likely. Someone would have had to be clever or desperate. Or both.

16

Molash arrived at the Gowers' house just after six o'clock. He had a good opinion of Fordham and Sayer and thought that if there were to be any obvious clue to be gleaned here, they would not have missed it. As he completed the near two-hour car journey he wondered whether spending nearly five hours of the first day of an enquiry on visiting Mark's parents was a smart use of resources. Mr and Mrs Gower would be arriving in the next day or two to identify the body. Should he have waited until then to meet them?

In part this was simple common humanity. The FLO concept is a good one, working especially well when the bereaved family lived so far from the investigating team. However, the bereaved family tends to gain a significant amount of comfort from a meeting as early as possible with a senior investigator.

In any case, Molash was spending the time in the car thinking about the case and that in itself might be more valuable than being in the incident room talking to colleagues about specific lines of enquiry. The deciding factor was that he needed as complete a picture of the victim as possible and speaking directly to the parents was a key part of that. The quicker he did that the better.

From the report from Fordham, Molash was expecting to like the Gowers, and he did. The reality of investigating major crimes such as murder is you are often dealing with people who aren't very likeable. That in no way lessened Molash's desire to see justice done, but meeting such a pleasant couple increased the pathos.

The Gowers had got out photo albums and were reminiscing when Molash arrived. After introductions Molash joined Lydia Gower on the sofa whilst Bob went to put the kettle on. The initial shock had subsided and the Gowers were much more in control of themselves than when the FLOs had visited earlier in the day. Over the next half-hour or so Molash discussed various episodes in Mark Gower's short life.

The anecdotes, promoted by photographs, just added to the overwhelming evidence. Mark was a bright, good-looking, fun-loving, kind and compassionate young man. He had never made an enemy as far as his parents were aware. He wasn't the type. He was open-minded and even when he thought someone was clearly wrong in their opinions he was an advocate of their right to hold those views. His parents reported him being as happy as ever at university when they had spoken to him a few days previously.

Molash was also shown Mark's room and found nothing in it that added to his impressions of the dead man. Bob Gower asked the same question of Molash that he had put to Fordham and Sayer, whether alcohol was the cause of Mark's death. Molash looked slightly surprised at the question and Bob Gower continued before Molash could reply, "Mark drank, often in a joyously, excessive way. Sometimes he would get on a table and sing. Not everyone commended him for this. I did."

Molash smiled and said, "I think I would have liked to go

for a few drinks with Mark. We'll confirm after the post-mortem but at this stage we have no reason to think it was alcohol that caused Mark's death."

The visit left him even more convinced that Mark had not killed himself. He was also of the opinion that Mark was unlikely to have been killed because of some grossly unreasonable behaviour that might have given someone a motive for his murder. It was going to be more complicated than that.

He shared some of his thoughts with the Gowers regarding Mark, including how unlikely it seemed that he had provoked someone unreasonably, which had led to them killing him. He emphasised that they would need the forensic results from the post-mortem before it could be confirmed, but at this stage Molash believed this would turn out to be a case of murder.

As the Gowers were seeing Molash out, he told them in his calm, authoritative way that he was going to find out who had killed their son. The Gowers didn't speak, but Bob shook him very firmly by the hand and there was a little thankfulness amongst the grief in the eyes of both of Mark Gower's parents.

17

Whilst Shah had been at the Union Bar and Molash had been with the Gowers, Woodcock had remained at 12 Newton Street and spoken to the remaining housemates. It was just after three o'clock when Owen Lloyd and Sam Taylor arrived home. They had clearly been talking to each other about Mark's death and looked to be bursting with questions when they entered the house by the street door.

Woodcock forestalled the questions, introducing himself and explaining that he'd like to talk to each separately. Given Owen had the sole room on the ground floor, Woodcock asked him to wait there, with the usual catechism about not contacting anyone.

He decided to speak to Sam Taylor first purely as his room was on the same floor as the rooms Jack, Danny and Ryan were currently occupying. Regardless of Woodcock's instructions there was a greater chance of Sam talking to them than Owen doing so.

One element of interviewing witnesses that makes life

complicated for an investigating officer is the fact that five people witnessing an event will often give five very different, and even contradictory, accounts. Sifting through those statements to establish an accurate fact pattern is one of the key skills of a good investigator. Woodcock was beginning to feel the opposite problem listening to Sam – everyone was saying the same thing, that everybody liked Mark.

An additional issue was that to start with Sam wasn't very communicative. He was a bit surly which Woodcock put down to having been on a protest march, where anti-police sentiment would be rife. His only response to why Chloe had not come back from London with him was a terse suggestion that Woodcock take it up with her and some muttering about the fact that he wasn't her keeper. He had nothing to say about the protest march. From long experience of dealing with anti-police sentiment, Woodcock's gut feeling was that Sam's attitude didn't ring true, that his heart wasn't in it despite the fact he was studying politics.

What Sam did have to say made Woodcock feel like he was trapped in a Groundhog Day scenario. Whenever he was asked about Mark, Sam just said he was a great guy and that it was inconceivable that anyone would want to hurt him. There was no way he would kill himself and so there must be another explanation.

Sam had little to add to what Woodcock knew about the previous evening in the bar. They had basically sat together all evening, a typical boys' night out, although Chloe had unexpectedly decided to come to the bar later on. Sam only recalled the interlude with the girls from the tennis club when prompted but did recall Jack's movements more clearly.

"Now you mention it, I think it was Jack that spotted those tennis girls and Mark and Ryan followed him over." He thought for a moment. "I think Jack got short shrift fairly quickly, though, and the next time I looked over he was sat with that Annette."

Sam pronounced her name with a touch of incredulity. Tall at around six foot one, with dark hair and a muscular, though not heavy frame, Sam Taylor was very good-looking. He had classical features and his olive skin was already well tanned from the early summer sunshine. Woodcock sensed that Sam would be in demand amongst the female contingent at the university and that he knew it.

"Tell me about Jack and Annette."

"God knows what he was doing. He has plenty of success with girls, it's not as if he needed it. But that's Jack, it doesn't seem to matter that much what they look like. Walking home they were a bit behind us and I had my back to them when we were having the nightcap so I didn't actually see how he was getting on. We left them on the sofa, but I did hear them come upstairs not long afterwards."

Woodcock asked Sam the same question regarding whether they'd consumed anything on the way home and got the same negative answer. He continued, "Did you help Mark make the nightcap?"

Sam was starting to thaw and Woodcock sensed that what he was now listening to was closer to the real Sam Taylor. Had he known Sam better, Woodcock would have realised that the prolonged, shrewd stare he was receiving was evidence of Sam's brain clicking through the gears. As it was, he just noted it mentally as Sam responded.

"No. Ryan pointed out it was Mark's turn and Mark went off to the kitchen. Sometimes we experiment, mixing something we've never had before from what's there. I went into the kitchen and asked Mark if he needed any inspiration mixing something, but he said no, he was doing gin and tonic. We'd had a big few days since the exams finished and a sensible nightcap suited me fine, so shortly afterwards I went back to the lounge and sat down with Chloe."

"Did anyone else go into the kitchen?"

"Not that I know of. Jack wasn't there when I got back. The other three lads were milling about and Chloe was at one end of the sofa and Jack's Annette at the other. It made me want to laugh contrasting the two of them, but I didn't want to be cruel. Annette looked terrified and so I gave her a quick smile and sat down and talked to Chloe. Jack came back not long afterwards and then Mark came in with the nightcap."

"If anyone had wanted to slip something into Mark's drink do you think they could have done it whilst you were all in the lounge?" Woodcock asked.

Sam didn't seem keen on this question. He embarked on another round of why nobody would wish Mark harm but caught something in Woodcock's eye and, pausing, stared at Woodcock again. "I wouldn't have seen much anyway, Sergeant," he continued. "I was sat side on and listening to Chloe talking through plans for today. To be honest I was thinking about the fact I was about to go to bed with Chloe and Jack was probably about to go to bed with that Annette." He grinned ruefully. "I was just smiling to myself about how lucky I was and I wasn't paying much attention to what was going on around me."

Sam hadn't noticed any change in Mark's behaviour through the evening, beyond the normal consequence of a few pints of beer. He had seemed perfectly lucid in the kitchen during their brief discussion about the nightcap. When they finished the nightcap all bar Jack and Annette went straight to bed. Sam and Chloe had followed Mark, Danny and Ryan up the stairs to the first floor. Danny and Ryan had gone into their rooms and Mark had climbed the stairs up to the attic. As far as Sam was aware nobody else had gone up to Mark's room.

Sam didn't seem to know how to take Woodcock's request for his phone and clothes from the previous night. He seemed on the verge of objecting and then thought better of it, handing them over in thoughtful silence.

18

Woodcock's interview with Owen Lloyd was very different to those with the other housemates. Owen clearly fancied himself as an amateur detective and Woodcock had only elicited that Owen was taking an English literature degree before his ideas began gushing out. Seemingly he had spent the journey back from London working on the case and arrived full of opinions to share with the police. Woodcock sighed inwardly.

Owen began by giving Woodcock a detailed history of how the six students who lived at 12 Newton Street had become friends. Of the six Owen had changed the most during their near two years at the university. When he'd arrived some had mistaken him for a pseudo-intellectual. Studying for one of the more traditional English literature degrees the country offers, he had been prone to quoting from obscure texts and using archaic words that nobody understood.

What he also possessed was a rock-hard head for alcohol and as friendship groups were being formed in the first term that had led him to the group that now lived at 12 Newton Street.

When they had all been in halls of residence during their first year he had initially been on the edge of the group.

On the evenings during the first term when they didn't go out drinking, they had needed something to do. They sat talking in each other's rooms in the halls of residence, drinking coffee or tea, occasionally indulging in legal highs. Even amongst a group of academic high-flyers they soon realised that there was nothing pseudo about Owen Lloyd's intellect.

Halfway through their first term at the university, Owen founded the Christopher Wren Club. This was based on the rather pompous conceit that, rather than simply being specialists in their degree subjects, they would be experts in many fields. In practice this involved them each sharing snippets of information they had learnt on their courses, that each deemed would be of interest to the wider group. It soon expanded to cover any subject of intellectual interest. The six residents of 12 Newton Street had been the members of the Christopher Wren Club.

For many undergraduates, starting university is the first time they live away from home for an extended period. The first couple of terms can be the transformation from adolescent to adult, learning in a fair bit more detail about sex, alcohol, drugs and the practicalities of looking after yourself.

As the six made their transition out of adolescence, the proportion of the nights spent in pubs or the Union Bar increased. In consequence, the Christopher Wren Club was quietly disbanded towards the end of the second term of their first year (somewhat to Owen's chagrin). However, it had helped to form the bond between the six of them and, when houses had to be found for their second year, there was little dissent to the idea that the six would live together.

Owen explained this at unnecessary length, concluding that the now-defunct Christopher Wren Club had given the housemates insight into the human mind that would help work out what had happened to Mark.

Desperate to cut in and stem the flow, Woodcock said that he thought the housemates' insights would be invaluable and took a deep breath in preparation to begin questioning Owen. Filling even the briefest silence quicker than nature abhors a vacuum, Owen continued happily, "I wouldn't say it will be invaluable but I hope that it will be valuable and I'm sure when this business is cleared up you'll be able to put a value on it. It's a real puzzle," Owen continued, the last sentence said with considerable relish. "I've thought about it and I think we can rule out suicide. Mark loved life. He was always saying how lucky we were, what fantastic opportunities we had ahead of us and how we could enjoy the here and now. Even when something went wrong Mark would always be looking on the positive side of it, emphasising what we'd learn from it.

"The first big question I'm wrestling with is whether this could have been an accident. Mark wasn't into drugs, though. We tried a couple of things last year." Owen looked pointedly at Woodcock at this stage. "I'm sure I can tell you about this, Sergeant, without repercussions. I know you're not interested in such peccadilloes. Anyway, Mark pretty quickly decided he preferred drinking. You won't find much in the way of drugs when you search the house, Sergeant." Woodcock fancied for a moment that Owen had winked at him as he said this.

"My initial theory therefore looks to fall to the ground. The most obvious solution is that Mark went upstairs, took something and overdosed. I wanted you to know that I just don't think that happened. As I say, Mark wasn't that keen on trying illegal substances in the first place and pretty quickly decided he wasn't going to do so again. I just can't see him having a stash of something in his room. You'll doubtless find them if I'm wrong about that," he concluded with a careless wave of the hand.

"He looked completely normal to me when we were having the nightcap, so unless it was some slow-acting drug it's less likely that he could have consumed it back at the Union Bar."

Owen paused for breath and Woodcock intervened, trying to get a foothold in what was in danger of turning into a soliloquy. Trying to remind Owen of his presence and that they were actually participating in an interview, Woodcock said, "That's a really important fact for the police, Mr Lloyd. How sure are you about Mark's behaviour being normal during the nightcap?"

Owen sailed on, "Oh, absolutely certain, Sergeant. I've got a decent head for alcohol and I was no more than a little merry at the time. Mark was very much in control of his faculties if I'm any judge."

"I imagine you want to know if we saw anything unusual during the evening, anything that might be a clue to what happened."

"I suppose it's possible that he died of natural causes. Mark looked really fit but you never know. Still, that will all come out at the autopsy. I think we can say it's pretty unlikely. That only leaves murder by some person or persons unknown. I think that must be it. We all loved Mark, so none of us would want to hurt him. The most logical explanation is that there is a maniac around and he poisoned Mark's drink at the bar with something that took a while to act."

Owen frowned. "That's just a theory, mind you. The forensics will tell more but if we have got a lunatic in our midst then we all need to be on our guard. He might do it again."

He thought for a moment and Woodcock, hoping Owen had run dry, tried to get the interview back on to solider ground. "Did you see anyone arguing with Mark at the Union Bar? Or anyone tampering with his drink?"

Owen shook his head reluctantly. "No, everything looked normal to me. I got the penultimate round in and I'm pretty sure there was no dirty work at the bar with that. Jack got the final round in, with a shot. It would be worth checking with him to see if anyone at or behind the bar behaved strangely when he was being served. If you didn't care who drank the poisoned drink, then slipping something into it would be much easier. That would get over the unlikelihood of anyone wanting to kill Mark too."

Woodcock was a patient man, but that patience was starting to run thin. "Let's go back to the nightcap. I understand Mark went alone into the kitchen to make them. Who, if anyone else, went into the kitchen and so might have had the opportunity to put something in Mark's drink?"

Owen answered immediately, "Well, we need to consider every possibility no matter how unlikely. Sam and I think Jack went into the kitchen. Sam certainly did because I heard him discussing what should constitute the nightcap with Mark. I was hoping it would be something a bit exotic, but Mark had decided on simple gin and tonics. That was his right. I guess you've heard about the house rules regarding the nightcap by now, Sergeant?"

Woodcock nodded and Owen continued, "Jack went out there too. He may have only gone to the loo, I'm not sure. The rest of us definitely stayed in the lounge. Sam came back and that was it: he was on the sofa listening to Chloe for the foreseeable. Mark brought the drinks in and Chloe got up and went and took drinks for her and Sam. Jack did likewise for himself and that librarian-looking lady he'd brought back. It's possible either could have slipped something into Mark's drink. Jack just took two glasses and immediately went to the sofa, so that looks less likely. Chloe stood by the tray for longer. She had better opportunity but surely one of us would have noticed?"

Without waiting for an answer Owen continued, "The rest of us were discreetly looking at how Jack was getting on with the librarian lady. It's theoretically possible someone poisoned Mark's drink whilst we were standing around drinking. Ryan, Danny or indeed I might have been able to slip something in unnoticed. I'd judge it a big risk, though."

Woodcock took advantage of another brief pause to ask another question. "If the four of you were discussing Jack and

Annette you might have been distracted and less likely to notice something being put into Mark's glass than if you'd just been chatting normally?"

This was a leading question, but Owen didn't seem to notice and he sought to quantify it. "Probably a little. It still sounds too risky to me. You have an innate sense of where your own drink is and I think Mark would have noticed even if nobody else did. We were all keeping an eye on how Jack was getting on with the librarian lady. Honestly, a penalty drink shouldn't be enough for that. He ought to be facing our kangaroo court," he concluded, a hint of bitterness in his voice.

Woodcock refused to get involved with the private versions of law and order that the boys of 12 Newton Street had invented, although he noted that Owen's tone might indicate jealousy. He established that Owen had seemed somewhat disappointed that everybody, except Jack and Annette, were keen to go to bed when the nightcap finished.

Given how loquacious Owen was, Woodcock decided to ask him about the dynamics of the group. Owen smiled, saying, "There's no need to be tactful about it, Sergeant. Mark and Sam call the shots around here. That suits me fine."

Woodcock said in a neutral voice, "You don't see yourself as a shotcaller then?"

This time Owen laughed out loud. "I go with the tide, Sergeant. Canute had the right idea. He knew you couldn't beat the tide so you may as well flow with it. He understood where his place was in nature's hierarchy and so do I."

Woodcock then turned to the current day. Owen seemed much less keen to talk about the protest march, describing his motives for attending as being to learn more about people's different views. Woodcock was conscious that Sam and Owen were the only two of the students who had appeared to be together all the time since leaving the house that morning.

If someone had poisoned Mark Gower's nightcap they

would probably have had to get rid of the receptacle that carried the poison today. In Trafalgar Square Sam had got restless and said he needed the toilet and Owen had lost sight of him for a while, as he'd wanted to stay whilst Chloe was discussing a speech someone was due to make. Therefore either would have had the opportunity to get rid of a hypothetical receptacle that had contained a toxin used to kill Mark Gower.

Owen nodded thoughtfully when Woodcock made the request for his phone and the clothes from the previous evening and handed them over without demur. Woodcock explained that they would be in touch about a formal interview at the station, at which time they would hope to return at least the phones. He left with a feeling that whoever interviewed Owen in a couple of days' time would be in for a lot of theorising about the case. He only hoped some of it might be useful.

19

Keith Bourne had already completed his forensic analysis of 12 Newton Street, bagged everything he needed and gone before Woodcock had begun talking to Sam and Owen. Mark Gower's body had long since been removed to the mortuary.

It was almost four o'clock as Woodcock gathered the five students in the lounge. He pointed out that they were all likely to be in shock and, whilst it was up to them, that it might be a good idea for them to stay in for the evening. Nobody seemed to object to this suggestion. Woodcock requested that they all think about the events of the previous day whilst they were still relatively fresh in their minds. He handed each a card and said they could call at any time of day or night if they remembered anything useful. The police would be in touch the following day to arrange formal interviews and the return of their goods, regarding which he thanked them for their co-operation.

Woodcock had a last look round the five young men gathered in the lounge. Danny was looking around at the others, perhaps to gauge who was coping and who wasn't. Ryan was looking contemplatively at Jack, who was clearly worried. Owen looked immersed in his own thoughts and Sam had put his hand in his pocket for his phone, only to realise it wasn't there. There was nothing obviously helpful there, but Woodcock memorised his impressions and said goodbye.

He returned to the station and spent the rest of the afternoon and early evening working with the team in the incident room and catching up on the meagre amounts of additional information collected thus far. At eight forty-five the DSIO strolled into the room and asked him if there were any major developments. Woodcock shook his head. Eliot had gone and Molash got the attention of the team.

"Thanks, everyone, for getting the incident room up and running so efficiently. This may be a case that takes a while to crack and so we could be in for some late nights. Unless you've got anything that needs setting in motion tonight, feel free to call it a day. I've spoken to the SIO and we'll have a daily briefing at 8am. In the unlikely event that anyone can't attend, please speak to me first. At the moment we know very little and have no obvious suspect so these briefings will be even more important than usual in terms of sharing information and ideas. Have a good evening, everyone, I'll be in my office for a while if anyone needs help with anything."

Molash was sat behind his desk when Woodcock entered about a quarter of an hour later. Molash was typing an email to a local divisional inspector complimenting PC Coleman for his work at 12 Newton Street, highlighting his initiative in preserving what might be important evidence in the kitchen and lounge. Molash went back a long way with the inspector in question and knew that he'd make a point of passing the gist of the message on to Coleman and seeing it formed part of his appraisal at the end of the year.

Woodcock waited for Molash to send the email and look up before saying, "What do you think, Guv, is it worth our running through where we are now or shall we start that tomorrow? I can hang around if you've got things to do first, I've got nothing on."

Woodcock was only a couple of years younger than Molash and had quickly become his right-hand man during investigations. Molash liked the way Woodcock's mind worked. In particular when they discussed cases they bounced off each other, the discourse often prompting new ideas and angles to explore.

Typically they would meet in Molash's office at the end of each working day to discuss the state of the investigation. At the very least these meetings provided a good summation of the day's events, which Molash would then spend the later hours of the evening at home running through. Woodcock generally headed for The Ship public house nearby afterwards, at which a good chunk of the Middleham Police Station employees congregated.

"Yes, I think so, Woody," Molash said. "As you say, there isn't too much for us to get our teeth into yet, but let's have a few minutes. My gut feeling is that this is going to be tricky."

Approximately two-thirds of murder cases are 'self-solvers'. Either the police know immediately who committed the crime or they can quickly work it out. In such cases their job is simply to ensure that they obtain sufficient evidence to secure a conviction.

The remaining one-third of cases are what Molash described as the tricky ones. This is the main reason why statistically if a murder isn't solved within forty-eight hours then the chances of it ever being solved decrease by half. In part that is because the evidential trail goes cold but the main reason is that it is not obvious who the offender is.

They began by running through the facts of the case together. Molash and Woodcock both enjoyed a flutter, being ardent horse-racing fans, focusing on jumps racing. They found it useful during an investigation to try to evaluate the odds of an event occurring or having occurred. Once one of them had made an estimate, they found that arguing that such odds overestimated or underestimated the actual likelihood helped them gain a better understanding of the real possibilities and probabilities. Natural causes were chalked up as a highly unlikely 33/1 shot.

Woodcock told Molash that he'd just called digital forensics and they were going through Mark's phone and social media in detail. They would report back in more detail the following day, but an initial trawl confirmed the impression that Mark Gower was an unusually happy and positive human being. There was no reason to suspect suicide, but there could be an explanation that was deeply hidden. Certainly it would have been much easier for Mark to take a lethal drug himself than for anyone else to poison him without anyone noticing. Suicide was tentatively quoted as an 8/1 chance.

Woodcock related Owen Lloyd's commentary regarding illegal drugs and Mark's lack of interest in them after a brief foray the previous year. Neither detective believed it likely that Mark had taken a substance, legal or illegal, in his room and accidentally overdosed. That feeling was compounded by Keith Bourne having reported that there was nothing in the house that looked like a receptacle for such a substance. He had bagged a couple of possibilities, but as he put it, only for completeness. There was definitely no such receptacle in Mark's room. Accidental overdose was priced at 12/1.

This left an approximately eighty per cent chance that Mark had been murdered. Woodcock ventured that that percentage was probably a bit high. He pointed out that Mark's phone records had led them to his voluntary work with the university's mental health helpline. The professionals involved were unstinting in their praise for Mark as someone who just cared about other people. Woodcock concluded, "I wouldn't want to bet the fours-on anyway." Molash was inclined to disagree.

"Given that we have no real positive evidence of anything at the moment, eighty per cent seems high, but actually I think it's on the low side. I just can't see any of the other three solutions as anything other than very unlikely."

Molash paused and added thoughtfully, "You know what it's like when there's a long odds-on favourite in a race. Once the price gets short enough then only the money-buyers want to back it. If it's a deep pool, for, say, the Gold Cup, it can keep the price too big because everyone is trying to find an each-way bet against it. We don't have evidence that Gower was murdered and so our police training kicks in, making us reluctant to conclude something is overwhelmingly likely. I think we've put a twelves-on shot in here at fours-on.

"We might find that he'd fallen out with one of his mates or that he knew something about one of them that made him dangerous to them. There is an almost infinite range of possibilities. Let's see what tomorrow brings before going through his housemates in detail, but even though this is officially a suspicious death at the moment, we should treat it as murder."

Next they discussed the timeline. None of the eight had consumed anything on the way home so if Gower had been poisoned it was at the Union Bar or at 12 Newton Street. Neither could think of a substance that Mark could have ingested several hours before going to bed which, when mixed so liberally with alcohol, would have had no noticeable impact on his behaviour but still kill him in his sleep.

That was one for forensics, but they would work on the basis he took it near the end of the evening. Owen Lloyd had seemed adamant Mark was behaving normally at 12 Newton Street. Whilst they wouldn't rely on the impressions of witnesses who had drunk that much, it was another pointer towards Mark ingesting any drug later rather than earlier.

Mark's room just before he went to bed would be the easiest place, but the initial evidence was that nobody else had gone up to the top floor. They debated whether, if they were trying to poison Mark, they would have preferred to try in the kitchen whilst he was mixing the drinks or in the lounge. They concluded that both would be risky, but if they were alone with Mark in the kitchen then that would be the easier of the two. The Union Bar might give more cover to actually poison the glass, but it was tough to then be confident of getting that glass into Mark's hand. This was definitely a point that needed further consideration.

Molash paused and asked, "What chance do we give someone in the Union Bar of bringing across a tray with six pints on it and by adroit handling forcing the poisoned glass on a specific individual?"

Woodcock considered and replied, "If you put down the tray and then took the drinks off it and handed them out to people sitting down then you could do it. If you were putting down the tray for people to help themselves then you could try and put it down so the poisoned glass was closest to the intended victim. It would be uncertain, though. Someone else could take a drink first and take the poisoned one." He paused for a moment and added, "Ryan Sandling phrased it in terms of the person buying the round putting the tray down on the table for others to take their drink when they were ready, but I should have asked about that distinction."

Molash replied, "Neither of us thought about it until now. It's a pretty fine distinction. Give their landline a call and see if any of them can remember."

Woodcock called 12 Newton Street and was glad that it wasn't Owen who answered. It was Danny who picked up the phone and he confirmed that whoever bought the round simply put the tray in the middle of the table so people could help themselves when they were ready. When Woodcock recounted this to Molash the latter shook his head thoughtfully.

"It's all too vague at this stage, but have a word with Yasmin tomorrow. She was talking to the bloke who runs the bar. It's even possible someone serving has developed a penchant for slipping something into pints they are pouring."

There was a brief silence. Woodcock said musingly, "Jack Freeman discovered the body and he's the most likely candidate at this stage. He tried to wash up but Coleman stopped him. That was a potential attempt to wash the evidence away if poison was in the nightcap. That said, arguably that might be a point in his favour. If he were guilty he could have done the washing-up before 'discovering' Mark.

"Jack was very nervous too, although that may have been related to the girl he brought home rather than Gower's death. That didn't quite ring true. I'll have a look at whether he's been in any trouble regarding his behaviour with women."

Molash nodded thoughtfully. "Good idea. He's studying chemistry. If it turns out that Gower was poisoned with something that's used in chemistry labs at the university then that would definitely point towards him.

"Owen Lloyd made a point to you about it being easier to slip the poison into a glass if you don't mind who gets it. If that was done late on at the Union Bar then Jack Freeman got the last round in. He probably had the best opportunity to poison one of his housemates if he didn't care which one."

There was a lengthy silence, eventually broken by Molash saying, "What's so interesting about this case is that it looks so ordinary. Murders aren't usually committed out of the blue by ordinary people on other ordinary people." On which point the two detectives called it a day.

*

*M*ark Gower's killer lay awake, revelling in complete and utter success. The roar of adrenalin of the previous night was gone but replaced with the tingling satisfaction of a job perfectly executed.

The police seemed to be taking little interest beyond the obligatory routine enquiries. With no discernible motive, Gower would soon join the list of students whose tragic demise periodically tugged the heartstrings of the bovine masses watching or reading the news.

Plan B was unlikely to be needed, which in some ways was a shame.

After so little sleep the previous night, the pleasure of a beautifully executed (that word again, enough to bring a smile to the lips) plan soon became a drowsier and drowsier pleasure. This really was the elixir of life.

Suddenly all were hailing a lauded genius. Standing at the front of the university hall delivering a wide-ranging speech with every word hanging on the packed audience's lips.

20

Jimmy Molash had a natural condition called short sleeper syndrome, which is exactly what it sounds. Molash could rarely sleep for more than five hours a night and during an investigation would typically feel fresh after about four. It was a characteristic he rarely ceased to be grateful for. He had been awake thinking about the case for about twenty minutes when he got out of bed at 5am on the morning of Thursday 13 June.

By half-past five he had driven into Middleham, parked at the police station and was making the short walk to the gym, just as it was opening. His gym routine varied hugely depending on his mood, but on that morning he used the treadmill, did a weights programme and was showering by six-thirty. It was already warm and he had his suit jacket slung over his shoulder as he walked back to the office.

Molash was at his desk at six forty-five and was getting stuck into rehydration with a two-litre bottle of cold water before the coffee round started. Unsurprisingly there had been few developments overnight and he focused on reading the information on HOLMES whilst the station was virtually empty.

The 8am briefings, usually the one time in the day the investigation team all got together, are crucial as they are the format for sharing information face to face, asking questions and swapping ideas. In the Mark Gower enquiry Molash knew the first briefing would be even more important than usual. At this stage it was a wide-open investigation. Getting the team into the right mindset in terms of how to approach the investigation and then directing resources in the right directions would be harder than usual. He went through a mental list of the key points he wanted made at the initial briefing.

By seven fifty-five Eliot's team were all present in the incident room, with the FLOs, Inspector Clinton and CSI Bourne also in attendance. Eliot cleared his throat to attract attention, the room fell obediently silent and he began.

"Everyone is already here so we can get going a couple of minutes early, which is great, thanks all. At the moment the intention is to have a daily briefing, always at 8am. I will let you all know if that changes and also on an ad hoc basis whether we are having them on weekend days. Please speak to me personally if you cannot make a briefing, so I am up to speed with your enquiries. For those of you newer to the team, can I remind you that there is no such thing as a stupid question during these meetings. An officer asking a seemingly odd question that nobody else had thought of has solved many seemingly intractable enquiries. From now on this is Operation Evergreen."

Eliot then ran through the facts to date. Naturally inclined towards verbosity, he had become aware that he not infrequently lost the attention of his audience during these briefings. He was therefore making a concerted effort to be more concise and was aided by the relatively simple initial fact pattern in Operation Evergreen. In less than ten minutes he was finished, having only had to field a couple of questions. He explained that if there were any material developments from the post-mortem at noon an update would be circulated, probably via a WhatsApp message explaining the cause of death, with the full details being put on HOLMES.

Eliot concluded his introductory remarks by emphasising the significance of documentation. "The Key Decision Log will be on HOLMES not on paper. Please input all relevant information from your day books before going off duty each day. I make no apology for reminding you all of the importance of recording the rationale for decisions, not merely the decisions themselves. As you know, as SIO I have to countersign all entries onto HOLMES and I will be looking hard at the rationale. At this stage this is a wide-open investigation and inevitably we will travel down some blind alleys. That's fine, but we want water-tight explanations in the documentation of why we took those routes, so that as and when we get to court it doesn't look as if we've just been trawling the sea and come up with least unlikely person to prosecute."

He continued, "Next I want to go through the lines of enquiry we've pursued so far and any initial information gleaned beyond what I have outlined. Jimmy and I will then discuss the strategy for the day with you. Let's kick off with CCTV – Jenny, what did you find?"

Detective Constable Jenny Martin had been tasked with securing both the CCTV from the hardware shop on Newton Road and any other footage she could find between the Union Bar and 12 Newton Road.

In her early forties, she had, after many years of apparent emotional heartache, fallen in love and quickly got married three years before. She appeared altogether more contented these days, which had made her much less abrasive around the office. She had good attention to detail and was reliable at tedious tasks, such as examining long hours of CCTV footage without losing concentration.

She spoke in a calm, efficient manner. "There is little CCTV between the Union Bar and Newton Street. The six residents of 12 Newton Street and two girls left the Union Bar just before twenty-five to twelve. They were virtually the last customers to leave. The two girls are Sam Taylor's girlfriend Chloe Hartwell and a girl called Annette Palmer. There is nothing of interest as they leave the Union Bar or on the one camera, on Mason Road, just over halfway home, although Jack Freeman and Annette Palmer are about twenty yards behind the others by this point.

"They arrive at 12 Newton Street at eleven forty-five. It looks almost certain that they walked straight there. The CCTV from the hardware shop on the opposite side of the road covers the entire front of 12 Newton Street and the last few houses they walked past to get there. They all went in and nobody other than them goes into or comes out of the house until Coleman got there after the 999 call. Nobody goes in or out any of the windows at any time.

"The door remains shut until just after two-fifty, when Annette Palmer opens it and leaves. We've only just secured her address in Garrard Street so we haven't yet looked for CCTV confirming her route home. At nine fifteen Sam Taylor, Chloe Hartwell and Owen Lloyd leave and head towards the campus, presumably to get the coach to London for the protest march. Shortly after nine thirty, Ryan Sandling and Danny Wilson leave together and head in the direction of the campus.

"All this is in accordance with the facts as the SIO outlined them. The only new fact is that Jack Freeman left the house at ten thirty-five and went the other way along Newton Street, towards the town centre. The CCTV only extends a few yards beyond number 12 in that direction so we don't yet know where he went. He arrived back fifteen minutes later and it looks like he's carrying a newspaper. That's it until Coleman arrives."

"Thanks, Jenny," said Eliot. "We'll ask Freeman about that trip."

Molash intervened to ask Woodcock whether he'd noticed a newspaper at the house and the latter confirmed seeing one in Jack's room. Molash said thoughtfully, "Do students buy newspapers anymore? Don't they just get any news they want on their phone? If Gower was poisoned at 12 Newton Street then there ought to be a receptacle that held the drug. Keith's been through the place with a fine-tooth comb and whilst there are a couple of possibles that have gone to forensics, there's nothing that looks likely. In that scenario the killer must have disposed of that receptacle somewhere the following morning."

He paused again before continuing, "The others all look to have normal reasons for having gone out of the house, but Freeman's is more questionable. Jenny, can you get a map out and then look for more CCTV between Newton Street and local newsagents, supermarkets, etc.? Let's see how far we can trace his movements."

Jenny Martin nodded and resumed, "I've got the timeline for the rest of the day, which I'll put onto HOLMES. There's nothing else startling in terms of anyone not being where you'd expect them to be at a certain time. Ryan Sandling is the potential exception in that he didn't return until just after two-thirty, but we have his explanation for that. Owen Lloyd and Sam Taylor got back shortly after three o'clock, which sounds about right given they were getting a train from London."

There was a pause and then Eliot continued, "OK, what about house-to-house? Where have we got to with that, Adam?"

Detective Constable Adam Cohen was a new recruit to the team, fresh out of uniform. He was a quietly spoken, nondescript-looking young man of twenty-two and the team were still getting a feel for him. He had been arranging house-to-house enquiries along Newton Street and also Stuart Street, which backed on to it.

"Nothing, Sir. Nobody heard or saw anything on Tuesday night. We've spoken to the houses on Newton Street close to number 12 and those that immediately back on to it on Stuart Street. Those that are student houses all knew Mark Gower. I didn't hear a bad word beyond the fact that some thought him and his mates were a bit crazy. The local residents had little to say. They were just glad there wasn't music going at all hours, I think. Where would you like us to go now, Sir?"

Eliot replied, "Thanks, Adam. I'm not sure how much value house-to-house can bring from hereon in. Let's continue for today. See if you can identify any student houses where people knew Mark Gower reasonably well and let's try and get to as many of those as possible today. We'll reconsider again tomorrow morning. Hopefully we can get a list of relevant student houses from social media – speaking of which, let's have a five-minute comfort break and then we'll hear what our young techies have got for us."

21

Still gritting his teeth at Eliot's description a few minutes before, nineteen-year-old Detective Constable Tyler Brennan stood up from where he'd been sitting behind a bank of terminals. He had spent his school holidays working in the Apple Store on the High Street and looked as if he would be more comfortable in an Apple-branded T-shirt than the ill-fitting suit he was wearing.

His computing skills and understanding of social media and the wider Internet dwarfed that of his colleagues on Eliot's team. With social media in particular having become such a crucial part of many investigations, Brennan had quickly become a core and much-valued member of the team, liaising with digital forensics by speaking their language.

"A report has just gone onto HOLMES and I've printed hard copies. We've focused on the victim and his housemates so far. We've delved as deeply as we can in the time into Mark Gower, looking for anything that might suggest suicidal tendencies or a motive for anyone to kill him. Nothing. The only caveat is that he's not a huge user of social media. It's mainly Snapchat and Instagram.

"He's got a Twitter account too but doesn't post much, nor does he 'like' or reply to other tweets very often. Where he does it's usually liking a tweet regarding a famous sportsperson. Rugby looks his principal interest, with other sports such as football, cricket and tennis not that far behind. His Facebook account is barely used, which isn't unusual for his generation. Seemingly he has no interest in political issues. His finances are that of a typical student, nothing unusual from his bank account. We'll keep at it, but everything we've seen backs up the profile of Gower that the SIO set out."

Brennan paused and Jenny Martin asked, "How many people are there out there that nobody dislikes? The few that I've met don't have big personalities like Gower."

There were some ironic grins around the room from officers that had worked with a younger Jenny Martin, who had made it clear that she didn't care who did and did not like her. Eliot looked nonplussed and Molash intervened.

"That's a really good point, Jenny. Mark had too big a personality to be universally liked, even assuming he's the good bloke he appears to be. We all need to try and dig out information that leads to someone who not only disliked him but wanted him dead."

Getting a nod from Eliot, Brennan continued, "Of Mark Gower's housemates, Owen Lloyd fancies himself as an intellectual and is doing well in his English degree. His younger sister is doing A-levels and is supposed to be Oxbridge material. Family life looks unspectacular but happy enough. He's inclined to post obscure literary references, although less so than when he first got to the university. He's the only one of the six that doesn't seem that interested in sport. Lots of references to drinking.

"Danny Wilson appears to be everybody's best friend. His father died of stomach cancer five years ago and Danny spent a lot of time with his younger brother and sister, dropping out of all his sports and neglecting his schoolwork. His mother and the three children are very close. He sorted himself out and got the A-levels to win a place at the university here. He's back into football now and plays centre-half for the university first eleven.

"He's always trying to help people out, in particular anyone having a tough time mentally. It's rarely anyone from 12 Newton Street, although he did look to be putting his arm round Owen Lloyd last winter when Owen fell for a girl, had a one-nighter with her and she wasn't interested afterwards. There's been a bit of an issue around a study group Wilson set up for law students, we'll go into that in more detail today."

Molash sounded interested. "Thanks, Tyler, can you give us a preliminary heads-up now?"

Brennan considered for a moment. "I think Wilson got about a dozen second-year law students to pool their lecture notes. The idea seems to be that everyone benefits from ideas each of them had regarding how to analyse the cases they were studying. One of them accused Wilson of plagiarism, of just setting the group up to steal his colleagues' ideas. Gower was invited onto it but refused. That's all so far."

Molash nodded in understanding.

Brennan continued, "Sam Taylor comes from a wealthy background. Family have a house in Central London and a spread in the country. He has an elder brother who has started a robotics company – they don't seem close but equally there is no antipathy. His posts during the university vacations are from luxury holidays, etc. He is studying politics but seems very much in third gear when it comes to work.

"He's good-looking and lots of girls were flirting with him on social media until he started seeing Chloe Hartwell. He used Snapchat a lot for that, but he's pretty much stopped now. One interesting item from his email is that he's got a summer placement at Goldman Sachs, the investment bank. They are like gold dust apparently as it's an almost-certain path onto their graduate training scheme. That doesn't look to fit with the protest marches and his recent 'liking' of left-wing articles on social media. He's not mentioned the summer placement on social media nor on WhatsApp, etc., with his mates.

"Jack Freeman is a ladies' man. So is his father, by the sounds of it. His parents broke up when he was a baby. Father has had a string of relationships since then. Mother remarried a few years later and Jack has a half sister who is eleven. Jack is close to his mother but seemingly nobody else in his family. He doesn't seem that bothered about his degree. He's had messages from tutors saying that he might not get an upper second if he carries on as he is, when he is capable of pushing for a first.

"The six of them set up Tinder accounts in their first year. Their interest didn't last long. Mark Gower and Danny Wilson entered into what proved to be fairly short-term relationships soon after so it lost momentum. Sam Taylor has shut his account, but the rest are still open, although not used much. Freeman is the exception. He pays for Tinder Plus."

Brennan looked round the room, sizing up the wide demographic, and continued with a wry grin, "For those without Tinder accounts Tinder Plus allows you to swipe right to express your interest in as many people as you wish each day. There is a daily limit on the standard, cost-free Tinder. Freeman swipes right to more profiles than almost anyone I've seen on Tinder. He does so especially when they are in a pub rather than the Union Bar, i.e. when they are more strangers around. Unlike his housemates Freeman is also registered for Bumble, OkCupid and other dating apps. He never mentions any of this on social media."

Eliot intervened, "From what Tyler has found and the interviews with the students yesterday, we have to consider the possibility that Jack Freeman is a sexual predator. How that would fit in with Mark Gower isn't clear, but it's possible that Gower knew something about Freeman's behaviour that provided a motive."

Like every other trade or profession, junior police officers have to be tactful when their superiors hold views they don't agree with. Brennan chose his words diplomatically. "His general social media profile is of a bloke just trying to get laid all the time. That's not unusual, although Freeman puts more effort in than most. However, as the SIO says, he could be much more than that. He's on a closed Facebook group with two friends from home. We'll be going through that in more detail today and the general social media profile of Freeman's two friends, but to give you an idea, there is a debate about who can be the first one to sleep with someone transgender."

There was a silence in the incident room. Everyone present knew that transgender issues were a tinderbox. The mood dropped like a stone.

Molash quickly said, "Thanks, Tyler. Whilst Jack Freeman discovered the body and there are some minor suspicious circumstances, it is nothing more than that at the moment. It's far too early to be focusing on him. Assuming Gower was murdered, it's more likely that someone else did it."

Molash nodded at Brennan, who continued, "Ryan Sandling's parents are divorced. He's an only child and lives with his father. He visits his mother but doesn't seem close to either. He isn't a big user of social media. There have been periods when he's gone off it completely for extended periods, both during his time at university and before. There's no explanation given: he just stops.

"He comes across as someone who doesn't like other people to know what he's thinking. He's working hard and doing well in his economics degree. He looks like he has a bit of a temper, though. There's the occasional brutal post, usually late at night – so it might be alcohol talking. I've put the detail on HOLMES; it's generally Sandling dismissing someone as an idiot. Nothing like that concerning any of his housemates, though, and specifically nothing negative about Gower.

"We'll get stuck in to Chloe Hartwell and Annette Palmer today as well. We should have everything on the occupants of 12 Newton Road for tomorrow morning's 8am. Is there anything else you'd like us to focus on?"

Conscious of Molash's comment on the likelihood of Freeman having killed Gower, Eliot said, "That's great, thanks, Tyler. We need to keep an open mind so keep focusing on all of them. As well as the two girls who stayed there on Tuesday night, do an initial profile on the other people who Gower regularly interacted with, especially those who were in the bar on Tuesday night, such as the rugby club captain and the girls from the tennis club. Also let's get some info on any girls it looks as if Gower had a relationship with, however brief."

22

One tactic sometimes favoured at briefings is to keep the order in which the SIO calls on officers to relate their findings, random. It's a matter of style. Some SIOs like the logical nature of a chronological agenda. Eliot was of the school that believed the random selection of officers/subject matter kept everyone sharper as they could be asked to talk at any moment. He asked the CSI, Keith Bourne, and DI Clinton to brief the team on the work done the previous day at 12 Newton Street that hadn't been covered by Eliot's introduction.

There wasn't much to tell. Clinton's view of Freeman was that his nervousness was well within the normal band of reactions to finding a dead body. Bourne talked about the house in more detail, giving a strong hint that he didn't expect forensics to turn up anything regarding contamination with a toxin from the samples he'd sent in.

Molash wanted the team to focus on this point and so summarised, "So if Gower was poisoned at 12 Newton Street, the receptacle has almost certainly been taken away and disposed of. We might get some contamination on the clothes once forensics have been through them, but I've got a feeling we won't. A small receptacle could be disposed of in a public bin, down a drain or just thrown away. I doubt we'll get anything, but we'll get uniform to check some of the most obvious places. If anyone has any bright ideas on that front, then please shout."

Bourne then gave a summary of the house, especially Mark Gower's room, aided by photos on the clearboard. He concluded by discussing the inventory of Mark Gower's room.

"I've put a full list on HOLMES. There was nothing obviously exciting from Gower's room. Clothes are pretty standard; he dressed smartly but in a classic way rather than fashionably. He had more shoes than most young men I've come across. Lots of sports kit. He even had his rugby kit in his room. Tyler informs me there is a Sevens tournament in a couple of weeks. He's also got tennis and badminton rackets, shuttlecocks and tennis balls, a golf ball, cricket kit – although he hasn't apparently played cricket.

"He did turn out for the university second eleven last summer with a fair bit of success, but he wouldn't commit to training so wasn't considered for the first eleven and it may be he'd lost interest. There were plenty of books, mainly a mixture of sports-based and classic fiction. Obviously happy to discuss anything of interest when you've had the chance to digest what's on HOLMES, where there is a comprehensive list of what was in Gower's room."

Eliot switched to the FLOs, who, with the odd additional point from Molash, briefed the team on Mark Gower's parents and family life, concluding that at this stage there was nothing suggestive from that home life.

Detective Constable Karl Denman then gave a brief report regarding criminal records. The evidence was scant. Sam Taylor had a couple of speeding fines from driving a sports car that apparently remained at the family home during term time. Chloe

Hartwell had a couple of minor convictions for public order offences when protesting and a more serious one for aiding and abetting an assault on a police officer at an Extinction Rebellion protest. The other six that had stayed at 12 Newton Street on the night Mark Gower died all had clean records. Molash asked Denman to find out everything he could about the Extinction Rebellion incident, suggesting he enlisted Brennan's help as needed.

Eliot summed up the state of play and implored everyone to keep an open mind. He then allocated the tasks and ran through the list of interviewees for the day, emphasising the importance of Chloe Hartwell and Annette Palmer.

In cases where there is not an obvious suspect the police method has traditionally been known as 'Trace, Interview, Eliminate', which is abbreviated to TIE. TIEs are conducted in categories. The investigating team believe the offender may be in a specific group of people so they TIE every member of that group they can find. A TIE group might, for example, be everyone who was in the Union Bar after nine o'clock the night Mark Gower died.

If Mark Gower had been poisoned it was almost certainly at the Union Bar or at 12 Newton Street. If the latter, then there were only seven potential offenders so the tracing would have already been completed. If the former, there were over a hundred and so the TIE process would be vital.

The investigating team will try and operate several TIE categories. If a single person appears in lots or all of those categories then the TIE process highlights that they are a person to focus on. A difficulty with the early stages of Operation Evergreen was a lack of TIE categories. If Gower had been poisoned at the Union Bar it would leave a wide field with little else so far to go upon.

Molash suggested that a nationwide trawl of murders or suspicious deaths with a similar modus operandi might prove a useful TIE category. If there wasn't a personal motive for Gower's death then there was the possibility of a serial killer, who may well have struck before in similar circumstances. Enquiries should be discreet given the need to avoid a public panic, but it would be as well to be ahead of the curve if the forensics pointed away from 12 Newton Street.

The good news was that there was swipe card system to gain entry to the Union Bar so there was a record of everyone present on Tuesday night. There was, however, no comparable system on exit so how long the students had stayed in the Union Bar would need investigating.

The data from the trawl of Mark Gower's social media would be used to identify students (and potentially staff) who Mark interacted regularly with. These would be cross-referred with attendees at the Union Bar on Tuesday night to produce a TIE category. Cohen was tasked with targeting house-to-house on that basis.

Eliot reiterated that the post-mortem was at midday and that an update would follow from it. If there was definitive news about a toxin from the post-mortem then that might lead to more TIE categories. With that the briefing broke up.

23

Despite being not much more than half a century old, Middleham University had long since earned itself a reputation for academic excellence, both in undergraduate teaching and postgraduate research.

This had led to a significant increase in the prosperity of Middleham itself in the previous few decades as the university expanded. The local council had facilitated the building of both a business park and a specialist 'science park'. Both were afforded attractive business rates and a sympathetic attitude from the council towards expansion. Each had flourished.

Both parks had forged strong ties with the university, with employers offering summer placements and one-year work placements for 'sandwich' courses. During the last three decades of the twentieth century this had led to plenty of the more commercially minded students settling in the town after graduating. This in turn enabled those businesses to grow significantly and also attracted professionals such as lawyers and accountants to the town.

This exponential growth of an 'imported' middle class had left Middleham with the classic split between a newer middle class in one section of the town and a deprived working class in the other, the latter having seen little of the benefits of improvement.

Middleham University was red brick in every sense. The monochrome buildings constructed almost identically for efficiency in the post-war decades now reeked of conformity. The university's cherished place in the Russell Group of universities, most of which were comparatively ancient institutions, was rumoured to be under threat.

The Head of the Department of Law, Dr Roger Bates, was giving a one-hour lecture beginning at nine o'clock in the Moot Room.

Detective Constable Karl Denman had left for the university almost as soon as the 8am briefing had finished. He'd had a quick word with Molash regarding the ten o'clock appointment that had been made with Dr Bates the previous afternoon. Learning that Dr Bates would be lecturing for the preceding hour Denman decided to try and catch some of the lecture and get a feel for Bates.

By the time Denman had got through the university's security and found the Moot Room, there were only ten minutes of the lecture left. He sat unobtrusively at the back of a half-full lecture theatre. In his mid-thirties and having joined the police force at eighteen, Denman had little experience of universities or of academics.

Bates was in full flow, talking through the introductory elements of the Law of Torts, which would form part of the second-year syllabus, beginning in earnest the following October. To Denman, who had expected the subject to be as dry as the dust he imagined pervaded a university law department, it was surprisingly interesting.

Dr Bates was telling an anecdote from a case where a blind

man had fallen down a hole and become deaf, due to the fact the workmen had gone to lunch and only left warnings that could be seen by those with 'reasonably unimpaired vision', as Bates put it. He concluded by explaining that this case, in 1965, was a relatively early indication of the court's willingness to impose a duty of care that sought to protect those who were vulnerable as well as the vast majority.

Bates hoped that next year the students would discover that both in law and in a decent society that they should learn to take reasonable care of their fellow humans. Ideally they would be inspired to think about how a legal system could be improved to fairly protect both those who get injured and those who might inadvertently cause such injury. It might have sounded trite coming from other lips, but somehow Dr Bates imbued a passion for his subject, which suggested that his lectures would be both entertaining and informative.

The first-year undergraduates filed out quickly and noisily into the summer sun when the lecture ended. Bates gathered his papers, spotted Denman and walked across the Moot Room. "Detective Constable Denman?" he asked with a smile, and upon receipt of some affirmative body language, continued without waiting for a reply, "Come along to my office. Apologies for not shaking hands, I'm always rather burdened with paper for my lectures."

Refusing a polite offer from Denman to help carry the books and files, they set off for Dr Bates' sanctum. Everywhere students bustled purposefully or meandered aimlessly according to their choice. The university embraced both contentedly, unaware that the outside world of work growled disapprovingly at the latter.

Given Bates' friendly manner Denman decided to share his own academic background. "This is the first time I've been inside a university. I joined the force after my A-levels and I've always been curious to see what I missed out on."

To his surprise Dr Bates didn't take the bait to talk about

the glories of tertiary education. "Wise man," Bates replied. "Far too many people go to university simply because there is a consensus that more education is de facto a good thing. Illogical when you think about it. Postgraduate research, where something new is learned, should by definition be profitable to humanity, provided it concerns a worthwhile subject.

"But unless you're in the sciences and can persuade, say, a multinational pharmaceutical to sponsor you, those research degrees have always had to be paid for yourself. Yet in different undergraduate degrees each year, thousands of people learn what hundreds of thousands already know. That apparently is worth the country spending vast sums of money on and, these days, saddling those taking those degrees with enormous debts.

"Not that I blame them for coming. We have a crazy system where employers demand degrees for the sort of ordinary clerical jobs that some decent GCSEs would provide perfectly adequate evidence of a person's suitability for. Until we change the recruiting system, we'll have about fifty per cent of young people in this country going to universities or colleges when little more than half that would be the ideal number."

As they walked, Denman drank in his surroundings. He'd imagined that universities comprised antiquated buildings with uneven spiral staircases. Middleham University was, he decided, very different to the depictions he'd seen on television of Oxbridge colleges, looking architecturally more like the local business park.

When Denman explained his impressions Dr Bates laughed, replying, "Yes, whilst the joke is that we are very close to Oxford and Cambridge, being just below them on students' order of preferred universities on their UCAS application form, you're right. It's very different here."

As Bates finished talking they reached his door, which he opened and then invited Denman in and offered him a seat. Bates' office echoed the wider surroundings, comprising a standard-issue pine desk and a small table around which were several modern chairs for tutorials. The walls were lined with bookshelves, most of the legal tomes looking to be of considerably earlier vintage than the shelves. Bates continued, putting his files and books away neatly as he talked, "I'm grateful to be in this department. If you want to be a solicitor or a barrister you do need to learn the law, so our degrees feel meaningful to me, compared to plenty of those the university issues."

Denman wondered whether Dr Bates was about to embark on a monologue about university life and if so whether it would be useful to listen. However, it seemed Bates was merely making small talk until they had reached the privacy of his office. He sat down and said, "I was devastated to hear about Mark Gower. How can I help, Constable?"

"We need to get to know Mark Gower as well as we can, Dr Bates," Denman explained. "Whilst we are waiting for the results of the post-mortem and forensics, I can tell you off the record that we are looking into the possibility he was poisoned. Either by his own hand or that of another."

Dr Bates laughed in a hollow fashion. "I'm as certain as I could be about any student that Mark would never kill himself. I've rarely seen a more positive, life-loving undergraduate. Of course, we can never know what goes on in another's heart and mind, but it seems incredibly unlikely."

Bates sensed Denman wasn't necessarily attributing him with the skills to spot depression in students many years younger than himself.

"We do get a fair bit of experience of mental health issues at a university, you know. Our pastoral care is far better than it was thirty years ago when I joined and from experience of those students who have had mental health issues, we've got sharper at spotting the less obvious cases. I keep an eye out in tutorials, where I put them under a fair bit of intellectual pressure. For what it's worth, Mark was in my tutorial group all year and I know him from the wider course too. He's about the least likely suicide of any student I could imagine."

"From what you say, Dr Bates, is it equally unlikely that anybody would want to kill him?"

Bates was silent for a few moments. It was the first pause in conversation since the two had met. Up until now Bates had seemed thoroughly in his comfort zone, a man both intelligent and articulate.

He frowned and began with the tone of someone slightly uncertain, who was used to being confident of his ground and who expressed himself carefully on rare moments of uncertainty. "I wouldn't say that. It's pretty unlikely anyone would kill Mark. I should think natural causes or an accident, perhaps a joke gone wrong would be more likely."

Bates paused again, thoughtfully as if attempting to articulate something that had hitherto remained in his subconscious. "However, he did sail through life and inevitably not everyone liked him for that. He was tall, blond, good-looking and he had the sort of easy, confident manner that enabled him to make friends easily. He was a star student in the law department. He'd have got a first back in the day when we didn't hand them out like sweeties."

Denman looked unconvinced. "I can understand that would make some of his peers jealous, but it hardly amounts to a motive for murder, Dr Bates?"

The silence was longer this time, but Denman was patient and sensed that pertinent information was imminent. Dr Bates eventually continued, "The way I would put it is that Mark was very happy in his own skin. He came from a grammar-school background and from what sounded like a lower-middle class family. He had neither the sense of entitlement that some of our privately educated students have, nor the chip on his shoulder that some of our working-class undergraduates possess.

"He was compassionate and open-minded. It didn't

really occur to him that others weren't. He was very good at empathising in one sense. In tort law we spend a lot of time looking at negligence cases. Mark was brilliant at putting himself in the position of both the person who had suffered and the person who had inadvertently caused the suffering.

"But he was much less good at understanding malice – in his first year the only subject he didn't get a first in was criminal law. In that narrow sense he was a bit naïve. I felt that he would need to get out into the working world for him to lose that naivety. He was the type of student that would occasionally upset his peers without knowing it, let alone meaning to."

Denman waited, assuming Bates would continue, but he didn't. "That's interesting, Dr Bates. If this is a murder, at this early stage it's one without a motive that we can see. Could you give me some examples, please?"

Bates seemed reluctant. Whether because he didn't want to paint a blemished portrait of Mark or that he didn't want to point the finger at other students, Denman wasn't sure.

Considering his words very carefully, Dr Bates eventually continued, "I think there were two ways it happened. The first was simple, in that Mark was just smarter than almost all his peers on this course. He never boasted; that might have been better somehow. It was more that he didn't seem to think about it. He was just learning the law and oblivious to the fact that some of his fellow students were unable to match him despite the fact that they had their brains in overdrive whilst his was in third gear.

"His housemate, Danny Wilson, for instance, is above average on this course, but Mark and Danny were always together and Danny was always in Mark's shadow. I'm not suggesting for a moment that gave Danny any sort of motive – he is a good lad, always helping everyone out. You get the gist, though. There may have been someone for whom Mark's attitude begat jealousy, out of which a more serious emotion developed."

Conscious that this seemed pretty thin as a motive for violent death, Dr Bates added, "It would take a certain type of person, what you might call an abnormal person, for this to lead to violence."

24

There was a lengthy silence as Denman tried to evaluate this nebulous-sounding information. He decided to be more direct. "Who did you have in mind, Dr Bates?"

"The second, more specific, way was that Mark angered the left-wing firebrands here in a serious way. The Haldane Law Society wields a lot of power amongst law students… and also staff here," Dr Bates added ruefully.

Denman still didn't seem convinced of the seriousness of Bates' point and countered, "Universities have always been left-wing, though, haven't they?"

Dr Bates looked at him thoughtfully. "You explained that this was your first time at a university, Constable, so stop me if I'm teaching you to suck eggs. I joined the staff here in 1990 as a part-time lecturer whilst I did my PhD. Thatcher was in the process of being kicked out and we all wanted to change the world through our teaching. The young staff here almost all voted Labour, but most of us were more centre-left rather than really left-wing. There was a feeling that something was wrong after a decade of Tory government and we wanted change.

"The difference between then and now was that then we looked at this country and saw that it was conservative with a small 'c'. We wanted to engage with people and see if they would change their opinions. Show them that the 'Who cares?' spirit of the '80s could be bettered. Of course, we didn't get a Labour government for seven years, but after we did universities almost become the last bastions of a failed socialist doctrine. Social democracy had won, the Tories were decimated as a political force and the small enclaves of socialist thinking looked quaint. Almost an amusing little corner of academic life.

"What has changed is not simply Jeremy Corbyn becoming Labour leader and offering a genuinely radical alternative to the centrist policies of the last couple of decades. It's the intolerance of other ideas. People like me joined the university to challenge the orthodoxy, to debate different ideas – some of which were radical.

"Now so much of that debate has been shut down. The ideas are radical but they are the only ones you are allowed to have. This sounds sensational but it is reminiscent of the Soviet ideologues responsible for dogma. It's shocked people like me who grew up when only the far-right wanted to stifle debate, never those of us on the left. The logical endgame is that we'll have broad swathes of society supporting measures to suppress free speech when someone says something they disagree with, whether via boycotts or employment contracts or a hundred other means.

"Ironically this has its roots in the Blair years. Because of the disaster in Iraq, it is unfashionable to remember the great things Blair's government did. Sure Start, the minimum wage and so on. However, it was also when a government-sponsored culture took off that basically said that 'if you don't agree with us you are a fascist/racist/homophobe, etc.' The day-to-day smearing of anyone who didn't agree with you meant people stopped listening. When you stop listening you eventually run out of ideas.

"This mentality festered and grew. Now there are many at universities, both staff and students, who think our purpose is to educate people as to what they *should* think, not educate them so they understand different points of view and so can make up their own minds what to think. When combined with the zealotry that is inherent on the radical left it has led to a culture of extreme intolerance. Universities aren't alone in that, you only need to go on to Twitter to see it, but it's particularly prevalent here."

Dr Bates sighed and continued in a different tone. "Every generation re-invents the world to some extent, and thank God they do. Perhaps I'm just the classic middle-aged fifty-something not liking the ideas of the young."

He paused and gathered himself, continuing in a steelier tone, "No, I'm convinced that is not true. I have always fought prejudice in all its forms in my teaching here. I'm going to keep on fighting the prejudice that says that only certain ideas are acceptable."

Denman was trying to get a handle on the social and political realities of university life. "You said the Haldane Law Society wields power over staff. Who exactly are they and how does that happen?"

Bates smiled for the first time since they had reached his office and his manner became conversational again. "Membership of the Haldane Law Society is open to anyone studying law at the university, whether undergraduate or postgraduate. They are very effective at intimidating staff whose views they don't like. For example, as head of the law faculty I give a speech welcoming the new students each year. It's not a political event as such. It is about explaining how a law degree works, but I always use some practical examples. Last year there was an element in the Haldane Law Society that tried to get me no-platformed as a first step to having me kicked out. I encourage the expression of subversive views, you see."

Denman, who had spent his career chasing kidnappers and murderers, felt like laughing but realised that for academics this was no laughing matter. "Could they really get you kicked out?" he asked.

"They wrote a letter of complaint to the vice-chancellor. He gave them short shrift but made it very clear to me that if I were to get involved in any material breaches of the university code of practice regarding debates, etc., that it would be hard to save my career if the mob were after me. Normally an academic has to get several raps over the knuckles for such breaches before there is any serious disciplinary action. The code of practice isn't supposed to stop free speech but that can be the effect."

"So what do you do?" enquired Denman.

Bates looked him squarely in the eyes, the hard edge back in his voice. "Constable Denman, I am fifty-one years of age. If I get kicked out it'll be with a pension. I am in the lucky position of being able to stick to my principles. I want to teach as many of the students here, those who are willing to learn, that all racism is equally bad. That antisemitism is equally as evil as Islamophobia. That only by freeing yourself from such prejudice can you practice the law well. So I am not going to be browbeaten by this intolerance. For my younger staff members it is harder, but I make sure they know I will support them to the hilt. For the students it is harder still."

Denman was starting to get interested. "So, how did Gower fall foul of this intolerance?" he asked.

Bates thought for a moment. "It started with his just being the sort of free-thinking student we should be encouraging. When analysing laws Mark would challenge neo-liberal policies and socialist ones alike. But of course, for some the former was just pointing out the obvious lies of the right, whilst the latter was unforgivable.

"Mark didn't understand this. He would say things to me such as, 'I like listening to their views, even when they all say the same thing. It reminds me that they might be right and I might be wrong.' He didn't comprehend that some of his peers had no interest in hearing different views.

"In each of the first two terms of the year we have a Great Debate in the Moot Room for each year group. It used to be the case that the department canvassed the opinion of students regarding the subject they'd like covered. We'd then frame an evenly balanced question and select two students to debate it in front of their peers, who would then vote on the motion.

"Now the Haldane Law Society holds a vote on not just the subject but also the question. Given that about four-fifths of the undergraduates in this department are members, the outcome is presented as the democratic wish of the year group. In reality it's decided by a core group of about a dozen within the Haldane Law Society, most of whom are also members of Momentum. Last year the third years debated *Are there any limits to what should be done to stop Brexit?* The whole concept of the Great Debate was becoming farcical and some of my colleagues wanted it stopped."

"Last term's subject for the second-year students was *Which new laws would help defeat populism in the EU?* It was actually an interesting question, if structurally rather different to what we were used to. As it wasn't the sort of 'yes or no?' question that these debates usually involve, we prepared two potential laws that might curb populism, with a view to each being voted on after they had been debated. I selected Mark Gower to be one of the two debaters.

"Both debaters had to argue in favour of and against one of the proposed laws. However, first they had to make an opening five-minute speech explaining their overall approach. Mark spoke for five minutes about the anti-democratic nature of the EU, eviscerating Juncker and company regarding their remarks such as, 'There can be no democracy against the EU treaties.' He explained that a bigger and bigger proportion of domestic laws would pass into a canon of EU law that could in practice not be changed. National parliaments didn't have the power to change them and MEPs don't have the power to draft laws, just critique those proposed by the unelected Commission.

"Mark's response to both of the proposed laws was to argue how populism would be best defeated by abolishing the EU and starting again with a new organisation of co-operation, based on democracy where national parliaments were supreme. He concluded by arguing that a monetary union could only survive with a political and fiscal union, which would involve the Germans taking an enormous cut in living standards to pay for the fiscal union and the Italians being forced to live by German rules in the political union. He described the 'inevitable' consequent surge in populism as the biggest threat to peace in Western Europe during his lifetime.

"It was brilliantly argued. I voted 'Remain' almost on principle, without really considering any of the points Mark was making. It's a moot point whether he was right or not, and if I had to vote again today I probably wouldn't change my mind, but it was food for thought, which is obviously one of the main points of having the Great Debates.

"Anyway, knowing Mark he may have just wanted to argue a radical and different view, to test it in his own mind. However, it incensed the firebrands in the Haldane Law Society, for whom being a Brexiteer is original sin. There was heckling throughout Mark's speeches once they'd realised what line he was taking, and he was abused and threatened afterwards. I walked out with Mark to try and diffuse the situation, but Shaun Roberts, the chairman of the Haldane Law Society, shouted that he would cut his legs off and we heard someone threatening to douse him in petrol."

"How concerned was Mark about this?" asked Denman. "That's pretty threatening language."

Bates laughed. "Much less so than I was, I think! Mark said

Roberts was full of wind and piss. Other than Danny Wilson, Mark didn't socialise much with his coursemates, I don't think. He was sporty and didn't get involved in political life at the university. I wanted to give him a lift home, but he refused."

"Did the animosity subside?" asked Denman.

"On the surface it appeared to. Mark wasn't a member of the Haldane Law Society, and Roberts and his allies rarely had anything to do with him. I'm careful when organising tutorial groups to try to ensure that…" Bates hesitated. "Well, let's say I try to avoid having groups that lead to people not fulfilling their potential."

"Is it possible that Mark might have got into further debates with someone like Shaun Roberts, maybe even on the night of his death? Or in the interim and that some of the hard left-wingers might have wanted to kill him?" asked Denman.

"It still seems pretty unlikely to me," said Dr Bates. "It is possible, though. The vast majority of the Momentum group here are good and peaceful people. As ever, the threats and occasional violence are a small minority."

"So there has been violence before then?" asked Denman.

"Very little," replied Bates. "Roberts got a warning last year. He got into a fistfight with someone from the Conservative Association. Roberts called him a fascist pig that deserved to rot in hell. The Tory lad looked a bit of a soft target, but he gave as good as he got. Roberts ended up with a black eye and a split lip. Both got a serious warning. It all just seems small-time compared to this. Maybe that's just wishful thinking. It was me who persuaded Mark to do the Great Debate. It is supposed to be optional. I'm feeling guilty that I might have initiated something that led to his death."

"Thanks for your time, Dr Bates," Denman said, getting up. "I wouldn't worry. As you say, it looks pretty unlikely that it was Roberts and his cronies, even if Mark was murdered, and it's certainly not your fault if it was."

They shook hands and Denman left and headed back to the station. He got himself a cup of tea and sat at his desk. He had a reputation as a tough nut within Eliot's group, someone who would go through the barrier for the team. He had worked on investigations involving organised crime groups and had refused to be intimidated.

His natural reaction was that what he had said to ease the conscience of Dr Bates was true. It seemed pretty unlikely that Mark Gower had enraged agitators like Roberts enough for any of them to want to kill him. Yet something lingered that prevented him from dismissing what Dr Bates had told him from his mind. It was like a bubble just floating away on the breeze that he kept nearly catching before a gust of wind blew it out of reach.

He'd keep at it, but in the meantime he went to brief Molash, prepare his report for HOLMES and look into Shaun Roberts' past. Whilst Denman had been with Dr Bates, a full trawl of Mark Gower's social media had come up with not the smallest reason why he would want to kill himself. The chances of it being a suicide were receding fast.

25

In every walk of life promotion and responsibility does not always result from achievement. Some are unfairly passed over for promotions, others over-promoted. The police force is no exception to this. Successful investigations tend to create a tide that lifts all boats. Eliot had been an inspector and DSIO on two of the most high-profile local cases towards the end of the first decade of the century.

He had in fact made no more than an adequate contribution to a seemingly unsolvable murder that had eventually been cracked by innovative forensic techniques and a couple of years later a kidnapping that had been solved by a lucky break, or inspiration of the SIO, depending on who you asked. That SIO had retired a few years later.

Chief inspector is the lowest rank for which an exam does not have to be passed. Instead a board interviews candidates, and Eliot was an excellent interviewee, being well versed in the county politics and the fashionable initiatives being championed by senior officers. He breezed through and with the SIO's role subsequently becoming vacant he was appointed.

Eliot had found the responsibility daunting in the first couple of years. Then Molash had joined the team as a bright sergeant with a flair for solving complex puzzles. An unspoken agreement had developed between the two. Eliot would champion Molash's cause and had indeed assisted Molash in earning early promotion to inspector and appointment as DSIO.

Eliot would then delegate a lot of the responsibility for the actual crime-solving to Molash, effectively giving him a free rein. This was officially framed as giving Molash the experience and opportunity to prove himself an SIO-in-waiting. The quid pro quo was that Molash was supportive in giving upward feedback on Eliot to the chief superintendent running the Serious Crimes Directorate. In practice it suited both well and the clear-up rate had flourished.

One of the areas where Eliot always let Molash gain more experience was by being the senior officer at the post-mortem. Molash and Woodcock arrived in plenty of time for the noon appointment. On television crime dramas, the detectives often arrive as the post-mortem is finishing, to be given a short summary by the pathologist.

In practice, a post-mortem tends to last around four hours and Molash and Woodcock would be present with Dr Patel throughout. Also present would be the CSI, Keith Bourne, plus a photographer, the exhibits officer and mortuary technician. Occasionally specialists in ballistics or other disciplines were also in attendance, but they were not required during the post-mortem on Mark Gower.

Dead bodies are infectious and where possible the police officers view the post-mortem from behind glass rather than being in the actual room. However, the SIO (or in this case DSIO) often wants to view something at close range as the post-mortem progresses and so, like everyone else, the police officers are dressed in full protective clothing. This consists of a full-length gown and mask, a faceshield, waterproof non-slip overshoes and nitrile gloves.

Woodcock's role was to take notes of what Dr Patel was saying, in a form that would be useful as a reference for the investigation on HOLMES. Such notes would be quite different in emphasis to the official post-mortem notes Dr Patel herself would dictate throughout.

Not wanting to give Dr Patel a half volley to stroke easily to the boundary, Molash and Woodcock were in place, behind the glass partition at ten minutes to twelve. Patel arrived a few minutes later. Molash wished her a cheerful good morning.

"Ah, *Detective* Inspector Molash," Dr Patel replied, taking twice as long as needed to pronounce the word detective, rolling the word around her mouth as you might a fine wine, as if she was considering what form of detective powers Molash might actually possess. She turned away and, as an aside, in principle to herself but actually in a voice loud enough for Molash and Woodcock to hear, added, "I wonder how much experience of being the senior officer at post-mortems one needs. I suppose it depends on how on the ball such an officer tends to be…"

The battle-lines set, Dr Patel announced that unless there were any objections she would break the seal on the body bag and begin the post-mortem. Greeted with acquiescing silence she played her opening gambit, not even bothering to mention Eliot's predictable absence. "So, Detective Inspector, seeing as you are here to gain experience, let's see how you have evaluated the situation thus far. What should I be looking for during the post-mortem?"

This was what Molash termed her crystal-ball question, but he knew better than to refuse to answer. "We've got a seemingly happy and healthy twenty-year-old man with everything to live for. His GP told us that Mark Gower had always enjoyed excellent health and his VO_2 max results from the rugby club at the university were around fifty, suggesting he was very fit."

Molash paused, but Patel wasn't having that as anything approaching adequate. She was circling the body, doing a preliminary examination. "Go on. I'm here to be illuminated."

"From the preliminary examination yesterday there were no obvious signs of assault of any description, unless today you tell us otherwise. However, there was pronounced cyanosis. His GP confirmed he didn't have circulation issues or any history of low oxygen content in his blood. It therefore seems possible that he's somehow taken some sort of drug that alone, or mixed with a liberal helping of alcohol, has killed him." Hoping to bounce the ball into the pathologist's court, he concluded by saying, "We're therefore hoping you will be able to enlighten us as to what, if any, such toxin he may have taken."

"Congratulations. You have mastered the art of memorising and repeating what you've been told by experts, James," Dr Patel opined, looking up with a smile that made Woodcock wondering if they were flirting after all. Her manner changed again and she added brusquely, "Now for some detection. If I am about to find a lethal toxin in this young man's system, how do you think it got there?"

Before Molash could reply, Patel decided to make it a bit more difficult for him, enquiring, "Would someone of your *eminence* be here if this was simply another student taking an accidental overdose?" Again she took plenty of time articulating the word 'eminence'. "Or are you suggesting someone killed him?"

This was a neat move in the game. From previous encounters Molash knew the dangers of Dr Patel leading him by the nose towards a theory that would then blow up in his face. He hesitated, and Patel looked up and was about to deliver a barb, so he plunged in.

"It looks as if the victim was happy and healthy, and with no apparent reason to commit suicide. Nor are we aware of any reason for anyone to kill him."

"Right, accidental recreational drug overdose it is then," concluded Patel, having neatly trapped him into a theory that both of them knew that neither believed was particularly likely. Dictaphone in hand, her manner imperiously demanding silence, she began to dictate the preliminaries of the post-mortem.

Given how complex post-mortem findings can be, the results in Mark Gower's case were remarkably simple. No signs of any physical assault on the body. No signs of recreational drug use, although forensic tests would be carried out to confirm this. Mark Gower had been extremely fit and healthy, to the point where a natural death would have been highly unlikely.

His stomach contents suggested that he had drunk several pints of lager and a smaller quantity of gin and tonic, with emphasis on the gin. He had also ingested a shot of Sambuca. However, he had also consumed a quantity of some form of sleeping draught (i.e. a liquid).

This might have been fatal without the alcohol, but the combination multiplied the impact of the sleeping draught. It was likely that the combination was considerably in excess of the minimum fatal dose.

Due to the amounts involved, the drug had probably been consumed in the hour before Mark Gower went to bed given that nobody had noticed it having any impact on him. Therefore if the drug were administered at the Union Bar it would have been at or close to the end of the evening. It was more likely that Mark Gower had consumed it at 12 Newton Street after returning home, either in the nightcap or later in his room.

Death was due to respiratory failure following acute pulmonary edema. Dr Patel asked the technician to take samples of the sleeping draught for forensic analysis.

Molash decided to chance his arm. "Would you care to give an expert opinion of what sort of sleeping draught this was and how it was ingested, Dr Patel?"

Without turning to face him, she replied witheringly, "Your line of work allows you to make wild guesses and then change your mind the next day when they prove to be predictably inaccurate. My profession does not."

"I guess we'll need to give the forensics top priority then, including the glasses and bottles from 12 Newton Street?" responded Molash, a twinkle firmly in his eye.

Dr Patel wheeled round and, briefly passing her tongue over her lips, smiled, acknowledging a hit. "Seeing as you clearly need all the help you can get, Inspector, I will stretch a point and mark it top priority. Shall we say noon again tomorrow, gentlemen, for the results?"

The journey back to the incident room was mainly silent. Woodcock liked to look through his notes whilst they were freshest in his mind, make amendments and ask Molash an occasional question. Molash therefore drove, deep in thought about what they had learned. When he parked the car, neither got out for a couple of minutes.

Eventually Molash said, "Woody, it's looking increasingly likely that whatever toxin killed Gower, he ingested it back at 12 Newton Street. Therefore let's go ahead and get all his housemates in for individual interviews tomorrow. Let's do it in the afternoon when we've got confirmation on the forensics."

"What about the two girls who stayed the night there?"

"Have a word with Clark about Annette Palmer and then take a view. You're off to see Chloe Hartwell shortly; I should think we'd want to see her tomorrow. I'll see you back here for a catch-up later."

26

Roy Clark rang the bell at 153 Garrard Street at precisely one o'clock. Garrard Street was comprised of Victorian semi-detached houses, which before the university had been built had been amongst the most desirable residences in Middleham. Obsolete chimneys that had once produced energetic clouds of smoke now poked vainly towards the fluffy clouds in the sky, never destined to approach them.

Most of the spacious semi-detached houses had been carved up into four-or five-bedroom, one-reception room student homes. Decades of hard student living and an often parsimonious approach to repairs had left the street with a resigned air of decay.

Clark had been selected to conduct the interview with Annette Palmer because, at fifty-four, he had the most naturally fatherly air of any detective on the team, with a long record of successfully extracting information from frightened witnesses. Molash had surmised that Annette appeared a periphery figure at 12 Newton Street, so it made more sense to utilise Clark's interviewing skills than the continuity of having Woodcock speak to her.

Annette had sounded nervous to the point of losing control when Clark had called to make the appointment. He had therefore made sure he was there in plenty of time, parking his unmarked car discreetly round the corner and remaining in it until just before one o'clock. Keeping Annette waiting beyond the time of the appointment would only be likely to increase her agitation.

He had looked at Annette's social media profile and seen that she was the daughter of a couple of local authority civil servants who seemed to live in a bygone era. The family lived in a small village in Shropshire, attended church every Sunday morning and returned to a ritual of a glass of sherry and the cooking of Sunday lunch. Annette's younger sister was still at home and, not yet eighteen, was still drinking heavily watered-down sherry.

The entire Palmer family appeared the personification of dowdiness. Annette's father wore the same jacket to church every week and Clark had swapped his blue suit for the nearest thing he had, an old checked sports jacket. To complete the ensemble he had found a tie of greens and browns that had hitherto been an unused Christmas present from a member of his extended family; he couldn't recall whom.

From every piece of information the police had acquired Annette seemed totally out of place at 12 Newton Street. Whilst Clark was prepared for the possibility she would turn out to be a consummate actress who was involved in Gower's death, much the more likely scenario was that she had ended up at 12 Newton Street by chance circumstances, probably fuelled by artificial stimulants.

His modus operandi was to assume she would be scared and embarrassed, and so he would be at his most fatherly, even 'her fatherly', as he put it ungrammatically to himself as he walked up Garrard Street.

"Good afternoon, Miss Palmer," Clark said gently as the door to 153 Garrard Street opened slowly, just enough for him to see Annette's nervous face. "I'm Detective Constable Roy Clark. Thank you very much for agreeing to give me a few minutes of your time," holding his warrant card up for inspection.

The door opened slowly and, with a watery smile, Annette invited him in. She led him to a small lounge, offered him a seat and, after some hesitation about the social etiquette (which Clark suspected had taken up a good proportion of her previous half-hour or so), asked whether he would like a cup of tea.

Suspecting that in the Palmer family all problems prompted a cup of tea he thanked her, adding with his most reassuring smile, "This should only take a few minutes so I think I've got time for a cup of tea – that's really kind of you, milk, no sugar, please."

Apparently freed from the prospect of prolonged third-degree interrogation, Annette scuttled off to the kitchen a little less timidly. Clark mentally summed her up whilst he waited. She was plain without being ugly. A little over medium height. Mousy hair worn in an unbecoming bob. Spectacles which had been purchased with a focus on practicality rather than fashion. Her T-shirt and jeans revealed a thin frame without anything much in the way of curves. Shy and bookish. Nowhere near a fool, without being anything spectacular intellectually. With over thirty years' experience of interviewing the public Clark had quickly surmised that Annette was exactly what she seemed and that kid gloves treatment was the right tactic.

A few minutes later Annette returned with two mugs of tea. Clark was relieved, having braced himself for a tray with a teapot, porcelain cups, potentially accompanied by seed cake. Armed with a mug of tea and seeing a friendly face, Annette Palmer steeled herself for the ordeal. She began by pointing to a bag on the sofa, explaining that it contained her phone and the clothes she had worn on Tuesday evening (which Clark had requested when he called to make the appointment). Her manner suggested that whilst getting the phone back would be useful, she'd be delighted never to see the clothes again.

The preliminary business being satisfactorily concluded she said, "How can I help, Mr Clark?" omitting any reference to his being a policeman.

Clark surmised that having 'dealings' with the police was abhorrent to the Palmer family code so changed his opening gambit. "That's very kind of you, Miss Palmer," he began gently and slowly. "I doubt you are familiar with this sort of thing, but when someone dies suddenly and unexpectedly then we have to have little chats with those who knew them so we can build a picture of the person who has passed away and find out what happened."

"But I didn't know Mark Gower," she burst out. "I'd never even spoken to any of them except Jack Freeman until Tuesday night and only a couple of times to him on…" She petered out as she realised that she might be painting a picture of herself as a scarlet woman.

"Ah, well, that will make my job simpler and I won't need to take up much of your time then," Clark said with another smile. "Why don't you tell me about Tuesday evening? You went to the Union Bar?"

"Yes, yes, that's right," replied Annette quickly, eager to move the conversation on. "You see, we don't go out to the bar or to pubs during the week much, but it was my housemate Alice's birthday and our finals had just finished so we thought we'd celebrate."

"A good idea after all the stress and hard work of the exams, I should think," Clark said encouragingly. "I shouldn't think you'd had much time for socialising during the previous few weeks."

"No, no, that's right," she replied a little breathlessly. "We haven't been out much this term, let alone during the we…" Again she ground to a halt. A few seconds later she continued,

"We generally stopped revising on Saturday evenings and went to the Union Bar for a couple of hours. It's the busiest night so there's more chance of seeing people you know."

"And that's how you met Jack Freeman and his friends?" Clark asked tentatively.

"Just Jack, really. The six of them always drink together but I had chatted to Jack a couple of times when we were in the queue for the bar," Annette replied, her answers coming more fluently now. "Jack was often chatting to girls so I didn't think anything of it the first time. Mark Gower and Ryan Sandling were often with him, but he always seemed to be alone when I talked to him."

"So when did you start speaking to him on Tuesday night?" Clark asked, taking advantage of what looked like a cue, but Annette seemed on the verge of clamming up. "Lovely cup of tea, this, Miss Palmer, thanks. I'm guessing you were on something a little stronger to celebrate Alice's birthday and finishing your exams?" Clark enquired encouragingly.

Annette took a deep breath and nodded. "Yes, Claire had bought a couple of bottles of Prosecco and the four of us drank them before we went out."

"Good choice, my wife and daughter love to celebrate with a couple of glasses of Prosecco, probably a bit more often than you do," Clark said, continuing to plough the uphill furrow of creating the impression that Annette's Tuesday night was nothing out of the ordinary. "What time was that?"

"Time?" stammered Annette. "I don't really know, the middle of the evening, I suppose. Does it matter exactly when? I can ask the others if that helps?"

Clark suspected that at least one of Annette's three housemates were in their bedrooms awaiting a potential summons for a rescue mission and wanted to avoid the possibility of them getting involved for fear Annette would become even more inhibited. "No, don't worry, Miss Palmer," he said. "All we're doing is trying to put together a timeline of what happened on Tuesday night. The more people who can tell us what was happening at different times, the easier that is, but don't worry, most people can't recall exactly."

"Well," said Annette, a little uncertainly but keen to be helpful, "I think we had the Prosecco about eight o'clock and walked down to the bar just after nine. It was rammed."

"That's great," Clark said. "Did you meet Jack Freeman right away?"

"No, not at all," Annette replied, the words gushing out again. "I didn't even know he was there. There were stacks of students. It was much busier than usual, as if everyone was celebrating the end of the exams. Sarah went to the bar and got some beers, bottles of Stella Artois, I think, and we found a table near a corner."

Clark nodded encouragingly and she continued tentatively, "When we had finished our drinks I went to get another round in. Jack saw me in the queue and came over and offered to buy me a drink, but I explained that I was getting a round in and asked if he'd like one. I'd never done that when we had met before, I don't drink a lot of alcohol generally, and…" Again she paused, seeking encouragement.

"That was friendly of you," said Clark, smiling his most paternal smile.

"He was friendly back – he offered to help carry the drinks to our table. He came over, but the others, well…" She dried up again.

This time Clark waited, calculating that what Annette's housemates thought and did wouldn't be beyond her descriptive powers.

"Well, you see, that household has a bit of reputation. Drinking, always doing something outrageous. My father would call them hell-raisers. The girls think they're trouble and had tried to discourage me about Jack."

"Discourage you? You didn't know him very well, though, did you?" asked Clark.

"No," she replied, "but I did talk about Jack a bit. I mean, he must have liked me, as it was the third time he'd come over to talk to me when there were loads of people around. Anyway, Jack was making what you'd call friendly small talk, I suppose, but the girls weren't keen and he kind of took the hint. He thanked me for the drink and said he looked forward to buying me one back."

"He sounds like a gentleman," said Clark. "What happened next?"

"Well, we sat and chatted for quite a while. The mixture of Prosecco and lager had gone to our heads a bit and we were reminiscing about our time at university, given that it was nearly over. I don't know how long that went on but eventually Alice said she was going to dance so we all went with her."

She took a deep breath, aware that she was coming towards the business end. "Anyway, it was when we were on the dance floor that I saw Jack again. He was with Mark Gower and Ryan Sandling talking to some girls I didn't know. Jack caught my eye and waved an empty glass at me and I nodded. A few minutes later he reappeared near the edge of the dance floor with a couple of drinks. The girls were lost in the music and I went and sat down with him."

Clark sensed that this would be the most difficult stage of the evening for Annette to talk about. The later events could be glossed over, but the bald facts were that she had spent a while talking with a young man she barely knew and had gone back to his house to spend the night with him.

Clark decided it was a good time to introduce the wider context. "So, there had been nothing unusual during the evening? You didn't see anyone messing about putting anything in someone else's drink or Mark Gower arguing with anyone for instance?" he asked.

"No, nothing like that," replied Annette, sounding shocked. "I hardly saw Mark. The only other time I saw him before we left was when he came over with an empty pint glass to remind Jack that it was his round. I'd just been explaining to Jack that I'd been doing my finals and Mark said, 'Hi,' to me in a friendly way and then went back to his friends."

"So you didn't see Mark drinking at all whilst you were at the Union Bar?" Clark asked. When Annette shook her head Clark continued, "Mark seemed on good terms with Jack then?"

"Oh yes, I think so," replied Annette, "though I think Jack was trying to make it clear that he wasn't inviting Mark to join our conversation. He was sitting in a chair facing out towards the main bar area. When Mark walked over Jack swung his legs round so his knees and shins weren't facing out towards the bar, which made it all a bit more intimate."

Annette seemed to be becoming less nervous rather than more so and continued, "Anyway, Jack said he'd be right back. I think he'd seen someone he knew serving behind the bar. I waited and he was back really quickly. He took a tray with six pints and six shots over to their table. He said something and they all downed the shots. He then left his friends and brought his pint over with a bottle of Stella for me."

She seemed almost proud of the fact that he had chosen her over his friends. Clark looked at her with sympathy. "What happened next?" he asked.

"Well, to be honest I didn't really want another drink and it was pretty late by then," she responded. "I took the odd sip out of politeness and we chatted but soon the bar was closing and everyone was going home. The girls were coming over from the dance floor and Jack said quickly, 'In our house we always have one nightcap before everyone goes home and we go to bed. It's kind of a ritual. None of us go to bed without it. Would you like to join us?'"

She was starting to lose her nerve again, the words stuttering out, and Clark moved in yet again to reassure her, saying mendaciously, "Yes, I've got some friends who do the same thing. They live opposite our local pub and we sometimes go for a nightcap there when the pub shuts."

This just seemed to tilt the balance, enabling Annette to continue. "Well, when we got to Jack's house I found out that someone chose what everyone drank. My head was swimming a bit, but I didn't feel too bad and the lounge was really quite clean and neat considering they were boys. As we'd walked to Newton Street I'd been apprehensive. I thought it might be, well, you know what boys can be like.

"Anyway, apparently it was Mark's turn to choose and sort the drinks. It was pints of gin and tonic. Jack whispered to Mark to make me a small one, without too much gin." She smiled nervously at Clark, seeking further justification. "I mean, it was really thoughtful of him – my drink was half full of ice. Lots of men having brought a girl home would have been trying to get them drunk to take advantage of them."

"This is a really important bit, Annette," said Clark, still friendly but now a little more seriously. "Did you see Mark drinking his nightcap? Did he put it down anywhere in that room?"

"I don't think I noticed. I'd forgotten to put my contacts in. I didn't want to go out in my glasses, so I couldn't see that clearly anyway. We stayed in the lounge whilst Mark went to make the drinks in the kitchen. He bought them in on a tray. Jack got mine for me and I sat at one end of the sofa with him. Sam Taylor and that Chloe Hartwell, in her skintight, fake leather trousers, sat at the other end. The rest of the boys were all standing up and moving around, I think. I was really nervous, being in *that* house, and I don't really like gin so I was wondering what I was going to do with my drink."

She paused, and Clark sensed that she was ready to conclude her story. "A while later Mark suddenly laughed, and as I looked over he had picked up his pint, which still looked to have plenty in it, and drank it down in one. Everyone suddenly started looking at Mark whilst he was drinking and Jack whispered to me and I poured almost all of my drink into his glass. Then everyone finished their drinks and I was really thankful I only had a little left.

"Anyway, Mark said good night and that seemed to be a cue and everyone else headed off to bed and within a few seconds we were on our own. Jack offered to walk me home but then said a little shyly that it would be lovely if I wanted to stay."

Annette looked terrified at the prospect of discussing subsequent events and Clark, a kind man where law-abiding members of the public were concerned, smiled again and said, "That's been hugely useful, thanks, Miss Palmer. Did the four of you stay on the sofa all the time from when Mark brought the nightcaps in until when he finished his drink?"

Annette hesitated. "I can't remember. Honestly. I certainly did, but I was talking to Jack. I think Jack might have got up to go to the toilet soon after he'd spoken to Mark about getting me a smaller drink. Yes, he did. I remember looking round the room and feeling intimidated, but he was back pretty quickly. I think he walked over to Mark when he came in with the tray and took our drinks, but I'm not certain."

Clark waited for a moment to see if Annette would recall anything else and then went on. "That's really helpful too, Miss Palmer. So you and Jack were the last to go up. Jack's room is on the first floor, but Mark's room was the converted attic. Did you hear anyone go up the stairs to Mark's room at any stage? I understand sometimes some of the housemates who wanted another drink would congregate in a bedroom after the others had gone to bed following the house nightcap."

Annette was stammering now. "I didn't hear anything like that. I think I would have heard as the walls seemed pretty thin. I could hear Sam and Chloe in the next room, pretty much as soon as we went upstairs. You could hear everything and I was nervous enough as it was, but what if they heard me? I…"

Finally her resolve broke and Annette burst into a flood of tears. Almost immediately the lounge door opened and Sarah Foster flew into the room and sat down next to Annette and gave her a hug.

Eventually Annette said, almost in a shout, the words that had clearly been uppermost in her mind all day, "The first time I have a one-night stand and the whole university is going to know. Everyone will think I'm a slag."

Clark had been expecting this ever since he had entered the lounge at Garrard Street and said, "If that's the first one-night stand you've had in three years then I should think the vast majority of your fellow students would see you as much more virtuous than them. In any case, it's much harder to pick a partner for life if you have no experience of different people."

Sarah gave Clark a grateful glance and looked Annette in the eyes. "You've had two boyfriends at university and you made them both wait several weeks. Nobody is going to think you are a slag because of one mistake. God knows what you saw in Jack Freeman. That lot are a bunch of arrogant arseholes. Strutting about like they own the place."

Annette was breathing heavily, but the tears were stopping and she seemed to want to unburden herself, both to her friend and to the policeman. "I was just fascinated. I'd never really known anyone like them. They were really clever and totally outrageous. It felt like Liberty Hall. I couldn't believe that Jack seemed interested in me, would leave his friends and come across a crowded bar especially to speak to me. But then… afterwards… he just went to sleep. He didn't even talk to me."

"There is one more question that I need to ask you, Miss Palmer. What time did you leave 12 Newton Street?" asked Clark.

Annette sniffed. "It was nearly three o'clock. Jack was asleep and it had been quiet in Sam's room for a while. I just wanted to get home. I didn't see or hear anyone. I'm pretty sure everyone was asleep."

"Well, you've been incredibly helpful in assisting us with building up a picture, Miss Palmer, I'm very grateful for your time. In a few days everyone will have forgotten you were even at 12 Newton Street. Trust me, I've seen enough to know," Clark said with his most reassuring smile. "We'll need a statement in due course and we'll arrange the return of your possessions. We'll be in touch about both. I'll see myself out."

Clark walked slowly back down Garrard Street in the hot sun, his initial thoughts summarised by the two words 'bless her'. *I must be getting old*, he thought. He drove back to the station, briefed Molash and inputted a summary of his interview onto HOLMES, giving his opinion that it was unlikely that Annette Palmer had anything to do with the death of Mark Gower. When the other students were interviewed again, confirmation could be sought that Annette had not left the sofa and had not had the opportunity to tamper with Mark's drink.

It was looking increasingly unlikely that anyone had gone up to Mark Gower's bedroom. If he had been poisoned in the house, it was almost certainly downstairs in the nightcap.

27

It was just before three o'clock when DCI Eliot received his first call from the press. Mark Gower had died in circumstances that could not as yet be explained. Whilst Molash had quickly decided this was likely to turn into a murder investigation and Eliot had acquiesced with that view, nothing to that effect had been made public.

The seven other students who had been at 12 Newton Street the night Mark died had kept to the police request to not discuss Mark's death and, in particular, not to post on social media. They'd had plenty of questions on social media and the silence with which they greeted them had fanned the flames of theories about Mark's death.

Those theories had been developing since word that Gower had died in unexplained circumstances had spread like wildfire through the university the previous afternoon and evening. The police cannot act in a vacuum and the presence of police officers making house-to-house enquiries, including at many student homes, meant that word spread. That would have happened in the pre-social media era, but it occurs more quickly now. Gradually word got out into the wider community in Middleham and the media picked it up.

DCI Eliot invested considerable energy in maintaining and improving relations with the media and with the different communities that Middleham comprised. As a result he had formed friendly relationships with a number of those employed in the local media. In consequence Eliot tended to have more direct conversations with the press than the typical SIO.

A golden rule for the SIO in dealing with the media is to keep all conversations 'on' rather than 'off' the record. No matter how much the officer may trust the reporter, they should not assume they can trust the reporter's editor.

This theoretical rule is difficult to maintain in practice as informal conversations can appear attractive and journalists will often want to have off-the-record discussions to better understand the circumstances of a case. It was into these murky waters that Eliot waded when Vivian Johnson telephoned him.

Johnson's parents had emigrated from Antigua in the 1970s, and as well as being a zealous journalist for the *Middleham Gazette*, Johnson had been a key figure in Eliot's relations with the black community within Middleham. Johnson was active in promoting the concerns of the black community and in dealing with the racism they experienced in the area.

In his mid-thirties he was both shrewd and experienced enough to know that good relations with a police force (where the black community remained significantly under-represented) was a big asset to the black community. He also knew that Eliot was a fundamentally decent man who was committed to helping all the communities in the area. So far the relationship had held.

There was no reason to imagine a racial angle to Mark Gower's death. Johnson was calling in the ordinary course of business to try and use his relationship with Eliot to get a handle on the case to see if it was likely to constitute a newsworthy story. He also had a tidbit of information to impart if needed.

As usual, Eliot was courtesy itself, enquiring after Johnson's wellbeing and his family. A couple of minutes later Johnson brought the conversation round to the point. Eliot was non-committal, explaining the basic details in what was effectively a private version of a holding briefing. He told Johnson that they were investigating the unexplained death of Mark Gower who lived at Newton Street and attended the university. It was being treated as suspicious. The post-mortem was going on as they were speaking and once it and the forensics were complete then a more detailed statement would be made.

Having got the stonewall treatment he anticipated, Johnson then imparted the information he had researched to try to get Eliot to open up. He had spent a few hours on social media and during the day there was an increasing debate amongst students regarding whether Mark Gower had been poisoned in the Union Bar.

This was the real power of social media at work. In a big town like Middleham many people have relatively little to do with their neighbours and, absent mass gatherings, information takes some time to spread. On social media it can spread in hours, sometimes in minutes. DC Shah's interview with the bar manager Les Christie had been the subject of much debate (not least because Christie wasn't on any social media to comment on that debate).

The result was a growing theory that there was a lunatic poisoner at work, and that nobody was safe, especially in the Union Bar. As is so often the case, it was hard to work out where the theory started. It seemed to come from various different similar conversations and spread like a virus. The more people who heard several other different people debating it, the more credence the theory developed. As far as Johnson could see this was not a rumour started through malice, the spread of which had been carefully choreographed.

Eliot was concerned. Naturally risk-averse, especially when it came to popular opinion, he feared this spiralling out of control. He asked Johnson to do what he could to convey the impression that this was not the police theory. However, he would look to arrange a formal press conference the following day. He also agreed to contact Johnson early the next day to update him on the state of play.

After Johnson had rung off, Eliot sat alone in his office thinking. He summoned DC Tyler Brennan and asked him to keep an eye on social media. In particular Eliot wanted to know if there was any evidence of a person deliberately spreading such rumours. He then left a message for Molash, who was still in the post-mortem. Molash would brief Eliot when he returned to the station anyway and Eliot now had an extra item for them to discuss.

28

As Woodcock had stayed behind the previous day at 12 Newton Street to undertake initial interviews with the students, Molash had decided that he should also interview Chloe Hartwell. It was not ideal. Molash had seen pictures of Chloe on the students' social media. Woodcock was something of a ladies' man and whilst Molash trusted his professionalism, he was less convinced about how objective he would be.

That said this was just an initial chat. Molash's hunch was that this was a 'personal' murder. As it may have occurred at 12 Newton Street the police would soon be speaking again, more formally this time, to everyone who spent Tuesday night there. For the moment it would be helpful to have as few interviewers as possible, to maximise the chances of any meaningful discrepancy being spotted straightaway. Molash needed a lead.

Woodcock drove to 18 James Street where Chloe Hartwell lived with three other girls also studying for degrees in social and economic history. Normally he would have driven all the way down to number 18, but the second half of the road looked a difficult thoroughfare to negotiate, with cars, including lots of 4x4 and SUVs, parked nose to tail on both sides of a street built when cars were much smaller and there were fewer of them on the roads. The percentage play was to find a space halfway down the street before it narrowed, and he duly parked the car and took the more straightforward option of walking the remaining two hundred yards or so.

The interview had been arranged for five-thirty and even in late afternoon the day was still hot rather than merely warm. It was a couple of minutes after half past five when Woodcock stood outside surveying the house Chloe lived in.

It was not an obvious student house. It was much further from the campus than roads like Newton Street, which were crammed with student houses. It was also rather more up-market, forming part of the 'new town' that had expanded during the last quarter of the twentieth century. It was the first student house Woodcock had seen with a sizeable front garden, which was immaculately kept. He surmised, rightly, that rather than one of the students being green-fingered, there was a paid gardener. Each house in James Street had only space for one car on the drive and few had sacrificed any of the garden to accommodate a second.

Woodcock had seen an online record of Chloe's political campaigning and the irony of her living amongst the beating heart of Middleham's bourgeoisie wasn't lost on him.

Chloe was alone in the house and it was some time after Woodcock had rung the bell that the front door opened. Given that Chloe Hartwell was one of the co-ordinators of the student-protesting movement within the university, Woodcock was expecting a welcome considerably cooler than the day. He got it.

"Yes?" Chloe asked aggressively, despite the fact that Woodcock was there by appointment. Woodcock already had his warrant card out and soundlessly held it up close to the door, forcing Chloe to look at it. "I suppose you'd better come in then," she said ungraciously, turning round and striding off to the kitchen, leaving Woodcock to follow and close the front door behind him.

When Woodcock entered the spacious kitchen Chloe was leaning against the granite work surface, the palms of her hands outstretched on the surface just behind her. She was wearing a very short cream cotton top, that helped emphasise the more than ample contents of the white uplift bra beneath, and a pair of blue jean shorts which zipped up at the back. Her glossy hair hung loose around her shoulders. She didn't offer Woodcock tea or coffee.

Woodcock realised that the pictures he'd seen from social media were, for once, not flattering. They failed to do her justice. She radiated sexual temptation. Not needing to flirt to create effect, she stood with an insolent look on her face. Woodcock programmed himself to concentrate.

He needed to gain the initiative. Whilst interviewing someone with Chloe's looks was a rarity, every police officer quickly gets plenty of practice in questioning those who don't like officers of the law. He used the time-honoured strategy of being polite and giving her as little as possible to complain about, whilst taking a no-nonsense, firm line.

"Thank you for agreeing to help us, Miss Hartwell, it's much appreciated. First of all, please could you tell me why you didn't come back with Sam Taylor and Owen Lloyd to 12 Newton Street yesterday as we requested?"

The contempt was obvious in her reply. "We don't yet live in a police state, do we? I was in London at the time, trying to do my bit to improve society. To help cleanse it of the fascist and oppressive forces which abuse their dominant position in this country. Why should I drop what I'm doing the minute you want to talk to me? There was no shortage of your lot in Trafalgar Square at the time if you had needed to speak to me."

"This is a murder investigation, Miss Hartwell," Woodcock

said, stretching the status of the enquiry slightly. "Mark Gower was a friend of yours, wasn't he? The housemate of your boyfriend, certainly."

The bluntness of his words moderated Chloe's attitude a little. She looked shrewdly at Woodcock. Her tone was less petulant, though hardly co-operative. "Murdered? Who would want to kill Mark? It doesn't make sense."

Woodcock agreed and said so. "I'm with you, Miss Hartwell. It makes no sense to me at all. That's why we need all the help we can get from Mark's friends." He waited, intrigued to see what effect this would have.

When she didn't respond he continued, "When we investigate a murder we're usually looking for a motive like money, sex, jealousy, love, revenge, hate and so on. Often the motive sticks out like a sore thumb. As an outsider, there seems to me a complete absence of motive for anyone to want to kill Mark. We need to know what he was really like, who loved or hated him, who was jealous of him or sought revenge."

A silence followed. At first Woodcock thought Chloe was just being unhelpful, but then he realised it was more than that. She was thinking too. His first impression of her was that she was sharp and understood people well, men in particular. He also thought that she'd assumed Mark's death was an accident, natural causes or suicide. Compared with what was happening in London, it hadn't registered. One life compared to millions.

Chloe had arrived back on the coach from London shortly before midnight. Annoyed that Sam had complied with the police request and got the first available train back to Middleham, Chloe hadn't communicated with him that night. Having not asked about Mark and now back in a different environment from Trafalgar Square, Woodcock wondered if she was feeling guilty about having ignored Mark's death. If she was, that guilt might be leading to a hint of rapprochement.

Eventually Chloe spoke again. "None of us have got any

money. We're students living in penury so the rich can get richer. Mark's parents haven't got money either so it won't be that."

It was as if it was obligatory for any helpful information to be couched in terms of a state of the nation address. Woodcock ignored the fact that even as a student Chloe was living in a house that half of the population of the country could never realistically aspire to. Instead he nodded and simply said, "You must be right. I can't imagine money being a motive here. Any other more feasible motives?"

Chloe laughed. "I can't imagine Mark having done anything to anyone for which they would want revenge. He wasn't the sort of boy you'd hate. He was decent-enough-looking and he was a laugh. I suppose someone might be jealous of him?" Chloe concluded doubtfully.

Woodcock picked up the doubt in her voice. "From what we've seen so far I think your instincts are right, Miss Hartwell. Even if someone was jealous of him, it seems unlikely that they'd kill him." He decided to test the waters by adding, "I mean, it's not as if Mark was an Adonis."

For the first time she looked Woodcock directly in the eye, flicking her lustrous hair, which fell alluringly back across her shoulders, and parting her lips. "Not even the best-looking boy in his household, Sergeant," Chloe said, delivering judgment. "He did all right with the girls, though, from what I could see."

"Mark didn't have anyone special as far as we can see. Is that right?" asked Woodcock, dry-mouthed.

The sexual pecking order at the university was one of Chloe's specialist subjects. She didn't bother looking too far down from the top of it, but Mark was within easy viewing distance and the truculence had all but gone from her manner as she continued, "I don't think so. Certainly he never bought anyone back to Newton Street on a regular basis. More often he wouldn't come back when we all went back there after a night out. It wasn't anyone serious, though."

Thoughtfully, she added, "He was a bit secretive about it. He'd get home the next morning and we'd be milling about and the boys would ask him how he'd got on. Mark would always deflect the question. I'm pretty sure there was nobody he cared about."

Woodcock wondered if there had ever been any sexual tension between Mark and Chloe. She was evidently too streetwise to admit it under direct questioning, so instead he asked, "What do you think about the others at 12 Newton Street, Miss Hartwell? You're the one person who doesn't live there but is there regularly enough to have a decent idea of what they are like. Off the record, what do you think of them?"

He wasn't sure whether she'd take the bait, but she did. She smiled. "Sam and Mark are the alpha males of the group. They led and the others followed, willingly or unwillingly."

Woodcock's interest was rising, but he kept his voice level, asking, "Who were the willing followers?"

"Butters Owen Lloyd for a start," Chloe said, making no attempt to keep the disdain out of her voice. "They'd outgrown him, really, but Mark and Sam were very loyal. He was one of the lads and that was it. Forever, apparently. Owen's clever, though, and I think he'd worked out that if he went with the flow, he'd stay in the group.

"Jack Freeman was a willing follower too, though of a different type."

There was a pause and, sensing that might be all the mention Jack Freeman warranted, Woodcock asked, "What type of willing follower is Jack?"

"Young men think with their cocks, right, Sergeant?" Chloe retorted, leaving Woodcock wondering whether that was intended as a classification not including him, on grounds of age. "Some will follow you on a day out they've no interest in, without realising that you'd rather take a lifelong vow of celibacy than let them touch you. Others will do anything to get their end away. Jack has literally no standards. It's not as if he's hideously ugly. He just seems to need to get laid with someone different every week. Provided he was in a pub or bar full of girls he wasn't bothered. Being one of the boys from 12 Newton Street helped him when he was smashing, I guess."

"So who were the unwilling followers?" asked Woodcock.

Chloe thought for a moment. "Ryan Sandling. You don't quite know where you are with him. He often seemed to be trying to muscle in on the Sam/Mark double act. He wanted to be calling the shots but doesn't have the same charisma. I sometimes thought he was annoyed when he'd been angling for them to do something and Mark and Sam had just made a different decision. It was nothing major – which pub they should go to, that sort of thing. You'd get a fleeting sense of irritation, but he'd always accept it."

"What about Danny Wilson?" Woodcock asked.

"Oh, Danny. He's the peacemaker. There are some big personalities in that house. Sometimes they'd bang heads and Danny would sort it out. Not often but you always felt nothing would get out of hand with Danny there. Sam and Mark would sometimes ask his view and they'd generally go with what he said, but Danny didn't force it on them."

"Thanks, Miss Hartwell, that's great," Woodcock said, allowing himself a smile, though one he was quick to lose in a thoughtful frown. "I also need to know anything you can tell me about Tuesday night."

Woodcock wondered whether moving on to the night of the crime itself might cause Chloe's hackles to be raised again. He was pleasantly surprised when she replied co-operatively.

"I hadn't been intending to go out. We had the march the next day and we were here planning that. We were all sorted about nine thirty, though, and so I thought I'd go up to the Union Bar as I fancied a beer. I messaged Sam to say I was on my way. It was packed for a Tuesday, post-exam celebrations, I guess. Sam got me a drink but I'd seen a few people in the bar that had been on protests in the past. I left the boys to it and did some recruiting. I didn't see them again until nearly chucking-out time."

"So you didn't see Mark having a disagreement with anyone? Or anyone putting anything in his drink?"

"No. People generally didn't start disagreements with them. Actually I did sit down at their table just after last orders. I'd had enough of talking to self-interested bastards for one evening, so I went to see Sam. It just looked like a typical evening. They were all half-pissed but nothing more than that. I didn't see anyone putting anything in Mark's drink, or anyone else's for that matter."

"What about back at Newton Street?"

"We had the obligatory nightcap. I fancied it actually. As soon as Mark came in with the tray I went and grabbed two for Sam and me. Mark's choice, and you never knew with him, but it was just gin and tonic. Industrial strength, of course, but I thought that would set me up."

She paused and Woodcock threw in another question, "Did anyone go to the kitchen with Mark and help make the drinks?" Chloe Hartwell was the soberest one in the lounge at 12 Newton Street that night. If anyone was going to have noticed someone slipping something into Mark Gower's drink she was the most likely witness.

"No, I don't think so," said Chloe, her eyes now faraway, trying to remember. "We all went straight into the lounge. Ryan reminded Mark that it was his choice of nightcap and Mark went on his own to the kitchen. Sam followed him into the kitchen to see if he wanted any help, but Mark must have said no. Basically that meant a normal nightcap rather than something they'd create.

"The rest of us stayed in the lounge until Mark came in with the nightcaps. All except Jack, who went to the loo, I think.

I didn't see whether he went into the kitchen. I think he was only away a couple of minutes, though. I was just toying with whether to ask that vicar's daughter he'd brought home whether she fancied being the centrepiece of a gangbang, just to see the look on her face, when Jack got back."

Woodcock gave her a 'man-of-the-world' smile and said, "So Annette Palmer definitely did not leave the sofa then?"

Chloe looked as if she was about to burst into laughter. "No. Annette, if that was the basic girl's name, sat like a church mouse. Jack brought her drink over to her. I could see her all the time. She didn't go anywhere near Mark or his drink.

"I was at the end of the sofa. Sam was next to me, and Jack and the vicar's daughter were at the other end. I could see those three well, although Jack had his back to me. The other four were all standing up. They seemed to be moving around the room a bit, not just standing still, but I didn't really notice what they were doing."

"Were the four that were standing holding their drinks all the time?" Woodcock asked.

"I didn't notice, but I doubt it. They'd have put their drinks down when not drinking them. House rules. I was talking to Sam about the next day and then suddenly Sam laughed and I saw Mark was downing his pint. I'd only had a couple at the bar so I was a fair way down mine and finished it off. Sam still had most of his and I thought about snatching it and drinking some of it. I wanted him on form. Then everyone went to bed. Except for Jack and the vicar's daughter. We left them on the sofa."

"Did Mark go upstairs to his room alone? Nobody went for another drink with him?" asked Woodcock.

Chloe considered for a moment. "Yes, I think he did. We went out of the lounge together and Ryan and Danny followed Mark up the stairs. Their bedrooms are on the first floor, same as Sam's. Owen's is downstairs and he'd waddled off. I'm fairly sure I saw Mark going up the next flight of stairs to his room and Danny and Ryan going into their bedrooms as Sam and I followed them up."

"Could anyone have gone up to Mark's room later?" Woodcock asked.

"They could have done, but the stairs squeak so I'd probably have heard if Jack and the vicar's daughter had gone up there for a threesome," Chloe said.

"Roughly how long were you awake for, Miss Hartwell?" Woodcock asked, resolutely avoiding catching her eye.

"I sobered Sam up by making him work hard on me first. He crashed out afterwards but I stayed awake for a while thinking about the next day. Probably an hour, I'd say. There hadn't been a sound I'd heard from upstairs in Mark's room. Jack was still pitching a woo to the vicar's daughter across the landing but other than that the house was quiet."

Woodcock decided that was sufficient. "Thanks, Miss Hartwell, I'm very grateful for your help. I think Sam has told you that we would like to borrow your phone for a day or two, please, and the clothes you wore on Tuesday night."

Chloe had intended to vocally point out her rights to the police but she'd quite liked Woodcock and used her other tactic. She looked at him with big eyes, swishing her hair beguilingly again. She gently pursed her lips, moistening them by running her tongue lightly over them for good measure, and said, in her most liquid and alluring voice, "Do you really have to take my phone? This is nothing to do with me and I need it."

"I'm sorry, Miss Hartwell, I'm afraid I do. Your voluntary co-operation is really appreciated," Woodcock replied. "We won't keep it long. We'll need a statement from you so I'll arrange it so that you can collect your phone at the same time to minimise the inconvenience."

As he was walking along the hallway to the front door with his new possessions he heard Chloe's voice from the kitchen. "If only I had known you were going to demand my clothes I would have worn something more exciting, Sergeant."

Woodcock walked up James Street to where he had parked his car, got in, drove round the corner and exhaled deeply. He thought about what he'd learned as he drove back to the station. If a drug had been in Mark's nightcap then, if Chloe's evidence was reliable, that eliminated Annette Palmer.

It had been difficult not to be dazzled during the interview. Woodcock arrived at the station, found a quiet room and wrote up a draft of his notes with particular care before going to discuss it with Molash. He'd seen the look in the DSIO's eye when he'd briefed him.

Woodcock wanted to be completely sure he'd not missed anything. If Mark Gower had been poisoned at 12 Newton Street, on Chloe's evidence none of the boys could be completely ruled out.

At least they now had some corroborative evidence that only Sam and perhaps Jack had gone into the kitchen when Mark was mixing the drinks. If Mark had been poisoned at the Union Bar they were no further forward.

29

It was after seven thirty by the time Woodcock had finished his report and spoken to Tyler Brennan. He went to see Molash before inputting his report into HOLMES. Molash was in characteristic pose with his feet on his desk, deep in thought. Woodcock arrived clutching two mugs of coffee and asked whether it was a convenient time. Molash took his feet off his desk and thanked Woodcock for the drink. He looked his sergeant squarely in the eye and asked how he had got on with Chloe Hartwell.

Woodcock had been expecting nothing less and replied, "She's a spanner, no doubt about that."

Molash didn't often go to The Ship after work, but he did attend the office Christmas party and celebrated promotions or the birthdays of close colleagues. Molash knew from seeing Woodcock off the leash on such occasions that he was no shrinking violet with women and it amused him to see the impact Chloe Hartwell had had on him.

"Well, she certainly seems to have made your nuts tighten. Did you get anything useful out of her?"

Woodcock recounted the salient points of the interview, which, unusually, he had been rehearsing. Whether or not Molash realised that, he reverted to seriousness and replied, "Good stuff, Woody. What's your gut feel – anything between her and Mark Gower?"

Woodcock had been considering this and replied, "Probably not. I wondered about the fact Chloe seemed so confident there was nobody special in Mark's life. Given that Mark was apparently cagey about his sexual exploits, that doesn't quite ring true if she was totally disinterested in him. That said, from what we know of Gower, he doesn't sound the type to shag a mate's girlfriend?"

Molash was inclined to agree but they decided to keep an open mind. "From what you've said she sounds like the sort of woman that a young man could completely lose his head over. That could lead to an uncharacteristic act of violence."

Woodcock hadn't yet seen Clark's interview with Annette Palmer and Molash recounted the details to him. Molash had plenty of faith in Clark's judgment. When coupled with Chloe Hartwell's evidence they both agreed Annette should be discounted.

Denman had sat down with Molash and discussed his interview with Dr Bates, emphasising that he thought there was something there that he hadn't quite grasped. Woodcock raised his eyebrows and the two officers went through the transcript from HOLMES. Woodcock said, "Karl has done a good job. It tells us a fair bit about Mark, but nothing jumps out at me as not feeling right. I'll get an interview with this Roberts arranged, but students don't kill each other in cold blood because of different political views, do they?"

Molash agreed that it seemed unlikely, adding, "Karl's got sound instincts, though. I wonder what it was that he thought he'd missed."

After a few moments he said, "Let's revert to how this was

actually done, Woody. We know from the post-mortem that Gower had ingested some sort of sleeping mixture, in liquid form. We'll know more tomorrow about what it was and perhaps equally importantly how much liquid it comprised. Ignoring the practicalities of how much liquid there was, the taste, colour and so on for a moment – just how do you get something into someone's glass without them noticing? Let's run through the possibilities, no matter how absurd they sound."

Woodcock started listing possibilities. "Firstly, as we discussed last night, someone behind the bar or a person buying a round could probably do it if they didn't care who drank it.

"Assuming Gower was the target, a second possibility is that you could hand a drink to someone, as Chloe Hartwell did to Sam Taylor with the nightcap. By sleight of hand you might poison the drink without anyone noticing, but nobody looks to have had that opportunity with Mark's drinks.

"Thirdly, there could be two people involved with one person getting the poison into the glass and another handing it to the victim, but that doesn't look to work here either.

"Fourthly, if Mark put his drink down somewhere – or potentially if he was the last to take a drink from the tray in the Union Bar – then someone might have taken the opportunity to slip the poison in when nobody was looking.

"Fifthly, somebody could have poisoned their own drink, say, holding it under the table, and then swapped glasses with Mark."

That was the sum total of Woodcock's possible theories, for the time being at least.

Molash nodded thoughtfully. "That covers the ground pretty well, I think, Woody. Let's keep an open mind, though. It may be that if we find another way for the poison to have been ingested, it will lead us straight to the killer. I agree the second and third options don't seem feasible here. We're therefore choosing between an indiscriminate killer, probably a maniac, poisoning drinks almost at random, and someone who took advantage of nobody looking at the crucial moment. Switching glasses at the Union Bar is an interesting theory – we can't trace the glass so it's quite neat."

Molash thought for a moment and added, "Gower apparently had about half of his nightcap left when he finished it and that meant everyone else had to as well. Did he finish it in one go because he was ready for bed or was there another reason?"

Woodcock replied, "According to the others he went straight to bed, and other than Jack and Annette the rest did too, so that suggests he was just ready for bed. It had the effect of leaving Jack alone with Annette, but I can't see that means anything. Let's look at it from the other end too – where it was done – and see if that helps. We've got four choices: the bar, the kitchen whilst Gower mixed the drinks, the lounge whilst they drank them and in his room later."

Assuming you could discount a conspiracy involving all, or nearly all, the students that were in 12 Newton Street with Mark Gower that night, it seemed very unlikely that anyone had gone up to Mark's room. Had someone done so then it would have been relatively easy to present Mark with a laced drink, though it would have probably required some ingenuity to dispose of whatever Mark drank out of. They priced it up at 20/1; it only not being made longer odds because of the fact that it would solve the knotty problem of why nobody saw the poison going into the drink.

There were two possibilities at the Union Bar. The chances of it being the location where Mark Gower was deliberately targeted looked slim. It seemed to require a lot of people to be looking in the wrong direction all at once, although if glasses were switched after the poison was added it would be less difficult. Someone indiscriminately poisoning whichever student took the poisoned glass was more practicably feasible, but as a motive was inherently less likely than a personal motivation. Gower having been poisoned in the Union Bar was a 9/1 chance.

The previous evening both detectives had believed that it was probable that a poison was administered in the nightcap at 12 Newton Street. The post-mortem and everything else that had occurred in the subsequent twenty-four hours had helped firm up that hypothesis. The results of forensics the following day should be definitive.

In the meantime they debated in more detail the respective difficulties of getting the poison into Mark's drink in the kitchen and in the lounge. Woodcock was inclined to have the kitchen the more likely of the two. His theory was based on the fact that there were eight people in the lounge whilst Mark was drinking and so the chances of being seen were too great. Sam Taylor had been alone with Mark in the kitchen and it was possible Jack Freeman had been too.

Molash agreed with the concept that the kitchen gave much better opportunity but countered with the fact that only Sam Taylor had definitely gone into the kitchen. His account was that he wasn't in there for long as Mark was already mixing gin and tonics. Would he have had that much opportunity? Woodcock recalled Chloe Hartwell's evidence, which indicated she'd sat on the sofa without Sam for minutes rather than seconds.

Jack Freeman had claimed not to have gone into the kitchen at all, but whether this was true or not wasn't clear. Jack's movements for the last hour and a half at the bar were pretty well accounted for so his story that he needed the toilet when he got back home sounded plausible. Woodcock was tasked with speaking to Annette Palmer to confirm Jack hadn't been to the toilet during the time the two of them were talking in the Union Bar.

Molash argued that a bunch of half-cut students, half of whom had been on the sofa seemingly talking privately in couples, would have a fair chance of missing poison being slipped into a glass. In the end they priced both up at 11/8 and decided to await the forensic results.

Molash concluded, "I think that's it for now on the practicalities of the actual poisoning. You could check if any of the students is a member of the magic circle and has sleight-of-hand prowess, I suppose, but I wouldn't count on it. What else?"

Woodcock smiled and replied that following their conversation the previous night he'd checked whether Jack Freeman had been in any official trouble regarding his attitude to girls whilst at school. The answer was negative, although the teacher Woodcock had spoken to at Jack's school had said he had a reputation during years twelve and thirteen for coming on strongly with plenty of the female pupils. There had been no official complaints at the university either.

Nevertheless, Tyler Brennan's report at the 8am briefing had made it clear that Jack's behaviour could have provoked a strong enough reaction to provide a motive for violence. Molash wondered out loud if it was possible Mark Gower had found out something about Jack that had made Mark dangerous to his housemate, who had poisoned him to keep him quiet. Molash tasked Woodcock to enlist Brennan and do a thorough investigation the next day and then asked Woodcock how Brennan was getting on with the general trawl through social media.

Woodcock replied, "Tyler's doing a good job, very thorough given there are literally hundreds of students who have interacted with Gower. Trawling through all those social media accounts is like reading one of Lydia Hislop's *Road to Cheltenham* columns – you know there's a load of gold there, but you need coffee by the flask-load to extract it. You're in the lucky position of getting an easily digestible summary."

Molash smiled and said, "Natch. Actually, there's an idea, Woody, you should ring up Racing TV and suggest they do a half-hour programme on the television channel each week for Lydia to do just that. It's odd nobody has thought of that, but if someone suggests it to Racing TV they may run with it. So what did you find?"

167

"I spent much of the morning with Tyler and have just been in with him. He's uploading the detail onto HOLMES as we speak. There are extracts from a dozen students who interacted with Gower in a wide variety of situations and the picture is consistent. Mark Gower was one of the good guys – he's just not the sort of person anyone should want to kill."

Molash summed up, "When we get the forensic report tomorrow we'll know more. At this stage we've got no reason to suspect there is a maniac on the loose or that Jack Freeman is a danger to the female population. However, Johnson from the local rag has been on to Eliot and told him there is a theory doing the rounds, mainly on social media, that there is a maniac out there poisoning random students. Eliot has sent Yasmin back to the Union Bar tonight to keep an eye on the students and make sure nothing gets out of hand.

"I'll put a Key Decision Log note on HOLMES saying that we don't have reason to believe that there is such a maniac or that Jack Freeman poses a risk. I'll have a chat with Eliot when he's back from whatever meeting he's in with the brass. We can't rule either out and I want our arses covered in the unlikely event either scenario turns out to be true."

30

Woodcock headed for The Ship to experiment with trying to pour little phials of water into his colleagues' drinks without being noticed. Eliot was back at his desk preparing to leave for the evening when Molash caught him to countersign the Key Decision Log note.

They had a brief conversation regarding the rumours of a maniac in their midst. Eliot prevaricated less than Molash had expected. He countersigned the Key Decision Log entry Molash had described to Woodcock fairly quickly and Molash headed home.

He was an only child and his father had had one, older, sibling, Molash's Aunt Kerry. Jimmy's parents still lived in the house he'd grown up in, in the next county. When he'd transferred to the Middleham team he'd ended up renting a flat in town, which was just a few miles from Aunt Kerry's cottage in the hamlet of Blakely.

Kerry Molash had been a sour, complaining woman for as long as Jimmy could remember. She had been divorced for as long as Jimmy could recall too and her husband had given her everything and emigrated to Tasmania. Jimmy's normally good-natured father had used to quip that her ex-husband had chosen the exact diametrically opposite place on earth to get as far away from Kerry as possible.

Jimmy had occasionally wondered if the divorce had caused Kerry's sourness but had never discussed the matter with her or with his parents when she had died after a brief battle with cancer three years earlier. The truth was that she was a part of his extended family and not an interesting part.

Much to Jimmy's surprise Kerry had left everything to him rather than his father. He'd offered to make a deed of variation to at least split the money down the middle, but his dad had laughed and told Jimmy to enjoy the financial security that his parents had already, albeit recently, attained.

This was one puzzle that Molash was destined to never know the precise answer to. He had never visited his aunt and saw her only at his parents' house each Christmas. They had shared a love of reading and so, for want of other subjects to converse on whilst his parents cooked Christmas dinner, he had always discussed with her the latest books and asked what she was enjoying. Kerry had rarely shown much interest in what Jimmy enjoyed, but Jimmy had been charitable and imagined that she may not have had many people to talk to, so he would ask questions and be content to listen. It was, after all, just once a year.

Aunt Kerry's birthday had been in late January and Jimmy had always sourced a couple of books based on their Christmas Day chat and sent them to her. It didn't seem much of a justification for such an inheritance, which had included around fifty thousand pounds in unit trusts as well as the cottage (once inheritance tax had been paid).

When probate had been granted he'd visited the cottage with a view to selling it, expecting it to be an outdated wreck after decades of Kerry living alone there. Much to his surprise it was tastefully decorated in a modern style suitable for a rural cottage and had clearly been entirely refurbished in the not-too-recent past. The setting was idyllic with a view over the fields and a well-run rustic pub less than ten minutes' walk away. He'd decided to move in for a while to try rural living and hadn't left.

He had decidedly mixed feelings about the will. He loved the cottage and, mortgage-free, for the first time in his adult life he hadn't been short of money. Equally, it seemed unfair that this mortgage-free inheritance should drop into his lap, when so many of his generation couldn't get onto the housing ladder at all. If it had been from his parents it would have been different, but this was from a virtual stranger.

Jimmy wondered from time to time why she had done it. Why not leave the money to charity if she didn't like her brother (as had been demonstrated only too clearly over many seasons of glad tidings and joy which the Molashs had shared)?

As he sat in the lounge drinking coffee and not being able to concentrate on the book that now lay in his lap, he started thinking about her again. The only downside to short sleeper syndrome was when you were waiting for something and would like to sleep the waiting away. Molash was waiting for the forensic report to point the investigation forward.

Thought processes analysing the remotest contingencies in the Gower investigation had been rattling round his brain like the multi-ball function on a pinball machine. The result was chaotic and he couldn't focus clearly. Every time he tried to consider a solid proposition it felt like attempting to grab globules of mercury, which duly slipped out of his fingers. He knew he would be better clearing his mind of the case for the next few hours and coming at it fresh the next day when the forensic report should make the position much clearer.

So Jimmy Molash wondered for perhaps the fiftieth time why Aunt Kerry had changed his financial life. Perhaps the fact he'd bothered to listen to her for one day a year and then remembered to send a couple of books she would probably enjoy a few weeks later was enough to have earned him affection. More likely she was too mean-spirited to want the money to be just a drop in the ocean of a charity. Perhaps she preferred to see herself as giving her only blood relation, other than her brother, a leg up. Jimmy also pondered on whether, if the cancer hadn't taken her so quickly, she would have changed her will.

At half past twelve Molash looked around the cottage and reminded himself that the best approach was to be grateful for his good fortune and most of all to enjoy it. He knew that he tended to get dragged down into a mental mire on this sort of subject when he didn't have something to concentrate on. He went to bed and fell sound asleep quicker than he had expected.

31

The five students still living at 12 Newton Street were all in bed (alone) before midnight. They had stayed in and it had been a tense evening. Sam had called Chloe using landlines, but nobody had picked up and the girls at 18 James Street had no voicemail on the rarely used landline.

There had been a debate about what they should do. Sam and Danny had suggested they went out for a quiet couple of drinks to unwind but Owen and Jack in particular were keen to avoid the Union Bar. Whilst this debate was ongoing, Ryan had been surfing social media platforms on his iPad. They'd tacitly agreed that none of them would post anything on social media for the time being, but having avoided looking at it all day (a process helped by not having their mobile phones), by early evening they had, somehow, decided that they did want to know what was being said.

The sheer volume of debate about Mark's death carried the day. Ryan had found a few references to people saying that if Mark had been murdered that one of his housemates had probably done it. Much the bigger debate was about a possible homicidal maniac with a penchant for poisoning students at random.

Fear had started to grip the student community. Some students were advising their friends not to go the Union Bar, or even leave their homes if they could help it. Others seemed to be teetering on the edge of suggesting vigilante justice, hampered only by having no clue as to who to impose their own particular brand of justice on.

A sense of foreboding had infiltrated the house at 12 Newton Street. Some of the students were already feeling steeped in it; others were only beginning to notice it. The five of them decided to stay in.

All five young men living at 12 Newton Street were intelligent and it hadn't taken them long to each work out several things. Firstly, if there was a homicidal maniac, he might be targeting their house rather than killing at random. Secondly, if Mark had been deliberately murdered they would be at or near the top of the list of suspects. They also realised that it wasn't taking long for the student community to work all this out either.

They sat in the lounge drinking coffee and tea for much of the evening. Nobody seemed to think alcohol was the answer – everybody wanted to stay alert. There had been some half-hearted cleaning but somehow each felt fatigued and domestic chores were quickly abandoned. They chatted occasionally, seeking reassurance from each other, but conversation quickly petered out and they were left with their own thoughts.

Owen Lloyd was sweating and his red face was purpling as the evening progressed. He went over and over the nightcap on Tuesday evening, trying to hoover up every nuance of behaviour, every word uttered which might be useful to him. From time to time, he cast brief nervous glances at the other four.

Danny Wilson was trying to work out whether he was in danger. No matter how much he told himself that everything was going to be all right so he could turn his mind to other things, it only took a few seconds for his thoughts to flick back. *It'll be fine*, he told himself for perhaps the twentieth time that evening.

Jack Freeman was thinking about himself. Was it going to prove a disaster or a godsend that he'd persuaded that Annette back to the house on Tuesday night? He'd had bigger fish to fry, but as it turned out she might prove a welcome distraction if the police were going to investigate them all. Or might it serve as a catalyst for them to focus on him, and then…

Ryan Sandling sat back in his chair, contemplating his housemates. He wondered what was going to happen tomorrow. Were they going to be confined to the house like rats in a trap? It was going to be vital how his housemates reacted over the next few days. It was annoying not to know whether they could be relied upon.

Sam Taylor was also thinking about the other residents of 12 Newton Street, giving them each in turn a lengthy appraising stare. Were they speculating what would happen to them all if it were proved that one of them killed Mark but it was never established which? He thought of his future, clearly mapped out and now in jeopardy. His face set a grim line. Nobody, he reminded himself, not even his friends from 12 Newton Street, was going to stop that future he'd planned from coming to fruition.

As the five of them thought more deeply about the situation in which they now found themselves, the first seeds of mistrust were being sown.

They benefited from having been a strong friendship group for nearly two years. The joy they had shared as young men exploring the adult world for the first time had bound them closely together. This was all going to be brutally tested in the days ahead.

A few days earlier 12 Newton Street had homed a group of

young men for whom the world was their oyster; now that world threatened to fall apart. They sat on, largely in silence, and time ticked on towards a reckoning for each of them.

*M*ark Gower's killer had lain awake, considering the day's events. The police were seemingly still investigating, though little was known of exactly what lines of enquiry they were pursuing. Only a fool would argue this was of no concern. There was that one piece of evidence that couldn't be retrieved and disposed of. Still, nobody was likely to think of that innocent-looking object being relevant.

Nevertheless, like all good military operations, a fall-back plan was ready. The threat was minimal and sleep would refresh the mind to counter it.

Sleep came.

Running through the woods, increasingly breathless from the indefatigable pursuit. That pursuit seemed never nearer, yet never shaken off.

The blue uniforms and shouts seemed to multiply as exhaustion set in. Turning round, the first policeman was close enough that the chevrons indicating the sergeant's rank could be clearly seen.

Any moment now the sergeant's face would be visible. Turning away to sprint one last effort, the sound of pursuit grew only ever closer. Lactic acid levels rising as oxygen levels fell, it was time to turn and see the lead pursuer – the fit, athletic frame of Sergeant Mark Gower closing in.

32

Friday 14 June dawned bright and sunny. Jimmy Molash knew this because he was up at the time. He had woken, feeling mentally fresh, shortly after half past four. The dawning day was anything but fresh as he opened his curtains, and then a window that looked out onto his garden and beyond to a field of wheat, another of recently cut grass silage and a small copse of trees. Molash had grown to love the view, but on that morning he could barely see it. His mind was full of the Gower case and the all-important forensic results that were due at midday.

What he was subconsciously aware of was the closeness in the atmosphere. Typically days in June dawned fresh, but this felt like the heat of deep summer. There wasn't even a gentle breeze and he could sense that the humidity was set to build during the day. He decided to skip the gym, showered in cool water and breakfasted in a leisurely way at home. He was at his desk at six, running through the HOLMES reports and preparing for the 8am briefing.

As had occurred the previous day, Eliot's team was all

assembled in the incident room shortly before 8am. Operation Evergreen was unusual in that, as Molash put it, it looked to concern an unknown ordinary person killing another ordinary person out of the blue. Interest was high for that reason and because the case was fresh. The mental and physical fatigue from the slog of a lengthy investigation had not set in.

The previous year, Eliot had persuaded the chief superintendent to invest a significant chunk of the station's buildings budget on high-quality air-conditioning. The postponement of other projects had been controversial, but the benefits were really felt on days like this. The room was pleasantly cool and attention levels were high as Eliot kicked off the meeting.

"Good morning, everyone. One preliminary point. Tyler can expand on this later, but the rumour mill has got into action on social media over Gower's death. The main strand appears to be a theory that there is a maniac on the loose who is poisoning students at random and may start attacking them with a meat axe at any moment. We all know the sort of thing.

"We will have the forensic results on the glasses and bottles removed from 12 Newton Street at noon. Our working hypothesis is that the toxin that killed Mark Gower will probably be found in his glass, which would restrict the list of potential offenders to those at 12 Newton Street on Tuesday night. That will present its own challenges, but at least I would then be able to say that there is not a serial killer on the loose, location unknown. I've therefore called a press conference to deal with the issue either way this afternoon. In the meantime, should the question arise, please play down the likelihood of a maniac being in our midst as much as you reasonably can.

"Let's begin with all the updates on action points from yesterday's briefing. Any order you like," Eliot added genially. "Let's go."

Woodcock was first, beginning in chirpy fashion. "I spoke

to Annette Palmer. She was quite clear that Jack didn't go to the toilet from the time she sat down with him in the Union Bar until they got back to 12 Newton Street. She admitted she hadn't taken her eyes off him whilst he went to the bar so she was certain. That suggests his rationale for leaving the lounge whilst Gower was mixing the nightcap was reasonable, for all we haven't tested his bladder functions."

There were a few laughs and Molash cut in to forestall the brevity. "We've had a search of the national database done and there is no sign of any murder, solved or unsolved, or a suspicious death with this modus operandi. If this is a serial killer then it looks to be either their first killing or they have multiple MOs. That points us more towards a personal motive."

Molash continued, "I think we covered the possibilities yesterday for disposing of a receptacle containing a toxin that might have been used at 12 Newton Street. Jenny, did we get anything more on CCTV, especially re Jack Freeman?"

Jenny Martin replied, "There is only intermittent CCTV, but Jack Freeman did go to a local Tesco Express on Sears Road. There is CCTV in the store and he seemed to meander around purposelessly until finally buying only a newspaper. If he took the shortest route he'd have passed a couple of public litterbins, but they've been emptied since. He also passed a few drains so he would have had ample opportunity to get rid of a small receptacle where there was no CCTV to record it.

"I've traced parts of the journey Annette Palmer made from Newton Street to Garrard Street in the early hours of Wednesday morning. She looked to go straight home, but she would have had ample opportunity to dispose of a small object. That goes for all the others. There's nobody whose movements we can trace sufficiently well to say that they didn't have that opportunity."

Detective Constable Karl Denman spoke next. "I spoke to Maddy Church, who was one of the three girls from the university tennis club that Mark, Jack and Ryan went to talk to in the Union Bar on Tuesday night. She was a bit odd on the phone. Her, Hannah Lewis and Zara Allen all live separately. I've arranged to see them all at Hannah's house this morning."

Molash asked, "Can you describe what struck you as odd, Karl?"

"I've been thinking about it and I'm not sure, Guv. It wasn't obviously to do with Mark Gower. She may just be an uncommunicative type, but I think there's some information to be got from her. Whether it's directly relevant to Gower's death I don't know."

Detective Sergeant Jessica Wade said, "The other person we know spent some time with Mark on Tuesday night in the bar was Rich Waters, who captains the rugby first fifteen. I spoke to him. The main rugby season is long finished but there is a sevens tournament coming up and Waters was trying to persuade Gower to play. Gower was non-committal. Waters sensed he was waiting to see whether they were going to field a strong side as they had to go to all the way to Bath University. He seemed confident that if he could get the rest of his first picks to commit then Gower would. According to him Gower was in his normal good spirits. Nothing of interest."

There was a brief silence and Eliot filled it, saying, "Thanks, Jess, who is next?"

Detective Constable Roy Clark said that he'd contacted Danny Wilson's old school. He'd spoken to a Miss MacDermott, who had been Danny's form tutor when he was doing his A-levels. Apparently there was a similar issue there about his running a 'tutorial club'. She seemed to have a bit of a downer on Danny. Felt he was too big for his boots and that it was the teacher's job to tutor and the students' role to learn as they were instructed.

"She reminds me of an old aunt of mine that used to terrorise me when I was a kid," Clark said with a grin. "She's a proper tartar and seems to think that the teenagers of today have far too much initiative and not enough respect for the elders and betters. It was a while since I'd heard that phrase, and I could see how Danny and her didn't hit it off. She said Danny was the type who would end up in the City earning a fortune rather than helping his peers.

"Anyway, I called the headteacher and got a more a detailed account. She said the whole affair was a storm in a teacup. There were four students involved. Danny was the brightest of them and duly got the best results. The head's view was that Danny was trying to help the other three rather than steal their ideas.

"She had, however, agreed with Miss MacDermott that official organisations weren't appropriate. If students wished to help each other they should revise together informally. Unfortunately Miss MacDermott took that as a cue to give Danny a public dressing-down in front of his peers. Apparently it was the first time any of them had seen Danny lose his temper.

"Miss MacDermott frogmarched Danny to the head's office. She wasn't at all pleased when the head sent her back to her class and spoke to Danny alone. I got the impression Miss MacDermott's impending retirement can't come soon enough for the head. The head defused the situation quickly, but she did remember how angry Danny was and how uncharacteristic that was. He felt that he was being accused of cheating.

"Tyler found out a fair bit about the equivalent study group formed here." Clark paused to see if Tyler Brennan wanted to take over the story, but Brennan signalled for Clark to continue. "A few of the law students had asked Danny whether Mark Gower would be part of the group and when the answer was that he wouldn't they didn't join. It looks as if Danny asked Mark two or three times but that may just have been because everyone knew Mark was a high-flyer and would feel the group would have more value with him in it.

"Anyway, the group met for one-hour sessions a couple of times a week. I spoke to one student, Kirsty Bonner. She openly said she's working her socks off to try and get an upper rather than lower second. She said she'd found it really useful and that it was a fair sharing of ideas. Danny often got the ball rolling; it wasn't as if he was just sucking up other students' thoughts and putting nothing back in.

"One student didn't agree, though. Chris Leeke had been part of the group and took the view that Danny was trying to steal his ideas. He complained to the law faculty and got the group disbanded a few weeks ago. This needs some context. I spoke to Dr Bates, who Karl interviewed yesterday. Dr Bates said that Leeke was heading for a third and had already made two formal complaints about members of staff about whose teaching Leeke wasn't happy with. Both complaints were chucked out in short order.

"Bates spoke to Danny and advised him to stop. He made it clear that he thought Danny's intentions were entirely honourable. Given that he'd prefaced his advice with that context, he was surprised how furious Danny was. When I told Bates about the similar scenario at Danny's school, his view was that Danny was probably seeking vindication via the university study group. Bates described him as a gentle giant but that this subject clearly touched a raw nerve."

"Thanks, Roy," Molash said whilst the team were digesting this. "A serious row between Danny and Mark over this looks unlikely. Mark probably was just confident in his own abilities and wasn't interested. The one point is that this does seem a big issue for Danny, one of personal pride now, so we'll pursue this with him when he comes in this afternoon.

"From what we'd seen Danny had arguably looked the least likely of the students at 12 Newton Street that night to have the mentality of a killer. It still looks unlikely, but it does now seem feasible. Is Danny in fact, behind the friendly façade, a manipulative type with a violent temper when challenged? Tyler, can you do some digging to see if there is anything in

Gower's behaviour regarding the study group that might have given Danny Wilson a motive?"

Brennan nodded and said, "A couple of updates from the social media trawl. We've spoken to both of Jack Freeman's mates that were on the closed Facebook group. Both were very defensive concerning the issue about wanting to sleep with someone who was transgender. One argued that it was no different to their having had a competition to be the first to sleep with someone who wasn't white. The other described it as a 'goalless draw so far' and thought Jack would have been straight onto the group to tell them if he'd succeeded or even found someone he was trying to hook up with. There's no evidence so far that anything practical has come of this as yet."

"Well, that's one relief," said Eliot feelingly. "Anything else, Tyler?"

"Yes. There is an embryonic mob forming on social media to deal with the perceived homicidal maniac in our midst. It's not out of hand yet but it could have got that way if we'd delayed the press conference a day or two. There's no evidence of anyone running an orchestrated campaign to promote this theory; it just looked fear-fuelled.

"We've put together a TIE of thirty-two people who had had significant interaction with Mark Gower, whether on social media or otherwise, and were also in the Union Bar on Tuesday night. If the forensics on the glasses at 12 Newton Street are negative then that will be a point of focus?" Brennan half asked and half asserted.

Eliot nodded and Brennan continued, "We've also completed the social media profiles. There's little more to say about the six residents of 12 Newton Street. Specifically, there's nothing new on Jack Freeman. We've looked hard for any hint of an episode with a girl that has been more serious in nature. Nothing. That's obviously not to say it hasn't happened, but if it has I don't think we'll get on the trail via social media.

"We've also looked at Annette Palmer and Chloe Hartwell. Annette's profile looks very simple. All the evidence is that she's exactly what she appears to be.

"Chloe's is more interesting. She's pretty ruthless at getting what she wants. She's broken a couple of hearts at the university and at home. She's been pretty contemptuous towards the men she's discarded. She's also not afraid to use her natural assets to persuade people, men especially, to do her bidding when it comes to political causes. She's left a trail of storm damage behind her since she was about sixteen.

"The incident at the Extinction Rebellion event Karl highlighted yesterday was a case in point. Word has it that Chloe egged on a lad called Philip Mortimer to make the assault on the officer, after which it really kicked off. A couple of girls who were there and don't like Chloe said she spent the day flirting with Mortimer and that he only punched the officer on what were effectively Chloe's instructions. She was verbally encouraging him at the time so was arrested, but Mortimer is a bit of a soft lad and broke down in tears when interviewed. It was clear he'd been manipulated and so Chloe was formally charged and both got a suspended sentence.

"There's nothing so far that links her sexually with Mark Gower. Shall I keep looking?"

"Definitely," said Molash. "Thanks, Tyler, that's good work."

"Anything from the house-to-house, Adam?" asked Eliot.

"Not much," Detective Constable Adam Cohen responded. "I spoke to Hayley Reynolds. She's the girl that Mark went out with for a few weeks in their first year, shortly after the Tinder accounts were opened. She's pretty in a girl-next-door sort of way but came across as a bit straight-laced. She'd been horrified that Mark had had a Tinder account and she seemed to keep her distance from his housemates.

"It fizzled out quite quickly. The way she put it was that they didn't have much in common. She thought Mark was a bit outlandish for her liking, which I took to be that they had different sexual tastes. She emphasised that he was a gentleman, though, which sounded like he'd suggested trying things she wasn't keen on but he didn't pressurise her."

Eliot looked at Yasmin Shah, who reported, "I spent the night in the Union Bar. Talking to Les Christie a fair bit of the time. It was much quieter than recent nights. He reckoned there was little more than half the number of students there compared to Tuesday night. He spent a good bit of the evening telling me how it wasn't like the old days. People wouldn't have been skulking in their homes then on account of some nonsense about a serial killer, etc., etc.

"Word pretty quickly spread about who I was, which kept a lid on things. The atmosphere was tense, though. Christie had sensibly instructed his team to open bottles of beer in front of the customer, but you could see people buying drinks wouldn't take their eyes off the glasses and bottles. Everybody seemed to be holding their drinks whilst they talked rather than putting them on a table, even to the point of putting their other hand over the top of the drink in some cases. It was under control last night but, similar to Tyler, I'm not sure how long that will last."

Eliot nodded. "We've got the press conference this afternoon and I'll deal with the matter then. What else have we got for today? Are the seven students who stayed at 12 Newton Street on Tuesday night all coming in today?"

Woodcock replied, "Yes, Sir. Chloe Hartwell seemed to think we should be couriering her phone and clothes round to her, but she agreed in the end. They are staggered between three and six o'clock so we'll have the forensic results by then. Yasmin and Roy will be conducting the interviews. The DSIO and I will be listening outside. If anyone has any suggestions or if there are any factual developments during the morning, please let me know. We spoke to at least one lecturer on each of their courses, except for Jack Freeman, where we are still waiting to speak to a

Professor Cassidy. Nothing startling from that, but the detail is on HOLMES."

Molash summed up, "If the forensics come back negative from the glasses at 12 Newton Street then we will be focusing on TIEs. We'll have those forensics in a few hours. In the interim let's stick to our working assumption that the forensics will come back positive and focus our attention on those seven students.

"Let's find as many people as we can that had close interaction with the seven of them. We'll talk to their peers from their courses, friends from the university, lecturers who taught them. If it is one of them who killed Mark, there must be a clue there somewhere."

With that, the briefing broke up.

33

DC Denman arrived at 9 Crowther Avenue at half past ten. Crowther Avenue was part of the original new town, built in the early days of the business and science parks before increased affluence had led to the building of areas like James Street. Nevertheless, it was one of the most sought-after roads for student housing and number 9 looked well cared for.

Hannah Lewis opened the door with a friendly smile and invited him in. It was becoming oppressively hot and Denman was grateful to get inside out of the worst of the heat. The lounge he was ushered into faced north and was less warm than the rest of the house, but after the air-conditioning of the incident room Denman felt uncomfortably warm.

The three girls were kitted out in loose cotton polo shirts and shorts with nothing on their feet. Hannah Lewis looked at Denman and said, "Normally I'd offer you tea, Constable, but we've got plenty of iced water in bottles in the fridge. Would that be better?"

Denman warmed (metaphorically speaking) to Hannah and

thanked her. He took the opportunity to take off his jacket and draped it over the arm of a chair. He only had a few seconds to assess Maddy Church and Zara Allen before Hannah returned with four ice-cold half-litre bottles of water, which she handed round. In those few moments Denman had badged Maddy as 'scared' and Zara as 'potentially stroppy'.

He thanked Hannah, drank deeply, introduced himself and explained the purpose of his visit.

"Firstly, thanks to all three of you for agreeing to see me together, I know you live in different houses. I'm part of the team investigating Mark Gower's death, which is being treated as suspicious. At the moment we don't have a motive for anyone wanting to kill Mark. We're therefore talking to those who knew him, especially those who interacted with him on the night he died. Anything you can tell us, even if it doesn't seem to be obviously relevant to Mark Gower's death, would be gratefully received. Perhaps you could start by telling me about Tuesday night?"

Maddy looked from one side to the other at her two friends, willing one of them to speak. Zara's cheeks were red and she was fanning her face with a magazine she'd found on a table, looking bored and impatient. It was Hannah who spoke, in a calm, matter-of-fact way.

"We don't go to the Union Bar much. None of us are big drinkers and when we do go out we prefer to go out to one of the bars in town. It's more our kind of scene. We got knocked out of the BUCS competition last week so..." She paused, seeing Denman's blank face, and smiled apologetically. "Sorry, BUCS is the British Universities and Colleges Sports competition – Nottingham University knocked us out. I'm chair of the tennis club here. We wanted some more fixtures and had a meeting on Tuesday to arrange dates, get in touch with local clubs, arrange an intra-club knockout and so on.

"We were at the campus and so afterwards the three of us

went to the bar and had a quick drink. It was heaving, though, so we had one drink and left. Mark and a couple of his friends, Jack Freeman and Ryan Sandling, came over to speak to us but we didn't stay long."

"What did you talk about?"

Hannah hesitated and Maddy was staring intently at her brightly painted toenails. Zara, impatient and grouchy in the airless room, drawled, "For God's sake, just tell the man, will you? Look, Officer, we don't usually go to the Union Bar because it's full of creeps. The whole campus is infested with far-left politicals that seem determined to take over this country and pauperise it."

Denman raised his eyebrows quizzically, which seemed to goad Zara into expanding on her theme.

"If you go to the campus you'll see. You can't walk more than a few yards without running into some gathering demanding the revolution, including the defunding or disbanding of the police by the way. We just steer well clear of that class of people. Although some people don't like to admit it, I don't mind saying it. I barely knew Mark Gower or any of that lot from 12 Newton Street."

Her voice was the epitome of the output of an exclusive public school, which Denman knew her to be. He therefore decided to be gently provocative to draw Zara out further. "Have you had trouble with these people, Miss Allen? We take harassment very seriously if you've been subjected to it."

Zara Allen snorted. "Seriously? I mean, seriously? There's no way I'd put myself in the position for any of those types to harass me. Look, Inspector, or whatever you are, I learnt when we were freshers here that you can't have a rational conversation with these people. They never listen to a word you say.

"I remember being caught at the campus when they were campaigning for something or other. They asked what sort of political priorities I had outside of university. I said it was about time we had a government that could arrange efficient bin collections and keep the roads free of potholes for five minutes.

"Do you know I've had two punctures in Middleham in the last year? I mean, tyres for a Range Rover aren't exactly cheap. All I got was a torrent of abuse about the supposedly inadequate Overseas Aid Budget. I mean, surely we should get this country running to a decent level of efficiency before worrying about other countries? This place could hardly be any more woke. Thankfully I'm leaving in a few weeks – I can't wait to get out of here."

Hannah had the patient air of someone who runs a sports team, where you have to put up with all sorts of different, and often difficult, characters to put out a winning side. She said, gently and patiently, "Zara, that doesn't have anything to do with Mark Gower or his friends, does it?"

"They were just as bad." She looked shrewdly at Hannah. "Well, not Mark, but that Jack Freeman is one of the biggest creeps on campus. He's such a letch. Ryan Sandling is almost as creepy. You get the impression he's there doing a time and motion study on Jack's pathetic attempts to seduce girls."

"Is that what happened on Tuesday night?" asked Denman. "Jack and Ryan were creepy and so you left?"

"Yes. That is it exactly. We were halfway through a drink and the three of them came and ambushed us. I was sorry for Hannah as Mark is a decent chap, but that Jack Freeman was round us like a dog on heat. At least he had the common decency to take a hint. He went off with some extraordinary woman who looked just like my Aunt Tamara's companion. We left and went and had a drink at the wine bar at the Juliet Street Hotel, where the clientele is just about civilised."

Hannah Lewis realised that Denman was struggling to keep a straight face and interjected, "We weren't really in partying mood as lots of the students were on Tuesday night, Constable. I had a quick chat with Mark but explained we weren't staying. He seemed fine to me, just as usual."

"Was there any tension between Mark and either Jack or Ryan?" Denman asked.

Hannah thought briefly but said, "I'm pretty sure not. Mark and I were having a separate conversation to the other four. I doubt Zara or Maddy said more than a few words to him." She looked pointedly at Denman, who interpreted her glance correctly.

"Well, thank you, Miss Church, thank you, Miss Allen. If you've nothing more to tell me I think that's all – I'll just have a few more words with Miss Lewis here." Maddy Church made a pleading eye contact with Hannah and left hurriedly, ironically, given Denman's last comment, having said precisely nothing at all. Zara Allen rose languidly and, having resumed her tone of boredom, said, "I'll see you at practice later, Hannah," and walked out, paying no further heed to Denman.

Denman was out of cold water and came straight to the point. "All right, Miss Lewis, what can you tell me?"

"I'm sorry about all that, Constable. Zara is abominably rude sometimes. It's my fault. We did the draw for the intra-club knockout singles this morning and I sent it round the WhatsApp group. Zara had been insisting the competition was seeded when we had the meeting on Tuesday night. She is our best player and so would have been the number-one seed. In fact we had an open draw and she's drawn another member of our first team. She was in a filthy mood even before you got here," she finished with a smile.

"You don't have to justify her to me, Miss Lewis. I'm only interested in anything you ladies could tell me that might be relevant to Mark Gower's death. Can we start with what your relationship with Mark was, please?"

Hannah was frank. "It was casual. I only really got to know him just before Christmas. I'd seen him around before then but as we mentioned we don't go the Union Bar much. He stayed here a couple of times last term and a couple of times this term.

I've never been to 12 Newton Street. I've just finished my degree and it would be ludicrous to imagine I could make a relationship work with someone like Mark whilst he was here and I was miles away with a job."

"I'm sorry to pry, Miss Lewis, but we believe someone deliberately poisoned Mark. We'll know for sure later today. If there's anything you can tell me about his character, in or out of bed, it might be much more useful than you imagine."

Hannah looked hard at him and thought for a few moments. "He was a good man, Constable Denman. His personal tastes weren't exactly missionary position with the lights off, but I'm not a girl guide. The thing about Mark was that he never put you under any pressure. He was gentle too. There aren't many men like that. Not in my limited experience anyway."

Denman returned her stare and seemed satisfied that she was sincere. "Did Mark tell you anything about himself, his housemates or anyone who might have had a grudge against him that might give us a clue?"

"Nothing. I've been thinking and thinking about it. It seems unreal. We didn't go out on dates as we weren't boyfriend and girlfriend, nor realistically were we going to be. So it was ad hoc, when we happened to be ships passing in the night, as it were. We generally chatted about sport. Mark liked tennis but had played cricket in his first year and had only played tennis casually this year. That's what we talked about. There's nothing about Mark that would make anyone sane want to harm him."

"What about his housemates?"

"I can't tell you much. When I first met Mark it was him and Sam Taylor chatting up me and another girl one night. Soon after Sam started going out with Chloe Hartwell and the dynamic changed a bit." She paused, searching for the right words, with Denman waiting patiently.

"Look, take no notice of Zara. Jack's all right. It's just that he's constantly looking to hook up with someone. Maddy had a recreational last term with a bloke who kissed and told. It did the rounds with all the gory details and Maddy is mortified, hence the Trappist monk act today. She's basically taken a vow of celibacy for the rest of the academic year. Jack heard all about it and has tried to sweet-talk her a couple of times this term. One occasion was Tuesday night. Given his reputation, Maddy made it very clear she wasn't interested.

"Zara said Jack is a letch and that's arguably true in that he's always chatting someone up. He understands how to take a refusal, though. I was keeping an eye on Maddy given what's she been through, and when she made it clear she wasn't interested Jack didn't push it. From what I've seen he understands about consent."

Denman thanked her and prepared to leave. Hannah smiled sadly. "I liked Mark, Constable. I can't believe anyone would want to kill him, but if they did – find out who did it for me, please."

Denman looked at her with a smile, assured her he intended to do just that and plunged out into the heat of the day.

34

The interview with Sean Roberts had been set for 11am as he had flatly refused to be available before then. It therefore clashed with the interview at Hannah Lewis's house. Molash decided it would be ideal for the person who interviewed Roberts to have no preconceptions, so whilst Denman went to Crowther Avenue, Detective Sergeant Jessica Wade was tasked with speaking to Shaun Roberts.

Hudsmith Street was a long row of terraced ex-council houses, sold off during the 1980s. When the houses were still owned by the state, Hudsmith Street had been only a stone's throw from the stadium where Middleham Football Club played, a fact proved at most home fixtures.

Middleham FC had moved to a new stadium on the outskirts of town and Hudsmith Street had gone gently and steadily downmarket in the intervening years. It was now a grimy mix of the working poor, a handful of low-rent student homes and even a couple of houses with the windows boarded up. The street felt as barren as Atacama.

Wade was hot as she knocked on the door of 70 Hudsmith Street on the dot of eleven o'clock. The sun was beating down with no breeze to alleviate it and she wasn't pleased by having to wait what seemed an inordinately long time on the pavement. When the door finally opened, Roberts was in a dressing gown and giving a good impression of someone who had just got up.

He looked Wade up and down and said, "You the copper?"

"Detective Sergeant Wade, Mr Roberts. Thanks for agreeing to give me some of your time."

He stood looking at her for a moment, grinned a rather lop-sided grin and said, "Well, you'd better come in then. Do you mind talking in the kitchen? I need tea." Wade, a tea junky, intimated that would be fine and followed him through a dirty-looking hallway into the small kitchen, which seemed slightly cleaner and was much cooler. "Would you like a mug of tea? Or don't you drink on duty?" Roberts added.

This was apparently humour. "Tea would be great, thanks. Milk, no sugar, please," Wade replied, ignoring the quip. Roberts made tea, putting three spoonfuls of sugar in his mug. He was short, very thin and wiry, or, if you were less charitable, scrawny. He looked to Wade as if he needed to put weight on but there was a latent physical strength about him. He had almost black hair, which was aggressively curly where it was allowed to run wild on the top of his head but which had been culled at the sides and back. He had a habit of running a hand through his unkempt hair as he listened, his body seemingly unable to remain immobile.

By contrast Wade, who was also short, was stockily built. This was part nature, part the result of her gym regime. At twenty-eight there wasn't much fat on her but her figure left the impression that plenty of work went into keeping that the case. Sugar in tea wasn't an attractive option.

"I thought you'd prefer Che Guevara to Jeremy Corbyn," Roberts said, handing her a mug adorned with the face of the

Cuban revolutionary. Wade smiled and took a lengthy draught of tea.

Having established lines of communication more easily than Wade had anticipated, she decided to get down to business without further ado. "We're investigating the death of Mark Gower, Mr Roberts. I wanted to—"

Roberts interrupted her, "Yeah, well, I didn't think you were popping by to discuss how we might improve community relations with the police. Mark Gower was an arrogant, capitalist, Brexit-supporting wanker. Message ends."

"I gathered you didn't like him very much, Mr Roberts, but I'm sure you didn't think he deserved to die."

Roberts didn't reply, much of his hair now standing on end as his hand frenziedly ran through it. Wade got the impression that anything that involved his backtracking was an anathema to him, so she continued, "At this stage we're treating his death as suspicious. Mercifully murders at universities are very rare. It's very unusual for anyone to have a serious motive to kill another student and there's no obvious motive here. We'd be very grateful if you could shed any light on a possible motive, Mr Roberts."

"Look, I didn't like Gower. He was smug and hedonistic. He didn't seem to care about the millions living in poverty in this country, the climate emergency, nothing. But if I was going to kill him because of that I'd have to murder half the bastards in this country, wouldn't I?"

Pursuing this logic, Wade said, "Agreed. If Mark was murdered then it seems very likely there was a personal motive involved. That could have been politically linked, though. Hatred for what someone represents can turn into personal hatred over a period of time. For example—"

Again Roberts cut across her. "Don't even try and pin this on any of us, you bitch." He appeared to have two settings when challenged, frenetic silence and abuse. "I know what the filth are like. Can't get a result so you fit up some poor sucker who doesn't know how to look after himself."

Wade had had plenty of experience of hard cases and was getting the impression that Gower had been right about Roberts. He was all mouth. "That could hardly be you, though, Mr Roberts, could it? You're doing a law degree and you don't look poor."

Roberts was back on silent mode, glaring at Wade. If the two of them had been in a cartoon she knew the bubble above his head would have contained the words 'You just wait'. She decided there was little point trying to be delicate about it so cut straight to the incident at the Great Debate. "I understand you threatened Mr Gower on at least one occasion, after he spoke at the Great Debate?"

More silence, but with Roberts calculating furiously now. "Yeah, OK. I shouldn't have said that," he eventually replied. "I was angry that he was using that privileged platform for right-wing propaganda. If you'd heard some of the shit he was spouting you'd have been disgusted. I lost my temper. It happens," he concluded with a shrug that cast off all personal responsibility for his actions.

Wade, who prioritised old-fashioned virtues like hard work and law and order, voting conservative without fail, wasn't impressed. "I understand that you weren't the only one to threaten Gower, Mr Roberts? Were all those threatening him men from the Haldane Law Society Committee?"

The silence was longer this time. Wade had gone onto the Haldane Law Society website and looked up the twelve members of the committee on the police computer. Seven had been at least cautioned for public order offences and Roberts had been convicted twice on minor charges. She had also noticed that eleven of the members were male, despite having found out from the university that the gender split of law undergraduates was approximately equal.

Roberts tried a different tack. "Look, Sergeant, perhaps it would be more useful if I tried to explain to you what we're trying to achieve. That way you'll understand that Gower was in no way important enough for anyone to waste their time killing."

Wade sensed that Roberts was well used to making speeches. In her view he was the sort who enjoyed making speeches, finding them a substitute for useful action. Still, the police hadn't dismissed the possibility that Roberts or one of his friends had killed Mark Gower, so she gave him an encouraging nod and prepared to listen.

"This country has been run by the right all my life. Firstly by Blairites when Labour was effectively a Tory party and then by increasingly far-right Tory governments. We want a gentler, kinder politics. OK, that shouldn't involve shouting abuse at people, even Tories, but those of us who really care enough to try and do something about the mess our country is in are entitled to get frustrated occasionally."

He paused and Wade sensed that he was used to testing the water with this line of justification so remained quiet.

"We're the fifth richest country in the world. We have hundreds of billionaires. We have multinationals that make billions a year and pay no tax. We have bankers on million-pound bonuses for placing one-way bets, knowing we'll bail them out if they guess wrong. Yet one in five people in this country officially live in poverty. That's fourteen million people. Kids brought up on estates with no chance of bettering themselves whilst the wealthy send their sprogs to private school to entrench their social status. People in care homes are left to rot."

Roberts sensed this would have to be a condensed version of the monologue. "I could go on, Sergeant. The injustice and inequality sickens me to the stomach. Yet if it is suggested that the rich pay a fair share in tax, even if it's couched in weasel words like 'those with the broadest shoulders should pay a bit more' there is a torrent of outrage from the privileged establishment."

"The top rate of tax in this country is forty-five per cent. You only pay that on what you earn over £150,000 each year. I mean – what is that? You're one of the privileged few with more money than you can possibly need. You could easily donate that entire chunk of your income to good causes, but if someone suggests that you should pay half of it in tax they are not competent to run the country. Apparently all the rich pricks would leave and we'd be bankrupt. Bullshit, Sergeant. You know it and I know it."

Even in this relatively short speech, Wade sensed the impact Roberts' oratory could generate. The full-length version might create an intoxicating atmosphere, especially for the young and impressionable.

When Wade didn't fall into the trap of disclosing what she knew on the subject, Roberts continued, "I spent last summer doing legal aid work for free in Manchester. I saw what the people of Rochdale have to put up with. Slum tenancies run by greedy buy-to-let landlords riding a housing boom that has fuelled inequality. Unable to fill in the forms to claim the paltry tax credits this country has decided they should be given. I'm entitled to be angry. People like Gower were part of the problem. I'm part of the solution. You either care or you're the sort of scum who don't."

Wade thought about pointing out that caring wasn't in itself an end. You had to actually come up with a set of solutions that in a democracy people would vote for. Most of all you had to get them to trust that you were serious about taking the hard decisions, not simply a protester who only pointed out what was wrong.

Like a billion people before her, she wondered if someone came up with a radical left-wing agenda that was rooted in what seemed to her some sort of economic reality, whether she would vote for it. Perhaps the whole concept was an oxymoron. She dismissed the thought from her mind on the basis that it was for people like Roberts to work out. Or more likely not work out.

Still, his pro bono summer work suggested that Roberts walked the walk as well as talking the talk and her attitude softened a little. "One day, hopefully you'll be part of peacefully bringing about a better world, Mr Roberts. Unfortunately in the meantime I have Mark Gower's death to investigate. Are you saying that you just lost your temper with him occasionally and that there wasn't a grudge held by you or any of your like-minded colleagues?"

"Amusing as this has been, Sergeant, I should tell you that Gower wasn't important enough for any of us to bother about, let alone kill. I lost my temper with him only the one time and have barely exchanged a word with him since. I hardly knew him or his sidekick Wilson. I've met Sam Taylor, who is one of Gower's crowd, a few times. Taylor at least seems to have some sort of conscience, although that may just be because he is giving one to that dime Chloe Hartwell with the great tits. She does some decent work helping arranging protests, but boy does she love herself.

"Gower had no interest in being part of any movement here – he wasn't even a member of the Haldane. If he was killed on Tuesday night then we're out of it. We tried the Union Bar and it was packed so we swerved it. We had an unofficial meeting to discuss the agenda for the next Haldane committee meeting.

"I've got ten good men and true who can tell you that I was in the Five Bells on Tuesday evening from about eight-thirty. Therefore my like-minded colleagues, as you put it, were there too. They know me in the Five Bells – it's a proper boozer, not one run by a multinational brewery or part of a chain. The landlord will back me up."

"Thanks, Mr Roberts, that's great. As you say, I will obviously confirm all this with your friends and at the Five Bells, but I don't think we'll need to take up any more of your time."

Roberts flashed her his wonky smile. "Any time, Comrade."

The Five Bells was a freehouse at the other end of Hudsmith Street, so Wade went straight there. It being a Friday, there were a few customers even though it wasn't yet noon. The young woman behind the bar summoned the landlord from the cellar and he greeted Wade cheerfully. He had none of Les Christie's fat from drinking whilst he worked, looking hard-fit and muscled from plenty of time spent at the gym. He gave Wade the impression that he'd have no hesitation in employing his physique at the first prospect of trouble.

He knew the lads from the Haldane Law Society Committee well. They were regular and valued customers. They drank plenty of beer and never caused any trouble. They always sat in the same corner, agreeing about how to put the world to rights. When Wade asked whether they were firebrands, the landlord laughed.

"They are a bunch of pussycats. If they've been at a meeting or a rally then they are animated for an hour or so, denouncing the Tory scum. Other than that they spend their timing discussing the idyllic workers' paradise they are going to build."

He confirmed that Sean Roberts and his mates arrived about half past eight on Tuesday and stayed until the pub shut. He explained that his normal closing time on quiet evenings like a typical Tuesday was eleven o'clock. However, he was licensed until twelve and even though the Haldane crowd were the only customers left, he'd sold another twenty-two pints in the extra hour.

With a mischievous smile he added that the flexible closing time was presented to Roberts and his friends as an example of the terms of a commercial enterprise being dictated by the people. To him it was good capitalist profit, so everybody went home happy. Sean Roberts and his friends hadn't left the Five Bells until about quarter past midnight.

Spotting some freshly made rolls on the counter, Wade ordered one with a Diet Coke and chatted to the girl serving. She'd been working on Tuesday night and confirmed the landlord's story. There was no question as to their alibi.

As Wade walked back to her car, the team WhatsApp message from Molash arrived containing the forensic results.

35

Molash and Woodcock cut it finer for their meeting with Dr Patel than the previous day, arriving at five to twelve. Woodcock remained intrigued by the relationship between Patel and Molash. Molash was inscrutable when it came to anything personal, in particular anything concerning his sex life, so Woodcock knew he would find nothing out by asking a direct question.

On the journey to the mortuary Woodcock had wondered out loud, "Why is a good-looking, smart woman like Grace Patel always single?" Predictably, Molash hadn't responded. Woodcock filed it under T for tomorrow, determined to one day get to the bottom of it, even though he suspected tomorrow was not going to dawn any time soon.

The meeting took place in Dr Patel's office and she was clearly relishing recommencing dialogue with Molash. To ensure that he didn't get to set the agenda, Patel had left her door open for the two detectives to walk in and she began talking as they entered her office. "What I find admirable about forensics is that they are not affected by faulty eyesight or a poor memory. In particular they are immune to the prejudices that cloud so many people's judgment."

She looked up, pretending to notice for the first time that Molash and Woodcock had arrived in her office, continuing, "Ah, speaking of such things, good day, Inspector. The forensic report is in. Something a little out of the ordinary for you."

She passed a sheet of A4 paper to Molash but carried on talking, ensuring he had to read and listen simultaneously. "So you've got it completely wrong again then, Jimmy. Your accidental recreational drug overdose turns out to be murder?"

Whilst the forensic report made it clear that recreational drugs played no part in Mark Gower's death, it did not unequivocally point to murder. An accident looked extremely unlikely, but suicide was still possible. Molash didn't for a minute believe it was suicide. All the evidence suggested Mark Gower was in excellent spirits. He wasn't going to fall into the trap of challenging the murder diagnosis, since he thought it overwhelmingly likely it was the correct one.

"I'll put my hands up to an error of judgment when suggesting it was unlikely he'd been murdered, yes."

He got no further as Dr Patel interrupted with relish, "You don't have to put either or both of your hands up to anything – I'm telling you that you made a complete bollocks of it! Fortunately for you and what passes for justice around here, we have experts who are capable of interpreting evidence."

Molash knew he'd been cleverly cornered the previous day and so took it on the chin and moved on to the details of the forensic report.

"Chloral hydrate. The original Mickey Finn. In Mark Gower's nightcap glass but not in any other glass or any of the bottles used to mix the drinks. Only Mark Gower's fingerprints and DNA on the glass," he said thoughtfully. "What's this about dirt in the glass?" he asked.

Patel grew serious. "That's interesting. There are minute traces of grass and more particularly earth in the victim's glass. There's none anywhere else. It's possible the glass was just dirty, but I doubt it. It looks more like something that was put into the glass was dirty. It's possible that the dirt came from the receptacle that the chloral hydrate was in, but there is no obvious reason for its presence."

Molash was serious now too and the repartee was temporarily shelved. "We searched 12 Newton Street on the day we found the body. We found nothing that looked like it could be the sort of receptacle we're looking for. This report says that the only couple of possibilities have come back clean and there's nothing on any of the students' clothes either. Still, any one of the seven students could have taken whatever the receptacle was out of the house and disposed of it the following morning."

With a ceasefire in operation Molash began to ruminate aloud, "Is chloral hydrate still produced commercially? I thought it was pretty dangerous?"

Patel agreed, "It is. Most doctors don't prescribe it. It's actually the oldest hypnotic that has been available constantly for prescription in this country. Since 1862 if you're interested. It's basically been superseded by sedatives that work at least as well and are less dangerous. However, it's still commercially produced in small quantities and some doctors will prescribe it."

Woodcock was pleased. "That sounds promising. If hardly anyone uses it and we can trace a prescription to someone, then that should be a big pointer. Much better than a mass-produced recreational drug. Can you talk us through the lethal dose, please, Doctor?"

Patel nodded and said, "I've been doing a quick bit of research since the results came in this morning, as I haven't had a case involving chloral hydrate before. Too young, you see, Sergeant, like yourself," she added with a smile, emphasising that she was a year younger than Molash.

Without waiting for a reaction, she continued, "A teaspoon of pure chloral hydrate would typically be fatal. It's therefore usually produced in an oral solution with 143mg per 5ml. An adult dose, taken at bedtime, is usually about 30–35ml. The maximum recommended daily dose is 70ml, about 2g of actual chloral hydrate.

"A lethal dose is typically 4–10g, so quite a spread and with the lower end quite close to the medicinal dose. You soon grow a tolerance to it and so patients increase the dose, hence the danger. The effect of mixing it with alcohol hasn't been scientifically quantified but it is dangerous even with small amounts of both.

"What is clear is that even a medicinal dose mixed with the sort of alcohol Mark Gower had drunk could well kill you. There is approximately 8g of chloral hydrate in the body, which therefore may have killed him if he'd drunk no alcohol. When you add the amount of alcohol he'd consumed it was very unlikely he would have survived the combination despite how fit and healthy he was.

"There is something surprising here about the chloral hydrate, though. It doesn't look to be the commercially manufactured oral solution. We could do more tests, although I'm not certain how much they would tell us, but it looks to be a stronger mixture. The analysis suggests it is several times stronger than the commercial solution. Additionally the commercial product isn't quite a clear liquid. It's usually got a red tinge from passionfruit extract that is part of the solution. There's no trace of that colour here."

Molash looked gratefully at Dr Patel. The fact that she worked through forensic problems with the investigating officers rather than merely offering facts like Dr Goodworth was a huge help to investigations.

"So what are the most likely possibilities for how this solution of chloral hydrate was produced?" Molash considered.

"Could someone have taken the commercial 143mg per 5ml solution and condensed it? Could you produce chloral hydrate yourself at home?"

Patel nodded. "Both are feasible. A fair bit of knowledge would be needed but not that much. A pharmacist with some basic kit could take the commercial solution and increase the level of concentration.

"It would be harder to make it from scratch, but it's not that difficult. You combine chlorine and ethanol in an acidic solution. You get chloral hydrate and hydrogen chloride. YouTube is full of videos on how to do it in your own garage. The results aren't very pure chloral hydrate but then that isn't needed.

"The 8g we found in the body would be about a third of a pint of liquid in the commercial solution. It wouldn't surprise me if the actual chloral hydrate mix used was only a few tablespoons' worth, something that could feasibly be added to someone's drink without them realising."

"What would it taste like? Poisons often have bitter and unpleasant tastes," Molash asked.

"Yes, chloral hydrate is unpleasant to taste. But it was used as a Mickey Finn and people often didn't taste it. That was a much lower dose, designed to cause unconsciousness not death, but it would depend a lot on what it was consumed with. The ideal vehicle to mask its taste is a bitter drink like coffee or gin. The nightcap would have been perfect, especially given how strong the drinks were."

Molash thought for a moment. "When I was a kid there was an old sweat at the cricket club. He came from the era where people drank for several hours after the game and drove home. He used to drink gin and tonic and once he'd had a few they used to give him tonic water with gin on the rim of the glass. He smelt the gin and he already had a strong taste of it in his mouth and he never knew he was drinking pure tonic water. Would it have been easier to have disguised the taste of the chloral hydrate by adding it to his glass once Mark had the taste of gin in his mouth from starting his drink?"

Patel looked at Molash appreciatively. "Ah. An intelligent question." She thought for a while. "An expert toxicologist could tell you more definitively, but I'd say yes. He'd be less likely to notice it, but it might be harder not to be seen putting it in the glass once they were all in the lounge drinking."

"Agreed," said Molash. "It's a balance of risks. Sam and maybe Jack could probably have slipped it into Mark's glass in the kitchen after he had tasted it to test the strength. They'd know which was his glass because he'd drunk from it and he might easily have turned his back getting ice or another bottle of tonic when mixing the other drinks. The downside is Mark is more likely to have noticed the taste of the chloral hydrate if all he'd done was to test the gin and tonic.

"It would have been harder for one of the others to slip the chloral hydrate into Mark's glass in the lounge without being seen. However, the accounts suggest he may have drunk about half of his drink before he suddenly finished it. He'd have been less likely to notice the chloral hydrate the closer it was put into the glass to when he finished his drink. Thanks, Doctor."

Molash turned over the page and quickly scanned the rest of the report. The samples taken from Mark Gower's body confirmed that he wasn't a regular user of recreational drugs.

Suddenly Molash whistled. "Chloe Hartwell's DNA is on Mark Gower's bed. It's on the top of the duvet but not the sheet or pillow. There were no signs of recent sexual activity in the bed. No other surprising DNA or fingerprints anywhere in the house."

Patel opined that this suggested that Chloe Hartwell had sat on the bed at some point during the days leading up to Mark Gower's death.

Molash prepared to leave, but Patel wasn't letting him have it that easy. "So, Jimmy, now you know he was poisoned, who did it?"

"One of his housemates, I should think."

Dr Patel was delighted. "Only seven other people in the house and Jimmy still hasn't a clue who did it, Woody? Thank goodness he's not in charge of a murder in a public place where anyone could have done it."

Molash smiled. "There's the answer to your pathology question on the way over, Sergeant, but there's no need to write it up on HOLMES – the whole enquiry team knows the answer already."

Woodcock could not prevent the escape of an initial peal of laughter. As an exit line it could hardly have been bettered since Dr Patel could not possibly know what Woodcock's question had been. Molash sauntered out.

This wasn't playing the game and Grace Patel vowed there would be retribution when play resumed.

36

The media briefing began at two o'clock. Plenty of other SIO wouldn't have called a press conference but instead would have issued a general news release, outlining the bare details and stating that Mark Gower's death wasn't being linked to any other fatalities.

Eliot believed that the SIO should stand up and face the press to aid community relations. One wag in the canteen at Middleham Station quipped that it freed Molash up to conduct the investigation. Some bruising experiences hadn't changed Eliot's view and he rose and introduced himself.

Interest in the case had grown and the room was fairly full. Other than Vivian Johnson, to whom Eliot had communicated the bare bones of the forensic results, the media pack was still in the dark. The story wasn't just being covered by local papers and radio stations. A team from regional television was present, as were a few freelancers who were hoping to sell the story to the tabloids.

Eliot explained the facts of the case briefly so that the basics of the case were clear in the minds of the assembled journalists. Eliot deliberately did not give the full details, merely explaining that Gower had been poisoned. As Woodcock had pointed out, the relative rarity of chloral hydrate was a key line of investigation.

Eliot did not know whether the killer would be aware of this and did not wish to alert them, potentially leading to the destruction of evidence. Given that enquiries would be made into the original source of the chloral hydrate he did not expect this to remain confidential for long, but a short time was better than none at all.

Instead Eliot explained that forensic analysis of the glass Mark Gower had drunk from when returning to 12 Newton Street on Tuesday evening, had shown a toxin had been mixed with his gin and tonic. The mixture of this toxin and the alcohol in Mark's system had led to his death.

To forestall some of the obvious questions, Eliot stated that forensic analysis of the toxin was ongoing, which in the loosest sense may have been accurate. To move on promptly from this point he then explained that whilst only the victim's DNA and fingerprints were on the glass, the evidence of the victim's wellbeing had pointed strongly away from suicide. Whilst this could not be ruled out the police were now treating this as a case of murder.

Eliot concluded by pointing out the obvious in that if this was murder, it was committed by one of the other students that had been drinking with Mark Gower at 12 Newton Street that night. The police were working on the basis that the motive was personal and that it was being treated as an isolated incident. Eliot made a point of stating that the police wished to allay fears in the student community by saying that they did not have any reason to believe there was a threat to the public of further attacks.

Eliot was aware that by telling the press that Mark had been killed by the nightcap, he was placing seven young people under intense scrutiny by both the media and the public. Nevertheless, he had decided (and had had that decision backed by the chief superintendent) that this was the lesser of the two evils. Killing the theory that there was a maniac on the loose indiscriminately poisoning students was the priority.

As soon as Eliot opened up to questions it became a scrum. The press bayed for details and Eliot stonewalled. He explained that there was no discernible motive at the present time and no suspect. He requested that the press did not pursue the seven students who had been at 12 Newton Street with Mark Gower the night he died, knowing that it would have little effect on their behaviour. On the other hand, any modicum of restraint was better than none at all.

37

Interviewing is a fine art and, whilst every police officer has to do it, like every other skill it attracts specialists. Just as it is a myth from television crime dramas that the SIO/DSIO spends their time running to and fro gathering evidence, nor do they conduct all the interviews.

Practice varies depending on the style of the SIO but typically officers of sergeant or constable rank, who have been trained as interviewers, conduct the bulk of the interviews, especially early in the investigation. The usual strategy is that one talks and the other listens and writes. If the talker misses something then the officer writing can pick it up at the appropriate moment. Various different tactics will be used to induce the person being interviewed to communicate. If those of the talker fail, then sometimes they will swap roles to try to build rapport.

Both detective constables, Yasmin Shah and Roy Clark, were trained and experienced interviewers. Whilst they weren't the only officers in the team with that training they were, in Molash's mind, the A-Team. There being no specific circumstances in

Operation Evergreen that suggested that any other officers would be more appropriate, Clark and Shah conducted all the interviews with six of the students that had been at 12 Newton Street the night Mark Gower had died (an interview with Annette Palmer was not deemed necessary). As was his way, Molash left it up to Shah and Clark how to approach the interviews, saying he was happy to discuss any issues they envisaged beforehand. There were none.

At three o'clock, a hot and distinctly bothered Chloe Hartwell was being escorted to an interview room where Shah and Clark were waiting. The incentive was that this would be where the students could pick up their phones and clothes.

With the heat of the day at its peak, tempers were in danger of fraying and Chloe was on a short fuse. Despite being shown through without the interminable delays that occur so often at police stations, Chloe clearly felt she was being messed about.

"Finally," she said loudly as she entered the room and spotted her belongings. It looked as if she intended to grab them and leave without further comment when Clark walked forward and introduced Shah and himself. He explained that there had been some developments which they felt it was important that Chloe should know and gestured to a seat. In an adjoining room Molash and Woodcock were looking in through a one-way mirror and listening via microphone.

"Am I under arrest?" Chloe demanded. "If not—"

Clark interrupted using his gentlest manner, "Absolutely not, Miss Hartwell. You are free to leave at any time. However, some information has arisen that is relevant to you and we think it would be in your best interests for us to share it with you. Obviously any help you can give us would be greatly appreciated."

Chloe looked from Clark to Shah, thinking quickly. "All right," she said, sitting down. "What is it?"

Clark modulated his voice so that it remained friendly but serious. "There is one piece of evidence that we need to communicate to everyone who was at 12 Newton Street with Mark Gower on Tuesday night. We also have one piece of information for you specifically, Miss Hartwell."

Clark explained about the forensics on the glass and that despite the fact that only Mark's fingerprints and DNA were on the glass, that the police believed someone had introduced the toxin into it. No specific mention of chloral hydrate was made, nor did Chloe ask what the toxin was.

Chloe narrowed her eyes shrewdly. After a lengthy pause she said, "So you are saying that one of us in the lounge that night deliberately poisoned Mark's drink? I don't believe it. The vicar's daughter wouldn't have it in her and the rest of us were Mark's friends."

"It takes a bit of believing, Miss Hartwell, I agree. However, the evidence is unequivocal. Unless Mark chose the nightcap as a bizarre way to commit suicide, which given everything we know about him looks most unlikely, one of the seven of you there that night poisoned Mark, either in the lounge or in the kitchen whilst he was mixing drinks. A few minutes ago a press briefing occurred and what I've told you will soon be common knowledge. You should prepare yourself for considerable media intrusion. You should also prepare yourself for an adverse reaction from some of your friends, fellow students and the local population."

Clark paused and let this sink in. Chloe Hartwell was well used to the fact that her looks endeared herself to vast swathes of the male population but had the opposite effect on some of the female populous. She was well used to manipulating both to her advantage and expressed her opinion that she was well able to look after herself.

There was a silence during which all three people in the room knew that they were coming to the main point of the conversation. Clark stared hard at Chloe and said, "We have completed our forensic report on 12 Newton Street and your

DNA was found on the duvet on Mark Gower's bed. Could you explain to us how it got there, please?"

Both the officers in the room and the two watching from next door were unanimous in agreeing afterwards that this news looked to come as a shock to Chloe Hartwell. She initially looked stunned, quickly recovered and lost her temper. There was no hint of the feigned outrage that Woodcock had sensed at times when interviewing her at her home at James Street the previous day.

"That's what fucking well comes of Big Brother, isn't it? Firstly you lot trump up spurious charges that I somehow held the arm of someone I barely knew and made him punch one of your lot, and then in complete contradiction of any decent level of human rights, you keep my DNA. Well, you can get lost. Given that I am here voluntarily, I am leaving. May I have my things, please?"

"Of course," said Clark, reaching down to the bag by his seat and standing up to hand it over. "If at any point you want to tell us how your DNA came to be on Mark Gower's duvet please get in touch. Both our cards are in the bag."

Chloe Hartwell took no notice, grabbed the bag and stomped out. The four officers had discussed her likely reaction before the interview. Molash took the view that if Chloe refused to discuss the fact that her DNA was on Gower's duvet, then letting her sweat on it for a day or two, possibly literally as well as metaphorically, would be no bad thing. As Chloe was leaving the building Molash introduced himself to her and gave her his card, saying that he'd be happy to talk to her in confidence if she'd find that helpful. She glared at him, took the card and left without saying another word.

Sam Taylor arrived promptly at three-thirty. Molash had waited to see if there had been any interaction between Sam and Chloe, and reported in the negative. Sam appeared to remember his initial frostiness with Woodcock two days before and was anxious to create a good impression.

He walked into the room and stretched out his hand to Shah and Clark, responding to the introductions by thanking them for getting his phone back to him so quickly. Shah explained the situation and Sam sat down promptly and said he would be happy to help in any way he could.

He didn't seem at all surprised to find out that Mark's nightcap had been poisoned, or that the police thought suicide unlikely. He weighed up both officers with a long stare and then asked what drug had been used. Shah was non-committal. Sam shrugged as if to say that he knew quite well that the police knew what drug it was but that he couldn't force her to tell him if she didn't want to.

He seemed to have already thought through the difficulties with the press and public that being one of a small number of possible people who could have poisoned Mark Gower would bring. When Shah outlined them he nodded in understanding without saying anything.

Thus far, Sam Taylor had been the model of a co-operative and relaxed person of interest in an inquiry. This changed dramatically when Shah told him about Chloe's DNA being on Mark's duvet. She simply told him the bare facts, sat back and waited for a reaction.

Initially it looked to be a mixture of shock and disbelief. Sam's astute brain was working frenetically. His response was an open question. "What exactly does that mean, Constable? I'm not familiar with how DNA samples work."

Shah replied, "The DNA was found on Mark's duvet. Sometime recently Miss Hartwell was on Mark's bed, Mr Taylor." She paused and, getting no response, eventually added, "Have you and your friends had a congregation in Mark's room recently where Miss Hartwell sat on the bed, so accounting for the presence of her DNA?"

There was a prolonged period of silence again, which in itself told the detectives that Sam Taylor had had no idea Chloe had been on Mark's bed. Sam was a man who naturally liked to get his ducks in a row before expressing a view. Having seen so many of his peers studying politics make themselves look foolish by shooting from the hip had just ingrained that approach further. Normally Sam was a sufficiently fast thinker that he could consider complex issues and come up with a reasoned response without delay, but the news about Chloe had scrambled his mind and he was staring into space rather than at Shah or Clark.

Eventually he asked in a low, husky voice, "You said Chloe was on Mark's bed rather than in it?"

Shah had seen enough so filled in the gaps. "That's correct, Mr Taylor. There was none of Chloe's DNA on the sheet or pillows. There was no evidence of recent sexual activity anywhere in the bed or elsewhere in Mark's room."

More silence. Whilst Sam was streetwise enough not to show his relief obviously, trained interviewers like Shah and Clark could see it. It wasn't total relief, only partial. Thoughts were flooding Sam's head. Even if Chloe hadn't been having sex with Mark in that room she had been there on his bed. Presumably alone with him in that room. Neither had mentioned it. If there were lovers then they would probably be careful to go elsewhere anyway.

He jerked himself out of his reverie and, with a massive effort at controlling his voice, said, "Thank you. I don't know when Chloe was in Mark's room. I wasn't there at the time. We are all in and out of each others' rooms all the time."

On balance Shah decided it was better not to tell Sam about their conversation with Chloe. Instead she said, "Had you had any falling-out with Chloe? For example, did she object to your summer placement at Goldman Sachs?"

It was clear that Sam Taylor had spent plenty of time preparing for a conversation about the summer placement, although not with the police. He smiled and replied immediately, "She doesn't know, Constable, trust me, she'd have raised the subject if she did." His eyes hardened. "She won't be pleased, but it's my call not hers. Some of the lads live totally in the moment. Don't get me wrong, I love the moment, at least I did until what happened to Mark, but you have to think of the future too."

"Thanks for your time, Mr Taylor. Our cards are in your bag of belongings – if you think of anything that might be helpful please give us a call."

Sam nodded, thanked them politely in a distracted way and left.

38

Molash had arranged the interviews so that the next three would be the three students who had been standing and moving around the lounge with Mark Gower on the night in question. The first in, at four o'clock, was a perspiring Owen Lloyd. Despite the heat, he was the only one (as it turned out) of the students not in shorts. He had full-length, loose cotton trousers, socks and trainers, with a polo shirt that looked designed for a warm rather than hot day. He carried a handkerchief with which he occasionally mopped his brow. Watching from the next room Molash idly tried to remember if he had ever seen anyone under forty doing that before.

The heat hadn't daunted Owen's enthusiasm. So far there was nothing beyond the fact that they shared a house and Owen's presence in the lounge on the fatal night, to connect him to Mark's death. Having explained the basic forensic results and the obvious consequences, the detectives had therefore decided to see what Owen had to say. It was quite a lot and Woodcock was grinning next door, having had a taste of Owen's stream-of-consciousness style of conversation. Clark's patience was legendary at Middleham Station and Woodcock wondered whether it could survive a prolonged interview with Lloyd. Molash looked at Owen with interest.

Owen recited out loud a summary of the facts surrounding the nightcap. He took not receiving any interruptions or corrections from the two detectives as agreement to the fact pattern he had described. The handkerchief was applied to his forehead again and he continued with gusto.

"I've been thinking over the theories your colleague Mr Woodcock and I were discussing on Wednesday," Owen continued, the slightly portentous note back in his voice. "We now know that Mark was poisoned on the ground floor of our house. Sam had the best opportunity given that he was definitely in the kitchen whilst Mark was moving about mixing the nightcap. There's no motive, though, unless maybe Mark and Chloe were having an affair and Sam found out."

He paused, considering the prospect of Chloe being unfaithful. Clark resisted the temptation to mention the presence of Chloe's DNA on Mark's bed. Owen smiled to himself and resumed.

"The trouble is, I can't quite work out if Jack went into the kitchen or not. My initial recollection was that he did, but he might have just gone to the loo. I remember he rushed back in, but that might have been because he was worried that that Annette would have made a run for it. He returned to the lounge after Sam, though, so in some ways he would have had a better opportunity in that Mark was more likely to have tested his drink by then, making it obvious which glass to poison.

"Sad to say, though, I think it more likely that the dastardly deed was done in the lounge. Time would have been short in the kitchen, but we must have been together for at least fifteen minutes in the lounge, which gave plenty of time." He paused and ruminated, "I was explaining to your Mr Woodcock that one has a sense of where one's drink is. That's not the case for everybody, but it is for drinkers. I suggested to him that it would therefore be difficult to poison such a drink. One of us, Mark especially, would be too likely to notice.

"I think I erred on that occasion." Owen leaned forward as if to part with some confidential but important information. "What I overlooked was the importance of a psychological moment when everybody would be distracted." Woodcock was chortling to himself freely in the next room, but Clark and Shah had to keep their faces straight.

"What sort of distraction did you have in mind, Sir?" Clark asked.

"That's the thing, Constable. It could be almost anything. It could be something obvious like a big noise, someone telling an amusing anecdote, an argument. Anything that would obviously ensure we were all looking with keen attention at a fixed point."

"And what such occasion have you remembered from the night in question?"

Owen Lloyd shook his head in a vexed manner. Reluctantly he said, "That's the problem. I've thought and thought, and there wasn't an obvious psychological moment where we were all looking at someone or something, that would have created the ideal opportunity to slip poison into a glass unnoticed.

"It was all, in fact, very normal. Chloe was talking at Sam. Jack was engrossed with a girl. The rest of us were chatting. Ryan was giving an amusing commentary on Jack's line of patter, and Mark, Danny and I were debating Jack's chances. Nothing unusual at all.

"I have therefore concluded that it must have been something subtle. The killer must have created a situation where we were all temporarily distracted without realising it and taken their chance. As far as I can see Mark's death wasn't urgent. The killer might have been waiting for days or even weeks. It's possible that the killer didn't want to leave a trail by conjuring

222

up a psychological moment that distracted us and just waited for such an opportunity to occur naturally or via someone else."

Clark blinked and smiled as Owen finally ground to a halt. "We very much appreciate your energetic assistance, Mr Lloyd." He picked up the bag with Owen's belongings and added, a touch conspiratorially, "In this bag I have placed Constable Shah's card and my own. Please give either of us a call, anytime of day or night, if you work out when and how that psychological moment was produced. Or indeed anything else that would help us."

Owen had effectively been forced to stand up to receive his bag of possessions and found Clark's arm around his shoulder, gently shepherding him to the exit.

Ryan Sandling was next and the detectives had only a couple of minutes' break before he entered the interview room, such had been Owen's loquacity.

Ryan was very different. Watching him, Molash recalled Tyler Brennan's comment at the initial briefing that Ryan didn't like other people to know what he was thinking. Ryan's body language was very open, though, and he had grinned in a friendly manner when shaking hands with Shah and Clark. Yet his initial answers were guarded and Molash wondered if this was natural reticence or something more relevant to the Gower investigation.

There was a definite tightening in Ryan's shoulders as Shah explained about the nightcap glass. Ryan was the first of the students to demand to know what the toxin in Mark's drink had been.

"Surely it makes sense to tell us what it is?" he claimed. "If it really was one of us then if we know someone was in possession of that chemical compound or had access to it, we can tell you? I mean, how many people have access to poisonous chemicals?"

Shah looked hard at him and said, "That's a good point, Mr Sandling. Who in the house did possess any form of drug?"

Ryan returned her stare. Slowly he said, "You've searched

the house – we aren't on the Calvin Kleins. I've never seen anyone with prescription drugs here either. None of us works in a pharmacy or a hospital during the holidays as far as I'm aware, so the possibilities are limited."

"Limited to what, Mr Sandling?"

Ryan shrugged his shoulders and smiled charmingly at Shah. "If I were trying to get hold of a poison I'd head to the chemistry labs myself."

"Could you gain access to them, given you are not studying chemistry?"

Ryan smiled again. "That's a good question. It would take some ingenuity, but obviously I would have the advantage of a housemate, in Jack, who is doing chemistry, which would help. I suspect I could find a way if I put my mind to it."

Shah switched tack. "When you spoke to Sergeant Woodcock on Wednesday you mentioned Rohypnol. Was there any reason for that?"

Ryan became more guarded again. "I suppose it's because that's what you read in the papers. I've never heard of a real case of anyone poisoning someone's gin and tonic. You read about date rape drugs, though."

Shah decided to have a shot in the dark. "Was that what you and Mark were doing, Ryan? Keeping an eye on Jack Freeman to make sure he wasn't doing anything untoward to girls' drinks?"

Ryan went very quiet, his eyes boring into Yasmin Shah's. Having waited too long to sound convincing, he finally said, "That was initiated by Mark, not by me. I just thought it was a result of Sam getting together with Chloe. Sam and Mark used to team up when chatting up girls, so with Sam out of action, so to speak, I think it was just a natural development." Ryan paused. "Look, Jack is a good lad, Constable. It's very easy for people who don't like someone to start spreading rumours. Jack's an easy target given how much he enjoys casual sex."

For the first time Clark spoke. "In any case, Jack Freeman

probably had the least opportunity of any of you to poison Mark's drink? There's no evidence he went into the kitchen and he just picked glasses off the tray for Annette and himself and then didn't leave the sofa."

Ryan's face wheeled round, looking at Clark for the first time. "I thought he went to the kitchen whilst Mark was pouring the drinks." He hesitated for a moment and, thinking it through, added, "I'm not sure, though. My memory is a bit hazy so don't quote me on that."

Shah brought up the subject of the row Ryan had had with Mark the previous week. Ryan explained it fluently. "We were pissed. We went on a pint-a-pub all-dayer to celebrate the end of the exams. We started at lunchtime and after a few pubs I was bored of trotting to and fro across town, looking for ever less good pubs. I suggested we head for the Union Bar. Mark told me not to bottle it and that we had another five pubs to go to. It got a bit heated, but that was just the alcohol talking. It was forgotten the next day."

Ryan seemingly had nothing more pertinent to say, so Shah handed over his possessions, for which Ryan thanked her courteously and left.

39

Danny Wilson entered the interview room at just after five o'clock with his naturally relaxed, friendly manner slightly on edge. As the conversation focused on the forensic results the tension went out of his voice. Something about Clark's manner created an atmosphere that he could be Danny talking in thirty years' time.

Danny still couldn't quite bring himself to believe that one of them had poisoned Mark. He repeated that there must be some other explanation, until a look in Clark's eye caused him to relapse into silence.

Clark didn't break it and eventually Danny murmured, "I suppose it could have been that Annette. We don't know anything about her. She did look a bit repressed." He caught himself and said in a much clearer voice, "What am I saying? That's absolute nonsense. I can't imagine that poor frightened girl doing any such thing. I'm sorry, Constable, it's just that I am utterly convinced none of us would want to hurt Mark, much less kill him. I was just desperately looking round for an explanation."

Clark gave Danny one of his fatherly smiles. "Don't worry, Mr Wilson, we understand. It's very natural. It seems incredible but there must be a motive somewhere, deeply hidden. You've been described as the peacemaker in the group, so you'd probably be as well placed as anyone to judge if there were any festering resentments."

Danny accepted the description without comment and replied immediately, "There just weren't, not unless one of us is a very clever actor. There was nothing on the night either that might have caused any short-term rage. I just don't understand it..." He tailed off.

Clark waited a moment and then said, "There's one other matter we'd like to discuss with you, Mr Wilson."

Danny ended his contemplations and nodded.

"We understand that you arranged and ran a tutor group for second-year law students here until it was shut down recently. Could you tell us what Mark Gower's involvement was, please?"

Danny's body had tensed whilst Clark was asking his question and, characteristically, he closed his eyes for a few moments before answering. After that brief hesitation, Danny replied simply, "Mark wasn't part of the group."

"That's a bit surprising. You were running this group and your best friend on the course and housemate wasn't involved."

Others in Danny's position would have remained silent but, his open and friendly nature battling with the anger he felt over the tutor group, he responded, "I asked Mark. A couple of times, but he said no."

"Why was that?"

"I don't know. Mark was a heading for a first. Easily. I guess he felt confidence in his own abilities and decided he didn't need any help."

"Why did you try to persuade him by asking him more than once?"

"Everyone on our course knew how bright Mark was. More

people would have joined if Mark had been part of it and we'd all have learnt more."

"Did you apply moral pressure on him? Did he get annoyed about it? Did he tell you that he thought you were trying to plagiarise other students' work and that he wasn't giving you his?"

Danny realised the purpose of the line of questioning and looked with horror at Clark. "Fucking hell," Danny exploded, the anger evident. "Are you serious? That I'd kill one of my best mates over something as trivial as this? You must be joking." He paused. "Please tell me you are joking."

Clark ignored the request and carried on calmly. "We spoke to your school about how you reacted when they closed down a similar group during your A-levels. We didn't just speak to Miss MacDermott – we also talked to the headteacher, who said she'd never seen you lose your temper other than on that occasion. Did you lose your temper with Mark Gower when he accused you of plagiarism?"

Danny was hyperventilating in an evident attempt to keep himself under some sort of control. His fists were clenched so hard that his knuckles were white. Eventually he said very slowly, enunciating each word, "I was not cheating. I do not cheat." A few seconds later he added, "Nor did Mark think I was cheating or that there was anything wrong with the group. He just told me that he didn't think it was a good idea."

Clark waited and, sensing there were no more questions to come, Danny said, "I am an honest man, Constable Clark. I try and help people. Now, unless there is anything else, I would like to leave." Clark nodded silently, handed him his bag of possessions and Danny walked slowly and heavily out.

40

The last of the students from 12 Newton Street to be interviewed was Jack Freeman. He entered the interview room looking wary and slightly dishevelled from the heat, as if his mind had been too occupied to consider his usually immaculate appearance.

Shah gave the same explanation as his four housemates had received. Reluctantly, Jack took a seat. He drank in the forensic results and the consequences. After a few moments he seemed to relax.

"Well, that lets me out, doesn't it? I had no opportunity to poison Mark's glass. The only time I went near him was to pick two glasses off the tray. There's no way I could have poisoned his glass, even if I'd been sure which one it was. What was used, by the way?"

Shah looked at him carefully, trying to decide if he was an innocent man, understandably scared and desperately hoping the police would accept his alibi. Or was he yet another offender protesting his innocence as naturally as breathing?

Ignoring Jack's question about what toxin was used, she said,

"I agree that you looked to have very little opportunity in the lounge, Mr Freeman. However, you could have poisoned Mark's glass when you went into the kitchen. It's arguable Sam Taylor and yourself had the best opportunity as you were both alone with Mark in the kitchen at different times. Mark only needed to turn his back to get ice or another bottle of tonic water and it would have been child's play."

For several seconds Jack Freeman had been bursting to interject and it was only a mixture of good manners and caution with a police officer that made him wait until Shah had finished. When he responded, his voice was rather shrill.

"I didn't go into the kitchen. I went for a piss. Sam was in the kitchen talking to Mark when I went. I came straight back. Annette was on her own on the sofa and she didn't know anyone. The lads are a great bunch, but they are piss-taking bastards. I wanted to get back there as soon as possible – I only left her as I was desperate for the toilet." Suddenly a thought struck him. "Who says I went into the kitchen anyway?"

Shah smiled. "Nobody is saying you definitely did, Mr Freeman. Unsurprisingly given that you had all been in the Union Bar all evening everyone's recollection is a little hazy. However, you did go in that direction and nobody could have seen from the lounge whether you went into the kitchen or not. Our understanding is that Sam Taylor was back in the lounge before you returned, is that correct?"

Jack thought for a moment and nodded.

"So you see, we cannot be sure that you didn't have the opportunity to tamper with Mark's glass in the kitchen."

"But why?" Jack responded hotly. "He was my mate, I have no earthly reason to want to kill him."

"That applies to most of the people at 12 Newton Street that night, Sir. We have to look for a motive somewhere. Did you and Mark ever fall out? Much better to say so if you did, we'll find out eventually."

Jack was firm. "Absolutely not. Mark almost never fell out with anyone, certainly not us lot."

"What about your womanising, Mr Freeman? Didn't Mark take a dim view of it? Wasn't he actually spending quite a bit of time with you when you were chatting girls up to see whether you were crossing the line? What did he have on you, Mr Freeman? What had you done that Mark found out about?"

Jack Freeman stared at Constable Shah, open-mouthed. Suddenly he smiled. "What evidence do you have to that effect, Constable? I'll tell you. None. That's because it never happened. I haven't crossed any such lines. With social media what it is, if I had you'd know about it by now, I'm sure. Mark and I were two normal blokes who liked girls. Given that it's how the human race is perpetuated, it would be nice if some people realised it's actually a positive thing and a natural one."

Shah changed tack. "On the morning after Mark's death you went out shortly before you found him. You went to the Tesco Express on Sears Road. Could you tell us why, please?"

Jack frowned as if puzzled. "I went shopping, Constable. I'm sorry if I am missing the point but that's what I always do when I go to Tesco."

"What did you go shopping for?"

"I can't remember. I bought a paper, I think. I wanted a breath of fresh air as much as anything. Look, Constable, I'm happy to answer any questions to help you find out who killed Mark, but I'm confused as to what my shopping habits have to do with it."

Shah thought for a moment. Molash had taken the view that the students would soon work out that if someone poisoned Mark at 12 Newton Street, there must have been a receptacle containing the poison, so she explained. Jack was horrified.

There was a slightly bitter note and Jack rose to his feet. "I had nothing to do with Mark's death. He was my friend and I would have done anything I could to protect him not harm him.

I did not take and dispose of any receptacle. I simply went to the shop. On that basis, please may I have my possessions and leave?"

"Of course, Sir," said Shah. "As I mentioned at the outset, you are free to leave at any time. We'll let you know as and when we would like to discuss this further with you."

When Jack got to the front entrance he found Molash waiting for him.

"Good afternoon, Mr Freeman," Molash said in a friendly fashion. "I knew you were coming in this afternoon and wanted to ask you a favour." Jack looked suspiciously at him in silence and Molash continued, "Would it be convenient for you all to be in this evening at, say, nine o'clock? I'd like to have a chat with you about the situation you all find yourselves in."

The categorisation of them all being in the same boat mollified Jack's attitude after what he considered barefaced accusations of murder from Detective Constable Shah. "Just the five of us? Or…"

"The five of you certainly. If Miss Hartwell can join us all the better. You don't need to bother Miss Palmer."

The relief on Jack's face was palpable and he promised to do his best to arrange it and call Molash if there were any problems.

Molash had deliberately arranged for Annette Palmer to arrive whilst Jack Freeman was being interviewed, so they wouldn't meet. He spoke to Annette himself and explained that whilst the forensic evidence proved that someone at 12 Newton Street was responsible, the other students, Chloe Hartwell in particular, had given Annette an alibi. Annette's frightened face relaxed just a little, thinking in wonder at Chloe Hartwell being her saviour. She signed a copy of her interview with DC Roy Clark hurriedly, paying the content little of her customary care and attention.

Molash explained that the press would be briefed accordingly, so Annette should not be subjected to the intense scrutiny that was about to come crashing down on the other six students who had been at 12 Newton Street with Mark Gower on Tuesday night.

Given that Annette was not exactly the epitome of worldly-wise, Molash also gave her some advice. He explained that it was quite likely that, as a witness to the events, she could be hounded by the press for interviews or 'her story'. When Annette's face froze in terror, Molash gave her a fatherly smile that Roy Clark would have been proud of. He suggested that she was lucky her exams were over and that if she wanted to return to the family home for a few days whilst this blew over, the police would have no objections. Annette Palmer was back in Shropshire before midnight.

41

It was just after seven o'clock when Woodcock and Molash gathered in the latter's office for their end-of-day discussion. The mood was very different to the previous couple of days. There was no longer the possibility that the Operation Evergreen was a manhunt, potentially for a crazed serial killer. It was cold-blooded murder by someone close to the victim.

When Woodcock arrived Molash was busy at the whiteboard. One of the basic building blocks for police investigation is the '5WH' method. These are the six basic questions, five of which begin with the letter 'W' and the other with an 'H'. Experienced officers don't need to consciously think in these terms as they do it instinctively. Nevertheless, in unusual situations, stripping a case back to basics can be an effective approach, which was what Molash was doing as he scribbled on his whiteboard.

Three of the five Ws had already been answered. Who the victim was, what had happened to them and when it had happened. A fourth, where it happened, was partially answered. The events had occurred on the ground floor of 12 Newton

Street. Whether the poisoning had occurred in the kitchen or lounge was still to be established and was crucial. If it occurred in the kitchen then Sam Taylor or Jack Freeman were guilty. If it was the lounge then the guilt lay with Ryan Sandling, Danny Wilson, Owen Lloyd or Chloe Hartwell.

The other two questions remained entirely unanswered. Why had any of Mark's six friends wanted to kill him? How did they manage to poison him with the chloral hydrate? The 'how' was in fact two questions. Firstly, how the drug was sourced, and secondly, how it was put into the glass without anyone noticing. Only by answering the 'why' and the two 'hows' could the case be solved.

Woodcock entered carrying bottles of cold water that he'd purchased as a replacement for coffee, given little of the heat had yet ebbed out of the day. Both men had their suit jackets off and Molash's top two buttons were undone, the now-loose knot in his tie several inches below his neck.

The title on his whiteboard was 'The Unusual Suspects'. The six names of the students were one below the other on the left-hand side of the whiteboard. Along the top were the three questions: 'Why kill Mark?', 'How did they get hold of chloral hydrate?', 'How did it get unseen into Mark's drink?'. Woodcock looked at the whiteboard, trying to decipher Molash's abysmal handwriting.

Molash was focusing on the motive. The obvious problem was the lack of one. He set the ball rolling by asking, "Is there a big motive we're just not aware of? Or is one of the issues we've been investigating in fact much more important to one of these students than we understand, therefore giving them a motive to kill Mark?"

Woodcock pondered. "If one of these kids was an embryonic Keyser Söze we'd know about it, wouldn't we? There would be traces on the computer. Their records are too clean, bar Chloe's protesting."

"Agreed. I don't think it can be anything like that. This smells of being personal. There is pure hatred somewhere here. I'm going to 12 Newton Street tonight to talk to them all together to try and get a feel for it." Molash paused for a moment and added thoughtfully, "Sometimes I think I can sense it but then it dissolves into the ether.

"What I'm trying to get a sense of is whether that's because the motive is obscure and so when we find it, it will look odd and disproportionate to us, but justified to the killer. Or whether we're dealing with someone very clever here who is adept at covering their tracks. This lot are a bright bunch academically. How that translates into the ability to cover up a murder is an interesting question."

Woodcock nodded. "Well, if we judge by the results then we'd have to give the killer high marks so far. They must know we'd find chloral hydrate in Gower's body. Yet we have no idea how it was sourced or how it got into the glass without anyone noticing. We've no realistic motive. So, yes, perhaps we are dealing with someone cleverer than we thought here."

Molash finished the column headed 'Why kill Mark?' and stood back nearer to Woodcock. Woodcock liked to think out loud and sometimes their discussions played out with his reading aloud what Molash had written, commenting on it, with ideas being batted to and fro.

Woodcock began, "Jack Freeman could have an iceberg motive. Is he just a normal young lad with a high sex drive? Or is he a sexual predator? Given how many women are unable to report rapes, it's not hard to imagine that he could have committed crimes against women that have not come to light. That's got to be the most likely motive and he's definitely the most likely killer."

Molash laughed. "Remember that lad Tony Keenan who wrote that article in the Cheltenham annual about how thinking biases impact punters' bets? He'd be saying you had confirmation bias by the bollocks! You backed Jack Freeman at the outset and now you're making wild surmises about him to try and shoehorn facts into your theory. We need to be open-minded to the possibility that he's predatory, but remember that both Hannah Lewis and Zara Allen made it clear he took no for an answer quite happily with Maddy Church."

Woodcock grinned sheepishly recalling his susceptibility to confirmation bias when betting. He shook his head ruefully and then suddenly looked sharply at Molash. "Wait a minute, I've just realised – that Jack Freeman is the spit of that Racing TV pundit you rate so much, that Tom Stanley. Are you in danger of an unconscious bias and falling into the oldest trap of all – backing the outcome you want to have happened rather than what you think actually happened?"

Molash raised his eyebrows and replied firmly, "There's no more room for sentimentality in murder investigations than there is in betting. If Freeman is the killer, we'll get him – magnificent quiff or no magnificent quiff.

Woodcock realised that he was getting the worst of the exchanges and said, "Right, let's look at motive again with an open mind. Tyler and I have been through everything we can online and have spoken to a few students on the phone. There's nothing to suggest any criminal misbehaviour by Jack or that Mark Gower had found anything that made him dangerous to Jack. That being the case, why did Gower suddenly take so much more interest in Jack's sex life?"

Molash replied, "That may just have been Sam Taylor getting together with Chloe Hartwell. The dynamic changed. Ryan Sandling became part of it too. What was it Zara Allen told Karl? Sandling was like a time and motion man evaluating Jack. Had Mark heard a rumour of Jack committing some sort of sexual offence and enlisted Ryan to investigate with him?" He shook his head in a dissatisfied manner. "That doesn't quite sit right somehow, yet I think there's something there."

Woodcock looked back towards the whiteboard. "Sam Taylor and Chloe Hartwell. If it's one of those two then the motive is probably sexual. Why was Chloe on Mark's bed? She could easily have just been having a chat with him. If she was chatting innocently I can see her plonking her bottom on Mark's bed – she'd always be giving a hint to boys on what they were missing out on. Probably does it without realising now."

Molash agreed, "Yes, it could well be that simple. There are other possibilities too. She might have been trying it on with Mark and got rebuffed. Mark sounds like the sort of bloke who might well tell Sam in that situation. I suppose that could lead to Sam ditching Chloe and her name being tainted around the university. Would Chloe really kill Mark for that? Maybe being queen bee really is that important to her?"

Woodcock replied, "I can see it. Equally I could see her being willing to have an affair with Mark Gower. Perhaps a one-off where she persuaded him not to say anything to Sam and then, once it was too late for him to do so, she tried to control him. There's no evidence of sexual activity on Mark's bedclothes, but if she swallows there might not need to be – equally it could have happened somewhere else. Perhaps that would give him a motive for suicide and not leaving a note."

Molash shook his head. "If it had been one of the others living at 12 Newton Street then maybe I could buy that, but I just don't see it with Mark. I think he'd have shown the backbone to face up to the situation. I think he'd have told Sam what he'd done and apologised. I think they'd probably both have kicked Chloe out of their lives, so that fits in more with her having a motive. In any case, if he committed suicide, where is the receptacle for the chloral hydrate? I don't believe any of his mates would have removed it to protect Mark's reputation from being tainted as a suicide."

Woodcock was fairly convinced. "You said yourself that Chloe is the sort of woman that a young man could completely lose his head over. Could Mark and her have been having an ongoing affair? We haven't spoken to Chloe's housemates yet. It's possible they went there?"

"Maybe. It's certainly worth speaking to them. We'll ask Tyler to go through their social media profiles too. They could have gone anywhere. If Sam Taylor found out he might be so besotted with Chloe that he'd not tell either of them and kill Mark to make sure he kept Chloe. That sounds plausible."

Woodcock said, "Just before we leave Chloe, could politics be a motive? We looked at that with Shaun Roberts, but could Mark have angered Chloe so much with their differing political views that she killed him?"

"No way. Chloe is far too into Chloe to take that risk for the cause. If she did it, which is plausible, it will be for a personal reason."

Woodcock smiled. It wasn't just his skin Chloe Hartwell had got under. "Ryan Sandling doesn't have an obvious motive, although he did have a bust-up with Mark a couple of weeks ago. His explanation to Yasmin and Roy was a little too slick for my liking. He's the type to bear a grudge and he is the only one we know that Mark argued with. There might be more to it then we've yet found out."

Molash nodded and Woodcock resumed, "Owen Lloyd looks the least likely. His Hercule Poirot act looks genuine enough to me."

"Yes, I agree he's the outsider of the field. I suppose Mark may have decided he didn't want Owen in the group anymore, for example if they were arranging accommodation for next year. Actually, let's look into that. Were the six of them going to live together again for their final year? They'd need to be sorting it about now and if there had been a bust-up within the group, their accommodation plans for their final year might highlight it."

Woodcock looked at the final name on the list and said

slowly, "Is Danny Wilson a bit of a dark horse? Does he use his everyone's-best-mate demeanour to manipulate people? Some notice, like Chris Leeke; others, like Kirsty Bonner, don't realise? It was just odd how upset Danny has got over this. From what Dr Bates was saying he seemed to be doing well in his studies so he shouldn't have been desperate."

"Mmmm," said Molash in non-committal fashion. "Let's look at the chloral hydrate side of it. But first of all let's have a coffee, despite the heat. I'll go."

42

A few minutes later the pair were back in front of the whiteboard in Molash's office, sipping strong coffee and trying to put more pieces of the jigsaw together (the results of which would be copied on to the clearboard in the incident room as an aide memoire for the team).

"Let's start with how you get hold of chloral hydrate, Woody," Molash began. "Our eminent pathologist suggested it's not too difficult to make. If any of them made it Jack Freeman must be an odds-on shot – he's studying chemistry."

"Agreed. We've dug into the others and none of them have shown any interest in chemistry. None even did it at A-level. I'd wondered if someone like Owen Lloyd might be the type to have a garden shed full of equipment to brew potions, just to see what he could make. He was the instigator of that Christopher Wren Club in their first year where they were supposed to be becoming experts in different fields. Do you think we should have their parents interviewed and see if we get a pointer?"

Molash nodded. "Yes, I think we're going to need to do that

in the not-too-distant future. We'll have to decide whether we go on a countrywide tour or use locals. To start with it is probably more important to speak to the parents regarding whether they had any chloral hydrate in the house. Or, going back to the home-brewed version, whether they have chlorine, ethanol, an appropriate acidic solution and so on.

"We've got big questions about the chloral hydrate itself. Firstly, why was it so concentrated? If it was a home brew then it explains it, but if it was a prescription, why was it so strong? Secondly, does the dirt in the glass have any relevance?"

There were several minutes of debate about these two questions without Molash feeling they were materially any nearer finding a solution. Nevertheless, his gut feeling was that if he could answer them he would have a clear path to the killer. He made a decision.

"OK, there's plenty of legwork to do on finding the source of the chloral hydrate. Let's give the six sets of parents a call ourselves in the first instance. Then we can get onto the local forces where each of the six of them live and get them to do some digging. Once we've got details of the family's GP, we'll check the stories we get from the parents re what sort of medication members of the family are on that our six would have access to. The team have already checked the GPs here and none of the six have been prescribed anything in Middleham.

"In addition, I think we should dig into any cases in the last few years that these six could have been involved in at home. Unexplained deaths or suspicious ones where the investigation never got anywhere. This is a pretty sophisticated modus operandi. Perhaps our killer has killed before. Perhaps they've seen something that put this idea into their head. Given how unusual it is for a teenager from the sort of backgrounds this lot have to be involved in a suspicious death or murder, it's long odds against it having happened twice by coincidence."

Molash and Woodcock spent a few minutes speculating

about all sorts of theoretically possible ways one of the six students could have got hold of the chloral hydrate. Eventually Molash called a halt on the basis that there were probably dozens of realistic possibilities. What they needed were the hard facts of investigation; hypothesising was adding little value to the process of answering this particular question.

Next they focused on how the chloral hydrate got into the glass without anyone seeing. It was probably not too difficult if it had been added to Mark's glass in the kitchen, so they focused on how they would approach the task in the lounge.

"I took some plastic specimen jars to The Ship last night," Woodcock said. "They only had water in them, before you ask," he added with a grin. "They looked the right size receptacle from what Dr Patel said, so I tried to slip the contents into different people's drinks on four different occasions.

"Jess spotted me once, and the lad working behind the bar noticed on another occasion and asked me afterwards what I was up to. I used some distraction technique to focus their minds elsewhere, but even so it felt too risky. There just wasn't a situation where I was confident I wouldn't be noticed. A couple of times I wasn't, but I just couldn't be sure enough to take that risk."

Molash digested this and said thoughtfully, "I think I'll openly raise this with the students tonight. Try and see if there was a moment where all their attention was attracted to somewhere else. Although Ryan, Danny, Owen and Mark were all keeping an eye on Jack and Annette, they would have to have been quite subtle about it, so it's questionable whether that would have been enough of a distraction.

"Going back to your five potential theories yesterday, I think we can conclude it's the fourth one. Mark put his drink down somewhere in the kitchen or lounge and the killer slipped the chloral hydrate in. The forensics suggest that poisoning your own drink and swapping it isn't feasible. The killer's DNA would have been on both glasses."

Molash picked up Dr Patel's report from his desk and nodded, continuing, "Yes, it says that each of the eight students had drunk from only one glass containing gin and tonic. Only Mark's fingerprints are on the poisoned glass. I'll see what I can get out of the students tonight re whether they'd have noticed someone doctoring Mark's drink in the lounge and we'll come back to this tomorrow. What else have we got?"

Woodcock thought for a moment. "Jack Freeman's trip to Tesco Express, which would have given him the opportunity to get rid of the receptacle that contained the chloral hydrate. He wanders about aimlessly and then buys a paper. That's arguably the single most suspicious act we've got."

Molash agreed. "His explanation this afternoon might be true, but it's exactly what he'd say either way so it doesn't take us any further forward."

Molash mentally went through the other students. "Something that I thought about after the interviews this afternoon. It may just have been a turn of phrase but Danny Wilson said that Mark 'didn't think the tutorial group was a good idea'. That may just mean Mark didn't think it was right for him, but equally he may have thought the whole concept was a bad idea and tried to stop it.

"It sounds pretty thin as a motive until you hear the effect the topic has on Danny Wilson. Mark was very bright and perceptive – maybe he saw through what Danny was up to when nobody else did. Let's get Tyler to go through social media again hunting for anything to do with that study group. We can look at interviewing more of the participants.

"I reckon that's it for now, Woody. When I see the students tonight I'll try and get them to start thinking about the night in question to see if anything jogs their memory. Can you get going on the enquiries back at the students' family homes please?"

Woodcock said, "Will do. We're speaking to the parents about any drugs in the house, finding out who prescribed them, etc. Getting the contact details of their GP regardless and asking them what they prescribed to double-check. Then also asking their parents if any of the students like doing chemical experiments in their garage or shed.

"The other half is speaking to contacts at local forces. That's to see if any of the students have been involved in unexplained deaths. It's also to see if they've been involved in any thefts, distribution, etc., of drugs, especially sleeping draughts and similar products. That the lot?"

Molash said that that was ideal. Before he left, Woodcock asked curiously, "What are you expecting to learn at Newton Street tonight?"

Molash had already put his feet up on his desk and replied in a deceptively languid voice, "Just the normal Routine Activity Theory."

Woodcock sought clarification. "You mean that in the same sense that a burglar will target a certain sort of premises, often at a certain time of the day, that you'll get a feel for what it would have been like when Mark drank the fatal nightcap because the students will behave in a similar fashion?" He sounded unconvinced.

"People are much more creatures of habit than we like to acknowledge, Woody, especially under stress. Just as your burglar is under stress when he's putting his liberty at stake, these kids will be under a serious amount of stress this evening. Hopefully an informal reconstruction of the nightcap will be revealing."

43

Ideally Molash would have liked to arrange a visit to 12 Newton Street at a quarter to twelve but he thought that an unreasonable request, even during a murder inquiry; hence the meeting was set for nine o'clock.

In any case, Molash expected that the students would be virtually, if not completely, sober whatever time the meeting was set for. In that sense it wouldn't resemble the night of the murder whatever time he went to 12 Newton Street. He just wanted to get a sense of what it had been like in that lounge on Tuesday evening.

When he arrived, Ryan Sandling opened the door and greeted him in a pleasant but guarded manner. He showed Molash into the lounge where the other four residents were waiting. There was no sign of Chloe Hartwell. Ryan asked who would like coffee. There were a few raised eyebrows amongst his housemates but everyone accepted.

Molash made small talk whilst Ryan was in the kitchen. Sam Taylor explained that he'd telephoned Chloe and messaged her on social media but hadn't been able to make contact with her. Molash sensed that Sam hadn't mentioned the presence of Chloe's DNA on Mark's bed to anyone else and indicated to Sam that that was fine.

The atmosphere was tense. Whilst they awaited refreshments there was a feeling amongst the students that Molash embodied the predator that was pursuing them. There was little that could be done to dissuade that predator, only hope that he would eventually leave to pursue other prey.

All five of the students were trying to protect themselves without it being obvious they were doing so. None of the students could outrun this particular predator, so camouflage, of different varieties, was their best defensive tactic.

In the meantime, the five of them had agreed before Molash's arrival that they would provide a united front to the police. Whatever they privately thought they all, at Danny's instigation, said that they didn't believe any of them had killed Mark. By being open and helpful to the police there would be the best chance to eliminate them from the inquiry and allow the police to find out what actually had happened.

It was a hot, muggy night but at least the brutal heat had gone out of the day. The students sat around in shorts and T-shirts, and Molash had left both jacket and tie in his car. Coffee was drunk partly as a formality and partly as everyone wanted to be at their sharpest, which given the heat was difficult. The strain and lack of untroubled sleep was having an impact on the students, who were fatigued.

Molash sensed the change in the students. Shocked and saddened as they had been at Mark's death on Wednesday, their youthful buoyancy had masked those feelings. They were under suspicion in the sense that they were close to Mark, but no more than that.

Since they had left Middleham Police Station earlier in the afternoon they were under suspicion in every sense. With

Annette Palmer ruled out, the police believed that one of the other six had definitely killed Mark. No matter how often they all said that they didn't believe it, it didn't make any of them think it wasn't true.

The strain was starting to show and nobody seemed to want to sit down, almost as if they would be more vulnerable seated. Molash put down his mug of coffee and said, "Thank you all for agreeing to meet me this evening. There are a couple of things I want to discuss with you."

Molash was standing by the sofa close to where Annette Palmer had sat so nervously three nights before. This gave him a view of all five men and his senses were on full alert to see if he could spot signs of guilt. The lounge looked as it had done when Molash had first seen it two days before, sparsely furnished with old but serviceable furniture and, by student standards, not too untidy. He had little difficulty in envisaging the scene on Tuesday night when Mark had drunk the fatal nightcap.

"Firstly, to give you some idea of what you are in for from the press and the community. It is unusual to have a murder where there is no obvious suspect but where the number of people who could have committed it is so small. This time yesterday, your fellow students, and to some extent the wider community, were working into a frenzy over the possibility that a lunatic was on the loose with a penchant for poisoning students.

"All that energy, some of it negative, will shortly be directed at the six of you. The press will harass you – if they haven't already?" Molash turned the statement of advice into a question.

It was Sam Taylor who replied, "We've had some phone calls already. Nobody at the front door yet, though. We discussed it earlier and decided to be polite and not get arsey with them but refuse to discuss anything."

"That's a wise strategy. I'm afraid it's not going to be pretty. If they can't get you to talk to them, they'll find others who will and they'll write stories about you regardless. The only comfort I can

248

bring you is that the media rarely focus on a case for more than about ten days, often less. After that, if they are still interested in the case they'll be switching tack, most likely to the mess we're making of investigating it," Molash said with a wry grin.

"What happens if the case is solved?" Owen asked. "Will they leave us alone then?" Five pairs of eyes swivelled to look at him, to try and establish any undercurrent in his words.

"No, they'll be wanting to know your views on the killer, albeit they probably won't be so aggressive. In the meantime you need to be prepared for hostility, especially from your fellow students. You may decide to try and lie low this weekend, but it's your call."

This time it was Danny who spoke. "We've basically avoided posting on social media. You asked us not to do that the other day and we've only just got our phones back. We've looked occasionally on tablets but we weren't sure whether that embargo still held."

"No, that was just to stop word getting out before, for example, we'd told Mark's parents. However, I think your discretion is better than your valour would be. You might prefer to know what's being said or just keep away from it, but if everyone can see none of you are posting then some of the furore will dissipate." He looked round at five faces with differing levels of anxiety. "You're doing the right thing, lads, it is a case of weathering the storm. Does anyone have any questions on that side of things?"

There were none, in part as the relevance of Molash's last four words sunk in. Molash continued, "If you get any serious problems don't hesitate to get in touch. The other reason I wanted to talk to you was to get your help in understanding what happened on Tuesday night, a reconstruction if you will. Do any of you object?"

Phrased like that it was very difficult for anyone to reasonably object and Molash watched them all carefully. He then continued, "I'll be Mark. Don't worry about Chloe and Annette too much – we'll say the cushions at each end of the sofa represent them. You all came straight into the lounge and then Ryan told Mark it was his turn to mix the nightcaps, is that right?" Ryan nodded and the others followed suit.

"I'm Mark so I walk into the kitchen," Molash continued, doing just that and setting the stopwatch running on his mobile. "It's just across the hall but you can't see one room from the other given the angle. Sam, you followed Mark in there fairly quickly?" Sam Taylor nodded and walked into the kitchen.

Molash switched from asking for confirmations to asking an open question: "What happened next?"

Jack Freeman got up from where he'd been sitting next to the cushion and explained that this was when he went to the toilet. He walked tensely down the hall feeling the eyes boring into him. Shortly afterwards, Sam Taylor explained he'd finished talking to Mark about the nightcap about now and so he went back into the lounge and sat on the sofa. Jack flushed the toilet for effect and walked quickly back and sat down.

"Jack had only just sat down when Mark brought in the tray of drinks. It was maybe thirty seconds in between," said Owen helpfully. Molash had spotted a tray in the kitchen and, having mimed the mixing of drinks, had placed eight empty glasses on it. He brought it in and they re-enacted the taking of the glasses. Jack grabbed two of them quickly and sat down staring at his cushion.

Sam explained that he'd play Chloe and so he stood by the tray, picking two glasses, chatting to Molash and then sitting down. It appeared that Danny, Ryan and Owen had waited as they were chatting and they had come over broadly together and selected a glass each. They'd then stood on the far side of the room, several feet from the two couples on the sofa. It looked like it would need considerable sleight of hand to poison Mark's drink without being noticed whilst he held the tray, with Chloe the only one looking to have a realistic opportunity.

"How long before Mark came to join you?" asked Molash. There was a pause as the students who were standing looked at each other.

Eventually Danny spoke. "Not long, certainly less than a minute. I think he turned to speak to Chloe briefly and then she went to the sofa. You have to understand that we'd been drinking and this seemed to be just a typical nightcap, Inspector, so we weren't paying close attention."

"Understood. You're proving much more helpful than the typical witness. Go on."

"Mark came over here, having put the tray down on that table by the far wall."

Molash obeyed, carrying his glass over, and asked, "What happened next? Did the four on the sofa stay there until Mark finished his drink?" Several nods and quiet affirmative murmurs.

Sam and Jack seemed comfortable on the sofa, but Owen, Danny and Ryan looked nervous. Molash sensed this concerned the banter about Jack and Annette, which they weren't keen to repeat in front of him.

Molash therefore said, "Rather than recount who said what to who, let's keep an eye on everybody's movements from now, when Mark has just taken his glass off the tray until he finishes his drink."

Owen piped up again, "Well if we're being pedantic I should be at this end, not next to 'Mark'. I remember as I had a good view of Jack looking at Annette when we were, er, chatting." Owen moved from his place next to Molash towards the edge of the group, diagonally opposite the door to the hall, with Sam and his cushion Chloe directly in between Owen and the door.

Danny closed his eyes and screwed up his face in remembrance. "Yes, that's right, Mark was at the other end of the four of us, where the inspector is now. He'd have had the best view of Annette as she was sitting side on with her left shoulder almost hiding her face from where I was next to Owen."

Molash said, "I appreciate it's difficult, but what can any of you remember about the remaining time? As I understand it there were no events to break up the fifteen minutes or so before you finished the nightcaps? By event I mean something like people moving around and handing out drinks. You were all in pretty much the same place?"

Owen couldn't resist. "Ah, you're referring to the psychological moment when we were all distracted, Inspector? The four on the sofa stayed there but the rest of us did move around a bit. You know what it is when you are talking as a group. I don't think anything happened to distract us, though, I've been trying and trying to remember."

Nobody else had anything to add. Molash said, "You're all holding your glasses, but I understand that you have a house rule that when you are not drinking you are supposed to put them down if there is table to put them on?"

Owen wanted the rules understood properly. "Not simply a table, Inspector, if you can put your drink down safely you should. For example, Sam was sitting on the sofa with his back to Jack. Sam put his glass down on the carpet by the edge of the sofa when he wasn't drinking."

Owen left a pregnant pause and Jack said in an irritated fashion, "What Owen is trying to say, Inspector, is that I held my drink throughout."

"What about the rest of you?" asked Molash.

Sam said, "Chloe held hers too – she didn't participate in our drinking games much."

Danny said slowly, "I suppose what matters most is what Mark did with his drink. There's the table Mark put the tray on, but we were over this side of the room." He sighed, "To be honest, Inspector, we were over this side as it gave us a better angle to watch Jack. If we'd been over the other side near the tray we'd have been looking directly at Annette and she seemed terrified as it was. We didn't want to intimidate her but we did want to keep an eye on how Jack was getting on."

"Thanks, Danny, that's very helpful. So the four of you stayed roughly where the four of us are now." Molash looked behind him, knowing full well what was there. "That highish table with the lamp on was presumably where the four of you put your drinks down when not drinking?"

Owen nodded. "I think that's right. In theory the glasses therefore should have been on the table behind us most of the time, but as you can see, Inspector, plenty of rule-breaking goes on."

"Did Mark play to those rules?"

Owen nodded again. "Yes, Mark was a big one for games and so he rarely broke the rules."

"Can you tell me when you all noticed that Mark was finishing his drink?"

Owen replied, "Well, I didn't notice immediately. Jack seemed to be making some progress and I was watching that. Suddenly I heard Ryan laugh and then Mark was brandishing an empty pint."

Molash turned to Ryan and asked him what was funny. Ryan looked uncomfortable. "I'm not sure, to be honest. It might have been the, er, progress that Jack was making. I had faith in Jack, the other three thought he might have taken on an impossible task, and so I was probably laughing at it getting more likely that I was right. I may just have been laughing at Mark deciding it was time to finish up. I'm sorry, I just can't remember."

Molash smiled. "That's very natural, Ryan, don't worry. I think that's it unless anyone else has anything to suggest?"

The tension, which had dropped as the students focused on the reenactment, was palpable again. None of them quite knew whether Molash had established anything from the reconstruction. Without that to focus on they started to look at one another uneasily.

Molash wished them a good night and reiterated that they

shouldn't feel afraid to call him or any of the team at any time. He walked up Newton Street to where he had parked his car and drove home.

Even amongst the one third of murder cases that are not self-solvers, there are often individuals amongst the TIEs that are immediately flagged as realistic possibilities. In the Gower case there had been none, nor a motive.

As he was driving home Molash suddenly realised that the Gower case bore some similarities to trying to find a bet in a horse race where, having looked at all the runners, his natural instinct as a punter was to oppose every horse.

Even where the evidence about each horse was in isolation negative, in every race there had to be a winner. When you didn't fancy anything, Molash had learnt that it was a mistake to automatically decide not to have a bet. Instead you should first try a process of elimination. Look at the runners you definitely can't see winning and the field could often be whittled down to a very small number of realistic winners, even though none looked particularly likely.

He realised that he'd been making a similar mistake in the Gower case. He had just been looking at each of the students in isolation and thinking how unlikely it was that they would kill Mark.

When he got back to the cottage he made a pot of real coffee and sat down to think. He went over and over the behaviour of the students and one by one he eliminated them as even unlikely-but-realistic killers.

As the night hours ticked past, Molash's thoughts gradually focused on one particular student who had been in the lounge at 12 Newton Street when Mark Gower had drunk his last drink. *Unlikely*, he thought, *but it is at least realistic and if it's the only realistic solution…*

He had a hunch who had killed Mark Gower and when, but exactly how they did it and why looked harder to fathom.

*

*S*leep would not come for Mark Gower's killer. That last drink with Mark seemed on a never-ending loop in the killer's mind. Too much had been drunk to expect any of them to be observant, even before you factored in that most of them had sex on their minds.

No, there was no suspicion. Yet. Plan B had begun smoothly, with the police being led nicely in the right direction. Assuming they had the wit to see it.

How to be sure that no genuine clue had been left, though? Go over it, check and check again. The impression was that the police would prove worthwhile opponents. That would make victory all the sweeter – providing no mistakes were made.

Eventually the endless repetitions brought sleep and dreams of nervousness of being seen naked, always in different locations.

Suddenly they morphed into a countdown.

It was impossible to say what or who was counting down, but the numbers could be clearly heard. Eight thousand, two hundred and twelve. Eight thousand, two hundred and eleven. Eight thousand, two hundred and ten.

It was also very clear what would happen when the countdown reached zero.

44

Jimmy Molash had gone to bed just after three o'clock, his brain still whirring like the electric fans being used across the country as people attempted to stay cool. The night had been sultry and Saturday morning was brooding, but as yet without the menace that suggested an imminent storm breaking.

Molash eventually got a couple of hours of good sleep and was pleasantly surprised to see the clock saying it was nearly six o'clock when he awoke. He bounded out of bed and into the shower. As is often the way with an experienced detective investigating a complex problem, the theory that had looked such a strong probability the night before seemed no more than a realistic possibility the following morning.

It was just before seven o'clock when Molash entered Middleham Station. Although it was Saturday morning, Eliot had decided an 8am briefing was justified. He arrived about half past seven and Molash, who had watched Eliot's car pull into the car park, was outside Eliot's office door as the SIO arrived clutching a Starbucks coffee and his briefcase.

Eliot was a little flustered to see Molash before he had settled into his morning routine. It was not helped by the fact that Eliot had attended a function at a local hotel the previous night to celebrate the elevation of a local assistant chief constable to the rank of deputy chief constable. There were few officers of rank as junior as chief inspector there and Eliot had seen it as an ideal networking opportunity. Most of those more senior officers had seen it as an ideal opportunity to get drunk. Eliot, generally a man modest in his potations, had a headache despite spending the evening trying to look as if he was drinking rather more than he actually was.

Eliot also recognised the gleam in Molash's eye – his DSIO had a theory and would try to persuade him what the next steps should be. Eliot's defences were low as he sipped his coffee and his rigour in challenging Molash's hypothesis was even lower.

Molash's theory had the added advantage that, whilst some of the team would have tasks that day, Eliot would not and he realised that Molash's plan would allow him to go home and have a nap. Molash reckoned it would take at least the rest of the weekend to seek the evidence he was searching for.

The team could therefore complete their allocated tasks and take the rest of the weekend off. Molash would enlist Woodcock and they would keep Eliot updated with a view to explaining Molash's theory to the wider team at the next 8am briefing on Monday (if the theory had stood up to the evidence gathered over the weekend). Eliot took a tired gulp of coffee and agreed.

The team were not as prompt as they had been for the 8am briefings on the previous two days. Some had been in The Ship the previous evening and others had been drinking elsewhere. There was a feeling that as Operation Evergreen had been narrowed down to six students, it would break but would need some legwork, which could be left until Monday. Despite the air-conditioning there was an air of lethargy in the incident room. It was nearly five past eight when Eliot began in what he hoped (vainly) was a bright and breezy fashion.

"Good morning, everyone. The good news is that forensics have narrowed the potential field down to the seven students who were with Mark Gower on Tuesday night at 12 Newton Street. At this stage we are not considering Annette Palmer, who has been given an alibi by the other six. Operation Evergreen has become a murder investigation with six potential offenders.

"We have some updates which we'll get to in a moment. What we need to focus on today is setting the wheels in motion to gather as much information about our six potential suspects as we can. We'll then take a break until Monday whilst we wait for that to arrive."

The team perked up like schoolchildren in class when the teacher tells them it's only a few minutes to go until break time. Suddenly everybody was keen to give their updates.

Tyler Brennan was first off the blocks. "I've been through Chloe and Mark's social media again and there's nothing even flirtatious between them. I can't find any rumours about the two of them either."

Molash replied, "Thanks, Tyler. Can you focus on Chloe's housemates over the weekend, please? Anything that suggests Chloe was unfaithful to Sam, even Mark visiting her house, would be interesting."

Brennan nodded and continued, "I've looked in more detail at Danny Wilson and his relationship with Mark Gower, especially regarding the study club Danny was running. Mark doesn't mention it at all on social media, but that was not his style so I'm not surprised. Danny pushed it quite hard but nothing to suggest he was obsessive about it. Lucinda and I have been through the social media of the dozen members and there's nothing startling. Chris Leeke tried to persuade two other members that Danny was a manipulator before he made the official complaint to Dr Bates, but they weren't convinced."

Woodcock said, "The DSIO asked me to check whether the six students at 12 Newton Street planned to live together again in their final academic year. The landlord confirmed that the six of them had already signed up for next year. They did it shortly after the summer term started, on the fourth of May. At that stage at least there had been no bust-up in the group."

The two FLOs, Fordham and Sayer, were there to give an update from Mark Gower's parents. There was little to tell. Lydia Gower had been angry when they had seen her the previous evening to give them an update. An accident with high-spirited students clowning around or a crazed lunatic poisoning students at random was something she could cope with.

Whilst Eliot had instructed the FLOs to keep the details as brief as possible to the Gowers, the conclusion was unavoidable and the fact that one of Mark's friends had murdered him in cold blood really provoked a reaction. It may have been nothing more than the likelihood her son may therefore have done something to goad the killer. Fordham and Sayer had arranged to see them again on Sunday.

Fordham concluded by saying, "One fact from last night is that neither of Mark's parents had heard of Chloe Hartwell. They knew all about his five housemates. The six of them spent New Year's Eve together and slept at the Gowers' house. Neither parent had a bad word to say about any of them. Neither Bob nor Lydia Gower had ever heard of chloral hydrate, let alone had it in the house."

Denman spoke next, rather hesitantly. "I spoke to Hannah Lewis, Zara Allen and Maddy Church from the university tennis club yesterday. I only got the report onto HOLMES last evening so some of you may not have seen it yet. A couple of points to highlight: firstly Hannah Lewis was having a casual relationship with Mark Gower. She basically endorsed what Adam reported from Mark's girlfriend from his first year, Hayley Reynolds – that Mark was a gentleman, albeit perhaps one with adventurous sexual tastes. Secondly, both Zara and Hannah said that when Maddy made it clear she wasn't interested in Jack on Tuesday night Jack didn't push it."

Eliot asked whether anyone had dug up any new information from speaking to university staff who lectured or tutored the students, or from friends or peers on their courses. There was some desultory discussion. The only really pertinent fact came from an interview Sergeant Wade had had with Professor Cassidy from the chemistry department.

Cassidy knew Jack Freeman well and said Jack would certainly have had the knowledge to make a rough solution of chloral hydrate. However, he thought Jack would have been taking a big risk if he made it on campus as it would be hard to do so without anyone knowing. It would have made much more sense to make the chloral hydrate at home, but that would clearly indicate significant premeditation. Molash's mind had already concluded that this was no spur-of-the-moment crime, so he thanked Wade and decided to bring the briefing to a close.

"OK, everyone, as the SIO said at the beginning of the briefing, the next step is to find out as much as we can about the home lives of the six students, which might be relevant. At this stage we are focusing on starting enquiries via calling and speaking to their parents, GPs, significant people in their lives back home and so on.

"We'll be speaking to our colleagues to find out if any of the students were close to anyone who died in an unexplained or suspicious manner, when they were living at home. By Monday we want to be able to decide which lines of enquiry warrant our travelling to those areas to investigate.

"One final point. The press has already got hold of the fact that chloral hydrate was used. Whilst this was inevitable given that we have started speaking to members of the public like Professor Cassidy about it, please can you all be even more discreet than usual about the details of the case over the next few days. My gut feeling is that the sourcing of the chloral hydrate could be crucial so please impress the importance of confidentiality when talking to GPs and so on. This is a murder case and public safety is a concern here, so there should be no issue with the doctors telling us the details of these prescriptions.

"Please could everyone chat with Woody after this meeting re what help he wants from you. After you've set the ball rolling, please be on call so you can share any responses you have with us. Otherwise enjoy the weekend and see you for the 8am briefing on Monday."

45

The five students at 12 Newton Street rose somewhat later than the officers in Eliot's team. All five had slept fitfully and the house was hot. The weekend stretched before them. Instead of the relaxed, post-exam party they had envisaged, they lay or sat in bed red-eyed, lethargic and fearful.

Each had replayed the evening spent with Inspector Molash numerous times in their head. None had forgotten what he had told them about the likely reaction of the press and their fellow students. Each, to a greater or lesser degree, was tempted to stay in bed as long as possible and hope the whole problem would go away.

All their thoughts had focused on the reconstruction they had played out with Molash the previous evening. The unity that Danny Wilson had created, in their agreeing that none of them had been responsible, had fragmented and crumbled. Suspicious thoughts began to seep through the house like fungi digesting wood and creating dry rot. None now completely trusted any of the others.

Only Sam Taylor had thoughts beyond the immediate problems created by Mark's death. He sat bolt upright in bed thinking about Chloe Hartwell. And about Chloe and Mark. Ryan Sandling lay on his back thinking of his four housemates, trying to evaluate them. Owen Lloyd was pacing around his room with his hands behind his back doing much the same. Jack Freeman lay in bed on his side with his eyes firmly closed considering what Molash's view was about Annette, and about the others: the nameless, faceless others.

Danny Wilson got dressed first. He was also the first to brave the checking of his phone. The days of having to go and buy a newspaper or turn on the radio or television to see what the media were saying are long gone. Within a minute Danny was staring in horror at his phone.

The story had made a couple of national tabloids, which had gone with headlines such as 'Student Poison Den' and 'Chloral Bye Mate'.

The local press was worse. The national press had gone for a formulaic description of the household that could have described most student houses in the country. The local press had dug up enough already to make innuendos.

Danny was described as Mark's well-meaning but much less bright coursemate. Sam and Chloe were the glamour couple of the university whose relationship now appeared under severe strain as Chloe did not appear to have seen Sam since the tragedy.

Lots of pictures of different groups of the students had been taken at a recent summer ball and posted on social media. One group shot, next to an article written by Vivian Johnson, was of Chloe in between Mark and Sam. It had been cropped down as if the three of them were the only ones there. The inference was obvious but not explicitly mentioned. Yet.

Jack Freeman came in for innuendo. It was implied that a girl he hardly knew had stayed with him at 12 Newton Street that night, and that that was what occurred most evenings.

Unattributed quotes from female students varied along the lines of Jack's reputation being such that they wouldn't dream of accepting any advances he might make.

Ryan Sandling and Owen Lloyd attracted less attention. There were some references to Ryan being Jack's wingman and unflattering ones about Owen's appearance. The media were keeping their options open regarding how Owen and Ryan would be categorised.

Danny went downstairs, into the kitchen and put the kettle on. Sam and Owen joined him and he showed them some of the articles online. It was the first the students had heard about chloral hydrate. Sam went to get Jack up to get his more knowledgeable opinion on chloral hydrate and put his head round Ryan's door too. Soon the five of them were in the kitchen, drinking coffee despite the heat.

Jack felt like he was up before the kangaroo court as he was explaining what little he knew about chloral hydrate. Danny sensed this and smiled and commented that hopefully this would help the police be more open-minded about who killed Mark as none of them had ever come into contact with chloral hydrate. His words rang hollow and tinny around the kitchen.

Nobody knew quite what to say next. Jack broke the silence by saying that they would benefit from knowing as much as possible, so they should go and buy as many papers as they could. Only Owen disagreed with this, not wanting to leave the relative sanctuary of the house. Danny put his arm round Owen's shoulder and said, "Come on, mate, let's go and face the enemy."

"United we stand, divided we fall, eh?" said Ryan in a thin voice.

When they opened the front door, everything got a whole lot worse.

46

Sam Taylor had been first out of the front door into the baking heat and uttered a stifled, "Jesus." There was brief moment when the five of them cascaded into each other and some cursing, but soon they were all outside on the pavement or road, standing in the blazing sun and looking in horror at the front door.

Someone had sprayed 'MURDERING SCUM' in red across the front door.

Ten eyes looked aghast at the vandalism, then five brains kicked into gear. Jack spoke first. "Let's get back inside and work out what to do."

As they were walking back in, the door about to be closed behind them by Ryan, who was last in, Sam suddenly thought of Chloe and yanked his phone out of his pocket and dialled her number. There was no reply and he left her a voicemail and messaged her explaining what had happened and asking if she was all right.

They walked like automatons back into the kitchen and

Danny picked up the kettle and refilled it. Owen burst out, "For fuck's sake, it's about thirty degrees out there, we don't want any more bloody coffee." He wrenched open the fridge door and looked at the array of bottles of cold water. "Who wants water?" he said as he grabbed one and started rolling the side of the bottle over his hot, red face.

It transpired that everyone did and Owen uncharacteristically threw bottles at each of them. Danny took a deep breath and said, in as calm a voice as could muster, "Good idea, Owen, thanks." He paused whilst they all took big glugs of water and then said, "What do we do now?"

They were all looking at each other, except for Sam Taylor, who said, "We call the police, call Inspector Molash and tell him, get his advice." None of the others looked sure but were certainly not confident enough to disagree. Sam took the silence as agreement, pulled out the card Molash had left the previous night and dialled.

Somewhat to his surprise Molash picked up and said, "Morning, Mr Taylor, everything OK?" *He's put all our numbers into his phone*, Sam thought with a jolt. Sam explained what had happened.

A couple of minutes later Sam cut the call and explained to the others that Sergeant Woodcock was on his way. Molash had advised them to remain calm, that this was probably just an isolated incident. He had, however, suggested they wait inside the house until Woodcock arrived.

Woodcock knocked on the door less than ten minutes later. He soon found himself in the kitchen of 12 Newton Street with five shaken young men. The difference in the five students compared to even the interviews at the station the previous day was palpable.

Owen Lloyd looked terrified. Ryan Sandling had an intense look in his eyes that was almost frightening in itself. Danny Wilson had the appearance of a man who had always provided comfort to others in times of stress but for the first time was at a loss what to do. Jack Freeman was on his guard and seemed unable or unwilling to take his eyes off Woodcock. Sam Taylor alone seemed to have the power of speech and in a tense voice discussed the situation with Woodcock, who felt as if Sam's intense stare was a direct challenge to break eye contact.

Woodcock had arrived with a big plastic bottle of what he described as graffiti remover, and a paintbrush. "The good news, lads, is that this is such a common problem that you can buy this stuff from any decent hardware store or online. Do you have a jet wash?" He noted the level of shock they were under, evidenced by the fact that nobody seemed to know. Eventually Sam pulled himself together and said he didn't think so.

"Well, it's some elbow grease for you lads then. Paint this stuff over the graffiti. It's fine, it won't harm the door. Then leave it half an hour and get some water and a sponge and rub what's left off. It's fresh so it should come off pretty easily."

Ryan thanked him with an attempt at a warm smile. Woodcock looked round the kitchen and asked, "You lads all right? Do you want me to get someone out by the front door for a day or two until this blows over?"

Both Jack and Owen looked gratefully at him and looked to be on the verge of accepting when Sam said, "No, thanks, Sergeant. We'll be fine. We're not going to be intimidated by scum like this," deliberately choosing the same noun as had been sprayed on the front door.

"Good to hear," said Woodcock. "But if you do have any more concerns just give us a call. It's absolutely part of our remit to make sure you lads are all right." Woodcock left them to it but made a point of finding Molash when he got back to the station and explaining the impact the case was already having on the five students living at 12 Newton Street.

Meanwhile, Chloe Hartwell had listened to Sam's voicemail. Ever since she had left Middleham Police Station the previous afternoon she had been trying to work out what to say and what not to say to Sam. His voicemail had seemed heartfelt, concern for her wellbeing trumping any other feelings he might be experiencing.

Chloe decided that it would have to be faced and it was better not to put it off. A simple explanation was the best one, ideally after Sam had had just the right amount of alcohol. She did an approximate Goldilocks calculation and messaged him saying "Morning, handsome. All good here, but been a bit manic with the Cause. Sorry to hear about the door. Can I cheer you up later? See you in the bar? If so what time are you going?"

47

The incident room was relatively quiet. Most of the team had set their tasks in motion and gratefully escaped for the weekend. The temperature had soared even higher than the previous day and many of Eliot's team headed for the coast or the countryside to enjoy the un-English weather whilst it lasted.

After Woodcock had explained the situation at 12 Newton Street he asked Molash whether anything of note had come from the enquiries at the students' family homes. Molash nodded and said they'd made pretty quick progress. They had already spoken to at least one parent of all six of the students that might have poisoned Mark Gower.

"None of them are admitting to there being any chloral hydrate in the house. Most didn't seem to know what it was. They seem a relatively healthy middle-aged bunch as they don't appear to be on much medication.

"I placed particular emphasis on sedatives. Danny Wilson's mother has been prescribed sleeping pills ever since Danny's dad died five years ago. She says she had anti-depressants for a while but that was some time back. I spoke to Ryan Sandling's father who said he didn't hold with popping pills but said that his ex-wife was just the sort to be taking them. We can't get hold of her but he gave me her GP's details and we've got all the other families' GPs too so we're talking to them now."

"What about any of these lads cooking up some chloral hydrate in the shed at the bottom of the garden?" Woodcock asked.

Molash smiled. "You should have heard some of the responses. Sam Taylor's father guffawed down the line. It doesn't sound like any of our students are practical types. If, and it's a big if, the parents are to be believed then Jack Freeman is the only one with the likely skill to make chloral hydrate. His mother said there was nowhere to make it at home, but he could have found somewhere away from prying eyes. I think whoever did this has been planning it for a while."

"Any more luck with finding any sort of suspicious death where one of our six had known the victim?" Woodcock asked.

"We've put in calls to all the local forces, some of which we've got personal contacts at. They've agreed to go through the files today and let us know – it shouldn't take long. In the meantime, shall we go and have a drink and get some lunch?"

Woodcock agreed with alacrity. Molash had a binge approach to many things, alcohol included. He seemed to have substantial periods of abstinence followed by enthusiastic sprees. Woodcock sensed that Molash was in the mood for speculating and so at least a couple of pints, and potentially several more, were in the offing to fire his imagination.

Woodcock lived in a flat about a mile away from Middleham Police Station and walked to and from work. After they'd washed down homemade sandwiches with a couple of pints of lager, he had suggested the excellent WiFi in The Ship meant that it might be the ideal location to spend the afternoon in creative and imaginative thought about the case, whilst waiting for information to arrive.

Tempting as it was, Molash had vetoed the suggestion on the basis one or both of them might be driving off to one of the students' family homes. A Cricket World Cup match between South Africa and Afghanistan was beginning on the big screen in The Ship and Molash wanted to get back to the station before there was any chance of getting engrossed.

At 12 Newton Street the five students were paying desultory attention to the same cricket match on Sam Taylor's iPad via the Sky Go app. All the household were sporty apart from Owen, and he was happy enough watching most sports, cricket included, even if he had no interest in participation. The game helped pass the time and reduce the brooding a little, and given that Mark had been the real cricket enthusiast amongst them, it seemed somehow appropriate.

Unfortunately, Afghanistan made only 125 and as a contest the match was pretty much over fairly quickly, so attention wandered. Between innings an argument developed over what they should do that evening. Jack and Owen, who had been getting on each others' nerves and bickering uncharacteristically, had found something to agree on – that they should stay in. Sam had been adamant that they should go to the Union Bar, saying he was going regardless and meeting Chloe there. Danny had thought hard and agreed with Sam.

Ryan had said very little all day. He had spent much of it looking at social media, where, if trends had been sufficiently localised, the phrase 'murdering scum' would have been at the top of the trending list. The accounts posting these messages were new with fake names but there was no shortage of their so-called friends 'liking' the posts. Irritated by Ryan's lack of contribution, Jack asked him, "Looks like you have the casting vote, mate. What's it to be?"

There was a pause that seemed to last an eternity, but eventually Ryan said, "Fuck it. Let's go to the bar and be there when it opens. If anyone's got an issue they can say it our faces."

48

The call came through just after four o'clock. After a brief discussion Woodcock handed the phone to Molash and could sense the latter's building excitement. The near-empty incident room fell completely silent around the DSIO. Molash's eyes were widening by the moment as he listened.

"So this eighteen-year-old lad committed suicide... Zopiclone... His foster mother's anti-insomnia tablets... The suicide note was quite clear... Yes, I understand... Even if you thought that you'd never prove it... They got to know each other at the local youth club. Tall, blond, good-looking... Yes, just the same, but Mark Gower had no history of mental health issues, quite the opposite, so this time it's murder... I need to find the source of the chloral hydrate... Yes, that sounds promising... Yes, I'll be down first thing in the morning... Don't worry, I'm an early riser... Yes, let's interview them both... That's fantastic, I really appreciate it. See you in the morning."

Molash hung up and slumped back in his chair, exhaling deeply and happily.

Woodcock smiled. "So it looks like your hunch was right, Guv. How much evidence have we got?"

Molash sat up and became serious. "Not enough. I think we've got the motive and it's looking promising regarding finding the source of the chloral hydrate. That's not enough, though. Unless we can show how it got into Gower's glass the CPS probably won't even want to take the case to court. We'd only have established access to chloral hydrate not possession. We're a long way from proof."

Woodcock frowned. "Let's focus on the chloral hydrate getting into the glass then."

They spent the next couple of hours role-playing the nightcap at 12 Newton Street.

49

Whilst Molash and Woodcock were theorising about how Mark Gower's gin and tonic was poisoned, the five students from 12 Newton Street walked into the Union Bar just after six o'clock that Saturday evening. It was virtually empty when they arrived.

The tension was blatant amongst the bar staff and handful of students already drinking. Les Christie walked out from behind the bar to greet them, shaking hands in an old-fashioned way and telling them that the first round was on him, pouring the pints himself.

The fans attached to the ceiling were working overtime in an attempt to stop the large room becoming a furnace. They sat at the table they often frequented in the middle of the bar and attempted to have the sort of normal conversation that had been beyond them at Newton Street. As the bar began to fill up the tension as well as the temperature ratcheted up. A number of students walked into the bar, saw the lads from 12 Newton Street, had a hurried conversation and walked out again.

Those that did stay, tended to sit on tables on the edge of the room. This led to the bizarre situation where there was a ring of occupied tables around the outside, an empty ring of tables on the inner, bar the one in the middle, which nobody approached.

Whispered conversations took places in huddles. When Ryan and Jack went up to the bar to get rounds in, they heard a low hum of 'murdering scum', once extended to 'murdering scum stick together and harbour the killer'. When Danny went to get the next round in there was silence.

Shortly after nine o'clock Owen was queuing at the bar. Just as he was about to order he was jostled from both sides, by two clearly inebriated first-years. One spat at him and the other shouted 'murdering scum' at him.

Les Christie was there in a flash. He had clearly been expecting a flare-up at some stage and physically Owen was much the most vulnerable of the five students so it was no surprise the heroes had decided to pick on him. Christie grabbed the two first-years by the scruff of their polo shirts, marched them to the nearest door and threw them out.

Christie walked back to the middle of the bar. He would have shouted for silence had he needed to, but you could have heard a pin drop.

He growled, "Anyone else who can't behave themselves can have the same treatment." He paused for a moment and then added, "Anyone have a problem with the way I run this bar? Anyone got any suggestions for me?"

The silence was broken as Rich Waters, the rugby club captain, walked up to the bar and said loudly, "Six pints of lager for me and my mates at that table over there in the middle, please." He put his arm round Owen, who was physically shaking, as the drinks were poured. Waters carried the tray to the table and sat down. He picked up a pint and toasted Mark.

Not long later Chloe Hartwell walked in and the bar fell silent for a completely different reason. She wore thigh-length, black leather stiletto boots and a dress that looked as if it had been sprayed on, which only just about covered her posterior. The evidence of a very brief G-string could be seen but it was obvious that it was the only underwear she had on. Often she didn't wear make-up, preferring a natural look, but tonight she was exquisitely made-up, and her hair was piled up on top of her head.

She walked to the end of the bar, where Les Christie was sitting on a stool and, taking no notice of the queues, ordered seven pints of lager, paid for them and took them over. Sam, smiling for the first time that day due to his girlfriend's new look, pulled up a chair next to him and Chloe sat down. With little left to see, conversation resumed throughout the bar.

As Waters was telling an anecdote about Mark from the previous rugby season, Chloe looked softly into Sam's eyes. The flick of the hair was gentle and subtle as her tongue slowly moistened her slightly pursed lips. Having held his stare for several seconds, she leant over and kissed Sam lingeringly on the lips, rubbing her chest against him, and then whispered in his ear, "There's nothing to it, I promise, and we don't discuss it. Agreed?"

Sam looked deeply into her eyes and lied, "I never thought there was."

"I never doubted that. Which means I can keep these new boots on later if you'd like."

Sam did like, very much. Waters left them after he'd drunk his two pints, and although it was little after ten o'clock, Sam's suggestion of an early nightcap was met with enthusiasm. His four housemates were keen to leave on a positive note and felt that it was wise to do so before the general scrum at chucking-out time. As they filed past the bar Les Christie managed to take his eyes off Chloe for long enough to shout, "Good to see you, lads and lasses, see you again soon," to which Danny replied with a thumbs-up.

50

Molash had sent Woodcock home around half past six but stayed in the incident room himself. His cottage dated back to late Tudor times and the thick walls helped keep the heat out. However, they were no substitute for the modern air-conditioning in the incident room, which made it much easier to think through problems. It was after eight o'clock when Molash left for home. He'd planned for the interviews he'd participate in the next day and, as he drove home, he tried to convince his brain that this wasn't the time for further speculation on how the chloral hydrate got into Mark Gower's glass.

Shortly before he got to the cottage he passed his local, The Barnett Arms, and saw Liam's HGV parked in the far corner of the large car park. Molash smiled and drove home, parked his car and took the footpath across the fields from his cottage to the pub. The evening was still hot and stuffy, and Molash ambled. The Barnett Arms was old, large and draughts proliferated. For much of the year three open fires would be ablaze to keep the customers warm. This evening it would at least be cool.

Molash reckoned it must have been three or four months since he'd seen Liam. Despite being born only a few months before Molash, Liam came from a different age. He had no mobile phone, participated in no social media and lived in the back of his HGV.

Despite having known him for several years Molash still had no idea what Liam's surname was. Liam had no bank account and so no debit or credit cards, dealing only in cash. Molash had surmised that Liam must have a driving licence, but he'd never seen it. He recalled someone in The Barnett Arms asking Liam what his surname was and receiving the serene reply that surnames were only needed: "When you were in trouble with people like Jimmy. I make sure I stay out of trouble."

Molash walked into The Barnett Arms and saw Liam tucked away in a quiet corner immersed in a book. Liam was tall and willowy and was dressed in a T-shirt, jeans and trainers. Molash had never seen him in anything else. He sensed Jimmy's arrival and jumped up with a wide grin on his face. A bear hug followed and Molash asked him what he was drinking.

Liam was having none of it, insisting that drinks were on him as he'd had a little bit of luck. Molash grinned, wondering what Liam had sold. He also braced himself. Liam could sit and nurse a drink for hours or consume vast quantities of alcohol, in a way that implied he thought prohibition was being reintroduced next Tuesday. Molash was hoping Liam wasn't on a binge given the early start and long drive the next morning. Molash was in luck.

"This new stuff from that micro-brewery down the road is decent, Jimmy," he said, ordering two pints. "I've had a week-long celebration so I've been enjoying a couple of quiet ones tonight."

They sat at the peaceful corner table and Liam explained his good luck. He'd been on his way north to sell his best piece, a walnut chair dating from around 1670, when he stopped for the night. The following morning there was a local auction, proper low-grade stuff, which had meant the pros were conspicuous by their absence.

Liam went on, his face animated in a way that only a truly beautiful object could animate it. "There was a piece of eighteenth-century soft paste porcelain, Jimmy. Decorated by Emile Renard from the Sèvres factory. It was a beautiful dinner plate, bleu lapis ground, cobalt, you'd probably call it, and flowers exquisitely painted in the centre. It even had Renard's running fox stamped on the reverse.

"It was amongst a load of junk from a clearance of a house where an old lady had died. God knows how it got there, so I bid for two or three items of junk first, paying twenty quid for things worth a fiver. Nobody blinked an eyelid when the Sèvres plate was knocked down to me for forty-five quid. I even paid another twenty afterwards for the sort of hideous modern picture your lad Eliot would put on his office wall, just to make sure nobody focused on the plate.

"It was beautiful, Jimmy, quite beautiful," Liam said, his eyes shining. "Still, needs must. I was only selling the chair at a knock-down price because I was short of funds. So I turned round and headed back to London and sold the Sèvres plate. The coffers are full and I haven't had to sell the chair to a bloke I despise for twenty per cent less than it's worth. Hence a little celebration was in order."

Molash smiled at the adjective.

"Afterwards I was coming back this way when I heard about the student case on the radio. How is it going?"

There was one area of police procedure that Jimmy Molash broke frequently. The details of the Gower case were confidential, but Molash didn't hesitate in discussing them with Liam. There were practical reasons for this. Firstly, from long experience he knew he could trust Liam. Some of what Liam knew about Molash would have caused Jimmy much more angst had it become public knowledge than his sharing of the facts of the Gower case, and Liam had never breathed a word.

Secondly, Liam had intuition to go with his undoubted charisma. He understood people brilliantly. He would often say that he had a decent eye for antiques but a much better one for the people buying and selling them. He would have made a good poker player had he not found the concept so boring.

Molash feared the classic detective's conundrum: that he would establish who had killed Mark such that every team member on the investigation would be happily convinced, yet he wouldn't have the evidence to secure a conviction.

So Molash talked Liam through the case and his theory. It took nearly an hour of Jimmy talking quietly and methodically and Liam listening intently. Bill Coulson, the landlord, knew them sufficiently well to see that there was little chance of the empty glasses being bought to the bar for refilling, so he poured two more pints and bought them over. Molash reached into his pocket but felt Liam's hand clamp on to his arm.

There was nothing flash about Liam, but since Jimmy had had his windfall there had been the odd occasion where Liam had been short and Jimmy had been discreetly buying the beer. Liam handed Coulson a tenner, thanked him and Jimmy went on with his story.

As usual Liam waited until Jimmy had finished to ask questions and, that done, said, "I can see why your mind is travelling that way – from a psychological point of view it makes sense. You'll have a devil of a job proving it, though."

They both relapsed into silence, Liam deep in thought and Jimmy wondering if Liam's famed insight into humanity would turn up anything of practical use for the investigation.

51

Liam eventually came out of his reverie to find that Jimmy had procured two more pints and had his nose in the froth.

Liam mused, "Putting what you may or may not find out tomorrow out of our minds for a moment, just how do you get something into someone's drink without them seeing? Your lad Owen has talked about a psychological moment where everyone was distracted, but there doesn't seem to have been one.

"Is it more a case of opportunity? Two lads went into the kitchen, or to be more accurate one, Sam, admits he did and the other, Jack, may well have done. It must be easier to poison someone's drink when you are the only other person in the room and they are moving about getting bottles, ice, etc.

"To do it in front of seven witnesses, including the victim, would take balls of steel. I know some of them were gazing adoringly into each other's eyes and they were mostly half-cut, but even so. If you get seen then you're facing a long jail stretch, whether or not the victim drinks it."

Liam relapsed into silence and Molash didn't respond. What

Liam had said was little different to the discussions he and Woodcock had been grappling with for much of the week. The pair sat in companionable silence. Both were thinking hard and their relationship meant they didn't feel it necessary to fill the void with unnecessary conversation.

Eventually Liam said, "I can only think of two angles to explore. The first is to find a Rohypnol rapist. There must be a few of them in jail? Ask them how they get the drug into the glass without their victim, or anyone else, seeing."

Molash wasn't convinced. "We can look into it, but that's usually one-on-one. A bloke is taking a girl out on a date or meets her in a bar. He buys them both drinks and can find somewhere between the bar and their table where with some dexterity he can tamper with the drink. If they are sitting alone at a table then when the girl goes to the toilet it's child's play."

Liam nodded slowly. "I see what you mean. Let's scrub that and look at the other possibility. If I was going to try and poison your glass in front of witnesses, I think I'd consider playing drinking games. They can provide an excuse for all sorts of shenanigans with other people's drinks. Do you remember when we were down in Dorset and we played that game with the depth charges?" Molash smiled at a long-forgotten memory and was trying to recall the details when Liam continued.

"Those two old boys who were playing skittles. We thought they were harmless and that the depth charge that was put in the pint was just a schooner of Drambuie. It was when they lost. When we lost the depth charge consisted of some potcheen that looked exactly like Drambuie, tasted a bit like Drambuie but definitely was not Drambuie."

The details were coming back to Molash now. The two local men, who looked well into their fifties, had had an arrangement with the landlord. Fortunately, Liam and Jimmy had smelt a rat and the games had ended abruptly. Another hour's play and even a couple of experienced drinkers like them could have been in trouble. As it was, a quick flash of the Molash warrant card had elicited a solemn, albeit almost certainly untrue, promise that such games would not be played for wagers in the pub.

Molash nodded thoughtfully. "There's been some talk of drinking games but in a negative sense that they sometimes played them but not on the night in question. Maybe the killer was playing a game with Mark Gower, one-on-one, and we don't have the details of it."

Liam shrugged his shoulders. "It's one possibility at least. It might give the killer the opportunity to be messing around with Mark Gower's glass in a way that wouldn't arouse suspicion."

There followed a lengthy discussion of drinking games they'd played but without an obvious candidate that was suited to this purpose. As Molash pointed out, twenty-year-old students were probably playing different drinking games than the ones he and Liam knew anyway.

When last orders were called, they drew the conversation back to more practical matters. Liam was off to the south coast for a series of antiques fayres. He planned on leaving in the morning, taking the view that it would be cooler by the seaside. The evening ended as it began, with a bear hug. There was never any sort of discussion about meeting up again. That was for the proletariat and the bourgeoisie, along with fixed places of abode and surnames. If you were a friend of Liam's you saw him when you saw him.

Molash walked back to his cottage, using the roads given that it was now dark, and made himself coffee. Liam's carefree, responsibility-free lifestyle was as alluring as ever. Molash knew that for the moment at least it was illusory for him. He had a murderer to nail.

At about half past twelve he sent a message to Owen Lloyd:

I'm sorry to keep messing up your social schedule but please could I come round for a chat over a drink on

Sunday night? I'll bring a bottle. I'd very much appreciate it if the five of you and also Chloe could be there. Will probably be mid-evening but I'll let you know. Regards, Inspector Molash.

There was no reply so Molash concluded Owen was asleep. He had an early start himself so drank his coffee and went to bed.

52

The lounge at 12 Newton Street was filled with six students, who were unusually sober after a night in the Union Bar. They'd drunk sensibly by their standards and left early. It was Ryan's turn to arrange the nightcaps and he disappeared into the kitchen and then reappeared with a rectangular tray with six pints of gin and tonic on it, saying, "I thought we'd stick with Mark's favourite drink."

The nightcap, the first they had had since Mark had fatally drunk his poisoned gin and tonic four nights earlier, was a tacit expression of trust in each other. Nobody had followed Ryan into the kitchen whilst he mixed the drinks. He held the tray so that there were five glasses in a row, with his three-quarters-full glass behind, making it clear that he was not trying to force any specific glass on anyone.

The bond between those living at 12 Newton Street had been encapsulated in the nightcap regime. Chloe Hartwell watched with a slight smirk on her lips as everyone hesitated before taking a drink. Five pairs of eyes looked at Ryan and gradually the students stepped forward to take a glass.

No matter how much they told themselves otherwise, once they held a drink that looked so reminiscent of the fatal one Mark had drunk, they all felt the nerves return. Even Owen wasn't following the rules about putting your glass down whilst you weren't drinking. Chloe sat down on the same spot on the sofa as on Tuesday night.

The five men stayed standing and subconsciously kept their distance from each other. Ryan took a sizeable gulp and said that it tasted like gin and tonic, not gin, chloral hydrate and tonic, so he didn't think that the mixer's curse was about to strike again.

There were some anxious laughs that were almost giggles. They gave way to a cautious optimism, the type that a reasonable amount of alcohol often produces, that the worst of the reaction from their fellow students was over. The actions of Les Christie and Rich Waters had thrown some sort of safety net around them, and Jack and Owen were inclined to be more bullish about returning to the Union Bar for the rest of term.

Paradoxically, the students weren't slowly sipping their nightcaps. They drank them as if it was as well to get them finished quickly. It was not yet eleven o'clock when they went to bed.

It was, however, a considerable time before the house went quiet. Chloe had never attempted to be discreet by keeping the noise down whilst she and Sam were in bed together. However, that Saturday night was different. Whether or not it was influenced by the paranoid thoughts of possibly having drunk a fatal dose of chloral hydrate, Sam and Chloe threw themselves into sex with the abandonment of those who think it might be their last time. How much it was the nervous strain of the previous few days or the hot, sultry night air wasn't clear, but Sam had never been like that with Chloe before and Chloe had never been like that with Sam before.

In the room directly below them, Owen Lloyd had never heard them like that before. As usual when he closed his eyes as he lay in bed he imagined that it was him rather than Sam with Chloe, but he had never imagined it like this.

Owen's fantasy, which he alone knew of, was that Chloe was faking it. Sam therefore would condone her coming downstairs to Owen afterwards, as that was the only way she could really achieve orgasm. As he lay in his bed, enacting his fantasy in his mind, Owen would listen and try to make his orgasm coincide with Chloe's.

*

*M*ark Gower's killer reflected that it was crucial to keep the paranoia at bay. That wasn't easy lying in bed in the dark at two in the morning and wasn't helped by the mindless abuse in the bar. There was evidence of Neanderthal thinking at every turn. The risk was of being lynched – a mob was a hard thing to control but equally it might be put to good use.

It wasn't just paranoia: anger was bubbling nearer and nearer the surface. The infantile scrawling of 'murdering scum' on the front door at 12 Newton Street. Honestly, the thought processes of these people. The half-wits in the bar were one level of irritant, but the police, as embodied by this man Molash, were on another plain.

Surely there was no chance of the chloral hydrate being traced? Surely nobody had seen the moment when it went into Mark Gower's glass? Surely nobody had any suspicions about motive? The police had been making enquiries but they were surely routine. Surely there was the clear evidence pointing in a different direction that Molash had been provided with? Surely...

After what seemed an eternity, fitful sleep came.

Molash was himself in prison and there was discussion of whether he should be freed as he had work to do. Suddenly Molash was sat at a table interrogating. Mark Gower's killer tried to speak, to explain to Molash, but couldn't get the words out...

Then the countdown began again. Seven thousand, eight hundred and forty-two. Seven thousand, eight hundred and forty-one. Seven thousand, eight hundred and forty.

The counting needed to slow down...

53

The previous days had been increasingly hot, but Sunday was baking and threatening, with the temperature predicted to peak at thirty-five degrees centigrade. For the time being at least it remained dead calm, with no breeze to take the edge off the heat. The atmosphere had got really close and when, at a few minutes after six o'clock, Jimmy Molash walked the few yards from his front door to his car he acquired several storm flies during the short walk.

He set his sat-nav, put his jacket and tie on to the passenger seat, and turned the air-conditioning full on. He had a two-hour journey ahead of him and it would probably be the most physically comfortable time of the day. He wished the storm would break and get itself done.

Molash's cottage had been comparatively cool. The house at 12 Newton Street was not and the students had passed a hot and sweaty night. Despite going to bed early none of the six had slept anywhere near soundly and they awoke hot, tired and grouchy, even before they had to face what the day had in store.

Sam Taylor had been awake for a while before Chloe Hartwell moved. Had he but known it, she had been awake for some time too. The two of them at least had had the physical release of passion well spent. However, the memory of it asked as many questions as it answered and both were concerned with how the other would view it. Eventually Chloe spoke, saying she was desperate for the toilet, and, having quickly pulled on a T-shirt and a pair of knickers from 'her' drawer, almost ran out of the room. Sam also donned a T-shirt plus a pair of shorts and went downstairs to the kitchen.

Danny was the only one evidently up and about when Sam reached the kitchen and he was busy checking the press and social media. The press coverage was more muted. The previous day's sensationalism had had nothing to feed it. Whilst there was mention of ongoing enquiries and the graffiti, in a country where the Prime Minister had resigned the previous week and politics was in turmoil, the Gower story quickly dropped down the agenda of the press.

"Oh, Jesus," said Danny suddenly. Sam looked up, concerned. Something in Danny's voice suggested it was serious. Danny showed him the image on Instagram on his phone and they both stopped, stunned. After what seemed an age they looked at each other and simultaneously said words to the effect that they should go and look.

They opened the front door gingerly to find the bottom third of it, the front doorstep and some of the pavement covered in vomit. Social media was awash with the 'Vomit on the Sickos Challenge', suggesting that students at the university should drink as much as they could and then register their disgust against the murderer and harbourers of a murderer at 12 Newton Street, by throwing up on their front door.

For the second day running the students wished they had a jet wash, or even a hose. As it was Sam fetched a bucket and spent the next twenty minutes filling it up, throwing it first on the door, then the doorstep and then the pavement. Fortunately that end of Newton Street was on slight slope and there was a drain in the road a few yards down the slope. Less than half an hour later the obvious traces had been washed away and, finding some disinfectant, Sam made up a couple of buckets of disinfectant and warm water and cleaned the front door and doorstep.

Meanwhile Danny had called the police. He'd wanted to wait until the police had seen the evidence before it was cleared up, but Sam had insisted he was clearing it up straightaway, telling Danny to take pictures first if those already on social media weren't sufficient.

Danny couldn't get through to Molash so he called Middleham Station. Tyler Brennan was there and called Woodcock, who was having a lie-in but said he would be round shortly. The noise had led to Owen Lloyd and Jack Freeman leaving their rooms and walking, bleary-eyed, to the front door to see what was happening. What Sam told them caused them both to become fully awake with a jolt.

Owen was shaking again, holding on to the top of the banister at the bottom of the stairs. Jack looked scared and frozen to the spot. Sam, already hot from even this minor exercise, said brusquely, "I'll sort this out and Danny's liaising with the police. We could do with a decent breakfast – can you three organise something?"

Jack muttered that Ryan was still in bed as usual but that the two of them could handle it and they disappeared into the kitchen. None of them argued with Sam. As their nerves were getting tauter they were, subconsciously, increasingly treating him as their leader and relying on his judgment.

Whilst dressing, Woodcock went onto social media and saw the 'Vomit on the Sickos Challenge'. Again this seemed to start from anonymous accounts and then gather pace. He called Tyler Brennan back and asked if he could find out who was behind this, requesting that he call him straightaway if he did find out. After cutting the call with Brennan, Woodcock stood considering for a moment and then called PC Coleman, who had been first on the scene on Wednesday morning.

Coleman, who lived alone in a bed-sit, was enjoying a leisurely breakfast when his mobile rang. He'd been pleased when he'd been put on the Operation Evergreen WhatsApp group and had taken all the mobile numbers of Eliot's team and put them individually into his contacts. He was even more pleased to see Sergeant Woodcock's name on the phone when it rang. When Woodcock explained what had happened and asked if Coleman would accompany him to 12 Newton Street he was positively delighted.

Woodcock was waiting for him at the top of Newton Street and they walked down together. Woodcock was hot in a polo shirt, shorts and flip-flops, evidencing that he was technically off duty but being the good neighbourhood bobby. Coleman was sweltering in his uniform. As they walked down Newton Street Woodcock explained the details and that that this was the second incident in little over twenty-four hours. The students had refused a police officer on the door after the spray-paint vandalism the previous day, but now Woodcock was going to insist.

He flattered Coleman by saying that the students would feel much more reassured by the presence of Coleman, whom they knew, rather than a stranger. Coleman thought for a moment and then grinned at Woodcock and said, "Yeah, right, Sarge. Nice day for it." Woodcock returned the grin and mentally noted that Coleman was intuitively sharp as well as good on procedure. He'd mention that to Molash so they could keep an eye out for an opportunity to offer Coleman a transfer to CID.

By the time they reached the house the smell of vomit had nearly dissipated and Woodcock noted that someone had done a good job of clearing up. At least one person at 12 Newton Street was coping with the situation reasonably well.

By the time the two police officers reached the kitchen, Chloe Hartwell, freshly showered and dressed in a T-shirt and shorts, and Ryan Sandling, yawning and still only clad in boxer shorts, had joined the other four students. Jack explained that they were making breakfast and offered some to the two policemen.

Woodcock politely declined and took this as an opportunity to explain that the police were not prepared to tolerate the sort of vandalism that had occurred at 12 Newton Street for the past two nights. He had therefore instructed Coleman to guard the front of the premises. He addressed his remarks largely at Sam Taylor, the pair staring at each other hard. What Woodcock was trying to communicate was 'I'd prefer not to explicitly worry some of your housemates that this might escalate from criminal damage to a physical threat to you all, but I will if you object'.

Sam glanced at Owen Lloyd, whose shaking had reduced to a twitch, and thanked Woodcock. Owen, quickly aware of the situation, looked at Coleman and said, with an unsuccessful attempt at nonchalance, "Don't worry, Constable, we'll keep you fed and watered."

Woodcock explained that he had instructed the team's social media expert to try and track down the source of this abuse and asked the six students if they had any idea who was behind it. Nobody did. Danny recounted the incident in the Union Bar but none of the six even knew the names of the two first-years who had abused Owen. The fact that their enemies were unknown compounded the fear and helplessness that was threatening to engulf them.

There was a brief hush and Owen mentioned the message he'd received from Molash regarding a visit that evening. This created a tense silence and Woodcock thought that twelve hours stuck inside with little to do but wait should bring the killer to a simmer nicely. He therefore suggested that they stay in as much as possible during the day and keep off social media. He concluded by saying that as tomorrow was Monday, hopefully the situation would calm down as the student community returned to lectures and preparing generally for the following academic year.

As he prepared to leave he said to Coleman that he'd arrange for relief that evening. Coleman said that he was happy to wait until the end of Inspector Molash's visit so the latter could make a decision if that was helpful. *Keen as well*, thought Woodcock, who thanked Coleman and left.

54

It was early afternoon and the hottest phase of the day had begun. Cumulus clouds began to form. The fluffy tops were growing into towering clouds that would spread through the afternoon to form the anvil shape that suggested a coming storm.

Conversation in the lounge at 12 Newton Street was stilted and all six students had given up any pretence of normality, such that the occasional stabs at cheerful discussion fell on stony ground.

The house was hot, stuffy and airless. Ryan and Chloe both sat silently using their phones hour after hour. Chloe had picked up one of Sam's books and regularly used it to fan herself whilst Ryan drank pint after pint of iced water.

Sam and Danny sat with their shirts off trying to immerse themselves in another Cricket World Cup match on Sam's iPad, this time a big clash between India and Pakistan. Neither could get comfortable and both would suddenly start as they realised they'd missed several minutes of the game whilst absorbed in their own trances.

Owen sat in his own world, desperately trying to rationalise every facet of the situation he found himself in. Increasingly red in the face, a small trickle of sweat ran down his spine as he failed to find the solution he sought.

Jack looked to have ants in his pants, jumping up and down every few minutes, offering drinks, going to his room to get a book or his phone before casting them quickly aside.

There was no fan of any type at 12 Newton Street and a suggestion by Jack that one be purchased from a shop in the town fell on deaf ears. Sam had ordered one online for next-day delivery to stop an argument developing, even though the forecast was for a storm to end the heatwave later in the day. They could all sense the fear-induced irritability that was bubbling under the surface, threatening to explode at any moment.

None of the six students could keep the impending visit of Inspector Molash that evening out of their minds. This visit wasn't just an issue for Mark Gower's killer but for the five innocent parties as well. Those five had all got past the stage of not suspecting each other on principle because of the bonds that tied them. As the long day, with little to do, dragged by there was more than enough time to speculate about which of them *might* have done it.

The thought that entwined those speculations was, *Do any of them think it was me?* For all six, there was a more practical related thought: *Do the police think it was me?*

Almost no matter how strong the bonds between you are, it is a rare person in this highly unusual situation whose mind would not get eaten away by such thoughts and speculations. The first and principal emotion is fear, fear of being accused. Innocence provides only partial protection from that. Each had thoughts along the line of 'one of us must have done it and it could as easily have been me as any of the others'. With nobody having an obvious motive, small things, well within the normal give and take of life as university students, could be taken out of context and justified as a motive.

Given the abuse they had suffered each knew that the wider student community would welcome an arrest and would assume that the arrested person was the guilty party. Such an accusation could grow a life and momentum of its own, roared on by thousands of scared students desperate to feel that there was no longer a killer amongst them.

The natural fear of being convicted for a murder they did not commit fuelled an equally natural desire to know who really did do it. Gradually it was becoming everyone for themselves.

When Molash had visited them two nights previously they had only found out about that proposed visit late that same afternoon. They had also only just found out that the forensic evidence meant that one of them had killed Mark. Molash had framed the visit to Jack Freeman in neutral terms – a visit to discuss the situation the students found themselves in.

If a week is a long time in politics, a couple of days can seem an eternity for a small group of people under suspicion of murder, when they know that one of them must have done it. The second Molash visit, now just a few hours away, shaped to each of them as a threat to their liberty.

Fleeting glances were cast as they considered reasons why one of the others might have killed Mark. When the recipient noticed such a glance they instinctively knew what it meant. And so throughout the day it grew.

All day they were clock-watching as the time ticked down towards the evening when Molash would arrive. Not knowing what time that would be just made the waiting worse. The fact that he wanted to see them all together again rather than their being interviewed at the station in the normal way must mean something, but what? Would the inspector's arrival herald a direct accusation? An arrest? All six were thinking, *What will he want to ask me?*

Gradually they began to also ask themselves what the inspector would want to ask the others. Self-preservation was kicking in and the prospect of giving Molash a nudge in the direction of one of the others, a tactic that would have seemed abhorrent a few hours before, was starting to appeal.

As the towers of cloud outside grew ever more threateningly, still the time ticked relentlessly on towards Molash o'clock.

55

The plethora of thoughts about him emanating from 12 Newton Street were not articulated out loud, and Molash's ears weren't burning as a result, but he felt as if they were the only parts of him that weren't as he climbed into his car to drive home.

The investigations had been a definitive success and, barring a freak coincidence, Molash knew who had killed Mark Gower. Proving it in a court of law would be a different matter. Molash was hot and sticky and he would have liked to sit for a few minutes in his car with the air-conditioning on full blast, before driving home and shelving the case until tomorrow.

However, some instinct deep within him was warning him of urgency. He couldn't articulate to himself what the danger was, but he sensed it was there. As he drove home he tried to evaluate that instinct. Woodcock had left a message explaining the 'Vomit on the Sickos Challenge', and Coleman's presence outside the front door. Was it a lynch mob that he feared? Was there a risk of a staged suicide and confession? He wasn't sure but his gut feeling was that going to 12 Newton Street that evening was important.

He made good time and decided to drive to his cottage first and shower and change. The atmosphere was menacing and there was now little doubt a storm was brewing. Molash arranged for a police constable to relieve Coleman that evening, suggesting to PC Williams that he arm himself with a waterproof coat and an umbrella. He asked Williams to pick him up from his cottage and drive him back, before beginning his sentry duties.

That enabled Molash to drink with the students, without having to worry about driving home. He messaged them all giving an estimated time of arrival, showered and changed, and collected eight bottles from a fridge in his garden shed, which was on the super-cold setting.

It was approaching a quarter past eight when Molash arrived at 12 Newton Street as thunder began to rumble in the distance. He exchanged some friendly words with Coleman, was pleased to find out that nothing untoward had occurred and explained that he would be about an hour, after which Williams would drive him home and then return to Newton Street to relieve Coleman.

In the lounge of 12 Newton Street the atmosphere was as brooding and tense as the weather outside. Jack Freeman had opened the door and invited Molash in. By the time Molash reached the lounge everybody had put down their phones, books or whatever else they had nominally been trying to concentrate on and he felt six pairs of eyes boring into him.

He opened the cool box he'd brought with him to reveal two litre bottles of Grey Goose vodka and a pack of six litre bottles of the Schweppes mixer Russchian. This mixer, not often available in supermarkets, was new to all the students and, as Molash hoped, there was some interest in a new drink that took the students' minds' momentarily away from the business to come.

Molash noted that the students had apparently been drinking coffee and tea rather than alcohol before his arrival. Given that Jack was still standing, Molash asked him to help him mix what he cheerfully described as 'hopefully another option for your nightcaps going forwards'.

As Molash walked round the lounge with a tray offering drinks he explained that it was a drink that needed to be served really cold, hence large numbers of ice cubes in each pint. The appreciative murmurs from the six students weren't those of politeness or wanting to curry favour with Molash. There was an element of finding something positive to focus on amongst the stress and angst. Owen Lloyd's eyes were alight. Chloe Hartwell sipped enthusiastically and said in a delighted voice that this could be her new drink going forward.

With plenty of ice in them the first pints didn't last too long and despite protests to the contrary Molash collected up the glasses, refilled them in the kitchen, and redistributed them.

"How confident would you all be that you'd got the same glass as last time?" he asked.

The illusion of normality, the delights of finding a new drink to enjoy, vanished like a puff of smoke. Suddenly all six students were strung up, alert again. The prospect of Molash being a friend who had come to share a new drink suddenly seemed ridiculous. He was hunting for a murderer whom they all knew to be in the room. Six pairs of eyes were riveted on Molash, sensing that he was about to spring a trap.

Owen recovered first. "I'm not sure. I was engrossed in the possibilities for this glorious, new imbibing pleasure." Some of the others looked at their glasses and nobody was prepared to assert whether or not they had the same glass.

"Actually, I swapped them," said Molash. "Everyone has the drink that the person to their left had last time." He wanted to create the impression that this demonstration was what he had come for, and that the debate to come was general background interest in the case. It was an old police diversion trick and he wasn't optimistic Mark Gower's killer would fall for it but he thought it might relax the others and the information he sought was more likely to come from an innocent party anyway.

"That's been very useful, thanks. I think this was the first drink of the day for all of you, unlike on Tuesday night? It helps show that it's harder than you might think to be sure about what's going on with your drink."

There were some nervous smiles and the students didn't seem to know whether to swap their glasses back or not. Molash took a swig, which seemed to answer that question. He looked at his nearly full glass as if thinking that he had another pint to drink and so some day-to-day chitchat was required.

He began by saying that the police were still looking into the social media abuse. The accounts used to start the campaigns were quickly closed once they'd gathered momentum and had been set up from pay-as-you-go phones, which were then discarded. The police strategy had therefore been to contact all students who had shared, liked or otherwise disseminated the abusive posts. The hope was that by putting the fear of being subject to the wrath of the police into those fanning the flames, the fire wouldn't spread but burn out of its own accord.

Whilst the students were digesting this Molash continued with a wholly mendacious anecdote about how he had first discovered the Russchian mixer, which revolved around drinking games. He hoped this would make him a more human figure, which could help the five innocent students relax a little and become more communicative. It also led neatly into the subject Molash wished to discuss.

Molash explained the drinking games in question, most of which were well known to the students but a couple of which were not. That fact allowed Molash to emphasise the joys of finding new drinking games as well as new drinks and so ask what the latest drinking games were, hinting at the fact that, in his thirties, he no longer had his finger on the pulse of such things.

Only Owen Lloyd engaged initially, his eyes shining. "The

important distinction, Inspector, is between games that are played at a specific time and games that are ongoing. Some of the games you mentioned, like 'I Have Never', 'Twenty-One', 'Drink While You Think' and so on, are games that are specifically played by everyone for a finite period."

Molash nodded in understanding and Owen continued, "Those games are pretty straightforward and you'd see them being played by hundreds of the local students in bars or pubs. The expert games player indulges in ongoing games where nothing might happen for hours but you have to keep your wits about you. That is what we do."

Owen paused for breath and Danny cut in, "Some drinking games can be played at any time, such as the Thumbmeister game. If someone puts their thumb on a table then everyone else has to; the last person to do so has to finish their pint. There's obviously some tactics to it. If someone," he looked at Jack with a wry smile, "is distracted by something then there's a good chance they will be the loser."

Sam picked up the theme. "A more dangerous game is 'Tell Her', which is where after you make a remark, usually about someone's appearance or that you find them attractive – someone says, 'Tell her', and you have to repeat exactly what you said to the person in question. It cuts both ways so 'Tell Them' is a better phrase, although I've never had someone actually come up to tell me anything, having been caught out at that game."

Chloe laughed and said, "If only I'd known that game before I met you…" Sam smiled cynically at the thought of what Chloe might have been prepared to say to his face before they knew each other.

Owen was keen to give a full account of the various games and said, "So what haven't we mentioned? Mark introduced the golf ball game, which was something he played at home. One person has the golf ball and if they drop it into your drink then you have to finish it. The recipient then has possession. The art is not to go too early. Getting it into someone's full pint right at the end of the evening is ideal."

"Then there is the 'Hats On' game that Ryan introduced."

Seeing that he was expected to comment Ryan said, "That's just played on official all-dayers. We sometimes go to the charity shop and each buy a hat for a quid or two. The odder the hat the better. It's rude to have your hat on indoors so you have to have it somewhere so that you can get it on quickly. This isn't a game where the last one to get their hat on has to drink. The person calling 'hats on' then counts to five. Anyone without their hat on has to finish their drink." Ryan's smile was broad as he added, "There's been known to be some hat hiding go on."

"We forgot the Freezemeister," said Jack. "Ryan should have remembered that, Inspector, after the Abbey Road incident." The smiles were more prevalent now and Jack explained how the game worked. "It's like musical statues except there is no music. Instead, when the Freezemeister becomes completely still the last person to stop moving has to finish their drink. Once when we were crossing a zebra crossing and Mark got safely to the pavement and froze. Ryan was at the back and had to stand still on the zebra crossing with cars hooting at him. Joyously there was a traffic warden who moved him on."

Owen added, "There's a tactic to these games in that you have a good slug out of your full pint straightaway. Then if you do get caught out at least you haven't got too much to drink."

Molash looked at his near-empty glass. "I suppose that means I should be suggesting playing drinking games now, but I'd better go. Thanks again for your co-operation and for helping with my little experiment. We'll be in touch during the week to let you know how the investigation is going."

Just as he had let Molash in, Jack Freeman escorted him out again. Molash said good night to Coleman, thanking him for his diligence. The storm rumbled louder and closer now and the wind had got up. Coleman grinned. "With any luck, Sir,

Williams will be back just before I get to use the umbrella he lent me!"

Molash smiled, climbed into the passenger seat of Williams' car and gave him directions to the cottage. As they drove out of Middleham the first flash of lightning lit up the sky, which although it was only dusk was now very dark. The thunder followed ten seconds later suggesting the storm was a couple of miles away. The rain began to fall as they approached Blakely. Molash thanked Williams when they got to the cottage and ran inside just as the rain became torrential.

Molash shook some water from his hair as he walked into the kitchen, grateful to have missed almost all the coming storm. He poured himself a drink and stood in the lounge looking out of the French windows as the rain sluiced down.

He'd missed the storm but Mark Gower's killer wouldn't. He called a friend in forensics and explained the test he urgently wanted done. His friend told him it wouldn't take long and he'd be happy to go in very early, make the test and call Molash with the results prior to the 8am briefing.

Molash thanked him and called Eliot and explained that he was confident he'd found out how Mark Gower was poisoned. They agreed to meet at seven fifteen in Eliot's office the following morning and Eliot said he would arrange for one of the CPS team to join them.

Molash stared out into the now-furious storm, his drink long neglected on the table as he planned the following day when he intended to trap Mark Gower's killer.

*T*his night was different. Mark Gower's killer lay awake, awash with sweat as the storm raged outside. Never having considered getting caught, that prospect was frightening. Frighteningly real now too. The crashes of thunder sounded like a herald of impending arrest. The relentless drumming of the rain appeared inescapable.

Calm. The way to brazen this out was to stay completely calm, no matter what the provocation. No matter what any of them might say. Molash was just waiting, biding his time, waiting for a mistake. Well, no mistakes would be made. Molash was dealing with someone too smart for the sorts of games that hoodwinked idiot low-life criminals.

Molash seemed to know, though. Those questions about the drinking games weren't casual. They were planned and Molash had the air of a man who knew. Would any of the others suddenly have their memories of the nightcap triggered?

All of them may need to be silenced. But who? And how? Shivering in the oppressive heat now. Or was it simply shaking?

That word a German exchange student had used. Torschlusspanik. The panic of closing doors. The idiot had been worried about time running out to decide on a career. But now the doors seemed to be shutting everywhere. How to reach one in time…?

Sleep was brief and troubled. In a car going to Molash's funeral. Sitting in the passenger seat but unable to see who was driving the car. Stopping at a crossroads. Which way would they go? An old childhood home was one way. Another led to a never-seen-before stretch of coastline. On another road was a gun shop.

Suddenly the countdown began again, drowning everything out.

Three hundred and twenty-six, three hundred and twenty-five.

Mark Gower's killer woke with a scream.

56

The morning of Monday 17 June was calm and fresh. The storm had blown itself out during the night and, at half past five, Molash was standing outside on the little patio in his garden in just a T-shirt and shorts. The ground was wet underneath his bare feet but felt deliciously cool after the oppressive heat of the previous few days. It was certainly easier to concentrate in the cooler air and Molash was immersed in his plans for the day.

He sensed Gower's killer was both dangerous and felt Molash was closing in, hence the emergency forensics. Now he had to convince Eliot to, at the very least, agree to an arrest to ensure no harm came to anyone else. Molash turned back into the house and headed for the shower.

The meeting in Eliot's office was fraught. Despite the forensics coming back positive, Eliot was indecisive and Peter Hanmer from the CPS wasn't much better. Hanmer was old-school and liked his cases neat and tidy. His attitude was that taking the Gower case to court was a lottery.

Eliot sat hunched over his desk like a cornered animal, his

eyes darting continually from Molash to Hanmer trying to find a way out of making the arrest decision. Molash sat, energy coiled, in stark contrast to his usually languid insouciance in internal meetings. Hanmer sat patiently like a bird in a tree, watching how it would play out.

Molash wore Eliot down and carried the day by convincing him that another killing was realistic and that with such a closed field of possible killers this wasn't a case that could be put into the 'won't be solved' tray. The nettle needed grasping now. The 8am briefing was therefore focused on the arrest procedure.

Police officers are sometimes heroic, but they don't act the hero. Tales of a lone investigating officer chasing a crazed, gun-toting killer through the streets or a derelict building, risking their own life in the process, are largely simply that – tales.

Officers experience more than enough unavoidable danger in police work. Molash's personal experiences of criminals trying to kill him had made him acutely aware of the dangers and when arrests could be planned, he made painstaking efforts to minimise risk.

A check with the university had confirmed that Mark Gower's killer had a lecture to attend at 11am. Molash was concerned that the killer might have armed themselves with some form of lethal weapon such that an attempt to make the arrest inside the house at 12 Newton Street would be dangerous. Whether they would risk taking any such weapon on to the university campus was another matter and so the decision was made to make the arrest en route to the campus.

Molash ensured that nobody connected with the case was involved and two officers from the divisional support unit were tasked to make the arrest. The surprise, when it came, needed to be total. The route to campus involved walking along Morris Street and then turning left at the end on to Goulding Road. There was a small café on Morris Street, ideal for a plainclothes officer to sit drinking coffee and keeping an eye out for Mark

Gower's killer. If all went as planned a discreet radio message would be sent to two taser deployed uniformed officers who were just round the corner in Goulding Road. They would make the arrest immediately once the killer turned the corner.

The café in Morris Street was owned by a gentleman not averse to it being used by a couple of local prostitutes, who would nurse a drink in a window seat whilst touting for business dressed as nurses. As far as Molash was aware his relationship with the two girls was nothing more than that, but a quick suggestion that he might be investigated for pimping was enough to ensure his co-operation in having a plainclothes officer sat in a window seat. The coffee was complimentary.

Round the corner in Goulding Road the houses were of the type where the front door is recessed so that there was an area on the front doorstep ideal for the concealment of one officer. After a brief discussion with the owner, the house nearest the junction with Morris Street contained one of the uniformed officers, to cover any attempt to turn and run. The other would be a few feet further up the road, ready to make the arrest.

Meanwhile Molash sat at his desk, the minutes slowing to seconds as his brain whirred, trying to assess the risks to the other students. He resisted the temptation to telephone to 12 Newton Street, despite his desperation to hear that everyone was safe, that there wasn't another bed with a young life snuffed out in its prime. He prowled round his office with the door closed waiting for news of the success or otherwise of the arrest.

57

In addition to his prime concern for the safety of the other students, Molash had been unusually twitchy in the run up to the arrest. He had a premonition that something could go wrong, that the killer had planned for this eventuality. In fact the arrest went smoothly and a few minutes later Ryan Sandling was safely ensconced at Middleham Police Station.

Sandling had made no protest when arrested. For a moment he seemed to be about to question the need for handcuffs but thought better of it. He remained silent throughout, other than to confirm that he understood what was happening.

He was already in the interview room when Detective Constables Roy Clark and Yasmin Shah entered to begin questioning him. Watching and listening in the next room were quite a crowd. Eliot, Molash and Woodcock were all there and, unusually, Hanmer from the CPS had stayed.

In addition, Claire Tanner had joined them. Tanner was one of the leading criminal psychologists in the country. Her hourly rate made Eliot wince when doing the accounts, but he accepted that she was first-rate and Molash had wanted her opinion concerning Ryan Sandling's potential psychopathy.

As news came through of the successful arrest and whilst they waited for the formalities to be conducted, Tanner had been explaining to a sceptical Hanmer.

"It depends on your definition of psychopath, but most estimates are that at least one per cent of the population are psychopaths. It's more common in men and some estimates put the male rate at as high as three per cent. This is much less rare than is perceived. We all know psychopaths; we have all worked with them. Only a relatively small proportion are violent; most use other means to get their way.

"Looking specifically at your profession, you'll all have seen plenty of obviously violent criminals who are psychopaths. The crucial difference here is that you potentially have someone who is aware of their advanced psychopathy and has spent their brief adult life covering it up. There is a good chance that Ryan has spent a lot of time researching how psychopaths behave so that he can dissimilate."

Hanmer asked whether dissimilation was important to a psychopath and Tanner nodded emphatically.

"Yes, to a sophisticated psychopath. The most important point to remember is that a psychopath manipulates. If that is what Ryan is then he will have spent his time at university manipulating his housemates, teachers, everyone."

"Note that I said housemates, not friends. Psychopaths don't have friends; they have people who are useful to them. As I've said, Ryan may have read up on the subject and so be able to feign the feelings of friendship, but under real stress his true character should become evident.

"The reason psychopaths don't have friends is because they don't feel positive emotions like love and warmth. They can feel a sense of satisfaction when achieving something but that's about as far as it goes. Psychopaths are often very charming, having the gift of the gab, and in day-to-day life it's not easy to see through that veneer of charm."

Eliot asked, "His parents broke up and from what we've gathered his mother is a bit of a mess. Is that likely to have caused his condition?"

Tanner shook her head. "No, Chief Inspector. People are born psychopaths; it is never caused by a bad childhood. Such life experiences can shape a psychopath, just as they can anyone else. For example, a violent upbringing might cause a psychopath to become a violent criminal. Had they had a good upbringing they may have become a white-collar criminal such as a con man. But no sort of upbringing will make them a decent human being."

It was at this point that Ryan Sandling had been shown into the interview room and offered coffee or tea, both of which he declined. Shah and Clark entered shortly afterwards and explained his rights to Ryan. He simply smiled when asked about a solicitor, saying, "I'm here willingly, Constable. I appreciate that this is the sort of case the police never do solve and you need all the co-operation you can get. I'm delighted to help in any way I can. You won't find any evidence against me as there isn't any, but if I can assist at all by answering your questions then I shall. I don't need a solicitor to help me do that."

Shah wondered for a moment whether Ryan was delusional and simply in denial about his arrest. She quietly reiterated the terms of Ryan's arrest, making clear that he was here because the police believed he had killed Mark.

Ryan smiled again. "Why would I want to kill my friend, Constable?"

"Was he really your friend, Ryan? What is your definition of true friendship anyway?"

"Of course he was my friend, ask anyone. A true friend is a friend when it is convenient and when it is not. They stand by you consistently, both when you are present and when you are not. They are honest and authentic with you. That's what my friendship with Mark was like, what my friendship with the whole house is like."

Tanner smiled in the next room and said, "If there was any doubt as to whether Ryan Sandling is a psychopath that dispels it. That definition is straight out of a textbook. If you google 'definition of a true friend', you'll probably find that he's quoted that verbatim from somewhere near the top of the search list. It sounds stilted to us, but because Ryan can't feel friendship he has to dissimilate by reading up on the subject. His problem is that because he can't feel emotions like friendship he can only spout quotes like this, without understanding how they come across."

Shah replied to Ryan, "We know you killed Mark, Ryan. Do you mind if we call you Ryan, by the way?" Sandling nodded and smiled as if to say that they were all friends and so that was fine. "We've traced the chloral hydrate that you took from your mother's stash of sedatives."

Ryan raised his eyebrows in an amused fashion. "My mother takes chloral hydrate? I doubt it. Her doctor is a stickler and from what I've read up on the subject in the last few days it's a dangerous drug. My mother takes sedatives, she's probably addicted to them, but not chloral hydrate. You've got your drugs mixed up, I'm afraid, Constable."

"Do you know the name of your mother's doctor, Ryan?"

Ryan looked amused. "Of course I do, as, I imagine, do you. My mother's mental health is not good, so when I go and visit her, medicine is a major topic of conversation. She often says that Dr Kelum doesn't understand her."

"What about her other doctor, Ryan? What about Dr Simons?"

There was a brief pause and Ryan asked who Dr Simons was. In the next room Claire Tanner said, "He had prepared for that, but it was still a bit of a surprise to him that we knew of Dr Simons' existence. Often younger psychopaths are easier to break down as they don't have much experience of interrogation, whether from the police or from ordinary life, but he's good. It may not be as straightforward as I'd hoped."

"Dr Simons is a close friend of your mother's, Ryan," explained Shah. "We spoke to him at length yesterday. His reputation is somewhat tarnished in the eyes of the British Medical Association. One more significant complaint and he'll be struck off. He was co-operation itself."

Shah paused, giving Ryan the opportunity to ask about Dr Simons' co-operation, but he remained silent, his body language implying that he was pleased the doctor had been so helpful, so Shah continued.

"As you said, Ryan, your mother is a regular user of sedatives. Dr Kelum has taken a stringent line in what he prescribes, but it isn't enough for her now. You may be right that she has an addiction problem. Dr Simons was prepared to prescribe a high concentration dose of chloral hydrate to your mother for use when her normal sedatives wouldn't do the trick."

Ryan was watching Shah carefully now, his grey eyes hard as granite.

"Dr Simons' practice is pretty small these days – the two other GPs left his practice a couple of years ago and set up separately. He says he was unaware that your mother was registered with Dr Kelum. That's dubious, but seeing as he was so co-operative we haven't pursued that point. He admits to having had an on-off affair with your mother and said that he acted as a friend who understood her needs as well as a doctor.

"He said he prescribed an unusually strong solution of chloral hydrate for use when your mother was really struggling, as he put it. He said that he had done so for nearly two years and that given she had only asked occasionally for repeat prescriptions he thought that she was getting on top of her addiction. That was before we explained to Dr Simons that Dr Kelum had been prescribing Zopiclone to your mother for daily use."

The word Zopiclone looked to jar a nerve and the team in the next room could see Ryan clenching and unclenching his fists under the table.

"We went to see your mother yesterday. We told her that we were checking the medicines in the homes of close family members of all six of you. She's not well, Ryan, as you probably know. She was dosed up and barely seemed to understand what we were saying. She showed us all the drugs she had, including the chloral hydrate, which she said she hadn't used for some weeks. Interestingly, there are virtually no fingerprints on the bottle. Someone has handled it with gloves recently. What can you tell us about that?"

Ryan stirred and said in a calm and measured voice, "Nothing. I had no idea that she had another doctor, much less that she'd been prescribed chloral hydrate. I've rarely been in her medicine cupboard; she doesn't like anyone going into her bathroom, let alone in that cupboard." He thought for a moment and then added, "I can't recall any of my friends going there either. When I've seen them during the holidays that's generally been at Dad's house."

"Here it comes..." said Tanner in the next room.

Shah and Clark had been briefed to remain quiet at this point and let Ryan keep talking. He said, screwing his face up in an apparent attempt at remembrance, "Actually, that's not quite correct. Jack came to my mum's at Easter. It was an ad hoc thing, he only lives about an hour away and he came down for the day. I'd already arranged to see Mum so we both went round there for a cup of tea before we went into town. None of the others have been there, I don't think."

Ryan Sandling was attempting to present himself as giving helpful facts to the police investigation. It was pretty clear to everyone listening to him that Ryan had Jack Freeman lined up to take the rap if the net started closing. At the very least Ryan's plan seemed to be to create enough doubt so that a jury could

315

be convinced that either of the two could have extracted chloral hydrate from the bottle at his mother's house.

Shah continued, "We've tested the chloral hydrate at your mother's house and there is no question it was the toxin used to kill Mark Gower. It was individually made up by Dr Simons' rather dubious pharmacist who happens to be his common-law wife.

"So you extracted the chloral hydrate at Easter and arranged for Jack Freeman to visit your mother with you so that, if needed, you could create the impression that he had stolen it. That shows you had planned to kill Mark for some time – it wasn't a spur-of-the-moment impulse. Why did you want to kill Mark, Ryan?"

Ryan Sandling smiled, a slightly supercilious smile that was close to becoming a smirk but was just well enough controlled to avoid that classification. His manner was that he was a good citizen helping some dumb flatfoots who had got hold of the wrong end of the stick.

"Why indeed, Constable? I didn't kill him, as I had no reason to. Mark and I were close. Since Sam had got together with Chloe, Mark and I had got closer. He wanted my help as he was worried about Jack's behaviour."

"This is the next phase," said Tanner in the next room. "There will be no direct accusation that Jack killed Mark, just sowing the seeds. Given that Mark can't bear witness to what went on between them, Ryan will keep it simple. Mark will have enlisted Ryan's help to investigate what Jack has been up to, but Ryan won't know all the facts."

Sure enough, when Shah asked what Mark was worried about, the story came out in apparently hesitating and uncertain fashion.

"I don't know all the details – Mark liked to play a lone hand in things. He was always very confident in his own ability to solve a problem." Ryan was struggling to keep the bitterness out of his voice. "He told me at the start of term he'd got hold of a

316

story from one of Jack's one-nighters that Jack had, well, forced himself on her."

Ryan paused and then added hurriedly, "Of course neither Mark nor I believed it. Jack's highly sexed, but I'm sure he'd never do anything like that. Mark wouldn't tell me where the accusation had come from, as I was all for going and confronting the girl. Instead Mark said we'd keep an eye on Jack and talk to some of the girls we knew he'd been involved with. Subtly, if you know what I mean."

"Do you think Jack is a rapist, Ryan?"

Ryan seemed horrified. "Of course not, Constable, that was the whole point," he said patiently. "People are very quick to cry rape these days when they regret going to bed with someone. I'm afraid Jack loses interest pretty quickly after he's got a girl into bed. Most just accept that – Jack never pretends he's looking for anything long-term." Ryan shrugged. "But in the sober light of day some will always feel that they've been taken advantage of and a certain type of woman will play the rape card."

There was a pause and next door and Tanner said, "This is classic psychopathic behaviour. Psychopaths can't empathise. You can see it with Ryan here: he can't see it from the women's point of view at all. To him it's just a man trying to get laid; the potential for abuse in practice doesn't really exist in his mind."

Shah was close to losing her cool. She'd been part of a number of rape investigations, most of which had been alleged rapes by men who knew their victims. Few had come to court and she had first-hand experience of how the system was stacked against the complainant.

"Playing the rape card, Ryan? Rape isn't a game. Do you really think there are stacks of women out there who regret a one-night stand and so decide to make a fictitious rape allegation in revenge? Have you any idea what a woman making an allegation of rape goes through?"

Ryan shrugged as if to imply that the conversation shouldn't be upsetting Shah. Clark spoke for the first time since the preliminaries in order to give Shah the opportunity to calm down. They'd both been warned that Ryan would be likely to try and manipulate them, but that knowledge didn't mean they were immune to such tactics.

He said, "So should we take it that Mark and yourself found no evidence of criminal behaviour by Jack Freeman?"

Ryan looked irritated as if his patience was being tried by having to deal with a couple of not very bright investigators.

"No, Constable Clark, we did not. Had we found any criminal behaviour we would have reported it. We are mates but there are limits."

58

It was at this point that coffee arrived. Shah and Clark took theirs gratefully. The uniformed PC who brought them in asked Ryan if he was sure he didn't want a drink and was rewarded with a curt shake of the head.

Shah's equilibrium had been restored and she remembered Claire Tanner's briefing about how Ryan would try to manipulate them. Tanner's advice had been to keep calm and accept that was what he was doing.

"Can you tell me again what happened on Tuesday night when you were having the nightcap, please, Ryan?"

The traces of irritation on Ryan Sandling's face were more obvious now. Tanner had warned them that if Ryan were a psychopath he would probably want to talk face to face with Molash. He would be likely to feel himself above the two detective constables. Psychopaths are only nice to people who are useful to them and Ryan was likely to decide at some point that he was wasting his time talking to Clark and Shah and demand to see the organ grinder.

However, the charm was turned on again and he ran through his recital fluently. He emphasised that whilst he appreciated the cleverness of Inspector Molash's swapping of the glasses the previous evening, he still didn't see how anyone could have poured something into Mark's glass in the lounge without being sure nobody would see, especially Mark. The inference was very much that the kitchen was the place where the poisoning had probably taken place.

Shah leaned forward and said, "Ah, but you see, Ryan, we know how you got the chloral hydrate into Mark's glass."

Ryan stiffened and was watching her like a hawk, a difference being that she was the predator and he was increasingly feeling like prey.

Clark produced a small forensic bag with a golf ball in it and Shah continued, not without a certain smugness in her tone.

"The golf ball game. You must have loved that moment, Ryan. Mark's own game was what you used to kill him."

Shah paused but Ryan had no intention of saying anything. He was trying to regain his composure from the shock of seeing the golf ball, another brick knocked out of his defensive wall.

"On Friday night Inspector Molash established that you were standing next to Mark as Owen, Danny and the two of you watched Jack and Annette on the sofa. You all had drinks behind you. A bit of well-practised sleight of hand and you could be pouring the chloral hydrate in as you put the golf ball in. The receptacle that contained the chloral hydrate could have been small enough to be hidden in your fist immediately afterwards.

"You gave a laugh, as if having caught Mark out at his own game. Owen and Danny were watching the sofa. Mark laughed too when he saw you looking over your shoulder and then seeing the golf ball in his glass. He took it out, put it in his pocket and that's why he drank his half-finished pint in one go. The rules of the game said he had to. You knew he wouldn't mention anything about the golf ball as the rules are that whoever has it in their possession can use it at any time. Mark had taught you all the advantage of others playing the game not knowing who had the golf ball."

"The golf ball was found in Mark's room despite the fact that there were no golf clubs there – his are at his family home. You didn't dare go up there and try and search for the golf ball in case anyone heard you and thought you'd been drinking with Mark in his room and therefore were the one with the golden opportunity to poison him. Equally you didn't want to create suspicions by sneaking up there the following morning. You had to leave it where it was. We'd probably bag it up but what were the chances of anyone making the connection between it and the poisoning?"

There was a sneer in Ryan's voice as he said, "Well, clearly not you, Constable. This appears to be a fiction in the mind of Inspector Molash. So that was the purpose of his questions about drinking games, was it? It's a nice theory, but it didn't happen."

"Your DNA is on the golf ball, Ryan…"

Ryan laughed contemptuously. "Yes, I should think it is. I should imagine that most of us had our DNA is on it. We've held the golf ball because all of us had been caught out at one time or another. If that's all Molash's theory is then the sooner you let me go and start doing your jobs properly the better."

He paused, and added, "I imagine you are watching and listening, Molash. Is that all you can come up with?"

Having got a couple of nods from Tanner and Eliot, Molash left the room, walked quickly down the corridor and entered the interview room. Clark got up and retired to a corner, taking his notebook even though the interview was being taped. He was the sort of detective that liked to write things down.

The light was in Ryan's eyes. His ego was working overtime and he regarded Molash as his opponent in this match. Shah and Clark had ceased to exist in his mind. The game had moved on.

Molash might know, but unless he could prove it, Molash would have lost and Ryan would have won.

"So let me summarise, Inspector, just in case you didn't hear everything your junior colleagues have been suggesting. I'm supposed to have pinched my mother's chloral hydrate, even though one of my friends had an equal opportunity to do so – if indeed my mother's medicine was really used to poison Mark. I was then supposed to have pulled off some sort of conjuring trick by putting both the chloral hydrate and the golf ball into Mark's glass without anyone seeing? Even though it would have been infinitely easier to poison Mark's glass in the kitchen?"

Molash looked hard at Ryan Sandling. It was at that moment that he felt disgust. Up until then he had been so focused on unravelling the crime and then gathering evidence, he hadn't prepared himself for the emotional side. This wasn't a crime born of desperation or circumstances. It was the cold-blooded killing of a young man who had everything to look forward to in life, for no other reason that Ryan hated Mark, with every fibre of his being.

Molash mentally shook himself and said, "That's a good start, Ryan, but there's more. The golf ball had been in Mark's glass. It had gin and tonic on it."

Ryan interrupted Molash by laughing derisively. "I should think it did. Christ knows how many times we've played that game, often when we've been drinking gin and tonic. You'll probably find lager on it too."

"We did, but that was from another night. From Tuesday night we found traces of chloral hydrate on the golf ball. However unlikely it may actually be, you might have tried to argue that chloral hydrate had got on the golf ball on another occasion, but we also found tiny traces of mud and grass from when the ball was actually used to play golf with. They correspond exactly to traces we found in Mark's glass. The only way that they could have got in Mark's glass was if the golf ball was put into that glass along with chloral hydrate on Tuesday night."

Ryan could feel his heart rate accelerating but he was determined to keep control.

"This is all fascinating supposition, but what does it prove?"

"I think we'll find out if we ask your housemates that the last person to be caught out in the golf ball game, and therefore the person who was in possession of the golf ball, was you. You'll doubtless argue that Mark asked for it so you gave it to him, but a jury won't buy that when they've heard the full story.

"It was a rather clever scheme, Ryan." Molash paused and caught sight of the faintest sign of Ryan preening. "It was well planned. You hated Mark so much that you revelled in the enjoyment of planning his death. You got Jack up to your mother's house so that he would be deemed to have had opportunity if anyone traced the chloral hydrate.

"You spent the term carefully crafting the illusion that you and Mark were keeping an eye on Jack because you thought he might be a sexual predator. As Zara Allen said to us it was like you were a time and motion man assessing Jack. You wanted to know exactly how he operated in case you needed to implicate him. You manipulated Mark so that the three of you were often chatting to girls together, so you could say that you and Mark were keeping an eye on Jack when it was nothing of the sort.

"I don't doubt that you've got plenty more up your sleeve. I imagine you found a reason to get Jack to go alone into your mother's bathroom. A few beers in a pub en route and then a hurried departure so that he was likely to need the toilet at your mum's house?

"You bided your time. You needed a night where Mark was making the nightcaps as that would hopefully indicate suicide and there might not be an investigation at all. Ideally he'd choose his favourite, gin and tonic. The gin would mask the taste of the chloral hydrate quite well, but the really clever touch was letting him drink half of it, getting the taste of gin in his mouth as he did so. Then the golf ball game meant he had to drink the rest down in one, so he's much less likely to notice the chloral hydrate than if he were sipping it in the normal way. Smart."

Ryan gave the ghost of a smile. It was gratifying to hear his opponent in the duel acknowledge how clever he'd been. Molash was dangerous, but there were other possible solutions, ones involving Jack Freemen in particular. Ryan was still confident he could put enough doubt in a jury's minds if it came to it.

"You were smart enough not to try and retrieve the golf ball, nor wash up. Apparently you never do your share of the domestic chores and it would have been suspicious if you'd washed the evidence away. When you offered to make coffee when I arrived on Friday evening it was obviously out of character judging by your housemates' reactions. In any case, it would have been hard to cleanse the glass completely of chloral hydrate and too risky to try and remove it. You hoped the glass would suggest suicide so it made sense to leave it for us to find.

"You made a mistake on the morning after you killed Mark, though. You rose relatively early, most unusual from what your housemates tell me. Sam, Chloe and Owen had left to go on the protest and you wanted Jack at home alone so he'd find Mark. The police are always suspicious of the person who finds a murder victim.

"You manipulated it so that you and Danny went up to the campus whilst Jack was still in bed. You dropped Danny off and then had plenty of time to buy some books, have lunch on your own and generally get your head and story straight.

"The really suspicious act was to have your phone off so nobody could contact you. You wanted to be away from Newton Street for as long as you could whilst the initial investigation was going on. It was a mistake, though. Criminals are always turning their phones off or leaving them at home to avoid

GPRS tracking. Anyone whose phone is off at a convenient time becomes an object of suspicion."

Ryan was starting to shuffle a little in his seat. Had Molash really suspected him immediately? Or was he putting the pieces together now with the benefit of hindsight? He told himself to concentrate. Molash was back to the nightcap now.

"You distracted Owen and Danny by making bets on what would happen between Jack and Annette. Owen's got an amazing memory, you know, he can recite the conversation almost word for word. It's pretty obvious that you were manipulating the conversation so that their attention would be fixed on the sofa.

"It didn't matter with Mark so much. Even if he noticed as you were doctoring his drink, which I don't think he did, provided you were careful he'd only see the golf ball going in, not the poison. The beauty of your plan was that if he, or indeed anyone else, saw you tampering with Mark's glass it would be readily explained by the golf ball in it. You were the one with the opportunity as you were standing next to him. It would have been hard for Danny or Owen to have reached."

"And why, pray, did I go to such elaborate lengths? Why should I want to kill Mark at all?"

Molash mused for a moment and replied as if he and Ryan were debating criminology in a pub over a pint. "I've seen a lot of anger in this job, Ryan. People kill or commit other serious crimes because circumstances, sometimes the behaviour of a single individual, have stretched them beyond breaking point."

"I've never seen such undiluted hatred as in this case, though. It's seeping out of every pore of you. You don't like anyone much, but you really hated Mark."

"You keep asserting that, Inspector, without giving any sort of reason. I repeat my challenge – why did I hate Mark and so want to kill him?"

59

Molash's smile was faint and sad as he continued, "To you, Ryan, life is a deadly serious contest. Every person for themself. You're in probably the most well-known student house in Middleham. To you it was important to be part of such a household. Your housemates were therefore useful to you. You'd won that battle for your place in the wider student community. You were part of the crazy household that a nice, quiet girl like Annette Palmer wanted to spend a night in just to experience how you lads lived.

"It wasn't enough, though, was it? Having won the contest in the university as a whole, you had to be winning the contest *within* the household too. You gradually realised that at that level you were inferior. Sam was dating the best-looking girl at the university. Jack was able to get a different girl into bed every week. Owen was intellectually superior. Danny was the bloke you all relied on and that everybody liked."

Ryan's face was pale now, adrenalin battling exhaustion. He was digging his nails into the flesh of his palms, with the knuckles white and protruding as if they were trying to break through his skin and escape him.

"That was bad enough. You weren't the best at anything. Mark was much worse, though. He was superior to you in virtually every way and you hated him for it. What I think you hated most of all was that he wasn't aware of it. He just took it for granted and sailed through life. He would talk about how fantastic all your lives were at university and all the wonderful opportunities you had when you left. You knew that his opportunities and experiences would be better than yours and you couldn't handle that, Ryan. It ate away at you, week by week, month by month. You had to win that contest and the only way you could do it was to kill Mark because you were so inferior to him."

Tanner had explained how hard it would be to ruffle Ryan with the evidence, as he would have prepared for interrogation and thought through every point of the killing. Probing into his psyche was her suggested way of making Ryan lose control and it seemed to be working.

"What's it like to have made it so close to the summit here and then find someone who had beaten you so effortlessly? Did it make you feel second-rate? A loser?"

It had been agreed with Tanner that they would try and goad Ryan before playing the trump card of the other death that lay at Ryan's door. The tricky bit was to judge the right moment. Keeping his face impassive but mentally taking the deepest of breaths, Molash showed his hand.

"Was it only by killing Mark that you could feel superior, sufficiently alive? Max Beaumont wasn't enough for you, was it?"

Ryan was starting to shake now. Whether with anger, fear or both, Molash wasn't sure. Ryan was making a colossal effort to control himself in face of this onslaught from an opponent who seemed to know everything about him. He was unable to speak and Molash pressed on, trying to tip him over the edge.

"We know all about Max, Ryan. Max was tall, blond and good-looking too, wasn't he? You got to know him at the local youth club. I spoke to Mr Barlow, who still runs it. He remembers you and Max. Always competing at everything. Every competition they ran you had to win. You befriended Max as he was useful. He was talented and the two of you practised every sport and game together.

"He was a bit too talented, though, wasn't he, Ryan? You couldn't stand the fact he would usually beat you, could you? But Max was very different to Mark. Max suffered from mental health issues and had a history of self-harming."

Molash paused briefly and looked Ryan hard in the eyes, daring him to break eye contact.

"Girls that self-harm typically cut themselves but with boys it is often different. The most common form of self-harm is self-poisoning. Increasingly we see a problem with boys taking ibuprofen or similar medication to knock themselves out at night. Often they end up in hospital having taken an accidental overdose, rather than a definite suicide attempt.

"It wasn't an accident with Max, though. He was already self-poisoning when you met him. You couldn't accept that he beat you so often so you dripped poison into his mind, drip by drip, to break him."

Molash opened the file he'd brought in with him and took out a small diary. "Do you know what this is, Ryan?" he asked.

For the first time Ryan Sandling showed real fear. Whilst he hadn't expected the police to discover so much, he had prepared ruthlessly to counter every small piece of evidence that might be uncovered. This was apparently an item that he had not even known existed. Everything was happening too fast. Suddenly he felt like he was swimming and being pulled down by a vortex and that damned man Molash was demanding that he speak. All he could do was shake his head.

"It's Max Beaumont's secret diary. His foster parents had four kids, all unrelated. A couple of them were real handfuls, as you

328

probably remember. They thought Max was doing well and were so busy coping with the other kids that they were completely unaware of the anguish and torment Max was going through. They only found this a year after his death when they finally felt able to clear out his room.

"I won't lie to you, Ryan. That wouldn't be playing the game, would it? I'll tell you what happened next. They took Max's diary to the police, whose view was that it wouldn't stand up in court on its own.

"However, it is clear to us that you egged Max on to start using his foster mother's Zopiclone. You knew exactly what that did, as your mother uses it; it's the most commonly prescribed sedative in the country. It didn't take you long, did it, Ryan? You're very persuasive and Max thought you were his friend. You'd done your A-levels and you were going to move on. Move on from Max, who had served his usefulness. You didn't like the idea of moving on with Max having kept beating you, though, did you? So you whispered poison into his ear and eventually he broke."

Molash opened the diary at the final entry and held it up so Ryan could see it across the table. It simply said, "He's right. I can't go on like this."

"That night Max Beaumont took a fatal overdose of Zopiclone.

"That wasn't enough, though, was it? To have talked poor Max into killing himself. Increasingly you wanted to do it yourself, to feel the real power of life and death in your hands.

"So you waited until you found someone you hated. A person that was better than you in virtually every way. Someone who, no matter how hard you tried, you couldn't match up to. Did Mark remind you of Max? Having seen a photo of Max, they were quite similar physically. They were both tall, blond and good-looking. Mark was made of stern stuff, though. He was the most unlikely suicide imaginable, so you had to kill him."

Ryan Sandling was running a dry tongue over even drier lips. His voice was little more than a croak as he asked for a drink. Molash sensed he was close to breaking him but that if Ryan was allowed to rest and regroup, he might never again have the surprises to be able to pile on enough pressure to obtain a confession.

"Of course you can, Ryan. We can get you food too if you're hungry." Molash looked over to Clark and said, "Would you mind, Roy?" with a meaningful look.

Clark interpreted it correctly and departed with a cheerful, "Won't be long." Rather than head to the canteen, Clark went into the next room to consult with Eliot and Tanner, the latter opining that Ryan was on the edge, so Clark should remain with them.

"I think a jury would convict you on the evidence we have for murdering Mark Gower. However, we will also be prosecuting you for encouraging or assisting the suicide of Max Beaumont. That way the jury will see exactly what sort of person you are. They will hear the extracts from Max's diary. There's no way in a million years they will believe your insinuations about Jack Freeman."

Ryan Sandling was hyperventilating. Somehow he had missed this point. Insinuations against him about Max in isolation were harmless. The police might believe whatever Max had written in his diary, but with or without the diary it wouldn't be hard to argue that Max was deluded, always looking for someone to blame. He could even argue that Max was saying those things to himself, rather than Ryan having said them, to justify his own desire to kill himself. Ryan had been through this broad thought process many times.

What he had not foreseen was the danger that Max's death would bring about in terms of convincing a jury that they couldn't be sure it was him rather than Jack that had killed Mark. That damned diary had just made it a whole lot worse. He was starting to sweat now and the room threatened to engulf him.

Molash played his final card. "You're going to be convicted of murder, Ryan. That means a life sentence and in your case it may well mean life. Not in prison, though. You're destined for hospital. We've got a psychiatrist who will look at you and you're going to spend the rest of your life strapped into the giggle-jacket."

Ryan was on his feet snarling, reminiscent of exactly the sort of madman that does end up in a padded cell. He inadvertently spat across the desk as he spoke. "I'm not ill, you idiot. Don't you even fucking think about trying to section me. I'm not going into a room on my own every day."

"So convince me, Ryan. I'm the only one who can save you from that now. The psychiatrist is here ready to examine you. Convince me that you are sane. Why did you do it? What reason could you have?"

Ryan Sandling bellowed across the desk. "You know why I killed him. I hated him. Mark bloody Gower with his blond good looks and his easy charm. Getting a top first with virtually no work before deciding if he'd pop out and score a hundred for the university cricket team or not bother. I hated his guts and I loved watching him drink that fatal drink. I wanted to be better than him. He had everything…"

Ryan petered out, the vitality ebbing from his face as he slumped back down into his chair, emotionally drained and physically exhausted.

In a cold, hard, emotionless voice Molash said, "Nobody has everything, Ryan, and those who try to end up miserable."

Molash got up and added, "Here's some paper and a pen. I want you to write it down and if I believe you I'll tell the CPS that I think you are sane. What I also need you to do is write about Max. So his family can understand what happened to him and get some closure."

Without waiting for a reply from the exhausted figure opposite him, Molash had the tape switched off and he and Yasmin Shah left, with a uniformed constable replacing them.

60

Eliot was effusive as they congregated in his office after Ryan Sandling's confession. It was only lunchtime, and on a Monday, but Eliot had his drinks cabinet open. Although he rarely drank alcohol for its own sake, he had seen its power in team-building, a topic concerning which his own inadequacies still rankled.

Tanner was driving and opted for coffee. Hanmer, who was also driving, compromised and had coffee with a tot of whiskey in it. He hadn't been looking forward to the case coming to a jury trial. He knew that under the circumstances the CPS would have had to go ahead with prosecuting Ryan Sandling even though he had felt that there was a good chance he would convince a jury to find him not guilty. To get a quick confession was worth a little celebration.

Eliot had picked out a bottle of the decent stuff from the back of the cabinet and poured brandies for Woodcock and himself. Knowing that Molash couldn't abide brandy, he poured him a large vodka and they raised their glasses and cups.

Woodcock asked Tanner whether she thought Ryan

Sandling was certifiable. Tanner smiled and said that it was a question with a very long answer. A quarter of those in prisons in the UK are deemed to be psychopaths so the bar is pretty high in terms of someone's psychopathy being too strong for prison to be appropriate.

Tanner was explaining her theory about why the prospect of being taken to a secure hospital so appalled Ryan. Many in his place would have jumped at the chance to avoid prison. The likely reasons for Ryan's preference weren't comforting.

Eliot congratulated Molash and thanked Tanner for what he termed 'her invaluable guidance'. He was adamant that Sandling should be in a Category-A prison and if that meant the prison staff would have to cope with the danger he posed to his fellow inmates then that was their job.

He had been concerned that Molash would argue that Ryan wasn't fully responsible for his actions and that they would soon be knee-deep in psychological evaluations. It had been pleasing that Molash was showing appropriate backbone with criminals.

The interview process with offenders can involve hours or days of exhausting conversation. A large proportion of offenders continue to deny everything even when presented with overwhelming evidence, the lies coming as naturally as breathing.

Despite the fact that it had been quick with Ryan Sandling, Molash felt tired. Throughout he had felt that he would only get one chance to break Ryan and the pressure he'd felt had been intense.

He was quiet as he sipped his vodka. One drink would be enough as he had a long drive ahead of him. He listened to Tanner and Woodcock discussing Sandling and heard Eliot's delight that Sandling would be in a 'proper' prison where he belonged. *Ah well*, thought Molash, *perhaps now there will be fewer of Eliot's little homilies on society's demands for retribution.*

He raised his glass slightly to Mark Gower and said to

himself, "We got him, Mark. I know it won't bring you back, but I'll soon be raising a glass to you properly. You knew how to live."

61

Molash was glad to get away from Middleham for a few hours. He'd leave the glory to Eliot. He'd got Woodcock to call Danny Wilson and tell him of Ryan's arrest and confession. Woodcock had also said that Molash would be happy to drop in that evening and give the students a more comprehensive update. During the journey to Mark Gower's parents a WhatsApp message from Danny had flashed up on Molash's phone inviting him round for Mark's wake that evening.

The two FLOs, Sayer and Fordham, had been stationed in a car near the Gower family home. When the arrest was made they were told and so went and informed Bob and Lydia Gower. Initially they couldn't tell Mark's parents much detail without risking prejudicing the case but whilst they were sitting in the Gowers' lounge the landline rang. It was Molash, who told Bob Gower that Ryan Sandling had confessed. Molash's offer to drive down and explain the details was gratefully received.

As he was driving Molash wondered what he should say to the Gowers. So often, when travelling to tell the bereaved of the death of a family member or the arrest of the offender, the officer had little positive to say about the victim. Molash had the opposite issue here. He desperately wanted to tell Bob and Lydia Gower that everything he'd learned about Mark pointed to a fantastic young man who had had the world at his feet. Only to be murdered by a psychopath for no reason that could be remotely justified outside the killer's own warped and savage mind.

Bob Gower opened the front door with a sad but welcoming smile. He shook Molash's hand, offering both his thanks and congratulations, and invited him in. As Molash was taking a seat in the lounge, Lydia called from the kitchen that they had real coffee on and could they tempt him with a cup and some fresh, homemade lemon cake. Molash indicated that he would be delighted to be led into such temptation and a few minutes later the three of them were sitting in the lounge.

As Molash was expressing his appreciation of the coffee and cake, Lydia Gower asked the question that had been keeping both Mark's parents awake at night. "Before you tell us the details, Inspector, we need to ask you a question. What, if anything, did Mark do that made Ryan kill him?"

Molash was relieved to be coming to the crucial point so quickly and looked Lydia straight in the eye and said, "Absolutely nothing. I cannot over-emphasise that. Ryan Sandling is psychopathic. He drove a supposed friend at home to suicide because he felt inadequate compared to him.

"Ryan hated Mark because Mark was very talented but also because he was a good human being. You will understand this much better than me, but everything we have learnt about Mark was that he loved life, always taking the positive view. He was caring and compassionate and seemed to have little sense of arrogance. The fact that Mark was such a decent bloke made Ryan hate him all the more. If it hadn't been Mark there would have been other victims; Ryan's a serial killer in the making."

Bob and Lydia Gower were sat on a sofa opposite Molash

and they had instinctively held hands as Lydia asked her epoch-making question. Those hands were squeezed now as relief flooded through their veins. Mark was gone, but their memories of him remained unsullied.

Lydia spoke again, tears in her eyes. "That's a wonderful way to put it, Inspector. You've no idea how much comfort we'll take from those words going forward, that our Mark was the young man we thought he was."

"He was the ultimate glass half-full merchant, from what I've seen, Mrs Gower."

Much to Molash's surprise both the Gowers burst out laughing. The sombre atmosphere was punctuated with a little joy.

Bob Gower had a grin on his face and explained, "Whenever anyone talked about your glass being half-full or half-empty, Mark would always say that his glass would be completely full in a minute when he took it to the bar and paid for it to be filled up. We always thought that phrase epitomised his attitude."

Molash smiled back. "It must have been all this delicious cake that he grew up eating that gave him that attitude."

Bob Gower rose and said, "I'd like you to see where Mark and I spent a lot of time, Inspector."

The three of them trooped out into the hall and Bob opened what looked like a cupboard door but in fact led down a flight of stairs to a converted cellar.

The light in the cellar flashed on and Molash uttered a slightly startled, "Wow."

Lydia laughed and said, "I am a bit of a sports widow, Inspector. I enjoy watching sport, but Bob and Mark absolutely adored it."

The cellar had been converted into an American-style bar. At one end was the bar itself, with a draught lager pump, a fridge full of bottled beers and another full of mixers, which were below a comprehensive array of bottles of spirits, some upside down in optics and others on a shelf.

The bar was curved with four high bar stools next to it. At the other end of the long, rectangular room was a huge widescreen projection screen attached to the top of the wall. Bob Gower pressed a button and the screen came down and flickered into life. He muted the sound on another Cricket World Cup contest, this time between West Indies and Bangladesh.

Along the two walls on the longer side of the room were lots of framed photographs. The pictures were of different vintages of the Gower sporting dynasty. Bob's hockey and cricketing career mixed with Mark's short, multi-sport career. Pride of place was a team photo of Mark's school first fifteen winning the county schools rugby trophy.

Mixed in with their own performances were photos of the three Gowers at famous sporting venues including Twickenham, Lord's and Wimbledon. As well as domestic sporting events the Gowers were clearly Americanophiles. There were pictures of a teenage Mark with his parents outside Yankee Stadium, home to the New York Yankees baseball team, and then a couple of years later at Levi's Stadium, home to the San Francisco 49ers American football team. Between those two photographs was a huge American stars and stripes flag.

Seeing Molash's interest in the photographs Bob explained, "We love America, Inspector, and have been lucky enough to go twice as a family. As well as the British sports we watch baseball, gridiron, ice-hockey, a bit of basketball. Mark and I shared a love of sport generally and we enjoyed the American sports too." His eyes twinkled and he had the cheeky smile of a much younger man as he looked sideways at his wife and added, "When Mark was at home we were always looking for an excuse to sneak down here in the evenings and watch sport over a couple of beers."

"Speaking of which, can we offer you a beer, Inspector? I know it's a bit early, but it would be good to raise a glass to Mark with you, and to thank you for catching the man who did it."

Molash would normally have declined the offer of alcohol in

this sort of situation, but the Gowers were different. He admired their backbone and gumption, their simple joy of life that Mark had inherited and which they had clearly imbued in him.

"I'd have liked to have known Mark and had a few beers with him. This is the closest I'll get, so I'd love to have a pint here with you now."

Bob poured two pints and an iced gin and tonic for Lydia, and they clinked glasses in a toast to Mark. Gritting his teeth to control his emotions, Bob Gower said, "It was a short life, but it was a full one, which is something to be thankful for. Some people live to be a hundred without experiencing half the joy Mark lived through."

"Sunspangled," Lydia said suddenly, and both the Gowers' faces were pictures of deep and happy memories again. Seeing Molash looking puzzled, she explained, "Whenever we took Mark as a small child to the park or the seaside, the sun always seemed to shine. We'd joke that because we'd planned something like that for the weekend that it was bound to be a sunny day.

"We used to tell him that he must be blessed by a sun god, for it always to be sunny when we took him out. He was at that young age where a child is experimenting with words and building out their vocabulary. One day when we were at the seaside in glorious sunshine, Mark declared that he was 'sunspangled' and we never forgot the word."

Bob's eyes were shining again and the lines of pain on his face were becoming lines of idyllic recollections. He said, "We never knew exactly where the word came from. It's like that with little kids, and Mark always had a lot of imagination. He used to love the spangles on the dresses Lydia used to wear in those days, so that may have prompted it. It may have been the star-spangled banner we've always had down here. He may just have liked the sound of the word 'sunspangled' – little ones are like that."

Lydia's face was animated with the memories of early

motherhood. "When Bob was at work and I was playing with Mark in the garden, when the sun came out Mark would say, 'Look, I'm sunspangled, Mummy,' and he'd jump up and give me a hug with his arms and legs around me. Thank goodness he always kept that sense of joy."

62

Jimmy Molash felt emotionally drained after leaving the Gowers' house. As he drove back towards the motorway he reflected that it was certainly emotionally simpler dealing with the killing of a career criminal who'd crossed the line once too often and suffered the vengeance of a nastier brethren.

He stopped for petrol and a sandwich halfway home and checked his phone. There was a message from Jack Freeman saying that the wake started at seven and that they hoped to see him at 12 Newton Street.

There was also a message from Chloe Hartwell saying, "Sorry I won't see you at Mark's wake tonight but the Cause calls! Thanks for solving the mystery, I owe you a drink next time we meet." Molash grunted and muttered to himself that he hoped that meeting would be a long way into the future. As he drove home he called his usual cab firm and arranged for a taxi to and from Newton Street.

By the time Molash had got home, showered, changed and been driven to Newton Street it was nearly half past eight.

Molash hadn't known exactly what sort of wake the lads at 12 Newton Street were planning. When Danny opened the door it was quickly clear this wasn't a party in the traditional sense.

"Thanks for coming, Inspector. The four of us are having the wake in Mark's room. It seemed appropriate somehow. We thought about inviting others, but we've had to re-evaluate who our friends are a bit in the last few days, so we thought we'd keep it simple and just have us here. We also hoped that would mean that you'd be able to speak more freely. We're hoping you can tell us at least some of what happened. Sergeant Woodcock gave us the bare bones earlier but we're still pretty much in dark."

Danny led the way into the kitchen and opened the large fridge. Food was conspicuous by its absence, but alcohol was not. "I'm just getting some more beers. Any preference, Inspector?" Danny asked as he pulled several bottles of San Miguel lager out. Molash indicated that San Miguel would do fine and Danny got a pint glass out of a cupboard and filled it for Molash, and led the way up the two flights of stairs to the attic clutching several more bottles.

Mark Gower's bedroom was large and the boys had brought some chairs up. As Molash entered Sam Taylor and Jack Freeman jackknifed off the bed and shook his hand. Rather more ceremoniously Owen Lloyd rose from a chair and did the same. The greetings of thanks were from the heart and the four young men looked as if the weight of the world had been lifted from their shoulders.

Danny offered Molash a chair and once everyone was seated a polite demand for facts was made. Molash emphasised that there was a lot that he couldn't tell them and what he did should be treated in the strictest confidence. He then proceeded to tell them all about it.

63

The relief at knowing their ordeal was over had been felt by the four remaining students at 12 Newton Street some hours earlier. By the time Molash arrived, four well-functioning brains wanted to understand what had happened. It wasn't so much the nuts and bolts of how the murder was done, although there was interest in this, and Molash's story was regularly interrupted by debates concerning such matters as whether they should have noticed the golf ball trick.

The big question focused on was, why? Why did Ryan want to kill Mark? And why had none of them realised Ryan was a psychopath who didn't like any of them but who hated Mark? These were deep questions, but Molash reckoned they were questions the lads needed to think through, and he wanted to give them a gentle shove in the right direction at the start of that process.

He explained some of what Claire Tanner had told the investigating team about psychopaths. He explained that they manipulated, felt above the rules and were only interested in people that helped them achieve their goals. He also told them that psychopaths cannot empathise and feel no pity or responsibility for the feelings of others. Typical phrases used by psychopaths such as 'Why are you getting upset by this?' rang plenty of bells and, gradually during the evening, the pieces started to fall into place in the students' minds.

Jack Freeman cut a very different figure visually. He was wearing an old, faded pair of tracksuit bottoms. He said, "It all seems so obvious now with hindsight but I had no clue, not even that he was setting me up as a patsy if there was an investigation."

Molash smiled and said, "Don't beat yourselves up over that, lads. Psychopaths, especially extreme cases like Ryan, are brilliant at dissimilating. That's all part of the manipulation process. We deal with loads of criminal who are psychopaths, but we still needed Claire Tanner's help to get Ryan to confess. They are incredibly difficult people to deal with.

"Oddly Dr Bates, from the law faculty, summed it up perfectly when he said that an 'abnormal person' could become violent towards Mark because they were jealous. On the plus side, as you go through life you'll all have a better idea of how to spot a psychopath now. There are milder cases in every organisation so you'll meet plenty more."

There was a brief silence whilst the students digested this and it gave Jack Freeman the opportunity to get something off his chest.

"I just wanted to let you know, Inspector, that I've always accepted it when a girl says no. Whether it's in a bar or when we're in bed together. No means no. I wanted you to know that."

Molash nodded. "I believe you. If it hadn't been the case Ryan would have probably found out and told us!"

Jack didn't smile. "I just don't want to live in a world where a girl says yes and I'm supposed to take it as a no." The other three students laughed at this and Sam told Jack to calm down, only to receive a retort that it wasn't him that the bastard was setting up for a life stretch. Eventually Jack laughed too.

Danny changed the subject and asked Molash, "Did you suspect Ryan straightaway, badging him as a psychopath?"

Molash resisted the temptation of apparent omniscience and replied, "Not at all. The only really suspicious fact was that he had let his phone die the following day. Even that wasn't a big issue really. I was telling myself that when a career criminal does it then that's suspicious but I shouldn't read too much into it when an ordinary member of the public does it.

"That was the fascination of this case. We fairly quickly got it down to the six of you that were in the lounge on Tuesday night, seven if you counted Annette. All of you looked really unlikely candidates to be cold-blooded killers. That was why I was keen to get to know you a little by coming here.

"The reconstruction we did on Friday night pointed to Ryan as having the best chance to poison Mark's glass if it was poisoned in the lounge. That was only suggestive, though. Sam and maybe Jack might have had a better opportunity in the kitchen as far as we knew.

"It was Ryan's behaviour on Friday night that made me start wondering whether he wasn't the normal student he at first sight appeared to be. The rest of you looked like innocent parties caught up in the maelstrom. Ryan looked like someone carefully co-ordinating what he did and said. When I thought about it I realised that the same was true in the interview we'd conducted with him earlier that afternoon. That combination was far from conclusive, it could just have been his natural manner, but, as I say, it was suggestive.

"We were going to investigate your lives at home anyway, but the following day I placed particular emphasis on Ryan. I got a break. My colleague that I spoke to used their initiative. They recalled an investigation into a dodgy local doctor a couple of years back and despite the fact he wasn't Ryan's mother's registered GP, they got in touch with him and found that he had prescribed chloral hydrate to Ryan's mother. That could easily have been missed. We might have searched her house and found it, but it certainly helped to confirm our suspicions quickly. Once we had the source of the chloral hydrate then we had the focus for the investigation."

Molash didn't mention the urgency he had felt because he feared that Ryan might kill Jack and frame it as a suicide and confession. Instead he explained the story of Max Beaumont.

Sam then asked about Mark's parents and Molash explained to them that he'd been to visit Bob and Lydia Gower that afternoon. He didn't want to discuss the details of the conversations he'd had with the Gowers and made the rather nondescript comment that he'd realised how happy a person Mark had been.

Sam looked keenly at Molash, his stare now steeped in empathy, no longer purely penetrative. He said, "Yes, we'd got used to Mark's love of life, the fact that he found happiness in everyday experiences. It's easy to forget that's not the norm. There's a lot of misery around. God knows why, this is supposed to be our time having fun but there are a lot of people around who seem to find happiness elusive.

"When we were all out together it wasn't as if you were convinced that today would be the best day of your life. It was just that it could be. Today you might fall into the deepest love of your life, you might have the craziest experience with your mates. There was something about Mark that made anything seem possible and the four of us love the fact we've been part of that. Life is short, we have to live it, but equally we live it better when we make the effort to understand each other."

There was a pause whilst they considered what Sam had said and then Owen pronounced, "For every one of us, living in this world means waiting for our end. Let whoever can win glory before death."

Molash looked at Owen, not without affection, and asked, "*Beowulf?*"

Owen was delighted, replying, "Excellent, Inspector. It's nice to speak to someone who is well read."

"I'm appallingly read," replied Molash. "But I love reading."

"Sorry about him, Inspector," said Danny with a glint in his eye. "Think yourself lucky, though, this time last year he was using phrases like 'Quomodocunquizing clusterfist'. These days obscure literary quotes are the limit of it."

Molash blinked and asked, "A what fist?"

Owen was blushing and Danny nipped in quickly, saying, "Apparently it's someone who makes money in any way possible and then is tight with it. Have I got that right, Owen?"

There was general laughter at Owen's expense and the ruddiness of his face deepened, but he retorted, "Us intellectuals have it tough, Inspector."

Molash smiled, not sure whether Owen was including him in that comment or not, and said, "It's good to see the banter is back. You've come through an ordeal, lads, banter will be a great antidote to it."

"Yeah, that's good advice," said Danny. "Before you got here, Inspector, we were talking about how we felt over the last few days. We'd all ended up suspecting each other and were apologising for it. We were stopping caring for each other too. It felt like we were being reduced to caged animals only able to consider our own survival. I feel dreadful for some of the thoughts I had over the weekend."

"Listen, this is important," Molash said, becoming serious. "Most households would have been at each other's throats in the situation you were in, making accusations and shouting abuse at each other. You may have wavered, but you never buckled, which shows that the four of you were worthy of being Mark's friends."

Sam said, "It's amazing what you start thinking. Now it's all over it seems ridiculous, but yesterday I thought Mark might have been shagging Chloe and that you might suspect me because of it. I remembered I'd been late home one night a week or so ago and she'd turned up and only Mark was in. When I got back they were in the kitchen chatting as Mark had offered to make her a cup of tea, but when I heard she'd been sitting on his bed I started wondering. I know there's no way he'd do that, but my mind was scrambled."

Molash agreed, "That sums it up perfectly. From everything I know about Mark he'd never even consider sleeping with one of his mates' girlfriends." Trying to be charitable, he added, "At most I'd imagine Chloe was doing a bit of harmless flirting in his room whilst she waited for you. She was probably annoyed you weren't here when you said you would be," he concluded with a twinkle in his eye that Sam did not miss.

Danny smiled ruefully. "I had a similar feeling. I wondered if you'd think I was cheating at my exams and that Mark had caught me doing it. It sounds absurd when I say it out loud. Mark didn't want to be part of the tutorial group simply because he preferred to do his own thing. It never caused a moment of friction between us. We all knew that, but over the weekend I just couldn't rationalise it in my mind. Ironically enough I wondered if you'd think I was some sort of psycho!"

More laughter ensued, including from Molash, who said, "Well, hopefully now you all know a bit more about the characteristics of psychopaths, you can be extremely confident Danny isn't one. You learn pretty quickly as a policeman that an apparently nice guy is almost always just a nice guy, so I always thought it was pretty unlikely you were involved."

Owen said, "I think we've all learnt plenty from this. My days of protesting for the revolution are over. Mark always said we'd achieve much more in improving society by listening to people rather than shouting at them."

Molash's smile had a tinge of frustration as he suggested, "Perhaps the revolution we need is a revolution in listening."

"You're probably right. We were just kids when it happened,

but I remember last year when Mark first saw the Gordon Brown/Gillian Duffy incident. He said that nothing summed up our inability to listen better than that. On both the protests we went on nobody other than Sam had any interest in listening to anything I said; they just told me 'the answer'. Half the protesters I met were self-righteous and there for themselves, not the people they were supposedly campaigning for."

Before they could debate the most appropriate strategy for peaceful, successful protesting, one of the most fundamental tenets of democracy, the front doorbell rang and Molash went downstairs to get his taxi. He shook hands with all four of the students and wished them all the best for the future.

"Life goes on, lads, it has to. You've all benefited from the privilege of knowing Mark. You've also learnt a lot about people like Ryan, that all the positivity in the world couldn't protect Mark against a homicidal psychopath. The crucial point is that you've now got a choice. You can spend your lives trying to minimise the chances that you upset someone like Ryan, despite the chances of you knowing someone like that again being infinitesimally small.

"Or you can try to emulate Mark's positivity. If you can emulate Mark, then Mark has won and Ryan has lost. Enjoy your time here. In the not-too-distant future you'll have jobs and then maybe mortgages and families."

Molash paused and, to hammer the message home, added, "Use Mark's memory as inspiration to do as many of the things that you all discussed with him as you can. Nobody ever died regretting having created too many good memories."

349

Epilogue

A few months later the Covid-19 coronavirus pandemic struck. The National Health Service made an appeal for 250,000 volunteers to assist the vulnerable. Within a week over 750,000 people had volunteered. Jack Freeman, Owen Lloyd, Sam Taylor and Danny Wilson all volunteered for the Royal Voluntary Service on the first day.

A few days later they arrived at Middleham Hospital. Whilst they were waiting to be assigned their duties a couple of young female nurses passed them, one nudging the other and asking, "Who are that mob?"

Jack Freeman called after them, "We're The Gower Mob," and the name stuck.

For writing and publishing news, or recommendations of new titles to read, sign up to the Book Guild newsletter: